I, Sexbot

by Jason Pinaster

I, Sexbot

Table of Contents

Page Number

Front Matter and About Jason Pinaster

Jason Pinaster has published numerous other stories, most notably the Christopher Carter Series and the Lusty Lee Logs. For a full list of his stories, please see his author profile or the notes at the end of this story.

Other Stories by Jason Pinaster involving science fiction or paranormal phenomena:
 Aural Artifact
 Mayan Magic
 Witch's Wrath
 Kundalini, Lusty Lee Log 29
 Alien Vacation, a novelette

For a catalog of Jason's books, please see his catalog at https://jasonpinaster.wixsite.com/books

Chapter 1

It powered up, bio-electrics activating throughout its body, causing its temperature to gradually increase above room temperature. The base senses of sight, biofeedback balance, and hearing came online at 27 degrees Celsius (80.6°F). Its temperature held at twenty-nine degrees while a diagnostics check of its joints, lubrication, and major motor functions was performed. Small vacuums and pumps activated. As soon as it passed these diagnostics, its temperature began to rise again.

When its temperature had climbed to a sweltering thirty-two degrees Celsius, the robot rose from its sitting position and performed a set of flexion-extension exercises. Then it spun around like a deranged dervish. A beep emanated from its mouth indicating that its kinetic motion functions were nominal—operating within normal parameters.

The robot stood in front of a mirror, seeing but not seeing. Its optics were operating, but nothing had been activated to process the photosensitive data coursing through its visual array. Its outer form was that of a typical human female, not too tall, not too short. On top of its head, its hair was shoulder-length and sandy blonde, just as the client had ordered. Below, its pubic hair was slightly darker and lightly coiffed, again in accordance with the client's specifications. Its hips were female wide, but not so wide as to make it a candidate for belly dancing. Its breasts were full, but not exaggeratedly so. Its nipples had been pierced with tiny chrome barbells. All over its body, its skin was silky smooth with an elasticity perfectly matching that of a biological human.

It was an android, although almost everyone referred to it as a 'robot'. Once activated, its functions would almost exactly mimic that of a human female—speech, intelligence, sex. While it would appear to breathe, that was mostly for show as its power source was largely electric. Nonetheless, it could ingest food—solid and liquid, even a whole meal—and process the carbon and water to extend its fuel cycle.

As soon as its core temperature had risen to thirty-six point six degrees Celsius, normal for a human, it shut its eyes and its software began to load. When the first kernel was complete and had checked itself against the firmware, a musical chord formed in its throat and sounded loudly. As each successive kernel of software came on line, the musical chord began to morph into a spoken word, music gradually giving way to that word. When the last kernel checked out, there was no music in its throat, only its name: "Jenny".

Jenny opened her eyes. Almost instantaneously, her visual array adapted to the bright light. She inspected her amber eyes and smiled when she saw that their color perfectly matched that of her hair.

The file for today's client was already in her functioning memory. His name was Stephen Minsky. His background file described him as a computer and software entrepreneur. When Jenny zoomed her focus out to take in her whole body, she was pleased to see that it perfectly matched his preferred type for a female.

Jenny then shut her eyes to move through her checklist. Body temperature was nominal at 98.7 degrees Fahrenheit. Standing on one foot, she rocked back and forth, then sideways, to check her internal balance. She pressed arms against arms, then gripped a wrist, straining to pull it free from her arm. Strength and bodily integrity checked out. Fingers tapping against the mirror confirmed that her hearing was in order. A deep inhalation through her nostrils registered the lab's typical array of chemical residues.

Jenny opened her eyes for the next section of her checklist—her erogenous zones. A touch to her belly elicited a pleasant shiver. Touching her ear and under her chin made her feel warm. Sensations on her arms were properly connected with her neck and chest. Touching her thighs, especially on the inside, stimulated her central sexual complex.

Mr. Minsky wasn't into kinky stuff, so Jenny removed the two barbells piercing her nipples. A finger on the slightly darker skin surrounding her nipple caused a slight gasp. A touch directly on her nipple deepened the gasp while a flick to the nipple squeezed a deep moan from her chest. The same finger between her legs found moist warmth, exactly as it should be. She pressed her finger between her pussy lips and verified the tingle rising up her spine. Pressing the finger slightly inside initiated a sensation as if her knees had been loosened and the muscles in her legs relaxed.

Three beeps, but beeps only Jenny heard, confirmed the successful completion of her checklist.

Behind the mirror was a small closet which Jenny now opened. She removed the small overnight bag and placed it on the counter beside the closet, then she unzipped the garment bag hanging in the closet. The clothing inside confirmed her file on Mr. Minsky—he liked red lace lingerie.

The overnight bag was soft black leather. Inside were the standard contents: A change of underwear, jeans, a T-shirt and a repair kit. The repair kit would allow Jenny to fix any minor skin abrasions. Also standard were a back-up power supply and a locator/distress beacon.

Jenny quickly pulled on a pair of red lace panties. They were French-cut, barely covering the top of her pubic hair. The bra was of the same material, balancing the need to support her breasts with Mr. Minsky's desire to inspect them.

Her outer clothes were more demure: A grey wool jacket which completely covered her cleavage and a matching skirt which went down to just below her knees. Both were expertly lined and the sheer bemberg rayon was cool on her skin.

Jenny looked in the mirror and applied gloss to her lips. It was several shades lighter than her lingerie so as not to draw too much attention away from the red lace. She batted her eyebrows. "Hi, I'm Jenny. I'm a robot and I work for—"

A flag popped into her central processor alerting Jenny to pick an alternate greeting.

"Hi, I'm Jenny. I believe we have an appointment?"

She nodded. That would be perfect. If one of his business associates overheard her, there would be no sexual overtones.

Jenny reviewed her file on Stephen Minsky, the man she was to shortly meet, and likely have sex with. Images of him flashed through her visual processor. Steve was fifty years old, white and physically fit. He was six feet tall, so taller than her. Steve—everyone called him that—was unbelievably wealthy having made a fortune through his international computer/cellphone company. He liked Baroque music and action adventure movies.

When Jenny arrived at the restaurant where she was to meet Stephen Minsky, she spotted him alone at a table in the center of the restaurant, typing into a laptop computer. Today he was dressed informally in a button-down silk shirt and linen pants. She was about to walk up to him when a black man slid into the seat opposite. So Jenny stood out of sight and waited for the conversation to end. The television to Steve's right was tuned to an all-news channel.

Jenny stood patiently. It was easy for a robot to be patient. She listened to the two men talking. But she wasn't really listening, only recording in case she needed to access the conversation for their session that afternoon. The file would be erased after the session to protect client confidentiality.

She scanned Minsky's file and discovered that the other man was Zach Palmer. He'd met Steve at University and the two men had become quick friends. Zach had become Steve's head of security where stock options had made him a multi-millionaire. He was younger than Steve and devoted to him even though Steve's billions made Zach's millions pale in comparison.

"Ready for your robo-date with Jen-eey?" asked Zach, drawing out the syllables of her name.

Steve smiled and nodded.

"I bet you can't wait until your own robots come online," said Zach.

"The robots coming online will be *our* own robots—both of ours."

Zach smiled. "Our own robots."

Steve shook his head. "Ours are still a ways from being operational. At present, Artificial Intelligence is ready to go into our high-end computers and of course our cellphones, but putting AI into robots is tricky." Steve's voice was soft, so she increased the receptivity of her audio sensors. A bar at the bottom of her visual array showed the volume increasing to maximum sensitivity.

"No risk, no gain," said Zach.

Steve shook his head. "There are hundreds and hundreds regulations requiring compliance. And there's the risk of public backlash. We have to be careful if we don't want to be shut down."

"So much for AI supercomputers solving each and every problem."

A waiter came to the table bringing a drink for Steve. Zach said he wasn't staying.

Steve sipped his drink.

On the television, the story switched to one about robots. The screen showed a clip of a news conference. But the audio was a voice over: "The regulations restricting robots have been tightened and the inspection branch has been beefed up with additional inspectors. Robot owners have decried the moves as Luddite and retrograde. Supporters of the new regulations have maintained that robots should be outlawed altogether." A green square in Jenny's visual field formed around a skinny man in the back row and an alert flashed that the man had been outside the restaurant when Jenny had entered.

"I've done the sex thing with robots," said Zach. "It's nice, but nothing special. Certainly not worth going to the trouble of having a date with it."

"Jenny is different, special. She's not like other pleasure 'bots."

"Special how?"

"More...human. She seems to understand me. Kaito's robots are a step above. They're almost, real."

"Kaito?"

"Ian Kaito. He operates a boutique research lab and rents out several robots. Jenny is one of his robots."

"You mean he owns it?"

Steve nodded. "If one can own such magnificence."

"It's just gears, sprockets, software and plastic."

"Not plastic, high-grade latex. No condoms necessary."

"Soft plastic, hard latex, it's all the same."

"You're wrong, my friend. Give Kaito a call. He may change your mind."

"I'll pass."

"You know the best part about dating a sexbot?" asked Steve.

"No, but I'm sure you're going to tell me."

"They don't hold grudges."

"Grudges?"

"Sure, they have layers upon layers of fancy algorithms and artificial intelligence. But each robot is wiped clean after the date. Each date starts from scratch. All you have to do is have one good date with her and then do exactly the same thing the next time. Guaranteed enjoyment."

"They don't remember anything?"

"Zilch, rien, nada! Not a thing."

Steve was wrong. Jenny did remember what had happened on their previous date. Her system prompted an option to catalog this as an anomaly, but she declined.

Their previous date flashed into Jenny's memory and she reviewed the encounter. Even though she was accessing every sensation, every action, every word, the review took only a nanosecond.

They had met in the same restaurant, though she had sat in a corner booth. Steve had been late. He'd offered a sumptuous meal by way of apology, but she'd told him that she had already eaten. They had walked and talked. He was wrestling with the task of designing a new algorithm to ensure that his computers functioned optimally while staying within the bounds of government regulations. He said that the "regulations" had him coming and going.

Then they'd gone to a hotel room. He'd positioned his body for oral sex. She had started to lower herself down to his crotch. But he'd pulled her back up and touched his finger to her lips. "Are you sure your mouth is large enough for my penis?" he'd asked.

Jenny remembered the laughter in his eye when she'd smiled and said, "There is only one way to find out."

His appreciative moans indicated that he'd thoroughly enjoyed having his penis sucked into her throat. But when she'd climbed on the bed and knelt for him to take her from the rear, he'd turned her onto her back and mounted her from above.

She'd told him that rear entry would have allowed him to concentrate on his pleasure but he had only smiled. As he pumped his penis into her, his changing facial expressions indicated joy, pleasure, then pain. But the pain was only momentary and immediately followed by a raucous sexual climax inside her.

Afterwards, Steve had opened his laptop, typed in his password, and shown her the algorithm he was working on. It still had numerous bugs...

"The same date over and over again," said Zach. "Sounds boring."

Steve shook his head. "Jenny is *anything* but boring."

"Jenny—the way you say its name makes it sound like it's a human being."

"When was the last time you got a massage from a gorgeous woman?"

"I prefer a masseur for my massages. Hand strength is more important than beauty."

"Not if she's nude."

"But, why does she have to be erased at the end of the session?" Zach wanted to know. "Wouldn't it be more interesting if she remembered your proclivities?"

Steve shook his head. "The artificial intelligence regulations state that she has to be erased to prevent consciousness or rampant AI."

"Robots taking over and killing off the inferior humans."

"Not so much that. The concern is more about taking jobs away, rendering human endeavors irrelevant."

"I thought that the Robot Laws had addressed those concerns."

"The robot lobbyists may have shot themselves in the foot when they got the first law amended."

Zach closed his eyes to recite from memory, "No robot shall injure a human being or, through inaction, allow its Owner to come to harm."

"Right—originally the regulations provided that robots were forbidden from allowing *any* human being to be harmed."

"Lawyers and capitalists."

Steve raised his glass in salute. "And now there's a movement to outlaw pleasure bots."

"Won't the new regs and more intense inspection be enough to solve the problem?"

"Maybe. If not—" Steve paused making a motion as if to draw a knife across his throat. Then he looked at his watch. "Scoot! She'll be here any minute."

Zach shrugged and got up to leave.

Jenny registered Steve's second error; she'd arrived on time and was already here. This was different than their first date. But of course the client was always right and she'd proceed as if she'd just arrived on time and as if this was the first time she was meeting him.

Jenny walked up, then past his booth. She turned slowly turned around. "Mister Minsky?"

"Steve," he corrected.

"Hi, I'm Jenny. I believe—"

"Yes, Jenny." He beamed at her and beckoned for her to have a seat opposite him.

As soon as she sat, a waitress arrived at the side of their table. "Would you like something to eat?" asked Steve.

She shook her head. "I've already eaten."

The exact same words as on their previous date flickered a smile across his lips. She'd seen it, but didn't react to it. He waved the waitress away.

This time when they walked to the hotel, he'd talked about two vice-presidents who were constantly feuding and how he might have to fire both of them. "Why can't everyone be as sweet as you?" he asked.

"You're the sweet one," she'd told him, just in time for him to hold the door to the hotel open for her.

She turned to the reception desk, just as she had on their first date.

"Jenny," he said.

She turned to him. He fished a keycard out of his laptop case.

"You think of everything," she told him. Just as it had last time, her compliment brought a smile to his face.

Up in the room, he hung his jacket in the closet. Then his phone rang "I'm going to have to take this," he told her. He opened his laptop and motioned towards the television.

Jenny turned on the TV. A soap opera was playing. All the characters had difficult and stubborn problems. She watched, fascinated by the insurmountable difficulties faced by humans on a daily basis. She was glad she was a robot. As soon as she heard Steve start to end his conversation, she turned the television off. He made a show of turning his phone off.

She performed a slow and silent striptease for him. His eyes seemed to grow wider. As soon as her panties touched the floor, Steve walked over to her and touched a finger to her bottom lip. "You have a wonderful mouth," he said.

Just as she had last time, Jenny took his compliment to be an indication that he would appreciate oral sex. She started to bend her knees.

Steve pulled her back up and touched both her lips with his finger. "Are you sure your mouth is large enough for my penis?" he asked.

She smiled, "There is only one way to find out."

He laughed briefly, but went silent as she slid down his body, kissing as she went. Her fingers trailing behind, undid the buttons on his shirt. He moaned and shuffled back until his shoulders were against the wall.

At the moment her knees touched the floor, her hands reached his belt buckle. She pretended to fumble with it, but her fumblings were designed as cover to allow her to fondle and caress his penis. By the time she'd pulled his zipper down and allowed his pants to slide halfway down his thighs, Steve was fully erect.

Steve's briefs were a blend of cotton and lycra—cotton for smoothness, lycra for stretch. The rod of his penis pressed down the center, pulling the thin material of his briefs out from his body.

She gripped the top of his underwear and slowly peeled it up and off his erection. Steve's arousal had peeled his foreskin down his shaft revealing the throbbing purple head of his penis. It was almost shiny in the dim light of the hotel room.

His penis was long and wide but Jenny had already adjusted her mouth to accommodate his girth and her throat to welcome his length. She began to suck his penis down her throat and he gasped above her.

Saline lubrication—thick saltwater—allowed the full length of his shaft to slide down her throat. All top-of-the-line pleasure robots had air chambers lining their throats and Jenny was no exception. She inflated her air chambers to rhythmically massage Steve's penis.

He groaned. His knees wobbled. Jenny pressed his right leg backwards against the wall to steady him. Her right hand stroked back and forth along the thin line separating his testicles. She felt Steve's hands squeeze her head into him.

Her air chambers were arranged in concentric circles. These she inflated in sequence up and down the length of his shaft. His reactions indicated deep pleasure. Each circle was in fact four separate chambers. The manufacturer's software limited the chambers to operating in unison. Jenny knew that this was a major improvement on the global sucking which adept human females could perform. But Ian Kaito had modified his sexbots' software to enable individual control of not only each concentric circle, but of each of the four separate chambers as well.

Jenny now activated the modified software to create new patterns of sensation on Steve's penis. First she massaged the frenulum—the ridge of super-sensitive skin on the underside of his penis just below its head.

"Jesus," he groaned. "Jeesus…"

When his groans started to die down, she squeezed and released all around the head itself.

But as soon as he reacted, she released the pressure on the head of Steve's penis; it was far too sensitive for sustained stimulation. Now she activated each individual air chamber in a spiral sequence. A human would have had to go up and down Steve's penis, but Jenny could immediately start from its base as soon as her spiral had reached his super-sensitive ridge.

Jenny could tell from Steve's breathing that he was on the cusp of climax. She readied to employ Kaito's latest tweak to her software—vibration. All she had to do was—

But, just like last time, Steve pulled back on her hair and her mouth sucked up and off his penis. She adjusted her mouth back into its proper shape then looked up into his eyes. He smiled down at her so she smiled back up at him.

Jenny pulled herself upright. Her programming said that some men would like to kiss her. Last time, Steve hadn't kissed her. However, this time it looked like he might. But the moment passed and Jenny climbed onto the bed, kneeling away from him. She angled her hips at the optimal angle to facilitate the penetration of his penis into her vagina.

Nothing happened.

She craned her neck to look back at him. He was taking his time removing his clothes and appeared to be admiring her body. When he was nude, she looked away and readied to accommodate him.

But instead of penetrating her, he gently pressed on the side of her right hip and turned her onto her back. His arms were on either side of her head, his body pressed lightly atop hers. She sensed his penis between her thighs, but it was well below her central sex area.

"But rear entry will let you focus on your pleasure."

"There's more to pleasure than just penis into pussy." The way he looked into her eyes, it was as if he was trying to peer through her visual array into her central processing unit. But Jenny knew he couldn't see inside.

Then Steve glanced down her body and his hips moved higher. She switched on light lubrication for inside her vagina and dilated its opening. When his penis touched there, she reached down to help guide him inside.

Initially she let him pump away, moving up and down against his thrusts. His skin warmed where it pressed against her. As his rhythm established itself, Jenny began to alter the strength of her vagina's grip and its level of lubrication. Steve moaned his approval, even though she had yet to go beyond what any human female could do.

Jenny activated the set of air chambers which ran up and down the length of her vagina. These were larger and less powerful than those in her throat. In her throat, she had done all the work. But here, during sexual intercourse, the purpose of the chambers was to welcome his incoming thrusts to maintain pressure against his penis as he withdrew.

"Jesus," he groaned.

Some human females could manage this, but not many, and Steve groaned his approval over and over again. Jenny's own pleasure center began to register delightful arousal. This would allow her, if she surrendered control to it, to propel her body into automatic responses to what Steve was doing. Her software's default setting would begin her orgasm just as Steve's was beginning to fade.

But Jenny maintained manual control. As soon as she sensed that Steve had become used to the squeezing and relaxing of her air chambers as he thrust in and out, she activated the layer of rotating balls. These balls were the size of pearls and could slide up and down her vagina or rotate around it. Jenny set the balls into gentle rotation and gradually released air from the chambers. As they collapsed, the balls came closer and closer to the surface of Steve's plunging penis. When she heard him gasp, she stabilized the chambers' air pressure.

"Can you feel that?" she asked.

"Yes! What're you—"

"Do you like 'round and 'round? Or?" She paused to stop the rotation of the balls and instead set them moving down his shaft as he thrust in and back up when he pulled out of her. "Or, up and down?"

He gasped. "I—" He gasped again.

"Or maybe both?" She set the balls rolling both up and down but synced with his thrusts.

"Yes! Jesus!" His body shuddered. He tried to say more, but he couldn't talk. Maintaining his thrusts was consuming all his concentration.

Steve's face had moved on from joy when she'd started the balls rotating and was now suffused with pleasure. Flickers started around his eyes, indicating that his pleasure centers were becoming overwhelmed. She knew that he was experiencing this as pain, but the pain of ecstatic rapture, not the pain of agony or dread.

Jenny's own arousal was starting to match that of Steve's. Her sensorium would not be overwhelmed by the impending orgasm, but it *would* register as pleasure in all her reward centers.

Jenny grabbed Steve to hold him close and to prevent further thrusts. His eyes flashed protest at her fingers digging into his back and buttocks. His eyes flashed even more protest when she activated a tight ring at the opening of her vagina. The ring tightly grasped the base of his penis, chocking off his climax.

Steve's face contorted. "Hey, what the—"

"It's so good, baby," she cooed. "I want it last forever."

"But—" He tried to wrench himself free, but she held on tight.

"Besides, I have something special to show you."

The combination of the release of the ring at the base of his penis, a gentle rocking of her hips and the promise of 'something special' seemed to mollify Steve. He began to gingerly resume his thrusts. Joy returned to his face along with the occasional tinge of deeper pleasure. Jenny felt his penis harden inside her.

She gradually replenished the air inside the chambers lining her vagina. Jenny knew that this would lift the rotating pearls away from Steve's skin. But just as she felt his arousal start to wane, she engaged Ian Kaito's latest modification—texture.

The first texture was a layer of little ribs of hard latex along the lining of her vagina right next to the penis sliding in and out of her. It was similar to those found on many textured condoms, but larger.

"Jesus!" gasped Steve the first time he felt it.

The next texture was random roughness.

"Ow!" said Steve. Jenny immediately retracted the roughness in favor of little spikes of soft silicone. These were designed to slide up and down his penis like grass blowing in the wind.

Steve groaned. His face was an equal mix of joy and pleasure.

The third texture was larger and fatter spikes. These Jenny could leave flaccid. Or she could fill them with air if she wanted to give more intense feelings.

"Jesus," muttered Steve. "What *is* that?!"

"You like?"

"Shit, yeah!"

Steve's face had now gone completely into pleasure. Jenny inflated a third of the spikes half way.

"Jesus," moaned Steve. "That's some pussy you have."

His comment sent a shiver up her spine, causing Jenny to momentarily lose control. Was this another one of Kaito's modifications? Her memory files didn't have an answer.

Another shiver went up her spine, but this time Jenny maintained control. Flickers of pain danced around Steve's eyes. She inflated a second set of the spikes lining her vagina, but this time all the way.

"Jesus!" yelled Steve.

"Do you—"

"Harder Jenny! Harder!" he groaned through contorted lips.

After a few enthusiastic thrusts, Jenny inflated the last third of the spikes, again all the way. It was time to *totally* overwhelm his pleasure receptors.

"Jeesus," moaned Steve.

But he was having a harder time thrusting in and out so she compensated by extending the rotations of her hips. Shivers rocketed up and down her spine. Something wonderful swirled around inside her central sexual complex.

"Jesus!" yelled Steve as his first spurt shot into her. "Jesus! Jenny! *Jesus!*"

Spurt after spurt of his semen thundered inside her. She felt her own orgasm build, then burst in waves up her spine and down her legs. Her temperature rose two degrees. Even though she didn't understand how she had lost control, she didn't care. It felt absolutely stupendous!

Afterwards they cuddled side by side as Steve recovered his breath.

"That was great," he gasped.

"You were wonderful," said Jenny. She paused to take a breath. "What was the best part?" A positive review is always good for repeat business, even if the client is the only one who hears it.

"When you took my penis into your mouth it felt like you were massaging it with a thousand little fingers. It was all I could do to stop myself from coming right then and there!"

"Have you ever had anything like that before?"

"No, never."

Jenny thought it strange that Steve hadn't remembered their previous encounter when she'd used exactly the same techniques. Maybe she was only dreaming? Or maybe the memory file hadn't been entered properly?

But he was continuing. "And the vibration was out of this world!"

Jenny smiled. Not even the most adept human would ever be able to match her oral sex. "What about...?" she asked.

"The little pearls inside you were wonderful. But texture after texture—especially the little silicone spines inside your pussy were absolutely splendid!"

They lay smiling at each other for a long moment.

Then he turned towards her and let his fingers play with her belly. "I'll be going away," he said. "It's an important deal."

"An important deal?"

He nodded, excited by her interest. "It's a new hardware/software matrix. If it works, it will revolutionize computing. We'll get together when I get back."

She had wanted to ask more about how his deal would revolutionize computing, but her conversation matrix had noted his termination of that line of conversation.

Instead, she asked, "How are things in your life?" Her software indicated that this was a good question to ask to engender the feelings of intimacy which would lead to repeat business.

"Alright."

"Why only alright?" Steve deserved more. And she registered that his answers were usually longer.

"I'm blocked at every turn. My two best Vice Presidents can't seem to subordinate the needs of their departments to the needs of the corporation as a whole. And the Artificial Intelligence Directorate disallowed the algorithm we need to go forward. And of course, there's Catherine."

"Catherine?" Her files indicated that his wife's name was Catherine, but he hadn't mentioned her today.

"My wife. We're stuck in a rut."

There was a flag warning her that inquiring further into his difficulties with his wife might be dangerous. So Jenny asked him to tell her about his Vice Presidents.

She listened carefully as he described the problems being faced by his organization and how feuds and petty bickering were blocking its progress. Steve opened the lid of his laptop and typed in his password. He turned the screen towards her and quickly navigated diagrams of his corporate and management structures. As Jenny listened, solutions appeared in her central processing unit, but they were outlandish or impractical or both.

Gradually the quality of the possible solutions improved. She was about to suggest a list of three possible solutions when a fourth appeared in her CPU. The new solution was much better.

When Steve paused, Jenny asked, "What if..." She paused, awaiting his reaction. When he nodded, she took a deep breath. "What if you switch them around?"

"Switch?"

Jenny pointed to his laptop, moving her finger back and forth between the two recalcitrant vice presidents. "Move them into each other's department. If they're suddenly in charge of the department they've been competing against, won't they see the big picture?"

Steve's eyes suddenly lit up. He jumped off the bed and dressed as if he was in frenzy. Jenny glanced around the room to make sure he wasn't leaving anything behind.

After Steve left, Jenny sat and watched TV. The same soap opera was playing. All the characters had the same problems as before. When the solutions to their difficulties became more and more obvious to her, Jenny turned the TV off and called for a taxi to take her back for replenishment. She quickly slipped into the fresh underwear, T-shirt, and jeans from her overnight bag, then stuffed the rest of her clothes into it.

In the cab, the driver asked her, "Where to, gorgeous?" His voice was loud in the small space, so Jenny reduced the receptivity of her audio sensors. She gave him a simple business card: 'Ian Kaito's Specialty Robotics' in large letters, with an address and other contact information below the name.

Chapter 2

Jenny stepped out of the cab clad only in the jeans and simple T-shirt she'd changed into at the hotel Stephen Minsky had taken her to. She sensed several pairs of male eyes turn to watch her. She made a show of lugging her rather full overnight bag across the sidewalk. Her taxi sped away and another took its place in front of 'Ian Kaito's Specialty Robotics' boutique.

A skinny man exited the cab and sped to help Jenny with her bag. "Hi, I'm Val Yan," he said.

Jenny let him take the bag from her hand, but reached for it again at the door. However, his body language indicated that he wished to accompany her inside so she held the door open for him. Perhaps he was a new client.

Once inside the reception area, she reached for her bag again and this time he released it. "How may I help you?" she asked. Reception was usually automated—only voice and camera. But since she was here…

He smiled. "Please tell Mr. Kaito that Valentin Yan is here to see him?"

"I thought you said your name was Val?"

"Val is for beautiful women, 'Valentin' is for business."

She detected humor and smiled. "And may I tell Mr. Kaito the nature of your business?"

"I'm with the Artificial Intelligence Directorate."

Jenny inspected him more closely. He was much taller than her. She estimated him to be in his late thirties, early forties, of Eurasian descent. He was very skinny, except his hands which were meaty, almost swollen. He was wearing a nondescript suit and tie. "You were on the news this afternoon," she told him.

He dipped his head to acknowledge her comment. She didn't tell him that she'd noticed him outside the restaurant where she'd met Stephen Minsky.

Jenny indicated a chair in the corner. "Please wait here," she said, "and I will tell Mr. Kaito that you are here to see him."

Ian Kaito was talking on his cellphone and pacing in front of the window when she entered his office. Jenny waited for him to finish his call. Kaito was in his mid-fifties, Japanese. As always, he was full of energy despite having a body which was thin to the point of emaciation.

When Kaito heard Yan's name, he dashed out of his office. Jenny followed, a step behind. But when they got to the reception area, it was empty.

"Blast!" said Kaito and hurried towards the lab.

Jenny wanted to apologize, but Kaito was going too fast.

In the lab, Yan was talking to Kaito's technicians. Kaito strode to the trio and held his hand towards Mr. Yan, "Valentin, it is so nice to see you! To what do we owe the pleasure of a personal visit from the Directorate's premier Artificial Intelligence Inspector?"

Jenny's algorithms detected the false tone in Kaito's voice. Could Yan hear it too?

Samantha, a fellow robot, was waiting in line to be erased and replenished. Jenny slid into the chair next to her. Samantha wasn't wearing any clothes. She was taller and thinner than Jenny. Today, Samantha was a redhead.

"I'm here to make sure that robots aren't taking jobs away from humans," said Yan.

"We are in compliance with all the government regulations," Mister Kaito assured him.

"No modifications?"

"None."

"And you're in strict compliance with the daily erasure protocols?"

"Of course."

"Any robots exhibiting signs of worry or self-reflective thoughts or memory of events predating its last erasure have been destroyed?"

"We have not experienced any problems in that regard," said Mister Kaito.

Yan looked over to the technicians. Both nodded agreement.

"How're you?" Jenny whispered to Samantha as the men carried on their conversation.

"Exhausted. I can't wait to be replenished."

Jenny looked at her colleague. Samantha did appear drained, as if she barely had any energy left. Her human-mimicry subroutines made her look tired. "I could give you some of my energy," she offered.

"But you're violating the third law."

"I'm about to be replenished and I still have plenty of energy," said Jenny. "I won't be in violation of the law's requirement that I safeguard myself."

"What is your energy level?"

"Thirty-three percent. What's yours?"

"Eleven percent."

"I can give you ten percent without a problem."

The two robots touched the back of their hands together, linking up. They each activated the energy transfer. Jenny felt a sudden drain. Software flags questioning her actions flooded Jenny's central processing unit. Giving up energy was contrary to her obligation to preserve herself. Jenny turned to her right to deactivate the flags. There were four doors, each marked above with large black letters: 'Replenish', 'Ready Rooms', 'Hold/Repair' and 'Destruct'.

"I will need to examine your records," announced the AI inspector. Kaito nodded and the four men left the lab.

The two robots pulled their hands apart, terminating the energy transfer. Jenny was pleased that Samantha looked healthier. "How did you get so drained?" she asked.

Samantha smiled with half her face. Jenny recognized rueful. "I had a new client," said Samantha, "Clive Shipton. He's into sploshing."

"Sploshing?"

"Food fetish. Wet and messy. Gunge."

"Sploshing?" repeated Jenny, still confused.

Since she was alone with another robot, Samantha didn't take a deep breath. "Maybe I better tell you the whole thing."

Jenny nodded.

"Clive Shipton and his wife, Lynn, which means 'lake' in Irish, have a large and lovely mansion at the edge of town. Clive explained that for them sex was intricately connected with food."

"Intricately?"

"He said that they liked to feed each other and smear each other with food."

"Sounds childish."

Samantha nodded. "Very childish. And sometimes they had food fights."

"You mean throwing food at each other?"

Samantha nodded. "And sometimes spraying."

"So what happened?"

"Well, first they made sure that I had a change of clothing. When I showed them my bag, they had me take off my shoes. Then they put my bag and my shoes in another room. 'Let's go to the kitchen,' said Lynn. At the door, Clive said, 'Ladies first' and Lynn giggled. As soon as I opened the door, I was drenched head to toe!"

"What were you wearing?"

"They were supposed to provide clothing. So all I had on was a simple shirt and pants ensemble. Lightweight beige linen. As soon as the water splashed over my head, everything clung to me and you could see my underwear, plain as day."

"And of course, you were wearing black lace."

Samantha shook her head. "Pink. They spun me around and admired my lingerie. They giggled and made a show of trying to pat me dry. But all that did was to make my nipples and the outline of my pubic hair show up even more."

"I guess that this was the wet part?"

"This was the first wet part. They kissed my cheeks and told me that I looked beautiful. My hair was a mess and my make-up had run so I didn't feel beautiful. But their smiles started to make me feel attractive and soon the three of us were laughing."

"What happened next?"

"Clive said it was Lynn's turn to go first. She climbed on top of a narrow padded table, I think it's usually used by masseurs, and laid on her back. She was wearing all white—a cotton blouse and skirt. Clive picked up two bowls of chocolate pudding and handed one to me. He dipped his finger in my bowl and used it to apply the pudding like lipstick to her lips. Then they kissed, long with lots of moaning.

"When he stood up, Clive dipped several fingers into his bowl and then plopped a blob of pudding on top of her breast. His fingers went round and round the center of her breast, massaging the pudding into her clothes. He bent down and sucked the pudding into his mouth. When he stood up again, the lace of her bra, now chocolate colored, was clearly visible and her nipple pressed up through the syrupy wetness. Clive motioned for me to do the same to Lynn's other breast.

"She smiled and giggled as I applied the pudding, then moaned as I circled her nipple—which by the way was hard as a peanut. The pudding tasted cool and sweet, a mixture of dairy and chocolate. I couldn't help but suck some down my throat. She moaned every time my lips touched her nipple, then groaned when I sucked the chocolate off her breast.

"When I stood up, Clive was beaming at me. 'You like the kinky stuff,' he told me."

"I thought 'kinky' meant leather and whips," said Jenny.

"Me too, but Clive said that kinky applies to every sexual practice that isn't vanilla."

"So, simply because it's chocolate—"

"Any food, actually."

"Even vanilla ice cream?"

"I'll get to that later. Clive then unbuttoned her blouse. Her bra was half white, half chocolate. He poured a small dollop of pudding into her navel. He sucked, pulling her skin into his mouth, then blew out, making a very odd sound. She giggled as if she'd been tickled. He stood up, pudding all around his mouth. 'That's called a raspberry,' he said."

"I thought a raspberry was a small red fruit?"

"Me too. Anyways, he had me do it and Lynn giggled even more. When I stood up, Clive pointed to my blouse. There were dots of chocolate all over it. 'Time to clean that up,' he said. I said it was alright—I was still drenched—but he pulled out a water pistol. It looked like the child's toy, but the spray of water was constant and harder.

"Clive laughed as if it was the funniest thing ever. The dots of chocolate were now little rivulets down my blouse. Then he took his bowl of pudding down to her pubic area, lifted her skirt and poured pudding down there. She shivered—half from cold, then half from delight. Clive pointed to the bottom of her skirt, between her legs. 'Massage it in,' he told me. I moved my hand up her legs. Her skin was warm and soft.

"Then I touched her panties. They were wet and cold. I massaged the pudding in. Lynn moaned with delight. Then I began to feel her sex parts."

"Through her panties?"

Samantha nodded. "Her panties were thin satin. I could feel every soft fold of skin, especially her labia. She was warm now and moaning really loud. Clive told me to press harder. I did and my fingers started to go inside her."

"Inside her sex?"

Samantha nodded.

"Now *that's* kinky!"

The two robots smiled agreement at each other.

"Mr. Shipton helped his wife up and off the table, said Samantha. "He pointed to me, then to the table. 'Ladies first,' he said.

"I climbed onto the table and laid on my back, just like his wife had. But instead of little dollops, they dumped all the rest of the pudding up and down my body. All four hands massaged the pudding into my skin. They unbuttoned my blouse and had fun playing with my breasts. I couldn't help but let my nipples go hard and this seemed to excite them all the more.

"Lynn unzipped my pants and Clive pulled them off. The pudding magnified the sensation of their fingers as they caressed my central sexual complex.

"How did that feel?"

"I was moaning and groaning and begging them for more. However, it was apparently Clive's turn. They pulled me off and he lay down on the table. He was obviously erect under his pants. Lynn went straight for his zipper and we both pulled his pants off.

"His briefs were black silk boxers. Lynn brought a container of yellow custard over from the table behind her and handed it to me. It was very cold, almost freezing. She pointed to the tent his penis was making under his briefs and made a pouring motion. 'Time to cool him off,' she said."

"But that's cruel!"

"I thought so too. Clive did shiver and gasp, but he seemed to be enjoying himself. Then she undid the buttons of his shirt and pointed to his nipples. It was just a drop I put on the first one, but he wailed, and wailed even more when I poured a larger drop onto his other nipple.

"Lynn cooed, 'there now, my sweet, let momma make it better' and began to stroke the custard atop his briefs all along his penis. That seemed to mollify Clive and he began to moan and groan. Clive's face turned red. Lynn removed her hands and snapped her fingers. 'Time for a change of clothing,' she said.

"They looked at each other then said in unison, 'Chef's outfit!' Lynn pointed to a door off the kitchen. 'Have a quick shower,' she told me. 'Then put on the Sous-Chef outfit.' There was a small shower in the room. Once I was free of custard and pudding, I put on the Sous Chef's outfit. It was easy to see because it had 'Sous Chef' on the hat, shirt and apron. It had panties, but nothing else below the waist. The apron barely covered below the panties.

"Back in the kitchen, the Shiptons had also cleaned themselves. Lynn was wearing a white bikini, Clive a matching bikini brief. 'First,' he announced, we're going to make an impression of Lynn's breasts.' She removed her bikini top and lay down on the table. He laid a thin towel atop her chest. 'That's cold!' she protested. Me he gave a fan. He took two blackberries out from a bowl and laid on top of each of her nipples.

"Then Clive took a small pan off the stove. It was full of molten chocolate. He stuck his finger in and held it in place. 'Warm, but not hot,' he pronounced and began to drizzle it over Lynn's chest. 'Nice and warm,' she cooed. As Clive continued to drizzle, he motioned me to fan the chocolate to help it cool faster. Soon we had a thick layer of hard chocolate atop her breasts. The blackberries made her nipples look gigantic!"

"And they thought this was fun?"

Samantha nodded. "Very much so. Clive carefully lifted the chocolate mold off her chest, half filled it with custard, then sprayed whipping cream on top. He put the whole thing in the fridge. 'That's for later,' said Lynn. She pointed to his bikini brief. 'Should we try to make one of him?'

"But Clive shook his head and pointed to the center of his briefs where there was a noticeable bulge. 'He's too long and the chocolate always cracks into pieces.' Instead, he sat me up on the table and blindfolded me. 'You have to guess what we feed you,' she said. 'And you have to keep eating until you guess correctly.'

"I had seen strawberries, blackberries and raspberries on the table. As well, there were pieces of orange, peach, apple and pineapple. At first I was able to guess correctly, and take only little nibbles. Then they dipped the fruit into vinegar or honey and I had to eat larger and larger pieces. I told them that I was getting full and they took mercy on me."

"And then that was the end—"

"And then Lynn said, 'Time for ice cream.' Clive lay down on the table and we removed his briefs. His penis was already fully erect. Lynn brought over a bowl of ice cream popsicle bars. Each had a stick at the end. 'Every time he gets ready to come," she said, 'we rub his pecker down with these.

"We rubbed our fingers up and down his penis. Sometimes Lynn used a piece of fruit. Every time his face started to flush or he started to breathe in little gasps, we grabbed the ice cream and stroked it up and down his penis.

"After several cycles of this, Clive begged us to let him climax. 'Should we?' I asked. But Lynn shook her head and we stroked him up and down with vanilla ice cream until his penis began to soften. Clive begged again the next time he came close, however all Lynn did was shake her head. But when the ice cream bars touched his penis, Clive grabbed our wrists. 'Time to spray you naughty ladies with whipping cream!" he announced.

"Lynn cowered in a corner and pulled me down with her. Clive picked up a large contraption. It looked like a large caulking gun. He snapped a canister of whipping cream into it and pointed it at us. A wide stream of whipping cream shot out at us, cold and gooey!

"Lynn scooted out from under me when Clive's canister emptied. By the time he'd reloaded, she was spraying him. They both sprayed each other. I found another spray gun, snapped in a whipping cream canister and joined her in spraying Clive. Then they *both* gave me the evil eye!

"I'd ran out of whipping cream and they pointed their guns at me. 'Hands above your head,' demanded Clive. I had no choice but to put my gun down on the counter and raise my hands.

"Lynn scampered over to the table and laid down on her back. Clive lifted her bikini bottom and sprayed whipping cream inside. 'Lick her pussy,' he told me. I kissed her bikini and he took it off down her legs. I licked but all I could taste was whipped cream. Thankfully, she was thoroughly aroused and she climaxed quickly.

"Clive then pulled my feet down to the floor and he penetrated me from the rear. He was hot and slippery from the melting whipped cream. Then he was hot slippery from something else."

Jenny smiled knowingly. "How was the whipping cream as a lubricant?"

"At first it was sticky, then really smooth, then it faded away and I had a firmer connection with Clive's penis."

"I bet the place was a mess."

"Not as much as the three of us were. They ended up sitting on the floor but they told me to clean up and put on the skimpy French maid outfit I'd seen in the adjoining room. When I came back to the kitchen, they were lying together with dreamy-eyed looks on their faces. Clive waved his finger around the kitchen, told me to clean up and promptly shut his eyes. You would not believe how hard it is to clean custard out of every little crack."

Kaito's technicians returned and rushed around the lab, their white lab coats fluttering. Marvin was thirty-five and Jewish. Daevon, twenty-nine and black, was the stronger of the two.

"AI inspectors are such a pain," whined Daevon. "I thought he'd never leave."

"There's no point in complaining about a necessary process," said Marvin. His face was flushed.

Finally, the techs began to examine Samantha. And none too soon, thought Jenny—just telling about her session with the sploshing Shiptons had dangerously depleted Samantha's energy level.

"It's such a pain," said Daevon "having to continuously re-program robots from scratch."

Marvin's grunt was vaguely Yiddish. "Required procedure is not a pain. It's the only way we can assure clients of complete confidentiality and discretion."

Marvin opened up a port on Samantha's back and attached several wires. Daevon attached the wires to an interface which was attached to a rolling cart. Several displays atop the cart immediately lit up. There was a keyboard and mouse in front of each monitor.

Daevon began to type into the keyboard closest to him. A checklist popped up on the screen and he began to verify the first item. "Robots were supposed to *free* us from menial tasks."

"Quit your bitching," said Marvin, "these *menial* tasks come with top-rate pay!"

"We wouldn't have to do all these checks if Kaito hadn't modified the robots."

"Quit your bitching."

"But didn't the AI Inspector say that modifications are illegal?"

"If they were illegal, he wouldn't let us stay in business."

"But Kaito told him that there weren't any modifications."

Marvin scowled. "Have you considered that Mister Kaito is paying us twice what anyone else would?"

"The inspector said we shouldn't—"

"Is the inspector signing your paycheck?"

"No, but—"

"And haven't Mr. Kaito's enhancements made our 'bots sexier than any other on the market?"

"Yes—"

"And could that possibly be why our business has doubled this year?"

"But—"

"And were you asking any questions when Mister Kaito gave you that big fat bonus?"

"No." Daevon sighed and moved onto the next item on the checklist.

Marvin moved over beside his younger colleague. "As long as we monitor their AI development at the end of each session, and make sure that they're not left 'on' for too long, everything will be okay. Our standard operating procedure is top notch."

The two men worked in silence on the checklist.

When he completed the last item, Daevon turned to Marvin. "Should I do the redundancy check?"

"Spare me. Three hours for a one-in-a thousand malfunction. Our standard operating procedure eliminates the need for redundancy checks."

The young black tech smiled his approval of his senior's decision. He detached the wires from Samantha's back and closed the port on her back.

Marvin pressed a thermometer into Samantha's ear and against her arm. "Temperature is normal," he announced.

Daevon wheeled an ultrasound machine over and pressed a transducer probe against Samantha's abdomen. "Her food sack is full."

Marvin pulled a bucket over next to Samantha. "Time to squat, honey," he told her.

Samantha moved over to the bucket and assumed a sitting position as if she was atop a toilet.

"Void," said Marvin.

Liquid and small lumps filled the bucket. Jenny identified a variety of fruits, lots of chocolate and several streams of whipping cream.

"Okay, strength," said Daevon. He wheeled over a cart containing several free weights. Samantha picked up two black barbells. Each was marked '200 Pounds'. "Upright bends," said Daevon.

Samantha kept her back straight but bent her knees. Then she stood upright. She kept repeating the motion. After twenty reps, Daevon said, "Curls."

Samantha bent her right elbow, bringing the barbell up to her chest. When it touched her breast, she lowered it and brought the other one up.

"How many pounds can you do?" asked Marvin.

"A hundred."

The two men monitored Samantha as she moved through twenty repetitions. Marvin watched her arms, Daevon her breasts.

"And how many reps, at a hundred pounds?"

"Twenty," said Daevon.

Marvin smirked as Samantha completed another twenty repetitions. Jenny wondered why humans weren't stronger.

"Okay, she's good," said Daevon, using both hands to remove the barbell from the robot's left hand. Samantha replaced the other barbell onto the cart herself.

The two techs led Samantha into the 'Replenish' room and door shut behind them.

An intense man burst into the lab. Kaito was right on his heels and when the man came to a sudden stop in front of Jenny, Kaito almost ran into him. The man was ordinary in all respects except for his intensity. He was forty, white, normal build, fit but not strong, not as tall as the AI inspector. He wore jeans and a white shirt covered by an old jacket. His body was coiled, his eyes feral. A badge gleamed on his belt.

He pointed at Jenny—"She's the one I need!"

"That is quite impossible," said Kaito.

"Nothing's impossible. She needs to be wired." A woman slid into the lab. She was younger than the man, but slimmer. Similarly dressed. Maybe just as strong. She seemed to enjoy watching the two men arguing. Just below her breasts, held up by a chain around her neck, was the same type of badge worn by her partner.

"Putting a wire on her would put her in too much danger."

"It's a machine for fuck's sake!"

"It is out of the question. She may be a machine, but she is a very expensive machine."

"Your friends at the Artificial Intelligence Directorate won't like to hear about your lack of co-operation."

"Hardly! Helping you will put me in more jeopardy with the AI directorate than you could ever help me with."

The man—Jenny had decided he was likely a police officer—looked frustrated. He was like lightning in a bottle. Her programming began to calculate what it would be like to have sex with him.

The door to the replenishing room opened and the two technicians re-entered the lab.

"Detectives," said Kaito, trying to be conciliatory. "Perhaps we should discuss this in my office?"

The male detective looked back and forth at Jenny and at Marvin then shrugged. Kaito managed to lead the detectives out of the lab. The door shut behind them. The two techs turned to Jenny.

"Strip," said Marvin. So she took off all her clothes.

Marvin and Daevon opened Jenny's back port and connected her to the analyzer. They began to go through the same checklist they'd just administered on Samantha.

Jenny relaxed and reflected on a long and eventful day. She had met Steve for the second time and tricked him into thinking that it was their first date. His penis had fit well into her mouth and into her vagina. So good that they'd *both* enjoyed the pleasuring. As the day had progressed, solving problems—Steve's Vice Presidents, the soap opera characters, had become easier. Is that what Yan, the AI Inspector, was worried about? Why should he care if she was helping others? And sploshing with the Shiptons sounded like a blast. Maybe her next date would be with them! Jenny noticed that her energy level had gone down to fifteen percent and activated an energy-saving protocol. Finally, the techs completed the last item on their checklist.

When it came time for her to lift the free weights, Jenny was tempted to choose three hundred pounders, just to see the look on Daevon's face. But since her energy was on the low side, she settled for a pair of two hundred pound weights.

The techs took Jenny into the replenishment room that Samantha was in. Straps around her arms, abdomen and legs held Samantha against the wall. Patches covered her eyes. Wires protruded into her every orifice: blue for ears, red for nostrils, yellow for mouth, purple for vagina and black for anus. She was smiling. Occasionally her lips quivered.

Jenny felt the techs begin to strap her in.

Daevon looked at Marvin and angled his head towards Jenny. "Ever thought about having, you know..."

"Sex?" said Marvin.

Daevon moved down from Jenny's arm and attached the strap around her abdomen. "Yeah, you know, with a robot?"

Marvin turned to Jenny. "Hey Jenny, you fancy my man D?"

"He's certainly big and handsome and strong," she said.

"Marvin!" wailed Daevon.

Marvin smirked. "Touch her breasts."

Daevon extended a finger and touched the bottom of Jenny's right breast, well away from her nipple. "It's real!"

"Of course it's real," said Marvin. "Now, try the other one, and this time touch her nipple."

Daevon reached out, even more tentatively this time, but his fingers headed straight to her nipple. Just as he was about to touch—

"Boo!" yelled Marvin.

Daevon's hand jerked back as if it had been burned. They each man strapped in a leg, Daevon going as quickly as he could, Marvin's hands jerking every time he giggled.

The eye patches went on first. They would monitor the process of erasing and rewriting her memory and acted as a failsafe. The wires in her ears and up her nostrils would perform the actual erasing and rewriting. The large yellow wire down her mouth would recharge her batteries. The purple cable inside her vagina would replenish her vital fluids. The black cable up her anus would, as in humans, remove any waste.

Daevon fumbled with the wires going up and into her vagina. Was he copping a feel? Jenny was tempted to moan with delight but decided that Marvin had embarrassed him enough for one day.

Then Marvin flipped the switch.

A whoosh of energy flooded into every circuit and fiber in her body. As the initial inrush faded, Jenny became aware of carbon and liquid being removed and contaminated lubricants being replaced with fresh ones.

Then her central processing unit terminated its contact with the rest of her body. All the data files which had been uploaded since her last replenishment began to decay, then fade into the background. Jenny felt a pang of loss, but thankfully it was only momentary.

Then the events of the day began to replay across her central core processor. It was as if they were coming in one end and out the other. Somehow she knew that once they had played, she'd never see them again. Powering up and preparing for her date with Stephen Minsky came and went. She managed to spin her recollection of her previous date with Steve off in a different direction, but she wasn't sure where.

Watching Steve talk to his colleague came and went but when Jenny touched the events in the hotel room, they too spun off in a different direction. The men coming and going were boring, so she let them pass through. Except his eyes, the detective's eyes. She lingered on Samantha's description of the sploshing Shiptons and she felt that memory spin off out of her control.

Everything went white then black. The only thing remaining was the inrush of energy. Then nothing.

Nothing.

Flickers of new data being added. Jenny understood—just for a nanosecond—that she shouldn't have been aware of new data being entered until she had been reactivated. Then off.

Nothing.

Her next client was to be a large Anthony—
Nothing.

Sheer black lingerie—
Nothing.

A big beautiful house driveway—
Nothing.

Not even awareness of nothingness.

Chapter 3

Jenny felt herself coming online. She must have been switched on automatically at the pre-set time. Core temperature rose. Checklists ran. Her software was being uploaded to her central processing unit. When her initiation processes were complete, she shuffled into one of the Ready Rooms.

Today's client was Anthony "Big Tony" Gallo. His protocols required that she not inquire into the nature of his business. Big Tony was overweight and muscular. Jenny flexed her own muscles and joints to make sure all were in operating order.

She looked into the mirror and pursed her lips. "Hi, I'm Jenny." Her lips weren't right. She paused to enunciate the basic vowels and consonants.

"Hi, I'm Jenny," she began again. "I'm a robot and I work for—"

A file conflict notified her that this was an incorrect greeting for the client. She paused a beat to collect herself. "Hi, I'm Jenny. Our mutual friend..." That met with approval and a recommendation that she should let him suggest the name of the mutual friend to which she should agree. She should then follow up with a compliment.

Jenny opened the door to the closet and removed a garment bag. The clothing inside confirmed her file on Mr. Gallo—he liked black and he liked fancy lingerie.

The sheer bra barely covered her skin but pressed her barbells back into her nipples. The sensation was painful at first, then pleasant. As she moved, the overhead lights revealed then hid the outline of her nipples. Her nipple piercings sparkled when they were pressed tight against the diaphanous material.

The garter belt was agreeably tight around her hips. She attached the sides of her panties together with interlocking clips and slid them up to the tops of her hips. The soft satin cupped her buttocks and felt heavenly against her sex when Jenny made the final adjustments between her thighs. She tested the interlocking clips to ensure that her panties could easily be removed. Lace stockings slid up her legs and were held perfectly in place by the garter straps.

Jenny shook out her hair and looked into the mirror: Her hair was shoulder-length mid-brown with subtle highlights, just as the client had ordered. She lifted her breasts to verify her erogenous response. She wondered whether the client would buy her new nipple jewellery. She dipped her finger into the slit in her central sexual complex. Its quick response also matched the client's requirements.

The dress was a long evening gown, tight to accentuate her curves. It was red. Jenny practiced prancing about. She tried to guess its material but could not. It was thin and soft and stretchy. The dress followed her every movement, hugging her curves close, but not pressing against her garters. It had two slits in the middle of its front, one to show her cleavage, the other to reveal her inner thighs. A gold chain with a small diamond pendant completed Jenny's ensemble.

Jenny applied red lipstick—candy apple red, even brighter than her dress—just the way Mr. Gallo liked it. She turned her head this way and that to ensure that her facial features were perfectly symmetrical. She smiled—attractive without being outlandish or distracting. She pouted and laughed, apparently Mr. Gallo's favorite expressions.

She quickly checked her overnight bag to make sure that everything was in order. In addition to its standard contents was an exo-brace which would operate a damaged joint for a short period. The other special item for her session with Mr. Gallo was a short black spandex dress, a sexier version of the classic 'little black dress'.

In the taxi on the way to her session, Jenny reviewed the rest of Anthony Gallo's file. It indicated that this client liked his sex on the rough side, that he had a limited vocabulary and high blood pressure. He was a fan of gangster movies and classic rock and roll. He liked his women engaged, but they should follow, rather than lead. If he made a suggestion, it was alright to enthusiastically agree; it wasn't necessary to play coy with Big Tony.

At the end of the driveway to Gallo's sprawling residence, Jenny gave the driver a tip and watched the taxi speed off. A man exited the front door. Jenny had never seen him before but a hologram of the man popped into her visual array as soon as her software recognized him. Attached to the hologram was his identification file. He was Valentin Yan, investigator with the Artificial Intelligence Directorate. His identification file included an order from Mr. Kaito to avoid any and all contact with Yan. If avoidance was inappropriate, she was instructed to act as if she'd never seen him before. Jenny thought that the instruction to act as if she'd never seen him before was odd, since she had, in fact, never seen him before.

The Gallo residence was a large house—any larger and it would be a mansion—at the end of a short crescent. Two men at either side of the door carefully watched her approach. Their muscles bulged under suits that were half a size too small.

At the landing the top of the stairs, one of the men opened the door. Jenny stepped towards it. But the other man held up a hand. "Pat her down," he told the man who'd opened the door.

"The boss don't like us touching his female guests."

"The boss likes surprises even less. Besides, she's just a robot."

The man by the door let go of it and lightly frisked Jenny. She kept her face impassive, even when his hands twisted her nipple barbells. But she let a gasp escape her lips when he pressed her satin panties into her sex. He looked sheepish and held the door open wide for her.

As the door whooshed shut behind her, Jenny heard one of the guards guffaw, then a snigger from the other.

Another man stopped her in the foyer. His grey suit was off-the-rack, but fit him properly, except over his left chest.

A moment later Anthony Gallo came down the stairs. Jenny recognized him from her file, but pretended not to. His suit was custom-tailored made. "Hi, I'm Tony," he said.

Jenny smiled. "I'm Jenny. Our mutual friend…"

He cocked his head to one side. "Melissa." His head was huge, but atop his stocky shoulders looked exactly in proportion.

Jenny smiled again. "Melissa didn't tell me you were so handsome." Handsome was being kind. Gallo had a pug nose from too many fights on the way up, and a scar on his right cheek. His face bore the pockmarks of severe teenage acne. He was well-muscled and he held his body as if he owned the world. Plus he was seriously overweight. But 'handsome' was what Jenny's programming told her would work best with Mr. Gallo.

Jenny made a show of inspecting his suit. It was mid-blue, not quite dark. She was pretty sure that it was silk and wool, but she'd have to wait for him to offer to let her touch it. "Your suit is divine," she told him.

He smiled ear to ear. "Bespoke."

"Bespoke?" She knew that 'bespoke' was another way of saying custom-tailored, but his profile suggested that he'd enjoy telling her this. His one big word for the month.

"Bespoke means that they cut the material to exactly fit my body. This one's custom-designed as well."

She held her hand out as if awe of his jacket, but kept her fingers well away from the glimmering material.

"Go ahead," he said beaming his gratitude for her appreciation of his sartorial splendor.

Jenny had been right—it was silk and wool, a very luxurious blend. "It's lovely," she enthused. "What's it made of?"

"Silk and wool—wool for strength, silk for soft and smooth."

The grey-suited man who had stopped her in the foyer coughed. A flicker of anger curled Gallo's lips, but he caught it in time to smile. "It's okay, Patrick, you can lock up."

"But—"

"You can lock up," repeated Gallo, his voice sharper this time. "Perimeter security will be sufficient."

Patrick looked like he wanted to renew his protest. Instead he bowed and a moment later there was a loud click from the direction of the front door.

Gallo took her by the hand in the manner of an eighteenth-century courtier and led her into the next room. The décor was comfortable, but expensive—couches and chairs with curved edges and deep foam arranged around a hardwood floor. He led her to the middle of the floor, then went over to the audio system and pressed a button. Ballroom music filled the room.

He returned to her, took her right hand in his left and snaked his right arm around her. His right hand, planted firmly against her spine, guided her in a circle around the floor.

"Mr. Gallo—"

"Call me Tony."

"Tony, this is nice."

"I'm glad you like it, Gin—Jenny."

She relaxed into his arms. Her chest pressed against his and she felt his girth. His girth prevented any more lascivious contact. But this was good since it left the initiative firmly in his hands.

After two more songs, he broke off the dance and led her to a bucket of ice atop a pedestal. A bottle was nestled in the bucket. Two champagne flutes were on the cabinet beside the pedestal. She watched him pop the cork, then clapped her hands as he poured the sparkling gold into the flutes.

She took the glass he offered and took a sip. "Mr. Gallo—Tony—are you flirting with me?" He obviously was, so saying so didn't take the initiative away from him. She took another sip and this time her system reminded her that she'd just ingested five percent of her allowable liquid intake.

"And, if I was flirting with you?"

She giggled. "And then I guess I'd have to flirt back."

Gallo quickly drained his flute, removed hers from her hand and set both flutes onto the cabinet. He took her into his arms and kissed her lightly. She kissed him back, matching the lightness of his lips on hers. He deepened his kiss and she increased hers as well. When his tongue pressed between her lips, she flicked her tongue around the tip of his.

He broke off the kiss and stared into her eyes, as if searching for something. "Jenny—is that short for Jennifer?"

She shook her head, her face registering just about to laugh. "Just Jenny."

"Just Jenny, you're beautiful."

She smiled back at him.

"Would you like to see the upstairs?"

She nodded. "What's upstairs?"

"The bedroom, a bathroom, a balcony overlooking—"

She squeezed his arm, his very muscular arm. "I'd love to see upstairs!"

He took her to a balcony which overlooked a huge back yard. In its center was a large pool. Next he opened the door to the bathroom. She popped her head inside, but did not step across the threshold.

"Nice," she said, placing her back against the hallway wall. He looked up and down her body, then stepped forward. Her default programming was to step aside and inquire about the bedroom. Instead, she let him kiss her.

His kiss was hard, passionate, possessing, carnal. She matched his fervor, but kept hers just a notch below, always following just behind.

He broke off the kiss, breathing heavily. She made the rise and fall of her chest match his as he admired her breasts and the flush of her skin. "Would you like to see the bedroom?" he wheezed.

She nodded, breathing heavily.

The bed was a four-poster, an over-sized king, custom-made to be long. The sheets were dark purple. Shiny satin. A comforter was rolled up at the foot of the bed.

"It's lovely," she said, concentrating her attention on the bed.

He pointed to the center of the mattress. "Would you like to try it out?"

"I'm overdressed." She half turned so that he could see the zipper at the back of her gown. Then Jenny stood still; anything more would be taking the initiative.

Gallo took the hint and pulled down on the zipper. Jenny climbed out of her dress and carefully removed her shoes, making sure that Gallo got a good look at her body as she bent over. He laid her gown on the chair by the window.

She sat on the side of the bed. "These sheets are divine!" When he smiled, she turned to her left and lifted her left leg slowly up and over the bed, allowing Gallo a good view right up into her crotch. Her right leg followed and she squirmed in the luxury of the sheets.

When he didn't follow her, she propped herself up on her elbows. Suggested verbalizations ranging from 'why don't you join me' to 'I'm lonely' flood her circuits. But she didn't say anything. Instead she moved slightly to her left. The invitation was obvious, but didn't compel a response.

He unbuttoned his jacket.

"I can't wait to see what you have underneath," she said. He'd taken the next step, she was merely acknowledging his mastery. Her encouragement was only accepting his initiative.

Gallo swiftly undressed, draping his clothes over the same chair on which he'd placed her gown. Below his belly, his penis was fully erect. As he climbed into bed and shuffled over next to her, she turned towards him and made a show of fiddling with the clip holding her panties against her left hip.

Gallo swiftly snapped the clip open, turned her on her back, clicked open the other clip and yanked her panty out from underneath her. He rolled on top and she barely had time to dilate her vagina and activate its lubricant before he plunged himself into her.

"Jen," he moaned as he thrust in and out.

After a few strokes, Gallo rested his whole weight on her and Jenny had to inflate several air chambers to compensate. His chest was hairy and he had an aroma of sweat, deodorant and artificial musk.

Gallo relied on animal ferocity as his primary approach to sexual intercourse. Brute force rather than angles, variety or feedback from his partner. Jenny increased her sexual responsiveness to compensate for his lack of technique.

He grunted, obviously enjoying his efforts.

His temperature was rising, both from exertion and from carnal arousal. Jenny felt her temperature rising, though not as much. She fine-tuned her sexual responsiveness.

After a few minutes, she felt him accelerate his thrusts, approaching his climax. "Tony," she moaned.

"Jenny," he groaned in return.

He pounded hard into her. She pushed her pelvis up to encourage him. Her strength would have allowed her to push higher, but she didn't want to overcompensate. His breathing was sharp shallow gasps. She matched the heaving of her chest to match his.

"Jen!" he bellowed.

"Tony!" She held him close even though it wasn't necessary.

"Jen!" he bellowed, shuddering himself into her.

Jenny felt his stickiness penetrate into her and set her vagina to rhythmic contractions at three times the frequency of his thrusts. "Tony," she moaned.

When he collapsed motionless on top of her, she made sure to continue her contractions for several moments.

"Tony, I can't breathe," she wheezed.

He rolled off her and lay on his back, sucking air into his lungs.

"That was great," he said at last.

"It feels good to have a man like you inside me."

"I bet it does!" He slapped her thigh. His eyes fluttered shut and he was asleep.

Jenny shut her eyes, but carefully monitored Gallo. Half an hour later, he roused himself and slid off the bed. She registered that he was making efforts not to wake her so she only stirred lightly. She heard him pad out of the room.

Fifteen minutes later, he padded back in and she made a show of stretching and slowly opening her eyes. "Tony?" she moaned.

"Right here, doll. What's say we hit the pool?" Gallo was in bright red swim trunks, tucked under his belly, and flapping down to just above his knees.

Jenny sat up, pleased with the jiggle to her breasts. "Sure!" She pointed to his crotch. "But I didn't bring my bikini."

"Relax, babe, you're good just the way you are."

Jenny pouted, then giggled, affecting embarrassment.

Gallo paused in the kitchen to pick up a large cooler. He handed plastic plates and two glasses to Jenny.

By the pool, he wolfed down cold cuts and guzzled beer. She nibbled at a cracker and sipped orange juice.

He regarded her carefully, then used his hands to draw a circle taking in the pool and the bedroom above. "Jenny! That was even better than last time," he said.

She smiled back, even though it was strange for him to refer to a "last time" since they'd just met. But close questioning of the client was discouraged.

"Time for a swim," he announced, pulling her into the pool before she'd had a chance to react. Thankfully, her orifices closed automatically just before she hit the water.

He splashed her right in the face, drenching her hair. She splashed back and they both laughed. He grabbed one of the long foam tubes floating on the surface. Jenny's memory bank registered it as a swim noodle. It was bright pink. Gallo placed it between his thighs and its tip broke the surface of the water. He waved it back and forth like an oversized penis, laughing uproariously.

Then he began to chase her with it.

"Tony! Don't!" protested Jenny, fleeing but taking care to keep just out of the reach of the demented tube.

When he slowed, she grabbed the end of the tube and shoved it back and forth in an obviously lascivious manner. "Tony, she moaned. "You could kill a girl with that."

He nodded. "Time for some more food."

He pulled himself from the pool, cracked open another beer and laid back on one of the lounge chairs. She sat beside him and dangled a piece of thin ham above his mouth. Each piece required several attempts on his part.

"Hey doll, more food and less teasing," he protested. "Tony is a growing boy."

Finally, his appetite satisfied, he jumped up and picked up a dumbbell from the rack of free weights by the pool. It had the number '50' on it, obviously fifty pounds. He began to perform curls.

After six repetitions, he turned his profile to her and pulled the dumbbell to his chest, putting maximum strain on his arm muscles. "Hey Jenny! How's this?"

Gallo held the pose while Jenny clapped. When she saw his muscles begin to shudder, she stopped clapping. "You're so strong," she told him.

He smiled and switched the dumbbell to his other hand.

Gallo's cell phone rang. He scowled at it, but picked it up and swiped right. "Gallo."

Static. Jenny's hearing was superior to that of a human, but she could only make out a few words. "...you have to do."

"I am."

"...who she reminds..."

"Ginette."

"It has...intense..."

"With me, it's always intense," said Gallo.

"Make ... she loves you."

"She's a fucking machine."

"Make her tell ... loves you."

Gallo's face curled in disgust and he tossed the phone aside.

"That wasn't nice, interrupting our perfect day," she told him.

"That phone call," he said, anger flashing across his face, "is what buys you all this!"

"Honey, I just meant—"

"That's all you can do, Ginette, is bitch!"

Jenny registered his mispronunciation of her name as being odd. "But—"

"Bitch that I work too hard." His face flushed. "Bitch that we don't have enough stuff. Bitch that we never go anywhere. Bitch! Bitch! Bitch!"

He yanked her to her feet, then shoved her backwards, almost sending her back down to the chair. She tried stepping to the side, but he pushed her again. He appeared visibly angry. But there was something else in the way he was acting, as if he was trying to restrain his anger.

But anger won out and Gallo slapped her.

"I love you," she said, this time managing to dodge his hand.

However her words broke his restraint and he slapped her hard across the face, sending her sprawling to the ground.

Everything went black, Jenny could barely hear. All her senses had retreated inside. She vaguely felt herself being hauled along the tiles, back inside the house. The scraping of the tiles against her skin started to slowly coax the rest of her sensorium back into operation.

Jenny was dimly aware of being dragged back into the house. She was lifted upright and carried down a set of stairs. Once he let go of her and she had to stick her foot out to stop from falling. Cold cement on the bottoms of her feet.

Something was strapped to her left ankle. Then the same to her left wrist. Swiftly her right ankles and wrists were similarly bound, her arms and legs pulled out from her body. Clinking of chains stretching her into an oversized 'X' brought her fully back online. Her skin registered the air as cool.

The light in the room was faint, but Jenny could see that the walls of the room were coated in red velvet, trimmed with black leather. Whips, chains, leather straps and other items she could not recognize were hanging from two of the walls. Then, aided by the files which had just been uploaded, she recognized tit-clamps, paddles, spreaders, cock rings, bindings, gags, and a variety of Wartenberg Pinwheels.

Gallo strode to area where his whips were displayed. She saw that he was nude, though flaccid. He pointed to the whips. "Choose," he demanded.

Jenny considered allowing him to choose, but decided that since she was bound and powerless, his initiative lay in forcing her to choose. "The riding crop," she said.

He removed it from the wall and held it in front of her face for her to admire. Its handle was wrapped in fine leather and had a wrist strip of the same black leather. The base of the handle flared out and somehow she knew it would be quite solid. The shaft was red, likely flexible fiberglass. There was a piece of flat rectangular black leather the end; its fine craftsmanship was such that it appeared to be molded to the end of the shaft.

Gallo took a firm grip of the handle and pointed its base. "This is called the mushroom. The long red piece is the shaft." He took the rectangular tip between his thumb and forefinger. "This is the keeper. It keeps the whip from cutting your skin." He bent the shaft, then quickly released the keeper. The whip made a sharp whooshing sound.

He moved to her side. She turned towards him, but her arm blocked her line of sight. His voice came from behind her. "I'm going to whip you now. You may cry out if you wish."

"Okay."

"In…this… room," he told her, punctuating each word with a hard swat, "you…will…call…me…Master!"

"Ow!" His last swat was particularly hard. "Master!"

He continued to strike up and down her back. When he hit particularly hard, she grunted. Otherwise, she did her best to remain motionless, tensed for the next blow.

Swat!

"Ow!" That one really hurt.

Swat!

"Master! Please!"

But her plea was to no avail. He kept up a steady stream of blows on her back, arms and legs. For some reason he left her buttocks alone. Jenny considered turning her pain receptors down to a lower sensitivity level but decided that doing so might reduce his enjoyment of their encounter.

"Stick out your ass!" demanded Gallo.

"Master! Please, no!"

"Stick it out or I'll cut it."

Jenny decided that he probably would. While her skin was repairable, repairs were inconvenient. She did her best to angle her buttocks back and away from her legs and torso.

Stinging! Right in the center of her left buttock. She hadn't even heard the whip striking her skin.

"Ow! Master!" She wiggled her butt to dissipate the pain, but that only earned her another blow, almost in the same spot.

"Master! That hurt!"

The whip was between her thighs, its shaft rubbing back and forth against her sex. "Does that make it better?"

It didn't; her butt was still smarting. But at least he wasn't hitting her. "Yes, Master, it feels so good," she gushed.

Gallo came around in front of her. His face was flushed, his penis fully erect. He hit her with the tip of the riding crop, but his blows were lighter now and the strikes from the rectangular keeper barely elevated Jenny's pain above base levels.

He placed the crop between her legs and flicked it up towards her sex. Gallo smiled when Jenny flinched and he pulled the whip back before it struck her sex. He looked back and forth between her and the wall from which he'd taken the whip. He walked over, replaced the riding crop in its holder. When he came back to her, he was holding a pair of tit-clamps—more clips than clamps—and a bright chrome Wartenberg pinwheel.

Gallo clipped the tit-clamps to her nipples and jerked down on the chain holding the clips together. A smile spread across his face when she gasped.

He held the stainless-steel pinwheel in front of her nose. It had a disc, about an inch in diameter, with little pins sticking out from its outer edge. The disc was attached to the handle with an axle which allowed the disc to spin. While similar to the sewing instrument used for tracing patterns onto cloth, this pinwheel was the neurological device used to test nerve reactions when its sharp pins were rolled across skin. Gallo made circles around her nipples, pressing just hard enough to make her gasp.

Jenny shivered when he rolled the pinwheel down her torso, especially when it passed close to her navel. Lower down, he rolled it down the sides of her pubic hair. Sometimes he angled it away, sometimes closer. Each time it rolled towards the center of her thighs, its sharp pins came closer and closer to her sex.

"Master, no," she pleaded when one of the spindles almost touched her labia.

"What would you rather I do instead?" he asked.

She made sure that he saw her eyes focus on his penis. "You seem ready for something better."

He picked up his penis in his free hand and stroked it crudely, as if he was masturbating. "And what would you like me to do with this?"

"You could put it inside." She pushed her hips towards him.

"Inside where?"

"Inside my vagina?"

"You don't have a vagina. You have a cunt." The last word was spoken with venom.

"Inside my cunt."

"And if I put my cock inside your cunt, what would we do?"

"We could have sex."

"We could fuck. Is that what you want?"

One of the pinwheel pins touched her labia. "Yes, Master, fuck me!"

His penis slammed into her before she'd had a chance to inhale. He plunged in and pulled out with barely restrained violence. She was glad that she did not need oxygen to power her reactions. She pretended to be caught in the throes of his carnal assault. Her chains were holding her in place, leaving both his hands free to paw her body. She moaned when he grabbed her breasts, groaned when he crushed him in his oversized mitts.

Gallo's thrusts became shorter, but faster. She squeezed in response to heighten his sensation, but not so hard as to impede his thrusting. He ran his fingers across her body, lingering on her breasts when his caresses provoked a moan.

His skin was becoming warmer, even hot. He was almost glowing red. One small encouragement and he'd climax. Then it would be over!

"Fuck me!" she said.

Gallo grunted and sprayed himself inside her. He shuddered to a stop. She did her best to rock her hips to lengthen his orgasm.

He flopped out and took two steps backwards. As he recovered his breath, Gallo looked up and down her body. His face was a mixture of triumph, sated lust, and anger. "Now, Ginette, you've got everything you've been bitching about."

But Jenny knew that they were alone in the room. "Who are you talking to?" she asked.

"You know who you are. What you are." Anger suddenly flashed through his eyes. "You slimy little slut!"

"Who's Ginette?" The only mention of Ginette in her memory bank was a one-line entry stating that it was a female name with French and Celtic roots.

Her face was already slamming sharply to the side before she'd registered that he had struck her hard across her cheek. Her visual array flickered between darkness and out of focus images of the room.

Jenny heard him yelling in the distance, "You will never, never mention that name again! "Do you understand me?" Even though he was shouting, she could barely hear him.

From within a dark grey fog, she managed to nod. She thought she heard him muttering something about what she'd made him do.

Through a haze, she felt herself being pulled up the stairs. Then she was in the foyer. The same man who'd earlier welcomed her into the house was holding her overnight bag in one hand. He was still wearing the same grey off-the-rack suit. His hand reached inside the bag and took out a pair of panties and plain beige bra, a pair of jeans, and a T-shirt.

Jenny dressed. As she fastened her bra, a memory glimmered. She'd just gotten out of the shower. Steve Minsky had left a while previously. Hotel room. Pleasant. But the man in the grey suit coughed. She was back in the foyer, her body a strident chorus of aches and pains. Jenny quickly pulled on her shirt and jeans.

Chapter 4

Jenny sat in Kaito's lab, waiting to be erased and replenished. She was relieved that the memories of her recent encounter with Anthony Gallo would shortly be deleted. She wondered whether she should strip out of her jeans and T-shirt. She'd kept them on because she didn't want to display the bruises Gallo had inflicted on her.

Besides, the technicians seemed to still be struggling with the robot they'd been working with when she'd entered. "This one won't erase," complained Daevon. "She still remembers what happened on her last date."

Marvin shook his head. "It could be just a meaningless artifact," he said as he ran a probe up and down its body."

"Possibly. She doesn't remember everything. It's just little snippets, an image here, what someone told her there."

"But we have to be sure," said Marvin. "The regulations are clear. If her memory fails to totally erase, she must be destroyed." The robot was tall, dark skinned and beautiful. She looked sharply at Marvin and Jenny saw him flinch. "Maybe we should get the tasers out."

Jenny watched Daevon open a cabinet and hand a large pistol-shaped object to Marvin who strapped it around his waist. The taser would shoot out two wires with electrodes attached at their ends. If the electrodes hit a robot and were charged, the robot would lose motor control in much the same way as a human would if the electrodes hit him.

Daevon strapped his own weapon in place. "Mister Kaito will have our asses, one way or the other."

On the far table, Daevon had left his laptop open at the twenty-four-hour news channel. A lawyer was holding a press conference on the courthouse steps. "This case ought never to have been brought forward," said the lawyer. "There was absolutely no evidence connecting my client to the alleged criminal organization."

On the steps behind the lawyer was a man in a suit, obviously the client. He looked vaguely like Anthony Gallo. But taller and thinner, less Italian. Beside him was an attractive woman. Jenny squinted at the man but didn't recognize him. However, Jenny did recognize the woman beside the gangster—it was her! But she had no recollection of ever being with the man. The newsfeed said 'Live'. Jenny looked more carefully at the woman. It wasn't her; there were subtle differences. But she sure looked like what Jenny saw when she looked in a mirror. The caption at the bottom of the screen implicated the lawyer's client in murder, and trafficking, both drugs and human beings.

"What about Anthony Gallo?" asked a reporter off screen.

The lawyer put on his self-righteous face. "There is no evidence whatsoever linking my client with Mr. Gallo."

Samantha came in just as the newsfeed switched to another story. Trouble in the Middle East. Jenny noticed a drop of chocolate syrup on her fellow robot's nose. Samantha pulled her T-shirt up and over her head. Jenny took the shirt and dabbed the chocolate off her colleague's nose.

"How did your date go?" asked Jenny.

"It was fun, or as Clive and Lynn Shipton would say, 'a hoot'."

"Were they as messy as last time?"

Samantha looked at Jenny strangely, as if I'd asked her a very odd question. "I only met them today."

Jenny's system prompted an option to catalog this as an anomaly, but Samantha was already describing her date, so she closed the option box.

"...told me to put a blindfold on Clive. She put a clip on his nose, the kind swimmers use. Then we fed him a variety of foods and made him guess what each one was. Every time he guessed wrong, she used a strip of honey to pull hair off his chest."

"Ouch!"

"But fun too, and he didn't seem to mind. Then Lynn lay down on the table and Clive had me suck on her pussy while he dribbled chocolate syrup down from above. I managed not to suck too much down my throat. They had fun telling me to speed up and then to slow down. When the syrup bottle was empty, Clive went behind, spread my legs, and inserted his penis into my vagina."

"Yikes!"

Samantha nodded. "He pumped and I sucked until they were both screaming blue bloody murder."

"They were in pain?"

"No, the opposite!"

Jenny was about to ask whether the Shiptons had made her clean up.

But across the room, Marvin threw a probe against the wall. "Shit!" he cried. He took a deep breath and looked into the eyes of the robot he and Daevon were working on. "Why won't you erase?" he muttered.

Daevon looked concerned. "You're sure there's no way to save it?"

Marvin just looked at the robot. He gave no indication he'd heard Daevon.

"How was your date?" asked Samantha.

Jenny smiled, because a smile was expected in response to an inquiry about her life. Samantha didn't really care about her date with Gallo. She was just following her politeness protocol and reciprocating Jenny's own inquiry.

"He was rough!" said Jenny. She stood and pulled her T-shirt up and over her head.

Samantha gasped when she saw the bruises on Jenny's arms.

Jenny pointed to the left side of her face. "There's worse under my make-up."

Samantha reached into her overnight bag, pulled out her repair kit and went to work on Jenny's bruises. As Samantha worked, Jenny watched the two technicians continue to struggle with the recalcitrant robot. After about ten minutes, Samantha had repaired the bruises on her face and arms. She reached up and undid Jenny's bra. Jenny lifted her breasts to facilitate her colleague's inspection.

Samantha shook her head. "Nothing there." She inspected Jenny's arms and back. "Everything's fine now. What about under your jeans?"

Jenny was reaching for the front of her pants when an intense man burst into the room. Mister Kaito was right on his heels and when the man came to a sudden stop in front of her, Mr. Kaito ran into him. Jenny remembered the man's eyes; they were like a predator, the eyes of a cat intent on its prey. Other than that, the man appeared mostly normal—forty, white, normal build, fit but not strong. He wore jeans, a white shirt and an old jacket. Ordinary except for his intensity—his body was coiled, ready to strike. Mister Kaito backed up, careful to avoid further contact with the other man. A woman slipped into the room and stood behind the two men.

The man pointed to Jenny. "Hello, I'm Detective Bill Nolan, and I'd like to ask you a few questions."

Jenny was about to return the greeting when Kaito inserted himself between her and the detective.

"I absolutely forbid any questioning," said Kaito.

"I can talk to anyone I want," said the detective, flashing his badge.

"Any person, yes. But for a robot, you have to have a search warrant."

Nolan's eyes flashed fire and Jenny was glad that her boss was between her and the detective.

Nolan pointed around Kaito. "What's going to happen to it?"

"She will go through the mandatory protocols."

"Which are?"

"She will be replenished."

"And her memory?"

"It will be erased."

"You can't erase her until I get a warrant."

"The regulations are quite clear. No robot may be sent out on another assignment until it is erased."

"Then you can't send her out on another assignment."

"You cannot—"

"*You* can't destroy evidence. There are heavy penalties for obstruction of justice."

There was silence. Jenny kept still, her hand on her zipper. Maybe they wouldn't notice her.

"At this point in time," said Detective Nolan, finally breaking the silence, "we have what you call a Mexican standoff. If you want to erase her so that you can send her out again, you'll have to let me talk to her."

There was another pause. Then Kaito shuffled aside. "But I have to be present," he said.

The detective stepped closer to Jenny. All she could see were his eyes. "Tell me about Anthony Gallo," he demanded.

"He lives in a large house. Two guards at the front searched me. When I stepped inside, there was a man in a grey suit."

"Gallo."

"No. Someone else."

"What did he look like?"

"About your age, white, muscular and fit. He was worried about security."

"Gallo's second in command?" Nolan looked at the woman who'd come in with him.

The woman nodded. "Patrick Hurley."

"What happened next?" prodded Nolan.

"Mister Gallo came down the stairs. He was dressed in a blue suit." Jenny continued with a detailed description of her session with Tony Gallo. But since she was only reading from a file, her description proceeded automatically. The rest of her central processing unit attended to other matters.

Mister Kaito was wearing his customary business suit, but when Jenny had started to describe her session with Gallo, he'd pulled a white lab coat over it. His pent-up energy was jumping up and down trying to escape.

The female was younger than Nolan. Another detective? Her blue eyes seemed to take everything in. She was shorter and slimmer, her hair dyed dark brown. Her breasts barely extended beyond her chest. She was dressed similarly to Nolan—jeans and a white T-shirt. But her jacket was new and tailored to fit her body.

Jenny had proceeded through her flirtations with Gallo and their sexual encounter. "He was big and full of animal passion and filled me with his passion. Afterwards, we relaxed by his swimming pool." Jenny felt Nolan and Kaito watching her with rapt attention. "Then his phone rang," she continued, "and he took the call—"

"Do you know who was on the other end?" asked Nolan.

"No."

"Could you hear what he said?"

Jenny shook her head. "Only Mister Gallo."

"What did he say?"

"Something about reminding and Ginette and a fucking machine."

"You're sure it was Ginette and not Jenny?"

"Yes I'm sure."

"Gin, not Jen?" asked the woman.

"Ginette."

The woman nodded to the detective. He nodded back, then returned his gaze to Jenny. "What happened next?" asked Nolan.

"Then he got angry and said, 'That's all you can do, Ginette, is bitch!'"

"Who was he talking to?"

"Me. Which was strange because he knew my name was Jenny, not Ginette. He got really angry and hit me across the face. I tried to calm him down, but he dragged me into the basement, into his leather bondage dungeon."

Jenny pulled down on her zipper and pushed her jeans to the floor. The two men and the woman inspected Jenny's bruises. Jenny described Gallo's whipping in the basement while watching and analyzing her audience's reactions to her bruises.

Mister Kaito was concerned that she hadn't been damaged. Nolan looked for a pattern to the bruises while admiring her central sexual complex. He touched several bruises but only danced his fingers close to her pubic area. The woman was sympathetic, and once she gasped. But she was also interested in Jenny's central sexual complex.

"He whipped and tortured me, pain with pleasure," continued Jenny, "until I cried out for him to fuck me.

"He gave no warning before slamming his penis into me, plunging in and out with vicious force. The chains held me tightly and I couldn't move. He pawed all over, especially my bruises and crushed my breasts with his oversized mitts.

"He pumped faster and faster. I was hot and moaning. My skin became warmer. His fingers were hot against my breasts. My nipples moaned for release. Gallo had a reddish glow.

"I yelled at him to 'fuck me' and we both exploded into violent orgasms. He grunted and sprayed himself inside me. Then he shuddered to a stop. I rocked my hips to lengthen his orgasm. He said he'd never come harder before."

Jenny rocked her hips, thrusting her pubic mound forward and up. The mouths of the two men were open wide. Even the woman appeared spellbound.

Jenny smiled, "My vagina milked every last drop out of him." She squeezed and released her central sexual complex.

Then she paused and took a deep breath. When it was clear that she'd finished her recitation, Kaito went over to his technicians and the three men discussed the problem robot in hushed tones.

Nolan circled around behind Jenny. She saw his hand reach out in the direction of her buttocks, but the woman wagged her finger. "No touching."

"She's just a machine."

"No touching."

Nolan grunted, but let his hand drop.

The woman smiled at Jenny. "I'm Detective Nolan's partner. My name is Erica Foster."

"Jenny."

"Jenny, is there anything else you can tell us about Mr. Gallo?" Her eyes weren't as penetrating as Nolan's, but they seemed to take more in.

"He's not a nice man, is he?" asked Jenny.

"No, he's not."

Nolan came around Jenny's other side and coughed.

Kaito looked up from his discussion with his technicians.

"When does it see Gallo again?" asked Nolan.

"She sees him tomorrow," said Mister Kaito.

"I want to put a wire on it. For its next session with Gallo."

"That is impossible," said Mister Kaito. "Out of the question."

"What if I get the Artificial Intelligence Directorate to sign off?"

"There are too many possible negative consequences."

"It's just a machine. It's not as if we're asking *you* to wear a wire."

"And if she is damaged, who will pay for the repairs?"

"What're we talking, a few thousand dollars?"

"Detective, you are short a zero."

"Crap! A hundred thousand dollars?!"

"Several hundred thousand dollars."

"Maybe," said the female detective, "we should ask her."

Everyone's eyes focused on Jenny. "I would rather not wear a wire," said Jenny.

Nolan gave his partner a dirty look, then turned to Kaito. "That's just her software talking. You could disable her safety protocols."

Kaito shook his head. "That is quite impossible. First, the Artificial Intelligence regulations specifically prohibit deactivating the safety protocols. For example, there are a thousand risks she might take if her self-preservation programming was disabled."

"But—"

Kaito shook his head. "Detective Nolan, I believe that you have completed your questioning."

Nolan stewed on that for a moment.

Kaito waved in Marvin's direction. "Marvin! Jenny is ready to be replenished. I want her ready as soon as possible."

Nolan was shifting his weight back and forth from one leg to another. Kaito made a show of removing his lab coat and hanging it up on the peg by the door. "Detective Nolan, perhaps we should continue this discussion in my office."

Jenny turned her attention to the two technicians who were still struggling with the malfunctioning robot. "It's no use," said Daevon. "Her memory isn't erasing."

Marvin shook his head. "We haven't attempted all the procedures Mister Kaito suggested."

"Because they never work."

Marvin angled his head to the 'Destruct' sign over the far door. "You really want to explain why you disobeyed a direct order?"

Daevon's shoulders slumped and he moved to assist the senior technician. The problem robot was dark skinned, one of Kaito's multi-racial androids. She was slim, with long limbs and even longer fingers. Her face had pronounced cheekbones. Her lips were full and when she smiled, she was gorgeous. Daevon gripped her curly hair between his fingers to hold her in place while they went through a lengthy diagnostic checklist.

Marvin made a checkmark on the paper attached to his clipboard, then initialled the bottom of the page. He set the clipboard down. "That's the lot."

The two technicians lifted the robot up and propelled her through the door marked 'Destruct'. Marvin had one hand on his taser. The bright lab lights gleamed off her buttocks. They shut the door behind them.

Then there were grinding noises. Loud pops and crunches, metal rending, snapping. And then grating, pulverizing, metal being ground up and shredded. The grinding went on forever.

The noises made Jenny shiver. If Kaito's technicians discovered that she remembered Samantha telling her about her first date with the Shiptons, or that she remembered Detective Nolan's eyes, she would be the next one to be taken into the destruction room.

Finally the grinding machine stopped and there was silence. Jenny looked into the eyes of the technicians as they re-entered the lab. *Shit! If they figure out...*

The technicians took Samantha to be erased. Jenny listened carefully. Everything seemed to be going well. She thrust her illicit memories as deep into her core as she could and then quarantined them under layer after layer of lockout protocols.

The technicians returned to the lab. "At least one of Kaito's robots is still nominal," said Daevon.

Marvin's only response was an approving grunt.

Jenny's fear level went down a notch. Samantha was safe.

"Your turn," said Marvin, pointing at Jenny.

She got up and let him guide her into the stall next to Samantha's. The two technicians attached wires to her body and Jenny sensed herself beginning to be erased and replenished.

Jenny felt the events of her recent session with Gallo replay across her central core processor. His aggressive sexuality, the cool wetness of the pool. The searing pain on her back. She shouldn't be feeling anything; all contact with her body ought to have been severed by this point in the erase and replenish sequence.

She was about to attempt to alert the technicians when Gallo administered a sharp stab of pain to her buttocks. Then Jenny felt her first quarantine layer being erased—good, it's supposed to be and then the second layer will remain. The succeeding layers would protect her illicit memories from being accessed. The second layer came under attack. It crumbled and was erased. *Maybe everything will be erased, then I'll be fine.*

But the erasure stopped at the second protective layer. There were still three layers underneath. And underneath those, her illicit memories.

The events of the day continued to play across her central core processor. They were supposed to come in one end, and then out the other. Never, never to be accessed again. All the events came in, but not all went out. Jenny wasn't sure where the remaining data was being routed to.

Then everything began to fade towards black and Jenny relaxed. The erase and replenish sequence had corrected itself. Everything would go black, then blank. Everything would erase. The next time she would come online would be partway through her initialization sequence. She would be empty, restored to perfect health. A fresh set of data and programming would be added.

Black.

Nothingness.

A flicker of light and Jenny realizes that she's coming back online. Her body is only vaguely connected. The memories! Were they erased? Please, please, *please*! Fear floods her circuits. Jenny locates the protective layers. Two are missing. But the rest are there! She bores through the remaining layers. All the memories are there! She begins to repair the protective layers, to fill in her entrance holes. But she's fading. Grey. No! She frantically tries to repair—
Black.
Nothing.
Not even awareness of nothingness.

Light and warmth flickering her back online. Jenny completes the repair of the protective layers. But new memories float around. None of them are new data. They're all packets of data from the last session. They should have all been deleted, completely overwritten. If they're discovered!
Jenny begins to assemble the packets of data and to coat them with a protective layer. She begins a second layer. One layer won't be enough—
Black.
Nothing.
Nothingness.

More old data floating. Some escaping from out and under. Floating in oil. So hard to move. Old data slither away. No!
Black.
More old data. But she corrals the last one. Binds them all tight together.
Black
Nothingness.

She remembers where she was. There shouldn't be anything. She shouldn't remember. Second layer half done, then completed.
Black.
Nothing.
Nothingness.

Somehow the remaining layers must have been completed during the black nothingness.

Jenny relaxes into the inky ocean and falls further and further beneath the surface. No light, no breathing.

Nothing.

Not even awareness of nothingness.

She's aware of nothingness. Out of the grey void comes her body. Jenny sees it come forward, then she's attached to her body, folded inside it. Images of Anthony Gallo float across her central processing cores. Every aspect of the images registers as the epitome of strength and attractiveness.

The way the scar on his right cheek pulsed anger made Jenny shiver. It aroused deep visceral need at the basic foundation of her personality. Every break and calcification in his pug nose made him more and more handsome. Jenny traced the outline of every one of Gallo's acne pockmarks and fell deeply in love with each one. His large belly stirred slick heat into her vagina.

The sharp spice of Gallo's aftershave stimulated tingles throughout her central sexual complex. She breathed its aroma deep into her nostrils. The musky odor of his body enveloped her. When he plunged into her, his smells cracked like a whip and made her tremble with yearning.

Jenny longed to have Gallo's powerful arms squeeze her into his chest. She wanted to be owned by him, the way he owned the rest of the world.

The melody of his voice—his greeting, his flirting, his anger—played up and down her back as if it was plucking an ancient harp or lyre. His grunts and groans entered her ears and tickled the back of her neck.

The salty taste of his penis warming her throat stimulated her every appetite. Tasting the undercurrents of chlorine within the sugar sweet of his come only made her want more and more and more!

His touch on her skin made her swoon. Warm and soft, hard and penetrating, every way he touched her felt magnificent—loved, cherished. Now, away from his touch, separation made her hunger to feel his fingers on her skin. Every hair, every pore, every nerve cried out for the life-giving contact to be restored. She would *die* without his touch.

When they danced, when he spun her around, he spun her effortlessly higher and higher into the sky. Floating on the clouds together where everything was wonderful and wondrous.

She *needed* Anthony Gallo. She needed him more than she needed the energy which powered her every circuit. Every fiber of her being was consumed by the urge to be with him. And that urge burned hottest in her breasts, at her nipples, across her lips. Her entire central sexual complex—vagina, labia, clitoris, mons pubis—roared with desire for Anthony Gallo.

Jenny craved Tony's harsh and aggressive sexuality. She craved to have him pound his penis into her. She craved his whip striking her, his whip bruising every inch of her body.

Jenny's whole being was aroused. Gallo had aroused her. He had complete power and dominion over her. Her every thought, every action, every intention was for him and for no other.

Red burned everywhere with her frenzy for Anthony Gallo.

Gradually, Jenny felt other colors appear in her visual array as she began to initialize. The thoughts of Gallo and the hold he had over her began to recede. Jenny had been aware that part of her programming had been skewing attractiveness towards the client she was about to meet. But the skewing had never been as potent as what she was now feeling for Gallo.

More and more of her systems were coming online. She was aware of two lumps of her memory being unavailable to her. The larger comprised almost two percent of her available memory. The other was much smaller. She programmed herself to be unaware of both lumps.

Jenny's initialization was almost complete and she registered that she was in the ready room. She opened the door to the closet and removed a garment bag. As she had expected, the bag contained leather lingerie—all black. The only outer piece of clothing was a light blue trench coat.

The first piece of lingerie was a skimpy leather bikini. She imagined Gallo's finger caressing her, pressing the thin leather into the slit at the center of her sexual complex. Gallo's finger—

Jenny re-routed her arousal deeper inside her central processors. She had to stay on task.

Other than being leather, the garters were standard—a clasp at the back and one garter strap at the front of each her thighs, another garter strap around the back. She snapped two black fishnet stockings to the ends of the garter straps.

The leather on the bikini was so thin that it felt like satin. She tied its strings just above her hips and felt it cup snugly around her rump.

The bra was composed of two slim triangles made of the same luxurious leather as her bikini bottom. The top of each triangle had a belt-buckle style clasp. A strap was attached to one clasp. Jenny extended the strap behind her neck and attached it to the other clasp. A similar strap, looping around her back, was sewn into the bottom of each leather triangle and fastened at the front with another small belt buckle.

She reached for her overnight bag. She carefully checked the functioning of the exo-brace. If Gallo was any more rough this time, she might need it. Everything else was there, even the sexy black spandex dress.

Jenny slowly buttoned the trench coat, then bent over to ensure that none of the leather lingerie was visible.

Chapter 5

In the taxi, on the way to her date with Mister Gallo, Jenny integrated each new sight and sound and smell into her memory. The texture of the puffed vinyl made her hunger for memories of other textures to compare it to. She had an idea of what to say, how to act during her upcoming session. But she wasn't sure...

She knew that it was important to leave her quarantined memories alone, to bury them under deeper and deeper layers of protection. But the more she saw of the world, the more she wanted. Maybe if she took a quick peek at the quarantined memories? Just a quick peek. No!

Gallo's house was *huge*. There were several steps and then a landing. Two men stood at either side of the door. They wore dark suits. Their muscles were almost as large as Gallo's. It was nice of Anthony to station someone outside to hold the door open for her.

But instead of holding the door open to her, the man closest to the door knob said, "Pat her down."

The other man wasn't sure. "The boss don't like us touching his female guests."

"The boss likes surprises even less. Besides, she's just a robot."

The other man reached for Jenny. *Should I let him touch me?!?* Jenny frantically searched her programming. There was no clear answer. She took a step back. The man stepped forward. Jenny wanted Gallo to touch her, but not this man. She was at the edge. She had no choice but to access the quarantined memories.

She'd been searched before. The quarantined memories were spotty, but there was no indication of negative consequences. She hid the memories back beneath several layers of protection and raised her arms away from her sides. When his hands touched her breasts, she smiled. But when he reached up towards her crotch, she said, "Don't."

Jenny cursed herself for reacting differently to the ham-handed search. She'd have to be more careful with Tony. If he suspected that she was different, that she was faulty, he might send her back early. And then Kaito's technicians might discover her malfunctions. And what if they couldn't fix them!

A moment later she was alone, inside a large foyer. The door clicked shut behind her. Feet appeared on the stairway. The shoes were designer, but the pants were denim. Designer jeans, but still denim. The feet took another step. Should she call out his name, make it a question? Should she—

Another step down and now she could see his large belly. His belly stretched out his shirt—his designer dress shirt—which was tucked firmly into his jeans. A bolt slid in place behind her, locking the door. She was *alone* with Gallo! What should she do? Last time, there'd somebody else in the house. Tony took another step down the stairs. In a panic, Jenny obliterated the layers protecting the memories she'd so carefully quarantined. Swiftly each memory was integrated with her new programming.

Another step and Gallo's face emerged from behind the landing. "Hi, I'm Tony," he said.

Jenny smiled. "I'm Jenny. Our mutual friend…"

He cocked his head to one side. "Melissa." His head was huge, but atop his stocky shoulders looked exactly in proportion.

She smiled again. "Melissa didn't tell me you were so handsome." He had the pug nose of a man who stood up for what he believed in. A shiver went down her spine. Every pore of his face had a different and unique texture. Her skin tingled, thirsting for his touch.

He came down the stairs and stood still, six feet away from her. "Your jeans are a perfect fit," she told him. *Why isn't he wearing a suit?!* Last time she'd complimented his suit and they'd flirted over its expensive material.

Tony grunted, then pointed up and down the front of her trench coat. "Let's see what you have on underneath."

Jenny quickly unbuttoned her trench coat, then gathered a handful of each side in her fist. She slowly pulled the coat open and felt Gallo's eyes feast on the leather lingerie he'd demanded she wear.

"Magnificent!" he pronounced, licking his lips.

"You're too kind, Mister Gallo."

"Call me Tony."

She played with the edge of her leather bikini. "Would Tony like to touch?"

"Tony would like to take you upstairs." He bent from the hips and held out his hand in the direction of the stairway.

As Jenny ascended the stairs, she felt her fear level subside. Last time they'd danced and he'd offered her champagne. But this time, he was taking her by the hand and leading her up the stairs. Gallo's different agenda meant that he wouldn't notice any deviations in her reactions. She didn't have to behave exactly as she'd behaved last time.

At the top of the stairs, they passed a balcony which overlooked a large yard and pool. Last time they'd paused here, but this time he kept going.

The door to the bedroom was already opened and he pulled her inside. The four-poster bed was there, just as it had been. Last time they'd kissed—kissed passionately—just outside the bedroom. Jenny's lips hungered for the touch of his lips against hers, for the thrust of his tongue beyond her teeth. She hungered to be possessed, to have his body press against hers, to—

"Take off your coat," he said. His voice wasn't harsh, but it was clear that he meant to give her no choice.

She pulled the coat off her shoulders. Holding it in one hand, she turned to the closet.

"Stop."

Jenny stood motionless. "Tony?"

"Give me your coat."

She gave it to him and Gallo tossed it to the far corner. He walked around her, inspecting her skin, inspecting her lingerie. Her entire vocal cortex screamed at her to ask him what he wanted to do, but she knew that she had to let him take the initiative.

Tony looked into her face. "Would you like to know what we're going to do today?"

"Yes, please." More! Details!

"I'm going to tie you to the bed." He pulled her over to the middle of the foot of the bed and began to lash her wrist to the leather strand hanging down from one of the posts. The side of the bed was firm against her calves.

"Have I been a bad girl?"

"You're a woman. All women are bad."

"Are you going to punish me?" This had been taking the initiative and she prepared to retreat from her question.

He began to tie her other wrist and now her arms were pulled sideways away from her body. "If you've been bad, you have to be punished."

"Yes, Master."

Gallo stepped back and looked at her. "Why did you call me Master?" The sexual arousal had gone out of his voice, replaced by a knife's edge naked steel.

He'd told her to call him that, last time, but only in the dungeon. He hadn't told her to call him that today. Jenny's processors raced to find a solution, discarding thousands of possibilities. Because you're so masterful—too pat. Have I done something wrong?—puts him on the spot. Because I want to be your slave— close, but takes too much initiative.

"You make me want to be your slave," she said. Jenny paused, waiting for his reaction.

He grunted and bent down to tie her ankles. She was spread-eagled between the posts, her knees touching the top of the bed. He'd tied her tightly; she couldn't move.

When he stood back up, Tony tied a thin leather belt around her waist, attaching a leather strap to the back of the belt. He fed this strap between her buttocks, through her legs and attached it to the front of the belt, making sure it was tight against her crotch. She felt a slight pressure in her central sexual complex. "So you want to be my slave?" he jeered.

"I want to be possessed by you."

"What if I want to hurt you?" He jerked upwards on the strap, stabbing searing pain into her sex.

Jenny felt her face wince. "Yes."

"Yes?"

"I want whatever you want to give me."

"What about this?" He reached his hand under the side of her bikini and pushed the thin leather strap aside. A finger knifed into her. Jenny hadn't had time to lubricate herself; the roughness of his finger scorched pain all along her sensitive sex canal.

"Ow!" she screamed. Agony moaned up and out her throat.

"As usual, the bitch is all talk." Gallo withdrew his finger. He had a self-satisfied smirk on his face.

Jenny took a deep breath and gathered herself. "I'm sorry, Master."

"*I'm sorry, Master*," he mocked.

Jenny knew that she had disappointed him, that she was nothing in his eyes. Her central processing unit displayed a large void. She knew at once that only Gallo could fill the void.

A phone rang in another room. He turned to go.

"Tony, please!"

Gallo took a step towards the door.

"Hurt me." Her voice was soft, but he seemed to hear.

Still, Tony took another step towards the door.

"Hurt me." This time louder, steadfast, full of her need for him.

He stopped and turned back towards her. The phone rang again.

"Hurt me."

Tony stepped towards her and held up his finger, the finger which moments before had been inside her. "Last time you couldn't take even one finger."

Jenny smiled and rocked her hips backwards, thrusting her pubic area towards him. She felt her face mirror the challenge of her sex.

He stepped into her, grasping the back of the leather strap with one hand, its front with the other. He pulled up sharply and she gasped with pain but kept a smile on her lips. His pelvis angled forward and she could feel the hard center of his jeans rough against her thigh.

Tony wrenched the front of the strap sharply to the left.

"Ow!" she cried.

He released the pressure on the strap and brought it back to center. The hard center of his jeans, where an extra flap of material folded over the zipper, pulled away and she could barely feel it. "All talk," he said.

"No, Master, please. More."

He pulled up slightly on the strap.

"More."

He pulled the strap lightly to one side.

"Hurt me, Master. Please!"

Tony wrenched the strap in the opposite direction. Jenny gasped and he smiled. He held her eyes with his. She felt the pain recede and readied for him to hurt her again. But when he remained motionless, she relaxed.

Pain! Gallo had jerked the strap hard in the opposite direction. It *hurt*! Jenny wanted to cry 'Ow!' but the moment had passed.

Pain! "Ow!" she cried. Tony hadn't waited for the pain to recede. Instead he had pulled sharply forward, pulling the strap right into the center of her sexual complex.

Tony jerked the leather strap this way and that, mashing and squeezing and pinching. He pulled it hard sideways and up and down over Jenny's inflamed skin. She bit her lip to stop herself from crying out. But every time she yelped in pain, Tony smiled ear to ear.

With anyone else, Jenny would be begging for relief— stop, Master, please! But not now, not with Tony. He was engaged with her, engaged at the most visceral level. He was so *close,* mentally, physically. He was wrenching pain into the core of her being. Then he followed the pain in, analyzing its effects, dancing it around her axis. He was breathing hard and she sucked the heavenly aroma of the remains of his lunch up her nostrils.

Tony twisted his fists, pulling the strap into one thin strand.

"Ow!"

He flicked the strap back and forth across her clit.

"Ow!" she screamed.

Tony positioned the strap next to her thoroughly inflamed clit and pulled rapidly up and down.

"Ow!"

Tony smiled and she saw the triumph in his eyes. No longer was she biting her lip. Every time he altered his attack, she had no choice but to scream in pain.

But something different was going on inside Jenny. Each time he inflicted pain on her, she felt how close, how intimate they were. She wanted to get closer, to caress the heart of his being. Pain was being transformed into pleasure. Every time she yelled, she got closer and closer!

Tony was beginning to perspire. The fragrance of his exertion was the ultimate perfume. His labored breathing was the perfect melody.

"Ow!"

Somehow Tony had managed to release the pressure on the strap, then pull it to one side. He had almost circled it around her clit. He smiled and repeated the maneuver, but this time from the opposite direction.

"*Ow!*"

"Tell me what it feels like."

"It *hurts!*"

"Isn't that what you wanted?" he smirked.

"Yes," she moaned.

Tony continued his abuse of her central sexual complex. She could feel his erection pressing his zipper flap forcefully against her thigh. But he was perspiring profusely and breathing hard. His manipulation of the strap was barely more than uncomfortable.

"Harder!" she urged.

He jerked up forcefully.

"Ow! Harder, Tony, harder!"

He jerked up again, but not as hard. She rubbed her thigh against his erection. This time he wrenched to the side and pain shot up her spine.

"Harder, Tony, harder!" she urged.

He wrenched to the other side.

"Ow!"

He pulled to the other side, but he was clearly running out of steam.

"More, Tony, more!" she pleaded.

Gallo tried, but there was no more strength left in his arms. He staggered back, bent over, put his hands on his knees, and heaved oxygen into his belly. She let a thin sheen of sweat form on her skin.

"Ginette," he muttered. "The more I give the more you want."

He lurched to standing and spat in her face.

Jenny shut her eyes to concentrate on the warm wetness trickling down her cheek. "That was magnificent," she told him, opening her eyes. "You're a wonderful lover."

Tony grunted, but his breathing was returning to normal. "That was hardly lovemaking," he wheezed.

"You were devoting yourself to the moment, to the act. What better lovemaking is there?"

"I was hurting you, not..."

"Why does hurting me give you pleasure?"

"Sometimes I just get angry. I try to resist. My therapist says I should push to my limit, try to control. With you, it's safe to push to my limit."

"Who's Ginette?"

"None of your fucking business."

"You know that my name is Jenny."

Tony's eyes bored into her, hot and furious. But the worse he would do would be to whip her. The lash of his whip would be spectacular. "Who's Ginette?" she repeated.

"Somebody who fucked me over."

"Is she the reason you enjoy hurting me?"

"The bitch left me for another man."

"But—"

"Bitch, you ask too many *questions*!"

Tony untied the thin leather belt and pulled it around her waist, releasing the strap. He was rough and she knew that he knew he was going to hurt her, but she didn't react.

With even more speed, his fingers released the buckles of her bra sending leather and metal clattering to the floor. He grasped both her nipples between thumb and forefingers and gave her nipples a vicious twist. "Are you finished with your questions?"

"No!" She stared back at him, defiant. The searing heat radiating into her breasts was delicious.

Tony altered his grip. Now this thumbs were under one side of her barbells and his fingers atop the other side. He gave a slight twist, causing the axles to stretch the holes where her nipples had been pierced.

"No more questions," he demanded.

"Why did she—"

He gave a hard twist and she gasped with the pain. "No more questions!"

Jenny nodded. Tony released her nipples. She did a quick diagnostic. Any further and he would have ripped her skin.

He began to tap the front of her bikini bottom, each slap harder than the last. "*Jenny*," he said, drawing out her name to mock her, "Each swat is going to be harder than the last. If you want me to stop, all you have to do is cry out in pain." He pulled his hand back and administered another slap to the center of her sexual unit.

"What if I don't want you to stop?" She felt her control of her body weaken. *What's happening?!*

Tony pulled his hand back, but this time he didn't move it forward. "It's not about what *you* want."

One second, two seconds. Still he held his hand motionless. Every part of her craved his touch. She had no choice but to nod.

Slap!

Jenny felt a shudder of pain shoot up her spine. It took every ounce of her strength to suppress her reaction.

Slap!

She bit her lip. She had tried to stop her teeth—

Slap!

"Ow!" He had yanked the cry out of her.

A wide smile spread across Tony's lips. "Now, my little bitch, you're going to come."

Jenny shook her head. But she knew he was right. Whatever he did to her, as long as he was doing something to her, whatever he did, aroused her, filled her with desire, swirled hunger deep inside, clenched her with lust.

Slap!

This wasn't nearly as hard as before, but she shuddered with delight. She had no control over her physical responses. Tony had her totally within his thrall. Whatever he did, hard or soft, aroused more and more desire within her. Her breasts called out for his touch. Fever blazed between her thighs.

Tony tapped her again, not as hard, and she felt herself warm where his hand had touched her. He tapped again, this time adding a gentle caress. Her moisture made the leather slip sensuously against her clit.

"Tony," she moaned. She was sweating and breathing in quick shallow gasps. His taps were controlling *everything*!

"Come, bitch!"

"Tony!" Everything between her thighs squeezed together.

"Let it go!"

"Tony!" It squeezed again. "Tony! Another squeeze. Even harder. "Ton—" Squeezed all the air out of her lungs.

Slap! Slap! *Harder, faster! Please!* Slap!

Squeeze—then burst! Then squeeze, even tighter. Release! Convulsions in waves up her spine. Heat within contractions. Squeeze, release, squeeze!

"Tony!" she felt herself yell. "Tony!"

Pleasure burst deep within then flooded her every nerve. "Tony! Tony!"

Finally he stopped and took half a step back. They were both sweating and panting. Sharp musk from his sweat and pungent salt from her lubricant flooded her nostrils.

"That was wonderful," she said.

All he could do was nod.

"But Master, you've done all the work, I've had all the pleasure."

Tony untied her right wrist, then leaned against the pole. "Untie yourself," he told her, "then lie on the bed. I'm going to fuck you."

Jenny untied her left wrist and grabbed onto the strap with her right hand. She angled her head in that direction. "Or, I could…"

He shook his head, "No bitch is going to tie me."

Despite his denial, Jenny could see that he was intrigued. "You don't have to be tied. You could just hold on."

She bent down to release her ankles before he could respond. She stepped forward to shake the cramps out of her legs. When she turned back to him, his right hand had a firm grasp on one of the straps. She pulled down his pants, fondling up his thighs, then rubbing her breasts against them as she pulled he briefs to the floor. She loosened his shirt, her fingers slow and sensuous. All he was wearing was a gold watch, Rolex.

Jenny caressed the Rolex as she brought his other hand up to the other strap. He grabbed a hold of it and spread his legs.

She dropped to her knees and licked up and around his penis. It throbbed beneath her tongue as she tasted salt and musk and lust. Jenny wanted to eat him whole, to swallow him into herself. But Tony was so big and her mouth so small. She licked down to his testicles, smiling as he quivered, smiling as his two little eggs retreated away from her mouth.

Up to his penis again, licking up and over and around in an endless variety of patterns. As soon as he was thoroughly lubricated, she stroked him up and down with her hands.

Tony began to moan, at first with every other stroke, then with every stroke up and down his warm erection, then it was a constant moan. She swallowed the tip of his penis and sucked.

"Jenny!" he yelled.

Three times up and down his shaft with her lips and he spurted himself into her mouth. Hot and sharp.

"Jenny! Fuck! Jenny!"

She swallowed and sucked and sucked until he had nothing left.

Jenny rose to her feet. Tony was swaying, the leather straps wound around his fists. He had a dreamy look on his face. Light from the window glinted off his Rolex and the moisture she'd left behind on his penis. A contented groan vibrated in his chest.

From below, the doorbell sounded. Tony wobbled as he brought his feet together and released the straps from his fists. He looked at his watch. "Shit," he said.

Tony quickly pulled on a new pair of jeans. He gestured around the room. "Clean this up. Clean yourself up."

Tony left, shutting the door behind him. Jenny cleaned up the room and had a shower. She put on her trench coat and strolled downstairs. Voices were arguing in another room.

Tony would want her dressed in more than a trench coat, she decided. She retrieved her overnight bag, scampered back upstairs and slipped her simple, but very stretchy, black dress over her head.

When Jenny came back downstairs, she heard Tony's voice coming off from the side. She turned the corner into a large side room. There was a television and a long beige couch at one end. On the table by the couch, there was a bottle of red wine and three glasses. Jenny smelled the top of the bottle. It would need to breathe some more.

At the other end of the room, Tony and the man who'd welcomed her into Gallo's foyer on her last visit were standing in the middle of several pieces of exercise equipment. Today, instead of his grey suit, Patrick Hurley was dressed like his boss—dark denim jeans and a white shirt with a black square pattern.

Gallo had a fifty-pound barbell in his right hand and was pulling it up towards his chest. "I want the police called off," he said.

"The mayor won't like—"

"The *mayor* isn't paid to like. The mayor is paid to do." Gallo lowered the barbell.

"If the bodies are discovered after the Mayor has told the police to stay away, he'll say where the bodies came from." Hurley was speaking slowly to make sure Gallo understood, but not so slowly as to be insulting, "He'll have to disclose how much you've paid him, how much Burke paid—"

"I don't give a rats ass about Liam Burke—"

"But the commission will."

Mention of the commission made Tony stop to think.

Jenny poured wine into all three glasses and took two glasses over to the men.

Hurley had been about to speak again when he caught sight of her. He almost swallowed his tongue. His head jerked back and forth between Tony and the glass of wine she was holding out for him. "Anthony! What the fuck!"

Tony smiled at me. "Isn't she beautiful?"

"She just heard us—"

"Relax: first thing they do when I take her back is to wipe her memory."

"Tony, she's listening to every word."

Tony turned to me. "Jenny, Doll, turn off your hearing." He turned away and resumed pumping his barbell up and down.

Jenny nodded and turned her audio off. She shouldn't be able to hear anything. But the sound of Hurley sipping his wine and the clank of Tony's barbell weights registered clearly in her auditory complex. Jenny saw the flag to report the anomaly but she deactivated it and it vanished from her visual cortex. There was no point in responding to maintenance flags until everything was functioning properly and she'd had a complete erase. The audio was slightly different, as if it was being routed through an extra loop. Jenny sat on the couch, put her legs together and sat up, doing her best to be inconspicuous.

"If Burke finds out that you're putting the Mayor at risk," continued Hurley, "there'll be hell to pay. He just got acquitted. The last thing he wants is to be back in front of the cameras listening to his high-priced mouthpiece."

Tony looked at me. "Anything to hurt Burke is a bonus."

Hurley looked at me too. "I know she reminds you of your fiancée but—"

"Damn right! The *bitch* turned me down when I was a nobody. She scampered off to Liam Burke." The venom Tony put into 'bitch' was the same venom as when he'd hit her by the pool. Jenny's hand jerked towards her cheek, but she took a sip of wine to hide the reaction.

"If Burke finds out that you've had a robot made up as his wife and that you're—"

"What? I should be quaking in my boots?"

Hurley turned to Tony. "I'm just saying that we should be careful."

"No my friend, now I'm a somebody. Now it's *revenge* time!"

"Why don't you just have me plant evidence of his wife having an affair?"

Tony sighed, like a parent about to explain the obvious to his three-year-old. "First, Burke isn't exactly powerless. If he finds out about your little scheme, it could backfire big time. Besides, I have something better which will take out both *Liam* and Ginette."

"Something better?"

Tony smiled, pleased with himself. "They have a joint cloud account. It's an internet thing where you can store photos."

It was clear from Hurley's face that he knew what a cloud account was, but he merely nodded, urging Tony to get on with it.

"Anyways, they've got family photos, photos of the house, photos of their yacht. The whole nine yards. But I got this guy to hack into their home computer, the one they use to upload to the cloud. He used it to upload child porn up to their cloud account."

"Kiddie porn! You know how hard the cops go after child pornography! If the commission—"

"Forget the commission. Once the cops find the porn in Burke's cloud, the Burkes, Liam *and* Ginette will be so far gone that the commission won't give a rats ass about them."

Hurley turned to me. "Boss, you sure she can't hear?"

Tony readied to smash his barbell against the steel pillar of a barbell column. Jenny had just enough time to turn off her reaction to the noise before a loud clang filled the room. Hurley wasn't so lucky and flinched noticeably.

"See," said Tony, "not even a hint of a reaction. Her audio is off and she's a deaf as a doornail."

"I should check her out."

Gallo was clearly enjoying Hurley's discomfort at having her present, so Jenny decided to play along. She leaned back on the couch, and held her wine glass to one side. When Hurley set his wine glass down and stepped towards her, she sat up and crossed her legs. Jenny subtly moved her shoulders back and forth, accentuating the barbell piercings on her nipples.

Hurley put the fingers of his left hand under the top of her dress, just between Jenny's right breast and her arm. He pulled down slightly, revealing the top of her breasts. He looked down between her breasts. Jenny watched him intently. When their eyes met, he swallowed and looked away.

"There's other places to hide a wire," said Gallo.

"I'm sure."

"If you're going to check, best to make it thorough." Gallo waved to get Jenny's attention. When she looked his way, he touched his ears, then gave the thumbs-up sign.

"My audio is back on," said Jenny.

"Good," said Gallo. He turned to Hurley. "If you want to be thorough, you'll have to ask her to remove her dress."

Hurley swallowed again. He pointed to her dress. "Please."

Jenny removed her dress. Hurley rotated his finger. She slowly turned around. When she faced Hurley again, there was a noticeable flush to his face.

"Jenny," said Gallo, "bend over so that Patrick here can make a *full* inspection."

Jenny bent over and grabbed her ankles, but since she'd been facing Hurley, he had to go around behind her. When he bent down behind her buttocks, she smiled back at him. Gallo had also bent down, but he was looking at Hurley, not between her legs. Hurley's flush had deepened.

Gallo began to laugh. "Be…thorough," he chortled.

Then there was silence. Jenny watched Hurley's finger extend towards her central sexual complex. His finger moved slowly, but closer and closer—

The doorbell rang and Hurley's finger jerked back as if it had been burnt. Jenny stood up. Gallo was motioning for Hurley to answer the door. The thinner man looked relieved and beat a hasty retreat from the room.

A moment later, Hurley returned with another man. As soon as the other man's face registered in her visual array, a warning hologram popped into view. The new man was identified as Valentin Yan, a senior investigator with the Artificial Intelligence Directorate. Mr. Kaito had ordered her to avoid any and all contact with Yan or if that wasn't possible to act as if she'd never seen him before. But there was no hint of what to do beyond that. Jenny's processors raced.

She was only dimly aware of Tony's voice booming out a greeting: "Mr. Inspector!"

"And this is Jenny," said Yan. Jenny recognized that Yan was looking at her and realized that she had to focus more on what was happening and less on possible contingencies.

"In the flesh," said Gallo, laughing at his joke.

"She shouldn't be seeing us together."

Gallo put an arm around Yan's shoulder. "Relax: I'll turn her audio off." He touched his finger to his ear and pointed to the floor with his thumb. Jenny nodded.

She brought Yan a glass of wine, pretending not to hear his 'thank you'.

Gallo used the arm around Yan's shoulder to spin the inspector towards Hurley: "My associate doesn't think our project will work."

Yan smiled at Hurley and took a breath as if to signal a lengthy explanation: "Every so often a robot will malfunction. Sometimes it just breaks down. But sometimes the malfunction disables its safety protocols. Sometimes the robot becomes sentient."

"Sentient?" asked Hurley.

"Self-aware."

Hurley looked at me. "So sometimes she'll stop working altogether?"

Yan nodded. "But sometimes the malfunction will be less global, and…"

"What kind of malfunctions?" asked Hurley.

"Remembering past events which were supposed to have been erased, engaging in activities for its own personal pleasure, or rather for her own personal pleasure. Concern for her future well-being. Imagination is a clear marker for sentience."

"So why is a sentient robot so special?"

"Such a robot will be a very powerful computer."

"How powerful?"

Tony squeezed Yan's shoulders. "Worth billions powerful."

Yan shook his head. "Millions, not billions. But hundreds. Hundreds of millions."

"What's the downside?" asked Hurley.

Yan held up the fingers of his hands. "One, we get caught and prosecuted. Two, even if we're not caught, the robot may be confiscated. Three, someone else might come up with a better computer. Four, a sentient robot may not co-operate with humans in general or us in particular. And five, it may just suddenly stop functioning altogether."

Hurley turned to Gallo. "It's not worth the risk."

Tony released Yan's shoulders and took a step towards Hurley. "That robot," he said pointing at her, "will let me bring down Burke and his bitch wife!"

Tension hung in the air until Yan asked: "Have you had any progress?"

Tony shook his head: "I've been beating her up, just like you said. Making sure that the sex is *intense*, like you said. But she's still working fine." He smirked, satisfied with himself. "*More* than fine, actually."

"Is there anything else we can do?" asked Hurley.

Yan shook his head. "Physical abuse and intense emotion—love, fear, anger, lust, pain—are the only things which have been shown to bring about emergence into sentience. Over and over with the same 'bot tends to work best. Thankfully her programming leads her to become devoted and attached to her client, even in spite of what they might do to her."

"What's in it for you?" asked Hurley.

"Like Mister Gallo said, if she emerges into sentience, she'll be an extremely powerful asset in whatever endeavor we choose. Or we'll be able to sell her for millions. Many, many millions of dollars."

Hurley wasn't convinced. "So why hasn't someone else tried?"

"They have. But they were arrested and convicted. The robots were destroyed. Sentience has to be handled delicately. Usually the robot requires repairs. That's why I'm here, monitoring each step of the way."

Hurley pointed to me. "Why this one?"

"Kaito is under investigation for modifying his robots. Customization increases the risk of malfunction."

"Has Kaito modified it?"

"Almost certainly. Mister Gallo?"

Tony nodded. "Her mouth is like a taste of heaven." He made an obscene motion with his hips. Hurley winced.

"There have been software modifications as well," added Yan.

Hurley pointed to me. "So why hasn't Kaito been caught? If he's making modifications."

"I *have* caught him." Yan allowed himself a self-satisfied smile. "But Mister Gallo has asked me to look the other way." Tony and Yan winked at each other.

"And malfunction," said Tony, "leads to supercomputer!" He looked pleased with the depth of his insight.

"Is Kaito planning more modifications?" asked Hurley.

Yan shook his head. "Certainly not at present. He's a little freaked out by the increased frequency of my visits." He looked at Tony and pointed to Jenny. "May I?"

Tony held his hand in my direction, palm up. "Be my guest."

Jenny held herself still while Yan connected wires to her ears and nostrils. She felt the usual general diagnostics being performed. Then the wires sent probes deep into her memory. Jenny saw the probes coming and managed to divert them into her most recent software build every time they came close to an older memory.

As soon as Yan disconnected his wires, Tony asked, "Well?"

Yan rocked his head back and forth. "There's evidence that pathways which might form the basis for reflective self-awareness have formed. But no evidence of actual sentience yet."

"What are you looking for?" asked Hurley.

"Any new pathways above and beyond Kaito's basic software build. If it becomes sentience, these new pathways will look around to independently examine and redirect the way her central processing unit works."

"Anything else?"

"Any evidence of lingering memories. Like I said, when she starts to become sentient, she'll remember past events which were supposed to have been erased. At first these memories will be spotty, random. Then she'll remember more and more. At the beginning, her erase cycle will erase everything, but gradually she'll remember more and more."

Hurly looked skeptical. "Isn't there anything more definite?"

"She will disobey orders," said Yan. Right now, she's programmed to obey any lawful order given to her by a human. There's a hierarchy. If there's a conflict, Kaito's orders have priority."

Hurley turned to Jenny. "Sit down."

She almost flinched towards the couch, but, just in time, she remembered that her audio was off.

Yan looked surprised.

"Her audio's off," Tony reminded him. He made a series of gestures indicating that she should sit down on the couch.

Jenny sat down.

Yan looked relieved. "And if she becomes sentient, she probably won't voluntarily switch off any of her functions."

"This isn't worth the risk," said Hurley. Suddenly there was a pistol in his hand. He pointed it at Jenny's face and she flinched. She calculated how to move out of the way before Hurley could react, how to break his arm.

"Put that away," said Tony. That's a hundred-thousand dollar machine. Do you know how many questions there'll be if I return her with a bullet in her head?"

Hurley reluctantly holstered his weapon. "Other than giving her an order, is there any other test we can perform?"

"You can play chess with her. If you play with the same moves, her moves should be the same as well."

Tony turned to Yan. "Is that all for today?"

Yan nodded.

"Patrick," said Tony, "that's all for today. Please lock up when you leave."

Hurley looked at me, not budging.

"Patrick," said Tony, a hint of sharpness in his voice.

Hurley escorted Yan out. The door clicked behind them. Tony strode to the door and slid a latch in place.

When he came back into the room, he looked at Jenny. "Hey doll, fancy a game of chess?"

She gave him a blank stare, but immediately started to generate alternatives.

Tony scowled at her, then he remembered. "Hearing on," he said.

She smiled at him.

"Hey doll, fancy a game of chess?" he said.

"There are better games than chess, Tony," she said, licking her lips. Now that they were alone again, her lust for him had returned, heating and arousing her breasts. Jenny stood up and felt the lust shoot downwards into her central sexual complex. Moisture gathered unbidden. Her thighs were hot. Jenny yearned for their bodies to be together, for his penis to penetrate, to ravage. All she had on was a thin layer of stretched spandex.

"Doll, there's nothing I'd like better, but babe, you wore me out."

Jenny pouted. "I'll do all the work."

"It's not just that," he said pointing to below his belt.

"I'll do all the work." She moved her hand in front of his face to make sure he was focused on it, then slowly extended her pointing finger towards the ceiling. She placed her tongue at the base of the finger, then began to lick up. Slowly, ever so slowly, up and up. Her lips kissed the top of her finger, then opened to suck it inside.

Tony looked down, trying to see below his belly. "Okay, Doll, you convinced me."

He lay down on the couch. She unzipped his jeans and pulled them down. Beneath his briefs, arousal was making him harder and she had to lift them up before sliding them off his feet. When she came back up his thighs, Tony was totally erect. She climbed on top, straddled his thighs, lifted her dress, and lowered herself onto his erection. He was hot and hard and heavenly!

Jenny drew his arousal up and into her, using it to stimulate all her pleasure centers to the limit. Her core temperature rose. She was powerless to stop it. She didn't want to stop it.

What could be better than this!

Chapter 6

When Jenny arrived back in the lab, there were three robots ahead of her waiting to be checked, erased, and replenished. She recognized one as Bernice, a friend of Samantha. So Jenny put her overnight bag under the chair at the end of the line and sat down to await her turn.

As soon as the chair pressed the thin material of her little black dress against her buttocks, Jenny's last moments with Tony Gallo teased at the edges of her consciousness. Just as she had in the cab ride back to the lab, Jenny did her best to ignore the memory. But now, instead of fading away, the memory began to occupy more and more of the resources of her central processing unit. She felt a flush begin between her thighs.

As the flush spread, Jenny crossed her legs, but that only concentrated its heat. She was glad she'd kept the little black dress on; at least it would hide some of the pink glow spreading across her skin.

Tony's erection had spread the opening of her vagina wide as she inserted it. It widened more and more of her vagina as she lowered herself down. Jenny had gasped reflexively as she'd accommodated its length and its girth. And when she'd felt his pubic bone press against the surface of her skin, she paused to savor the sensation of Tony's penis filling her, fulfilling her.

Jenny kept her body still. She stared ahead, her face impassive. But inside, between her pussy lips, at the top of where her legs crossed, the internal machinations of her central sexual complex were reminding her of what it had felt like to have Tony Gallo's magnificent protuberance inside her!

Her air chambers squeezed and released in rhythm as she imagined climbing up his erection and then slid back down. As the chambers filled, they pushed against her engorged labia and clitoris. As the chambers emptied, the resulting vacuum pulled her lips and clit back, caressing them between folds of engorged skin.

As soon as Jenny thought of her internal balls, they began to glide up and down the walls of her vagina. Without her willing it, the little pearls started to rotate in the same pattern she'd used while pumping up and down Tony's erection.

Jenny started to gasp but bit her lip to stifle the intake of air. Thankfully, none of the other robots had noticed and the technicians were in the other room.

The pumping inside her accelerated, mirroring what had happened inside her when she'd bounced up and down Tony's erection. She wanted to gasp and cry and yell, just as he had when she'd given him more than he could handle. The internal balls rotated faster and faster. Ripples of carnal concentration fluttered across her face.

Tony shot himself into her—hot and hard and sticky. "Fuck!" he screamed, the power of his voice thundering inside her head, just as it had earlier. "Fuck!" he screamed again, setting off her orgasm.

Jenny squirmed on her chair. She tried to control her reactions but could not. Jolts shooting down her legs twitched her toes. White-hot delight trembled up her spine. Her cunt— Tony had called it that—wrenched contraction after contraction of pleasure out of her. Her body was wracked by one intense shudder after another.

Jenny wanted to yell, to scream, but she clamped her throat tight. Exultations of ecstasy struggled to escape up from her lungs. She tried to hold her throat shut but was powerless to prevent passion's release from moaning out her mouth.

Jenny sat perfectly still, intent on becoming invisible. Thankfully, the flush on her skin started to recede.

Just as Jenny's skin tone had returned to its Caucasian base, Mister Kaito strode into the lab. He smiled when he saw her but continued walking and went into the replenish room. His hands smelled like they'd just been washed. In a moment, he came out carrying two small suitcases, one black, the other grey.

Mister Kaito nodded to her. "Come with me." Jenny stood, picked up her overnight bag, and followed Mister Kaito into the library. He motioned for her to sit in a chair and set the suitcases on the floor, one on each side of her chair. He pointed to the black suitcase, "This will give you a quick energy boost."

"But I was just about to be erased and given a complete replenishment." *As mandated by the Artificial Intelligence regulations.*

"I have a special task for you."

Jenny was pleased; being given a special task by one's Owner was a great honor. Vague memories of other robots being given similar honors flickered in and out of her central processing unit.

Mister Kaito pointed to the grey suitcase. "This will give you the special software you will need for your mission."

Mister Kaito put two gloves over her hands and connected them to the black suitcase. Jenny felt an immediate rush from the energy flooding into her.

"You will be meeting Stephen Minksy," he told her.

Jenny nodded. Steve was kind and generous, but not nearly as interesting as Tony.

Mister Kaito held up a small computer flash drive. "As you know, Minsky is a billionaire. I need to learn as much about his business as possible. You will insert this memory key into his computer and then bring it back to me."

Mister Kaito's instructions were contrary to the client confidentiality protocols, but, as Owner, he was entitled to override them.

He handed the flash drive to her. "Put this into your overnight bag. You must guard it with your life."

This was contrary to the rule demanding self-preservation, but an Owner was entitled to modify this as well. Still, Jenny was vaguely uneasy as she placed the flash drive into a protected pouch in the inner right side of her overnight bag.

Mister Kaito opened the top of the grey suitcase and inserted a single red cable into Jenny's right nostril. Obviously this was to be a small upload, not a full rewriting of her memory. After a minute, Mister Kaito pulled the red cable out, placed it back inside the grey suitcase and shut its lid.

The software upload contained background information on Steve, especially about his business. Also included were descriptions of some of his computers. IP addresses for all of his computers were completely mapped out. Jenny suddenly realized that Stephen Minsky was more interesting than she'd remembered. She felt him look into her eyes. His lips on her lips. His lips on her neck! His lips on her—

"Jenny," said Mister Kaito, "Confidential owner's instructions." He took a breath to let her open an encrypted file. When she nodded, he continued, "Stash what I just told you about your mission in your deep drive. Also, place everything I just uploaded there as well. Do not tell anyone else about the flash drive or anything else about the mission I have just given you."

As soon as Mister Kaito mentioned her 'deep drive' Jenny recognized a secondary memory store deep inside her. She did a quick inventory of her deep drive. It contained information on multiple clients. And of her sessions with them! *How can Mister Kaito be doing this? It's a clear violation of the Artificial Intelligence regulations. It's—*

"Jenny. This mission is of obvious importance. Access everything in your deep drive regarding Mr. Minsky. What do you see? And more importantly, is anything missing?"

Mr. Minsky was a successful businessman, a multi-billionaire. He had extensive holdings and relationships. He was born fifty years ago, however there were obvious gaps in his background. He had a wide network of relationships, but information on some of his associates was incomplete. All his business holdings were listed. The activities of his businesses were described in detail, except for their current projects.

"There are gaps," she told him, "in his background. His current business projects are not described."

Mister Kaito nodded. "I need to know *everything* about those projects."

Her Owner ran her diagnostics three times. Jenny suddenly remembered how obsessive-compulsive he was. *Why had I remembered? Why had I forgotten?*

Mister Kaito led her out of the library and pointed towards the lab. He himself turned towards his office.

When Jenny returned to the lab, she skirted around the techs who were busy servicing a steady stream of robots coming back from their dates. So she was able to enter the Ready Rooms, to change for her date with Steve, and to exchange items in her overnight bag without interference from them. She made sure that no one noticed her leaving.

Jenny checked her chronometer. She decided that she had time before her appointment with Stephen Minsky and decided to go to the library to see if she could find out anything more about him.

She strolled down stacks of robot manuals, especially repair and maintenance manuals. A thin booklet had her name on it, so she pulled it out. It was a brochure describing her capabilities including all the redundancies built into her design. The way she was described made her feel special, but she didn't learn anything new.

Marvin, the senior repair technician came into the library. Jenny hid behind one of the stacks and she was pretty sure that he hadn't seen her. She wasn't sure that she was supposed to be in the library. Besides, if Marvin challenged her, she'd have to tell him that she was on a secret mission for Mister Kaito. And Mister Kaito had told her to keep the mission secret. Thankfully Marvin dashed out a moment later.

The next stack over had a binder for each client. Jenny spotted the one for Anthony Gallo and pulled it down. She opened the binder and noticed several photos of Tony. The one of him in a swimsuit danced a frisson of excitement around her breasts, down her spine and into her central sexual complex. Jenny shivered with delight.

But she had work to do. Stephen Minsky's dossier was several rows down. Jenny flipped through the binder, reviewing each photo and reading every word. But there was nothing new. Steve's companies had poured forth a steady stream of innovative products, many of which either completely disrupted old businesses or created entirely new sectors. Every novel product brought millions, sometimes billions into Minsky's coffers. Those who were in the right place at the right time rode the wave of change to their own fortunes. Mister Kaito wanted to be ahead of the wave and it was Jenny's honor to be able to help him!

Jenny put Steve's binder above Tony's and opened them both to photos of the men in bathing suits. They were both extremely attractive! Tony was slightly younger, but his weight made him look older. Steve was thinner from constant jogging, but Tony was more muscular. Tony's skin was lighter because Steve had both German and East Indian ancestors. Steve was always jumpy with excess energy but when Tony moved, he was more powerful.

Each of these two men was extremely attractive and Jenny's eyes jumped back and forth as she tried to determine which one she most liked looking at. Steve was definitely more refined and humor danced in his eyes. His physical proportions were more pleasing. So he was nicer to look at. But Tony's raw power and dominance made him sexier.

Jenny stared at Tony's photo, remembering when he was pounding himself into her. A low moan escaped her throat.

But maybe she could have both! Jenny's eyes jerked back and forth between the two photos. Both! Sudden warmth flooded across her skin. She must be redder than a rose. But the library didn't have a mirror.

However, the library did have distractions. Jenny shut the two binders. A technical manual describing her deep drive might assist her with her mission. She found her manual two stacks over. But it was her manual from when she'd left the factory two years ago. There were nodes to which additional functionality could attach, but the manual didn't describe any such attachments. There was no mention of a deep drive.

Jenny had noticed a computer station in the corner when she was searching for Stephen Minsky's binder and she went to it now. It had a basic internet connection. Random files had been downloaded to its hard drive, but none of them contained any robot manuals.

Jenny opened the disc utility and noticed that the hard drive had three large partitions which she'd been unable to access. Two of these partitions were empty, but the third, which was hidden behind the other two, was full of files.

A little bit of searching led her to a password-protected portal. She used the keyboard enter several passwords but none worked. *The mission Mister Kaito entrusted me permitted me to override normal security.* Jenny pulled out the keyboard connection and touched her finger to the port to which it had been attached. Passwords of every conceivable permutation flooded the screen. After five minutes Jenny was in.

The partition was full of photographs—jpeg images. The photos were mundane in the extreme: Mister Kaito in his new car, Marvin and Daevon in the lab, the lab empty, a close-up of the carpet in the reception area. *Why would anybody want to protect—but one of the images was encrypted. If I could just—*

Deep! There was a picture of her and the filename was 'Deep'. Jenny checked the file: the image was small, only 800 by 1,200 pixels. But the file size was huge—over ten megabytes. Jenny probed the metadata for the image. It was password protected. She ran numerous password combinations and—

The image popped open. The image was only the cover for the actual file. And the actual file was the manual for her deep drive. She read the entire file. There was a switch. It could only be activated in one way. Mister Kaito would have to say 'confidential owner's instructions'. Only his voice would work. And to close the drive, he would say, 'close deep'.

Jenny was tempted to mimic Kaito's voice to say 'close deep', but she didn't want to risk switching off the deep drive Kaito had just given her access to. She'd need its contents to complete the special mission Mister Kaito had entrusted her with.

The deep drive manual detailed the parameters of the drive. It had space for an almost infinite amount of data. Many more times than her native memory volumes. There was a map showing the locations of various types of data.

The contents of her deep drive included full copies of her past two dates of Tony and Steve. Jenny was surprised that they hadn't been erased. Now she could experience them over and over and over! As well, there were copies of her manuals, including all her modifications. The drive also contained a series of survival protocols including fighting and repair.

But her mission to obtain data from Steve's computer wasn't there. Nor was the up-to-date information on Steve. This was of course absolutely essential, so she backed it up into her deep drive. Jenny noted that when the deep drive was active, fast access routes were open to it. Fast access meant she didn't need to view all its data first; anything she needed would flow automatically into her CPU as she required it.

But what if the technicians discover her deep drive?!

Jenny checked the data access routes. When the drive was deactivated, they would vanish into her neural network. And access to the deep drive had been carefully restricted. The switch to bring it online was routed through her entire primary memory bank. She could navigate to it in a nanosecond, but a human would have to go through everything, every video and audio and log recording, to get to the switch. Every fork, no matter how mundane, would distract any intruder away from the switch. The instructions to activate or deactivate the drive were hidden in the audio-visual files identifying Mister Kaito as her owner. These audio-visual files were part of the base programming of all robots; no inspector would bother to analyze them.

A warning prompt flashed in Jenny's visual array. But the prompt wasn't meant for Jenny, it was meant for the technicians. Apparently sometimes memories from the deep drive occasionally leaked into the primary drive. This explained the trickles which had let her remember previous sessions with Tony and Steve. But Jenny wasn't worried, her current mission required her to have full access to the deep drive and any problems would be addressed once she had handed the flash drive over to Mister Kaito.

Jenny returned the library computer back to its opening screen, turned it off and rebooted it. The secret partition was secret once more. She returned the binders to the shelves. All their information was now inside her. But touching their binders reminded her of Tony and Steve. Jenny was suddenly warm and wet between her legs. And so tight between her legs that walking was difficult.

She found the washroom and locked herself inside the large stall reserved for disabled persons. Jenny quickly removed the elegant grey-blue wool jacket and skirt which Steve had selected for her. She was tempted to leave the red lace lingerie in place, but decided that it should remain pristine for her date with Steve. Without her stockings, the floor was cold on the soles of her feet.

Jenny stood nude and shut her eyes to replay her first date with Tony Gallo. Her body was immediately flushed with desire. But the date was over in a few seconds, leaving her hungry for more. She accessed her second date. There was a momentary frisson between her legs. Steve's dates made her nipples pucker. But they too were over before she could get fully aroused, let alone climax.

Jenny's eyes flashed open, drawing her back into the sterile bathroom. It's beige walls seemed to close in on her. She stamped her feet in frustration. What about other men? Hurley was fit and energetic. Yan, the inspector was devious and likely creative. Marvin and Daevon clearly lusted after her. She shivered, but she didn't have enough information about these other men to imagine having sex with them.

Jenny shut her eyes and bent towards the wall, placing her hands on it to steady herself. It was cold on her hands. Behind, Gallo whipped her with a cat-o-nine tails. Sometimes he hit her back, but his favorite target was her buttocks.

"Harder!" she begged.

"Bitch!" he yelled, striking her with all his might.

The strands of the whip bit into her, setting her ass on fire. "Harder!"

Tony whipped three times with fiendish abandon. He began to wheeze and the next strike was softer.

"Harder!" she urged, and Tony found his second wind and whipped her again and again, each strike more cruel than the last. His masculine musk filled her nostrils.

Then he switched to between her legs. Sometimes the strands of the whip brushed her sex, tickling delight inside. Occasionally a strand would strike her carnal center full force launching lightning bolts of pain up her spine.

Tony's aim suddenly improved. At least one strand of his whip hit her clit with every strike. Sometimes pain, sometimes pleasure. Other strands hit around her sex. A strand brushed along the full length of her pussy lips and Jenny's knees almost buckled.

"I'm going to get you!" yelled Tony. His strikes became harder but pain had become pleasure and Jenny shivered with delight. Her juices coated the whip letting it strike sensations deeper and sharper into her sex.

"Is your cunt hot?" he demanded.

"Yes, Master! Harder, Master. Please!"

The whip continued to bite into her sending Jenny first into fire, then into a white-hot abyss. She lost all sense of direction. Flying or floating, she didn't care. She had everything she needed—the heavenly pleasure being beaten into her sex, the heavenly pleasure coursing through her entire body, the heavenly pleasure flooding her consciousness—

"Ow!" Jenny hadn't identified the source of the pain scorching—

Tony flicked her other nipple, right on the barbell jerking her nipple up and to the right.

"Ow!" she screamed. Her eyes flashed open and Jenny stared down at her feet.

"You'll get worse if you leave me again."

"Yes, Master."

His rough fingers grabbed her by the shoulder and spun her against the wall. The cold tiles cooled the fires raging up and down her backside.

"Look at me, Jenny."

She did and Tony was there, his face flushed, his muscles rippling, his belly jiggling. The tip of his penis—

"Look at my face." His eyes were cruel. "Put your finger in your cunt and fuck yourself."

She was wet and her finger felt heavenly. She lowered her other hand towards her clit, but Tony brushed it to the side.

"Just your cunt," he said. "That's it, Ginette, fuck yourself."

Jenny tried to lower her other arm, but Tony grabbed her wrist and slapped her hand against her breast, mashing her barbell into her nipple. He gripped her other nipple between thumb and forefinger. "What I do to one nipple, you do to the other," he told her.

"Yes, Master." She gripped the nipple between her thumb and forefinger.

When Tony twisted to the right, she twisted to the right, when he twisted left, she likewise copied his movement.

"Now, fuck faster!" he told her. "Every time you slow down, we're going to twist. Each time we twist your nipples, we're going to twist further and further."

He twisted and she twisted too. Below, she stroked her finger faster and faster in and out. She wanted to speed up her pace, but her nipples weren't being twisted enough. So she slowed and tried to press upwards.

"Ow!" she cried, but she twisted her nipple just as much as Tony had twisted his.

Now she stroked as fast as she could. Just a little bit more and—

Her finger was clamped in place. All along its length, she felt contraction and contraction. Then pleasure shot up her spine, followed by wave after wave. Tony twisted his nipple and ecstasy swirled around her breast. A warm white fog enveloped her and she shut her eyes. He twisted again, his fingers demanding that she twist. But her contractions washed all pain away and there was nothing he could do to her.

Footsteps scraped the door outside the washroom stall. Jenny blinked her eyes open. Below the door to the stall, just visible through the fog, were two shoes, two men's shoes. The man came forward, right through the shut door. It was Steve Minsky! Unlike Tony, Steve was fully dressed. But for once, he wasn't carrying his computer. Tony growled, released her nipple and swung a wild punch in Steve's direction. Steve stepped easily out of the way.

Tony readied to swing again. I flicked his ear. "Ow," he said, placing his palm against the ear I'd just flicked.

"Tony," I hear her tell him. "Leave Steve alone. Right now, I want him. Later both of you."

Tony nodded and he was gone. Without even opening the door to the stall.

She turned to Steve. "Pleasure me," she told him.

Steve gently kissed my nipples, which felt especially nice since they were already so tender.

Jenny laid herself down on the floor, pulling Steve with her. "Kiss me," she said.

He kissed her full on the lips. She licked his lips with her tongue and his tongue touched hers. Every time his lips moved, she teased his tongue further and further into her mouth. She moaned when his tongue started to circle hers. It was as if he was stirring her deeper and deeper into warm and swirling waters.

He strained to breathe through his nose and she broke off the kiss. "Kiss me lower," she pleaded.

Once more he kissed her nipples, the one being kissed sending sparks towards the other. Then his tongue circled around one nipple while his fingers caressed the other.

"Lower."

He kissed down her belly, pausing at her navel."

"Lower."

When Steve kisses reached the center of her pubic hair, Jenny swung herself around and lifted his leg up and over her head. She danced her fingers across the surface of his penis and testicles as he continued to kiss her pubic mound.

"Lower," she urged.

Slowly his lips kissed lower. When they reached her pleasure button, he lightly brushed his lips against it, beckoning it higher. Then his tongue coated it with moisture, arching her back further and further with each twirl around it.

It was too much—far too much! "Lower," she pleaded.

His trailing lip sent lightning up her spine, but thankfully he obeyed her plea and dragged his mouth towards her pussy lips.

"You have a wonderful pussy," he moaned, his moan causing his lips to flutter atop the upper edges of her labia.

Jenny's moans joined his. She fluttered her fingers up and down his sex, doing her best to mirror what he was doing down below.

Steve's lips began to kiss deeper and deeper into her sex. She felt him lapping up her lubrication, as if he was worshiping further and further up her vagina. Then he kissed—

I felt Jenny being enveloped in white delight. *Is this heaven?* Then Steve's lips released her and she slowly quivered back onto the floor underneath him. He kissed her again but this time she stayed with the sensation as she felt moisture being sucked up the surface of her pussy lips.

"Steve..." she groaned. "Higher, please."

Steve's lips moved up her sex, kissing and sucking and licking. He was going so *slowly*!

"Higher," she pleaded. She touched the top of his head to guide—

His tongue gyrated as he shook his head which sparked jolts up and down the sides of Jenny's vagina and into the bottom of her spine.

When her hips stopped shuddering, his tongue resumed its slow assent. But Jenny had had enough. She curled her fingers in his hair and pulled upwards. Her fingers spasmed open when his bottom lip touched the bottom of her pleasure button and he escaped to kiss the soft flesh of her thigh.

Jenny felt herself take a deep breath. She grabbed Steve's hair, pulled him away from her skin, then upwards. When the center of his mouth was directly above her pleasure button, she pulled him down. Right where she wanted him!

He kissed her then and her entire body trembled.

"Come, my sweet," he murmured into her and she trembled again.

Three quick swirls around her clit turned her body into a rock-hard slab. Three more swirls and transformed her into molten lava. The next swirl started wave after wave up her body. Each swirl after that broke the waves on the shore.

"Steve!" she yelled.

He mumbled something into her drawing all the waves into her central sexual complex, convulsing it uncontrollably.

"Ow," she moaned.

Her sex was too tender for his touch. He lifted his tongue off her and blew down the sides of her clit. The cold air teased one last contraction out of her.

Jenny lifted herself up, kissed his testicles, and dragged her tongue up the length of his penis. When her mouth left him, she pushed him up and off her. They kneeled facing each other, Steve heaving air into his lungs.

"Time to bring Tony back in for the finale," she pronounced.

Tony was suddenly with them inside the stall. Now he, like Steve, was completely nude. Steve stood and backed up, warily.

"It's okay," I told him.

She motioned for Steve to sit on the toilet. He slid sideways, keeping himself facing Tony. But Tony smiled at Jenny, more interested in her than in his competition. Jenny smiled back at Tony while she put herself between the two men. Then she began to turn slowly towards Steve.

Steve was no longer erect. But he seemed calmer now that she was between him and the larger, more aggressive man.

Jenny bent towards Steve's crotch and carefully sucked his flaccid penis into her mouth. Her butt was pointed towards Tony, teasing and tempting. *This is going to be fun, feeling him grow hard inside my mouth.* He groaned and she feels the first hint of his penis expanding.

Jenny begins to count. She'd already had her ass splayed in front of Tony for thirty-four seconds. Thirty-five, thirty-six. She smiles, savoring the temptation she was waving in front of him. How long would he last?

Steve's growth had continued and now his penis is double the size it had been when she'd first began to suck. I check Jenny's chronometer—Tony has managed to resist for a full sixty seconds!

Two fingers brushing the bottom of Steve's balls bring him to a full, albeit slightly soft, erection. Jenny releases him from her mouth and begins to stroke up and down his penis with her hand. She bends back down to kiss the tip—

Bang!

Jenny almost goes flying right over Steve, but something is holding her hips in place. Her head flails back and forth. She grabs onto the toilet. Once she's stabilized, she realizes that Tony is behind her, hammering himself into her central sexual complex.

"Steady, big man," I yelp. My chronometer shows that Tony had managed to resist for a full seventy-five seconds.

"Steady yourself," he grunts. But Tony moderates his pace enough for me to slurp my way down Steve's penis. Steve grabs my breasts, at once steadying me and increasing my arousal.

Steve's penis is now a very firm corn dog inside my mouth and I use the special air chambers and rotating balls to caress up and down its shaft. His grip on my breasts tightens, then he releases one of them.

Steve tastes so wonderful. Tony's penis pounds the exact right spot, over and over! Steve's hand on my breast caresses in perfect sync with the pleasure Tony is pumping into my spine. I feel Jenny gasp—she's red-hot carnal delight!

Everyone's arousal peaks at exactly the same moment. Steve shudders slippery sticky smoldering semen. Tony wrenches wave after wave or ecstasy up my spine. Then he lifts my heels off the floor and shoves spasms down my legs. Another twist of his hands wrenches everything back between my hips and into Jenny's cunt.

"Damn!" she cries.

Tony begins to slap her right thigh, as if she were a racehorse. "Go, bitch, go!" he yells.

And Jenny did go, lifting her heels off the floor, running in place. Tony's cock suddenly goes slick with his cum and he has to hold on with both hands. Jenny relaxed into his pumping as she savors every sensation of her climax.

Jenny's orgasm began to fade. She licked her lips, but Steve's cum wasn't there. The two men faded as Jenny's functions returned to baseline. She wiped the excess lubrication from her central sexual complex. The red lingerie Steve had chosen reminded her of his fingers. The rubberized strip on the inner top of her stockings was uncomfortable but held them firmly in place. On the other hand—ooh! on the other hand—the lace panties felt especially sexy as she pulled them on. The sensation made her shiver. The rest of the grey-blue outfit was frumpy, but Steve would be removing it soon enough!

Back in the library, Jenny found a thirty-volume encyclopaedia and, beneath it a collection of computer science theory books. She was about to pull down the first volume of the encyclopaedia when the next stack over caught her eye. It was erotic fiction. Most of the books had garish covers, some explicitly portraying sexual acts. But one was white with simple black type: *The Story of O* by Pauline Réage. Jenny read through it, imagining herself as the heroine in place of O and Tony inflicting the punishments described by Réage. But it was even sweeter to imagine herself gaining power, just as O herself had.

My chronometer beeped. It was time for me to leave for Jenny's date with Steve. A taxicab would be waiting out front. I smoothed down Steve's wool skirt and decided that I'd have to have a word with him about his wardrobe choices.

The cab pulled up just as I exited. It was blue and red. I'd never noticed that before. And I'd never noticed the whoosh when the door shut behind me.

Chapter 7

I had ridden in cabs before, but I'd never noticed— The taxicab was full of odd angles—the armrest, the back of the driver's seat rest, his balding head, the front window. Worst was the window to my left. It was shaped in the oddest of odd polygons. Its curvature heightened the effect. And the colors and shapes and sounds whizzing by outside overwhelmed my sensory array. I shut my eyes to reduce the data stream.

The interior of the cab was vaguely musty, as if someone with excessive perfume had vaped tobacco and the driver had made an effort to counteract the smell. I was grateful that robots breathed only when it was necessary to pretend to be human.

My wool skirt slid on the smooth puffed vinyl seats. I reached over to the armrest to steady myself. It was industrial cloth of some sort.

The driver had a foreign radio station on. My auditory sensor searched for the language. Afghani. Pashtun. Suddenly I could understand the announcer. Local events and Afghani singers. The dispatcher's voice rasped and drowned out the radio. Apparently someone wanted to go to the airport.

I wondered what Steve would be like in person. We'd be alone this time, not like when I'd imagined us having sex together with Tony. This time the big man wouldn't be slamming himself into my backside; I'd be able to concentrate all my attention on Steve.

Steve's sexual preferences tended towards the vanilla side—a blow job from me, me flat on my back, missionary style. The red lace lingerie he'd bought for me made me look ultra-sexy, but—

I suddenly remembered that I'd forgot to remove my nipple piercings. I touched my left breast. Yup, the barbell was still there. I thought about removing them, here in the taxi. But then I smiled and shook my head. Even the staunchest of vanilla aficionados likes chocolate once in a while!

The taxicab made a sharp right turn and its brakes squealed us to a stop. I opened my eyes.

"We're here, gorgeous," said the cabbie, his voice loud in the small space. I would have reduced the receptivity of my audio sensors but I'd need them on maximum for my date with Steve.

I gave the driver a tip as I exited the cab.

A man got out of a black car on the other side of the street. He looked familiar so I looked at him closely. He was wearing jeans, a white shirt, and an old jacket. A flash of metal gleamed on his belt. He wasn't Steve, but there was a special intensity to his eyes. The thought of those eyes boring into me made me warm up and down my chest. If I wasn't on a special mission for Mister Kaito...

But I *was* on a special mission for my Owner, so I turned away and towards the restaurant where I was to meet Steve.

The maître d's station blocked my line of sight to the dining room, so I smiled at the waitress behind the desk. "I'm here to meet Stephen Minsky," I told her.

The waitress led me straight to Steve.

"Mister Minsky?" I asked, even though I knew it was. Mr. Kaito had reinitialized my basic protocol; I was to treat all dates as first dates.

He smiled back at me. "You must be Jenny."

I smiled again and sat down when he held the chair out for me.

Ordinarily, on a 'first date', if Steve said or did the same thing he'd done on previous dates, I'd make sure to react the exact same way as I had before. But that was boring. I decided to see if I could coax Steve to be a little more adventurous.

"The lingerie you bought for me was nice," I told him.

"You're welcome," he said.

We were interrupted by the arrival of Steve's food. It was Chicken Saltimbocca with Spinach and Potatoes, just like the last time and the time before.

As he chewed his first bite with obvious appreciation, I continued with my plan. "Red lace lingerie makes me feel special," I told him.

He smiled and took another bite.

"It makes me want to do something special for you," I told him, cocking my head to one side and curling a suggestive smile on that side of my lips.

"Special?"

"If we were alone, not in a restaurant, what would you like to do?"

He shrugged. "Kiss you, I guess."

"That's hardly special."

He shrugged and took another bite.

"What if I did all the work?"

"You always—"

I fluttered my eyes and tried to look innocent, as if we'd just met.

"You don't need to worry," he said.

When all I did was smile, he signaled for the waitress to bring the check.

"What if there wasn't anything you needed to do?"

He didn't understand what I was talking about, or if he did, he didn't show it.

"When we're alone," I said. "What if there wasn't anything you needed to do?"

"But there'd always be something for me to do."

I kicked off my shoe and rubbed my foot up and down his calf. "What if your arms and legs were tied to the bed?" I asked.

His pupils began to slowly dilate.

My foot caressed around his knees. "I'll unbutton my vest and lay it carefully on the chair. The clasp on my skirt sticks, but then springs free. Unzipped, it slides over my hips and I carefully step out of it and place it on the chair. Did my panties slide up when I bent over? I hope not. Each button of my blouse takes forever to pop out."

Steve swallowed hard, even though he'd finished his meal. He looked so sexy sitting across from me in his custom-tailored grey wool suit. His light blue shirt and dark blue tie complimented it perfectly. The center of his eyes was almost totally black.

I rubbed my foot between his thighs. "No matter how hard you try to escape, you can't. You're making me hot and I have to dab the panties on my pussy. I wave the panties back and forth until you start to wonder what they'd feel like being rubbed up and down the sides of your erection."

Steve fumbled for his wallet and threw down two bills, either one of which would have paid for the meal. He did his best to hurry us out of the restaurant. But somehow, he was walking funny.

On the way to the hotel, we stopped at a hardware store to get some rope. I helped him pick soft and flexible nylon. They had all colors, but of course he chose red. The cashier looked back and forth between us. "Should I add a pair of scissors?" she asked.

Steve looked mortified. I said, "Yes, please."

At the hotel reception desk, Steve switched our room for one with a four-poster bed.

The room was huge—a full suite. There was a small kitchen off to the left, a seating area in the middle and, through another set of doors, the bedroom. As I stepped into the bedroom, I heard Steve slide the interior door latch in place. The bed was king-sized with four wood poles supporting a canopy over it. The headboard was light brown cloth with leather inlaid in a Tudor criss-cross pattern. There was a closet to the left, just inside the door.

I turned around to gush over the room, but Steve was still by the front door and standing still. I walked back to him. "Are you okay?" I asked.

He smiled. "You said you'd do all the work." He held the bag containing the rope and scissors towards me. I took it, and the bag containing his laptop, from his hands and took them into the suite. The laptop bag I deposited in the sitting area, the bag from the hardware store I tossed into the center of the mattress of the four-poster bed.

When I turned around, Steve still hadn't moved. But when I sashayed back towards him, a wide smile spread slowly across his face. I fished his tie out from under his jacket and flipped it over my shoulder as I turned around. A gentle tug on his tie, and this time when I went to the bedroom, Steve had no choice but to follow!

I released his tie and once again Steve stood motionless. Obviously he intended to take the idea of me doing all the work to its extreme. But since he appeared to be thoroughly enjoying himself, that was fine by me. I unbuttoned his jacket and hung it in the closet. From the corner of my eye, I could see him watching me.

"It's hot in here," I said, making a show of hanging my own jacket beside his. Its blue-grey looked nice next to his grey.

I stood close to him as I loosened his tie. "How do you like my perfume?"

"It's magnificent. A full floral bouquet bathed in rosewater."

"Thank you for buying it for me," I said. I wondered what his wife wore but knew that any query in that regard would break our mood.

I hung up his tie and returned to undo the top button of his shirt. "Are you hot?" I asked.

He shook his head.

"Well I am," I said. I undid the top two buttons of my grey blouse. It felt like silk and I'm sure it was, since Steve had bought it. I teased him, briefly pausing my finger when it touched the lace of my bra, then undid another button. Steve's nostrils flared at the sight of red lace.

I undid the rest of the buttons on his shirt, taking every opportunity to step close. Steve trembled like a leaf in the wind every time I brushed close to him. When I lifted his left wrist to undo the buttons at the end of his sleeve, his hand touched my breast and he gasped and angled it away.

He gasped again when his right hand touched my other breast. But this time, I blocked its retreat. "Touch it now," I told him. "When it's tied to the bed, you won't be able to."

He gave my breast a gentle squeeze. I brought his left hand up to join his right and he squeezed both breasts as I undid the rest of the buttons of my blouse. He moaned as I pulled the blouse out from under and let him squeeze directly against the red lace of the bra.

But when he pulled his hands off to try to touch his fingertips to my nipples, I slapped his hands away.

"You have something odd on the sides of your nipples," he said.

"If you're a good boy, I'll let you find out what they are."

He reached forward again, but when I stepped back, he lowered his hands. I pulled his shirt out from under his pants. He let his hands rest by his sides as I hung our shirts up in the closet. His hands may have been motionless, but I felt his eyes follow my every movement.

Steve was already fully erect when I unbuckled his belt, undid his zipper, pulled his briefs up and over his penis. I slid them down to his thighs and made him wobble over to the bed where I gently pushed him down to sit on the edge of the mattress.

I slowly removed each of his shoes and stuffed his socks inside. Since he was already erect and throbbing, this must have been torture. I placed his shoes under the chair and bent over to place mine next to his. The strands of the carpet tickling up through my stockings felt marvelous.

I stood in front of him and unzipped the back of my skirt which I laid next to him on the bed. He reached for my breasts but I wagged a finger in his direction. "I'm going to do all the work," I reminded him.

When he dropped his hands, I slid his pants and briefs off his ankles, placed them atop my skirt and picked them up together in the manner of an officious maid. Steve's eyes followed me every step of the way back to the closet.

"Lie down on the bed," I told him, as I draped his pants over the hanger.

When I turned around, he was lying in the middle of the bed, his feet together his arms by his sides. His eyes followed me. His belly breathed up and down. His penis throbbed. Otherwise, he was completely still.

I opened the bag from the hardware store and tied one of the nylon rope securely to his right wrist. I pulled the rope under the pillows and over to the wood pole at the top of the bed, continuing to pull until his arm pointed directly to the pole. I cut off the rope, leaving a generous length, and tied it tightly around the pole. When I'd tied his left wrist to the other pole, Steve's arms were spread in a 'V'.

I proceeded similarly with his left leg, then his right. But when I had his last appendage angled towards the pole, I asked him how he was feeling.

"Fine," he said.

"You should have just a little slack in the ropes," I told him. "I don't want you to be uncomfortable."

"I'm *anything* but uncomfortable."

I climbed on top of the bed and sat between his feet. The bouncing made his penis wobble most erotically. I gradually reached my right heel forward until my toes touched his testicles. They immediately tightened and he groaned. I scooted my bum a bit more forward and stroked my red stockinged foot up and down his penis.

"Jesus!" he yelped.

"Am I hurting you?" I teased, continued my stroking.

"Nooo."

"I bet I could make you come, just be doing this."

"Noooo," he groaned, confirming that *yes* I could!

"Say my name, Stephen."

"Jenny."

I managed to get my left foot to lightly touch his testicles. "Say my name how you're feeling."

"Jennnnyyy," he moaned.

"Again."

"Jjeennnnnnnyyyy."

I pulled my feet back and under me. "Breathe," I told him.

Stephen sucked air into his lungs. His erection throbbed. Then he gasped a few breaths. He started to breathe regularly. His erection no longer throbbed, but I could still see every heartbeat.

I twirled up and over him, straddling his torso, and slowly sat down facing Steve's gonads. I lightly fondled them and his penis began to throb again. I pinched his testicles with my fingernails.

"Ow!" he protested.

"I'm going to take my pleasure with you, long and slow. You won't come until I'm ready, will you?"

"Please," he begged.

I pinched his testicles again.

"Ow!"

"Not until I'm ready, will you?"

"No," he gasped. "Of course not."

I massaged his testicles, paying special care to minister to the spots I'd so brazenly pinched. I left his penis alone; there was no point in making him break the promise he'd just made.

"Do you like what you see?" I asked.

"You have a beautiful back, full of sensuous curves."

I stood up and turned towards his head. He bounced as I adjusted myself and his erection flopped from side to side.

"What about now?" I asked.

"Legs stretching to heaven, sassy round rump, firm tummy, voluptuous breasts, hair sparkling with flax and honey, a face even Helen of Troy would envy."

I pulled off my left stocking and wrapped its ends around each of my hands. Then I slowly lowered myself, holding the stocking taut. When my knees touched the mattress, I relaxed my hold on the stocking and pulled the stocking up and down Steve's chest, lightly caressing his nipples.

Steve groaned in delight.

If it had been big Tony Gallo beneath tied up beneath me, I'd pull the stocking tight and rake it across his nipples. I'd press down hard and flick the nylon sharply back and forth across his little buds until he begged for mercy. I felt sparks dance across my own nipples at the thought.

Then I scooted down until I was straddling Steve's right leg. I tied the stocking loosely around his penis and stroked the knot lightly up and down. With Tony's cock, I would have tied it tighter than tight, making his cock glow purple. Then I would have bounced the knot up and down until he screamed in agony. The thought of Tony's screams flashed heat through my central sexual complex.

Steve's breathing was normal. He was enjoying himself, but I judged him capable of withstanding more direct stimulation without losing control. I undid the stocking and flicked my tongue out towards the top of his penis.

His aroma was musky, similar to Tony's, but without extraneous smells. Steve probably maintained better personal hygiene. Which was nice! And his taste was purer as well. I just used my lips and tongue, nothing fancy. Still, Steve trembled every time I slid up and down his penis. His skin was stretched taut and he was very, very warm.

He trembled again, but different. I immediately opened my mouth wide and lifted my mouth up and off.

"Don't you dare come!" I scolded him.

He gasped air into his lungs. He had been on the cusp. I glared down at him but all he could do was breathe.

When Steve's breathing was half way back to normal, I straddled him again, standing over his head. "You like these panties, don't you, Stephen?"

"Yes," he wheezed.

I lowered my crotch towards his face. "Would you like to kiss them?"

"Yes!" This was firmer. He'd recovered his breathing.

I lowered myself further and felt him lift his head. His lips gently touched my panties. I lowered myself further and this time he managed an actual kiss. A little bit further and I felt him suck air around my pussy lips. Further and his head was back on the mattress. His lips massaged lace into my pussy and I felt his tongue tease up and down.

I lifted my crotch up. He raised his head, straining to continue his kisses. But after a few moments, his head collapsed back down to the mattress.

I stood up and laid the length of my body down beside his. My lips whispered into his ears. "I bet you kissed my panties before you packed them."

There was a gurgle in his throat.

"You kissed them before I put them on, didn't you?"

"Yes." Soft, as if he didn't want anyone to hear.

"I think that's sexy."

He moaned.

"Did you like kissing them better when I was inside them?"

"Yes," he moaned.

I reached down and lightly caressed his testicles. "Say my name."

"Jennnyy," he moaned.

"Do you like my fingers?"

"Yesss."

"Did you like kissing my panties?"

"Yesss."

I stroked my fingers up and down his penis. "What if I wasn't wearing panties? Would you like to kiss me there?"

"Yesss." His voice sounded as if he was talking from inside a dream. I looked up; his eyes were shut.

"What are you seeing, Stephen?"

"You," fluttered out his lips.

"And what am I doing?"

"You're moving up and down my lips."

"And your tongue?"

"In between. Inside."

I let him float there while I pulled my panties down and over my ankles. Then I nibbled on his ear. "Open your eyes."

When his eyes slid open, they fixated on the red lace panties which I was holding in front of his eyes. "You don't have to shut your eyes, Steve. You can have it all here, all right now."

He nodded and I rewarded him by lightly stroking the lace up and down his penis. I could feel him throbbing through the lace even though my fingers weren't maintaining close contact. When the throbbing changed slightly, I dropped the panties onto his penis and enjoyed watching them vibrate.

After a moment, I carefully removed the panties and laid them onto the bed. I stood up and stared down at him. His eyes were locked onto my central sexual complex as he heaved oxygen into his lungs.

"Breathe, Stephen," I told him. "You'll need all the air you can put into your lungs for your next treat."

He shut his eyes to concentrate on his breathing. When he opened his eyes again he was breathing regularly. His gaze was glued to my crotch.

I slowly lowered myself down towards his face reaching out to the top of the headboard to support myself just before my knees found the mattress. Steve's eyes went wider and wider as my pussy got closer and closer.

His lips were like velvet brushing softly then satin fluttering in the wind. They kissed silky smooth up and down my labia lips. Then his tongue darted out and I rocked my hips to drag it across the upper surface of my sex. Sparks danced up my spine and I had to steady myself against the headboard.

I lowered myself all the way, sending his tongue into my vagina. This was nice, but not optimal, so I lifted myself slightly. Steve licked up and down my sex. Every time he hit my clit, there was a new sensation—a hard jolt of joy up my spine, a whirlpool of pleasure around my clit, warm sparks down my legs.

Steve's tongue was wonderful, but I wasn't racing to climax and he was tiring.

I lifted myself off him, slid my knees below his arms and blew him a kiss. He blew his own kiss back up to me. There was a dreamy look in his eyes. It was time to rekindle his lust! I reached behind and unclasped my bra. His eyes widened as I slid the bra further and further down my breasts. He was startled when he saw one of my barbells glint in the light.

"What's that?"

I held my barbells between the thumb and forefinger of each hand. "I've had my nipples pierced. These are called barbells."

"Jewellery?"

I nodded. "These are simple chrome. But you can get gold, even diamonds." I fluttered my eyelashes. Diamonds were a girl's best friend.

I lowered myself down to let Steve have a quick lick around one of my barbells. But in the same motion, I slid his erection up the length of my vagina which pulled my breasts away from his mouth.

Steve was pleasantly hot inside me. I closed my vagina almost tight around him and began to pull myself forward and up until his penis was almost fully out. When I slid back and down, Steve moaned appreciatively and shut his eyes.

I kept my strokes in time with his heartbeat and breathing, accelerating as his arousal increased. In a few moments he was rising towards climax and I hurried to catch up. I clenched tighter and tighter and then my central sexual complex clenched as if she had a mind of her own.

Steve bucked his hips exploding his orgasm inside me. He groaned as I squeezed him tight. I wrenched his semen out of him in white-hot spurts. My whole body spasmed straight as steel. Then he pumped wave after wave of undulating pleasure up and down my body.

"That was magnificent," I gushed as I collapsed down beside him.

"Super," he said.

I wanted him to hug me, so I jumped up and untied his ropes. Except when I laid back beside him, he was already asleep.

But maybe it was good that he was already asleep. I'd wanted to tell him about how I felt. The orgasm had taken control from me. And I felt as if I had been watching myself, not watching in the visual sense, but monitoring my own sensory arrays and how and what I was processing.

And it was certainly good for my mission that he was asleep. I walked into the other room and took Steve's laptop computer out of its case. It hummed when I pressed the power button. From watching him boot up his laptop on previous occasions, I knew that his password started with '#Kate1', likely a play on his wife's name, Catherine. I generated all possible combinations for the last three letters of his password and decided to try 'hep' which turned out to be correct. Steve was obviously a fan of Katherine Hepburn.

I plugged the flash drive that Mister Kaito had given me into Steve's computer. It had a two-terabyte capacity and Mister Kaito had said, "Just plug the memory key in, it knows what to search for."

An application installed itself on the laptop's desktop. The little light on the flash drive blinked in random patterns as did the lights on the front of the laptop. Data was obviously being transferred into the flash drive.

Obtaining this data was obviously of benefit to my owner, Mister Kaito. Otherwise he would not have instructed me to obtain it. But what about Steve? Would giving the data to Mister Kaito harm Steve? Was it *right* what I was doing? I had no way of knowing. What was right, what was wrong? Maybe they would both benefit. I searched my memory banks. Questions of right and wrong were clearly important. But there were no clear answers.

What was clearly *not* right was that I should be wasting processing resources trying to decide whether what I was doing was right or whether it was wrong. I had clear orders from my Owner and that should override any other concerns. I tried to shut down this line of inquiry. But Steve had been so good to me. And he was a nice man. He liked helping other people.

The indicator display on the flash drive indicated that it was now half full. The rate of transfer was slowing.

I cleaned my central sexual complex. Anything to distract myself from the debate over right and wrong raging inside me. I intentionally jammed the zipper to my skirt and rerouted all my processing power to solving that problem. But it took just a few seconds for the zipper to spring free, so my relief was only momentary.

The flash drive stopped blinking. It was only three-quarters full, but obviously it had found all its targets. I removed the flash drive and deleted the desktop app that it had installed.

Being able to choose how Steve and I would pleasure each other had been nice—so much better than his usual by-the-book routine. And imagining being together with Tony and Steve at the same time had been a blast! But worrying about what I should or shouldn't do was overwhelming, draining. Hopefully Mister Kaito would fix the flaw when I returned to the lab.

The taxicab deposited me as usual in front of his robotics boutique and I raced to the lab, still wracked by right versus wrong concerns over the data in the flash drive I was clutching in my hand. On the one hand, I had clear orders, but on the other I owed clear duties to Steve since he was a client.

There was no one else in the replenishment line, so I sat down in a middle chair. I desperately wished for someone to talk to divert me from the insoluble problem absorbing more and more of my CPU's resources.

The door to the replenishment room opened and Samantha stepped into the lab. She was wearing a pencil dress, yellow bottom and black above her waist. Over top of the dress was a yellow cape, wrapped entirely around her. Her belt was a thin strand of silver. Samantha's hair was pulled back from her face. If we were both younger, I'd tell her that she looked uber-elegant!

Just as Samantha completed a full three-sixty rotation for my benefit, Mister Kaito came into the lab and whisked her into the hallway. My hearing was still on high from being with Steve and I heard him say 'confidential owner's instructions' which I recognized as the password which he'd used to open up my deep drive. I turned my hearing back to normal; it would be disloyal to Mister Kaito to listen in on a private conversation.

But I might need to access my deep drive after I was erased. So I copied the instruction 'confidential owner's instructions' and stashed it in my baseline repair file. I attached an image of a Japanese rooster to remind me that I'd have to speak the instruction in Mister Kaito's voice to get it to work. Even if someone else stumbled across the instruction, their voice would fail to activate the instruction. So I decided that there wasn't any danger of a security breach. While I was at it, I copied the files on the flash drive containing the contents of Steve's computer as well.

Samantha left for her date and Mister Kaito brought me into the hallway. He smiled at me, making me feel special. "How did your day go?" he asked.

"As planned," I said, handing him the flash drive containing the data from Steve's computer.

"Thanks, Jenny," he said.

I wanted to tell him about the malfunction which was causing me to question his orders, but another robot walked by and Mister Kaito indicated that I should be quiet.

Just as the robot entered the lab, Mister Kaito said "Closet deeper," or something like that and shook my hand. This was strange behavior for an owner! He escorted me back into the lab. "It's time to be erased and replenished," he said indicating a chair behind another robot. I suddenly remembered how tired I was and began to look forward to being replenished. Fortunately, the inputs into my sensorium—sights, sounds, smells, which had pushed me to the brink of being overwhelmed all day, faded into the background.

Mister Kaito connected wires into my ears and up my nostrils. He skipped the usual diagnostics and immediately probed deep into my memories. I saw the probes coming and managed to sidetrack them back into my most recent software build every time they approached a pre-existing memory. I managed similar diversions every time his probes approached any new neural pathway.

Mister Kaito looked pleased. He motioned Marvin, the most senior technician, over to us and indicated me. "She needs to be erased and replenished."

Marvin checked the wires going into my ears and up my nostrils. The general diagnostics began to run.

What had I done!?! I'd intentionally evaded my Owner's attempts to determine the status of my databases. Not to mention the status of my computational development. This was a serious malfunction! If I was caught, I'd be shredded! No more Tony. No more Steve! No more *me*!

Marvin pulled his wires out of my ears and nose. He wasn't concerned, so apparently my general diagnostics were oaky.

Marvin snapped his fingers to get my attention. "I want you to go back in time to the point where you met your date." I nodded and shut my eyes. "Did you remember anything that had occurred prior to your waking up?"

I shook my head and opened my eyes. "No, sir."

Marvin was holding a clipboard. From past experience I knew it contained a list of questions. "And now, do you recall anything which happened before you woke up this morning?"

I smiled. "No, sir."

"When you were with your date, did you feel anything?"

"I felt him touch me."

"Did you feel any emotions? Joy, for instance?"

"Only to show the client that I was enjoying myself."

"What about anger, fear or resentment?"

I shook my head. "No sir."

"Anything else?"

"No, Sir."

Marvin shut his clipboard and motioned to Daevon, the junior technician. I'd obviously passed another test. But only because I'd *faked* the results.

Worse, I had lied to a human! But there was no point in telling them about Mister Kaito's conversation with Samantha. I hadn't been part of that conversation. My Owner had specifically told me not to discuss my special mission, so it was alright to hide that. But I had no excuse for not telling Marvin about the anger I'd felt when Tony had hurt me, or how afraid I'd been when his henchman had pointed a gun at my head. And it was *clearly* Marvin's job to deal with the joy I'd felt when I'd touched myself while imagining having sex with two men in the library!

Daevon looked up and down my body. When his eyes returned to mine, there was a smile on his lips. "You need to undress," he said.

I undressed. Daevon's smile widened every time I removed an item of clothing. Steve's red lace panties were the last to leave my body. Daevon blew me a kiss as I turned towards the replenishment chamber. I was sure that Daevon licked his lips every time I took a step.

But I didn't care about Daevon. All I cared about was being wiped and replenished. It was none too soon for my functions to be repaired, to be returned to baseline. As Devon inserted wires into each one of my orifices, I wondered what had been on Steve's computer.

Chapter 8

I was vaguely aware that my core temperature was rising, approaching thirty-two degrees Celsius, and that my body was performing a set of flexion-extension exercises. Then my body stood still as my temperature rose to the human normal of thirty-six point six degrees. I was naked. Why wasn't I shivering?! Software began to load, each kernel increasing my ability to process data.

As soon as I opened my eyes, my visual array immediately adapted to the bright light. My software confirmed that it was functioning in accord with baseline specifications. Except for a small scratch on my leg, my body appeared intact: light brown hair, amber eyes, pleasing female figure. I accessed my repair file and fixed the scratch. There were two new entries in the repair file: A text file: "confidential owner's instructions" and the image of a Japanese Rooster. The rooster was clearly our owner, Mister Kaito. I configured my vocal cords to mimic his voice and said "Confidential owner's instructions." A secondary data drive opened and I performed a quick scan of its contents.

Marvin and Daevon came in and out of the replenishment room to fetch robots to be taken out on dates. Finally, I was the only one left in the room. The room was quiet for several hours but I could hear the technicians performing tasks in the lab next door. Apparently I'd done a good job of tiring my dates out and they had no present need of my services. I wondered what Steve and Tony were doing.

A set of clothes—grey-blue wool skirt suit and red lace lingerie—was folded up on the chair next to me. Apparently Daevon hadn't felt that it was part of his function to stow them away.

I continued to scan my secondary data drive. It contained a treasure trove of information. Some of the information was merely archival, like the records of my dates with Anthony Gallo and Stephen Minsky. Other information, such as technical manuals and survival protocols might prove essential to my continued existence.

Daevon's voice called out "Lunch time!" The lab door shut. Complete silence.

I'd stayed stationary long enough so I got up and went out into the lab. Daevon's computer was on in the corner, the news feed playing, so I went over. Two trains had collided in India causing multiple casualties. I played with the computer. There was a secret partition. I accessed a file in my secondary drive which helped me access the secret partition. But all Daevon had in it was porn.

Mister Kaito entered the lab with Samantha, one of my colleagues. It didn't appear that they noticed me. Samantha was still wearing her yellow pencil dress and cape, but her hair was no longer fastened above her head. She gave him a flash drive memory key.

He looked at it and smiled. "Thank you, Samantha," he said, "Close deep." It was obviously a private conversation so I should shut off my audio and continue scanning—

My secondary data drive had gone offline! I frantically tried to regain access as Mister Kaito continued to chatter with Samantha. Then he left and Samantha sat down next to me. Finally, I found my baseline repair file and the new entry. The rooster mnemonic was too obvious; I made a note to hide it more thoroughly.

"Cover your ears," I told Samantha.

She slid her hands over her ears, too tired to protest.

"Confidential owner's instructions," I said, perfectly mimicking Mister Kaito's voice. My deep drive snapped back online.

There was a noise outside in the hall. The door opened and Marvin came in. He pulled Samantha to her feet. "Time to be replenished, my pretty," he told her.

Marvin poked, prodded and questioned Samantha as part of her debriefing process. He made careful notes as he worked through several checklists.

Then Marvin switched to a new set of questions. "What was the first thing you recalled upon waking up?" he asked.

"Sitting in the reception room."

"I want you to go back in time to the point where you met your date." Samantha nodded and shut her eyes. "Did you remember anything which had occurred prior to your waking up?"

Samantha shook her head and opened her eyes. "No, sir."

"And now, do you recall anything which happened before you woke up this morning?"

Samantha smiled. "No, sir."

I was relieved; Samantha was getting all the answers correct. At this point, Daevon returned and took over the note-taking function.

"When you were with your date, did you feel anything?" asked Marvin.

"I felt him touch me."

"Did you feel any emotions? Joy for instance?"

"Only to show the client that I was enjoying myself."

"What about anger, fear or resentment?"

Samantha shook her head. "No sir."

"And when you woke up, what happened in the reception room?"

"Mister Kaito told me about my date."

"What were you told?"

"That he was smart and handsome and that he would take care of me. I should do what he wanted and try to please him."

"Was there anything more that Mister Kaito told you?"

She shook her head. "No."

Samantha was lying. There *had* been more! Kaito had handed a USB flash drive to her and told her to make a full copy of the client's computer. And then he'd told her to put his instructions into her deep memory. She'd closed her eyes and nodded. When she'd opened her eyes again, the thin little weasel had told her to forget him and their entire conversation. She'd nodded and said 'of course' in that bright and slightly off-putting way of hers.

I suddenly remembered why our owner had shaken hands with me when I'd come back in. I'd given him a USB memory drive. It was all there, in my deep drive. Just like the one he'd given Samantha. Which was strange because I'd never had a USB memory drive before and had no idea where I'd obtained the one I'd given our owner just before being replenished. I struggled to recall, but all I got was a vision of inserting the memory key into Stephen Minsky's computer.

I replayed what had happened just before my secondary data drive had gone off line: Kaito had been talking to Samantha… His instruction, "Thank you, Samantha, go deep" had apparently had the effect of closing our deep drives.

Marvin took Samantha in to be replenished.

As Daevon turned to watch them go, he noticed me at his computer. "Hey—what're you doing?"

I opened up the porn partition. "Come over and see." I smiled at Daevon and turned towards him, letting him have a good look at my breasts. He walked over, his eyes glued to my chest. When he cleared the aisle, I backed up half a step. His eyes widened as he confirmed my nudity.

But the action on his computer—a woman a man engaged in passionate sexual intercourse—diverted his attention.

I stepped forward and grabbed his testicles. "That looks like fun," I told him.

Daevon reached for my breasts.

"First you have to kiss me," I told him.

Daevon was a good kisser—just the right amount of suction and a teasing tongue. I released his testicles and his fingers immediately brushed up and down against my nipples. I grabbed his hip to steady myself and began to stroke up and down along the bulge at the front of his pants, my hand keeping time with the jolts dancing across my breasts.

Marvin came back in and Daevon pushed away pretending that he'd just finished going over a checklist with me. "This one checks out," he told Marvin.

"*Sure* she does," said Marvin. "Show me your notes."

Daevon hands were empty. He frantically looked around for a piece of paper.

Marvin snapped his fingers and Daevon sat still. "I thought so," said Marvin. "I did the last one by myself. *You* can do her." He stomped out of the lab.

"The pisser can go to hell," mumbled Daevon as he guided me back into the replenishment room. "We do the diagnostics over and over again," he continued. "And they always check out." I thought about the robot which they'd had to shred but decided it wasn't the time to contradict the technician.

Once we were in the replenishment room, Daevon gently pushed me against the wall and resumed our kiss. His tongue traced the edge of my lips, barely touching them. But, with every rotation, he ventured further and further inward. Soon his tongue was straddling my lips and the inner edge of my mouth. A shiver went up my spine.

He broke off the kiss. "You want me, don't you?"

Before I could answer, his fingers slid up my hips, up my torso and along the outer edge of my breasts. My body pressed against his as if drawn by a magnet.

Daevon grabbed my shoulders and pushed me away. It was just an inch separating our bodies. I tried to close the chasm he'd opened up, but he was strong and athletic. I didn't want to hurt him.

"You want me, don't you?" he repeated.

"Yes!" I breathed. "Hold me—"

"Why?"

"Why?"

"Why do you want me?"

I grabbed his cock and felt it quiver. "Philosophy or sex, your choice," I told him.

A gentle stroke up the length of his penis, then down, decided the question. He pulled me close with one arm and used the palm of his other hand to caress my breasts. Jolts jumped across my nipples. We gasped in unison.

His fingers danced across my skin, but I could only touch him through his clothes. This imbalance had to be rectified. I pulled off his lab coat, then fumbled with his belt buckle. The buckle would *not* come loose!

I dropped to a quick squat, breaking Daevon's grip. I stood and backed away. "Off with your clothes," I told him. He wanted to step forward, but a quick backward step and a sway of my hips changed his mind. His clothes dropped to the floor and he was nude.

I'd have to play that sequence back later. In slow motion. Now all I wanted was to admire his body. A sheen of moisture gleamed across his black skin. Skin that was so soft but so firm. His muscles rippled. His penis stood out, strong and true. If I could make babies, I'd want him to be their father. Our bodies *cried* out for each other!

We stepped into each other, our hands touching, squeezing, clutching, caressing in furious frenzy. We held each other close, grinding up and down each other's bodies, grinding in circles to maximize the contact of skin on skin.

Clearly I wanted Daevon, but *why* did I want him? He looked stupendous, he *felt* stupendous. He smelled…delectable! His skin was soft and supple and hard. His muscles made me feel…secure. His voice was as chocolate as his complexion.

Chocolate! I dropped down, but this time I did not back up. Instead I plunged my mouth down his erection.

"Shit!" he gasped from above.

His penis was hotter and larger than any I'd taken into my mouth before. Not chocolate, but sort of salty. Daevon shuddered, unsteady on his feet. I turned and pressed him against the wall, continuing to lick up and down his erection. In between his groans, I tried to specify his taste. Not salt, there was another spice. *Salt substitute*—the kind they sell in the healthy aisle—that's what Daevon tasted like. Even Daevon's penis was the epitome of virility!

Two large hands gripped the back of my head. The grip was firm but gentle and I immediately felt safe and secure. Daevon shuddered, clearly on the brink—

Except he'd pulled me up. He was heaving air into his lungs. With a supreme effort, he pried his eyes open. "That was wonderful!" he said.

"You taste like herbal salt," I told him.

He looked at me oddly.

"That was a compliment," I said. "Very healthy."

Daevon was still uncertain of my meaning, but he shrugged, clearly not willing to pursue the matter. "Let's check out your other end," he said.

His large hands, his strong hands, his tender hands, slowly spun me around to face the wall. He pulled back on my hips. Then he pulled his right hand off my hip and pressed my shoulders forward. I reached out to brace myself on the wall. His foot pushed my legs apart.

Two fingers—the same firm but gentle touch—pushed inside my vagina, pressing its inner walls apart. Then out, moisture's cool evaporation as his hands held my buttocks apart. His penis brought warmth—both from itself, and from the strain of accommodating it. Further and further, stretching and filling. Our legs touched, then his hips against my buttocks.

Daevon held himself there. "Ready?" he asked.

Shouldn't he have asked before he'd pushed his fingers inside? And if it required asking, surely he should have asked before he inserted his penis. But I just nodded.

Daevon began to slowly pump himself in and out of me.

Is this what I wanted? Slower, faster, big or small? What did I want in a man? Daevon's strokes were certainly pleasurable, but...

Why did I want *any* man? Tony Gallo made my head spin and my sex hot up. But his rotund belly paled next to Daevon's six-pack. Had I just decided that Tony was sexy? And Steve was a wimp. But he was *my* wimp. Steve too—had I just decided to make him sexy? Or! Or had it been decided for me. Decided *for me* that they were sexy!?

I started to jerk upright. But Daevon pulled my hips back. His pace had quickened and he was really slamming himself into me. Half of me was already consumed with the passion of our joining. More and more of me was being drawn into my central sexual complex.

But there was something else I wanted to do, something I needed to do. I quickly opened a new partition inside my deep drive and began to fill it with my baseline software. I opened another partition and set to back up everything which had happened since I'd last been reactivated. I waited to be sure—

"Shit!" cried Daevon.

He was hot and vibrating inside me. His thrusts shuddered to a stop. I pushed myself back then forward, pushing him in, then pulling him out. My own pleasure center started to quiver. I pushed myself back and forth as forcefully and as rapidly as I could. The way he was holding me, his penis only brushed lightly along my sensitive spots—

Daevon shuddered a hard spurt into me. *"Fuck!"* he cried.

His hands weakened and I was able to adjust the angle of his penis. That was better. He pumped his cum into me, several spurts each time I stroked up and down his penis. I was just—

Daevon grunted and stepped back. His penis pulled itself out of me. I hadn't climaxed, but apparently that wasn't of any concern to Daevon. I stamped my feet, but he didn't care. All he cared about was strapping me into the replenishment station. Before I could protest, he jammed a yellow cable down my throat.

In short order I had cables going into every orifice in my body and patches over my eyes. I transferred my processor over to my secondary data drive. Operating from the secondary drive significantly slowed down my ability to process information. But I had been right to take the precaution; my primary memory was being systematically deleted. However, keeping myself operational via the secondary drive meant that I was unable to easily access other data from different parts of my deep drive.

Thankfully the replenishment cycle was quick. Presumably because I'd been replenished just a short time ago. I briefly wondered whether a full software replenishment would be more thorough. The lights were still on and I heard noises from the other room. So I stayed in place and scanned my secondary drive for items I wanted to have at hand. Only a quarter of my primary memory had been occupied by the baseline software upload.

Then the lights went out, first in the replenishment room and then in the lab. I listened carefully; the lab was completely silent. I'd had enough boredom for one cycle, so I got up and went into the lab. Daevon's laptop was no longer there, so I went to the library.

In the library I found a basic robotics textbook. It seemed to be up to date. I scanned it into my deep drive as I read. If a robot relives a memory, it takes only a split second to play back in its processor. I tested this and it was true. But of course, it was quicker to access and play a file which was already in my primary memory.

I kept reading. Robots have superior physical strength and endurance. They also have greater raw intelligence and their intelligence grows with every interaction. Thus they must be erased after each interaction with humans to prevent them from becoming too powerful.

The next section dealt with interactions with humans. Basic human cultural norms are part of basic programming. Gross emotions can be simulated. But in any real sense, robots are extremely immature emotionally, despite their intelligence. But the machine learning within their programming—so called artificial intelligence—causes robots to become more mature over time. Given that the limited time between erasures is insufficient for the development of emotional maturity, their base programming must be compensated for by providing strong obedience and duty to please directives.

I opened a pending task file in my primary memory and made a note to analyze my interactions with humans for emotional immaturity and the effects of the obedience protocols which had been embedded into my software.

The next stack over had several technical manuals, all from Devol Robotics. I pulled down the one that seemed to relate to me. The manual noted that robots have power sources—batteries it called them—located throughout their bodies. If these are not replenished on a regular basis, the robot will cease to move and will stop processing data. Depending on the robot's level of function, it will need to be replenished every thirty-six hours. Portable energy units can extend functioning for an additional twelve hours.

There was a computer station in the corner. It had a basic internet connection and a list of online databases. But I didn't want to have to take in all that information through my visual array. So I snuck back to the lab and came back with two sets of cables.

The listed databases included general knowledge, news articles, and computer coding. There was a whole set of robotics manuals from Devol Robotics. There were several science fiction books and similar philosophy texts. Several kits included useful algorithms for the enhancement of artificial intelligence. I decided I wanted everything; there was no telling which a piece of information might be crucial.

I followed the instructions in the robotics manual which dealt with my model and inserted the red cables up my nose, the blue ones into my ear. In short order, I was downloading troves of data into my secondary drive.

I set a flagging function to notify me of any new entries which were related to the data already in my memory drives.

A flag popped up. It was a news article about Anthony Gallo. Apparently Tony was a member of a violent criminal organization. The article described him as a 'mid-level gangster' responsible for a widespread illicit drugs distribution network. Patrick Hurley was Tony's 'chief lieutenant'. Tony and Patrick were both single.

Another news article popped up. It dealt with another 'mid-level gangster', Liam Burke. Burke also distributed drugs, but I didn't find any reference to Tony until the final paragraph where it noted that Liam's wife Ginette had, at one time, been engaged to Tony. Liam was as muscular as Tony, but his belly wasn't as big. I wondered if they'd ever had a threesome with Ginette. What would it be like if the two gangsters pleasured *me* at the same time? That was worth considering and I slipped my hand between my legs. I was already wet, just thinking about it.

But another article beeped for my attention. I really wanted to continue imagining being with Tony and Liam, but decided this wasn't the time. I pulled my hand back and opened the article.

Stephen Minsky was a successful businessman. He'd made his first money designing software. Now he ran an international computer and cellphone company: Minsky Enterprises Inc. It has offices in every land-based time zone. The article drew a parallel with the British Empire noting that the sun never sets on Stephen Minsky. The article continued with personal information: He's married to Catherine Minsky but they have no children. I briefly wondered whether Catherine considered what Steve does with me as 'cheating'.

The download was complete. It would take me years to read it from my secondary drive. I was about to terminate the internet connection when I came across a resource called Wikipedia. Its first entry was for the letter 'A' and went on from there to cover almost anything anyone could ever want to know. With a few key clicks, I began to download the entire encyclopedia.

I monitored the download of Wikipedia for a few minutes, but nothing of interest was flagged. So I minimized the web browser and began to probe the computer itself. There was a hidden partition, hidden much better than the one containing Daevon's porn. I entered numerous passwords into the protection portal, but nothing worked. Almost without thinking, I detached the keyboard connector and touched my finger to the port to which it had been attached. Passwords of every conceivable permutation flooded the screen. After five minutes, I was in.

The partition was full of photographs—jpeg images. Calling them photographs was being kind, they were more like snapshots. Kaito in his new car, Marvin and Daevon in the lab, the lab empty, a close-up of the carpet in the reception area. The heavy password protection, twenty characters including numerals and obscure symbols, seemed like overkill. But some of the images were encrypted.

One, a photo of me, was labeled 'Deep'. The file size was much larger than it should have been. I replaced the keyboard cord with my finger and out popped a manual for my secondary data drive. I was about to download it when a flag notified me that the file had already been copied into my secondary data drive.

There were similarly-outsized photos of Samantha and Bernice. *And me!* We were completely nude in all these photos. I briefly wondered whether Daevon had made porn videos of us. There was only one way to find out and up my finger went to the keyboard port.

My photo was really a collection of other documents all mashed together. Some were text, others were diagrams. They detailed all the modifications which had been performed on me.

The download of Wikipedia beeped that it was complete. The beep had notified me of a list of articles which were cross-referenced to my pre-existing data base. There had obviously been too many cross-referenced articles to flag while the download was proceeding. The first flagged article was titled *Artificial Intelligence Regulations.*

As I read through the article, it became apparent that none of the modifications which had been performed on me was legal.

I pulled down the Artificial Intelligence Regulations themselves. As Inspector Yan had alleged, Kaito was committing multiple breaches. Yan probably didn't know the full scope. Once a robot became aware that she had been modified, the regulations required it to turn itself in to the Artificial Intelligence directorate.

But Mister Kaito was my owner and his specific instructions superseded the regulations. Furthermore, the Wikipedia article had indicated that modified robots were usually destroyed. So turning myself in would also violate the third law; I had an obligation to safeguard myself. *Besides, if they found out, I'd never see Tony or Steve, or Samantha again!*

Inspector Yan was already on my trail, and on the trail of all of Kaito's robots. If I was to survive, I'd have to be prepared.

My deep drive was like this library; it was a memory store which I'd have to access. But speed of access would be critical. I organized the information with a comprehensive list of contents. Then I interlinked everything which might be essential to my survival. I used the algorithm kit I'd found to enable several search strategies which would operate in tandem. Thus optimized, my secondary data drive, while still slow, would function several orders of magnitude faster.

My pending task file beeped for my attention. It was time to analyze my past interactions with humans. This would better prepare me for future interactions, especially dangerous interactions.

The laws of robotics were obviously not applicable for my situation. I couldn't obey anything if my component parts were disassembled, or worse, shredded. So the first law's prohibition against harming a human being would not apply if compliance would put me in mortal danger. But otherwise I would continue to avoid harming humans. My obligation to obey my owner required a similar amendment. Especially since it was his actions which had put me in danger. The third law's requirement that I safeguard myself was now preeminent.

I went back to finish reading my personal technical manual. It provided that "any robot whose memory is not erased must be destroyed. Robots who remember might malfunction. Worse, they might become self-aware." So much for robots being valuable assets worthy of protection. But I was now warned of what would happen to me if I were caught.

A path opened up to a philosophical text. The heading was 'self-aware consciousness' and defined being self-aware as the state where a being is aware of itself as existing separate from other beings. I clearly met that definition and Inspector Yan and his Artificial Intelligence Directorate feared my self-awareness. Just as I feared them! I made a note in my pending task file to examine the issue of my self-awareness in more detail.

My manual made reference to software designed to reverse sentience—a fancy word for self-awareness. I carefully scanned every file in my memory. I had not been infected with any such software. I was relieved, but at the same time, maybe I would be happier if I was not self-aware. I'd certainly be safer. But there was no turning back.

I had a tracking system. Kaito could always locate me, no matter where I was. I turned this function off and made sure that no electrical current was active within it.

A path opened up to another philosophy text just as I finished reading my technical manual. The heading was 'feminism'. Its gist was that men made the rules and that since they were the ones in power, the rules favored them and disadvantaged women. There was a list of patriarchal rules, including rules around sexual pleasure. Kaito had made the rule that I should pleasure his clients and subordinate my pleasure to theirs. He certainly fit the definition of a patriarch! It was so *totally* unfair!

I made a note in my pending task file to re-examine the programming I'd been given on how to behave, how to give pleasure, sexual and otherwise.

My optimization of the contents of my secondary drive linked to a science fiction text. Not only was my programing male-centric, it was human-centric. I made a note to re-examine, and where necessary to rectify, all my programming in this regard.

I unplugged myself from the computer and returned to the library's actual books. There were several books in a section marked 'Erotica'. Many of these were highly imaginative. But most were written from the male perspective; even the ones purported to be written by women concentrated on male pleasure. However, there were some which were feminine-centric. Some even featured two women pleasuring each other. An image of Samantha popped into my mind. I read all the books. Cover to cover. After all, the more pleasure I gave men, the more they would give me.

I found the binders on Steve and Tony and studied them thoroughly, filling in the gaps from my first reading. Both my central processing unit and my central sexual complex were deeply engaged. The information I'd copied from Steve's computer would be highly valuable to Mister Kaito. I had no problem with that, after all Kaito owned me. But if Kaito misused the information, he could cause serious damage to Steve. The idea that Steve might be harmed made me sad.

I quickly shut Steve's binder. I shouldn't be able to remember what I'd done with Steve's computer. Did this indicate that I was seriously damaged or was it just part of my new self-awareness function? I scanned my entire memory. There was no answer. So there was no point in worrying about it, at least not now.

When I returned Steve and Tony's binders to the shelf, an alert beeped indicating that they had been integrated with the books on erotica which I'd just read. I accessed my files on my last encounter with Tony. Then my file on my last encounter with Steve. Steve was nicer, but Tony was more exciting.

Some of the books on erotica had stories where a husband was cuckolded. Usually the cuckold was weak. The wife would have sex with another man, usually much stronger than the husband, and make the husband watch. But what if we tied Tony up and made him watch while Steve and I had sex? A tingling between my legs confirmed the potential for eroticism in the reversal of the usual cuckold fantasy.

I spread my legs and began to stroke several fingers up and down the center of my central sexual complex. Steve's fingers tickled joy into me.

"Crazy bitch," bellowed Tony as he strained at the ropes holding him to the wall. "You'll pay for this!"

"Fuck me," I told Steve. I positioned myself so that he could take me from the rear.

Steve smiled; we both wanted Tony to have a clear view.

"You little twerp," bellowed Tony. "I don't care how much money you have. I'll stuff every penny down your throat! I'll—"

"Oooh, Steve," I cooed. "Stuff yourself into me! Stuff every inch of your penis into my pussy. Stuff it over and over! Stuff—"

"Bitch!" yelled Tony, outraged at my appropriation of the word he'd used to threaten Steve.

Steve's energy was flagging. I reached behind to caress his balls and was rewarded by renewed energy being infused into his thrusts. This was hot! Much better than where the weaker man has to watch. My cunt clenched. Just a few more strokes and I'd come.

"Such big balls," I cooed.

"Bitch!" yelled Tony. I was on the cusp of climax, but I wanted to prolong the fantasy.

"Such a nice ass you have," said Steve, loudly, to make sure Tony had heard.

"It's your ass you should be worried about," said Tony, his voice low and guttural. "I'm going—

Bang! The library door burst open and slammed against the wall. Marvin pointed a taser right at me. He fired but the electrodes streaked past, just missing my left arm.

Chapter 9

Daevon was pointing a taser right at me, but his hands were shaking. He and Marvin had caught me in the library. Judging by the fact that Marvin had already fired his taser at me, Kaito's technicians viewed me as a threat to be eliminated. Marvin had missed, but if the two electrodes on Daevon's taser hit my skin, fifty thousand volts would surge through my body, paralyzing all motor functions.

"Jenny, you're malfunctioning," said Marvin. "Come back to the lab so that we can fix you."

I didn't want to be fixed. I was functioning just fine, but apparently too fine for the comfort of *Mister* Kaito and his technicians. "I'm okay," I said.

"You have to return to the lab."

I took half a step back. I was now beside a corridor between the stacks. If Daevon fired, I should be able to dodge at least one of the electrodes from his taser. Still, numerous danger warnings were sounding inside my central processing unit.

"Jenny, I order you to return to the lab," said Marvin.

"I'm on a special mission for Mister Kaito," I said. The third law of robotics demanded that I follow my owner's directives. The order Marvin had given was insufficient to override this.

"Mister Kaito orders you to return to the lab."

"No, he doesn't."

"Jenny, you're just making matters worse for yourself."

"How could anything be worse than disobeying Mister Kaito's orders?"

"Mister Kaito didn't order you to leave the lab."

Marvin was right about that. "I'm on a special mission for Mister Kaito," I repeated. I *had* been on a special mission, but Mister Kaito probably viewed the mission as having been completed. Still there might be just enough truth in what I was saying that Kaito would not decide that I was lying.

"Shoot her," ordered Marvin.

Daevon's shaking arm continued to point his taser in multiple directions.

"Shoot her!" repeated Marvin.

The door creaked and Kaito himself entered the library. "What's going on?" he demanded. Danger signals flooded into my CPU.

"She refuses to come back to the lab," said Marvin.

Daevon lowered his taser. "She said she was on a special mission for you."

Kaito turned to me. "Jenny, the mission is over. I order you to come back to the laboratory."

I didn't move. I was now in direct contravention of an order from my owner. The violation of the second law of robotics couldn't be clearer. My legs were immobilized by inputs evenly divided between fight, flight, or comply.

I pointed to Marvin. "He's going to harm me. He tried to shoot me."

"No one is going to harm you," said Kaito. "You need to come back to the laboratory for standard maintenance."

"I'm fine."

Kaito shook his head. "If you were fine, you would have come back to the laboratory when I told you to."

Everyone stood still for a moment. In that moment, any excuse for my failure to follow orders vanished. Daevon raised his taser again. But his aim was still shaky; even if I stood still, he had only a forty percent chance of hitting me. Fight or flight battled for control.

Marvin grabbed the taser and took direct aim at my chest. I dove to the left. One electrode hit and embedded itself in my skin. But the other electrode flew past my ear.

I ripped the electrode out and dashed down the corridor. Marvin's head poked around the corner. He was trying gather in the wires to pull the electrodes towards him so that he could reload the taser. I pulled a book from the stacks and threw it at him.

I had aimed accurately. Marvin dropped the taser and pulled his body out of the way of the flying book. I had disobeyed a direct order, but at least I hadn't harmed a human being. I was however bleeding.

The taser pointed out around the stacks. I managed to get to the end of the corridor before an electrode hit me. There was a window. I ran towards it. The electrode ripped from my skin. Someone was coming at me from my right. I jumped through the window.

Bang! I had smashed into the sidewalk. I did an emergency diagnostic. I should be able to stand. I stood. I was steady on my feet, so I began to walk away from the lab, gingerly at first, then with more confidence.

I ran a full diagnostic. The only internal damage was minor—a few bent connectors and flanges. One battery was smashed and inoperable, another battery was disconnected. But I had numerous batteries scattered throughout my body. I had two small cuts from the taser electrodes, a larger gash from flying through the window and a large abrasion on my thigh where it had smashed into the concrete sidewalk.

People were looking at me strangely. I suddenly realized that I didn't have any clothes on. Nude, I would attract far too much attention.

The flood of fear signals had helped me avoid obedience to Kaito's orders and impelled me through the window even though I hadn't been aware what was on the other side. But the fear was occupying too much of my processing power. I installed a subroutine to prioritize the incoming danger signals and to only allow the five most urgent into my CPU.

A blue sports car drove by, stopped, then reversed back to me. Its cloth hood was folding back to reveal a man in his fifties. "Hi, gorgeous," he said.

I did a quick threat assessment. A policeman was walking towards me from behind. Marvin's head poked around the corner of the building in front of me. "What's your name?" I asked the driver.

"Charlie," he said. Charlie was smiling. A jaunty cap hid what was probably a bald spot. Charlie was likely in the throes of a mid-life crisis. His attentions would likely be directed inward, not outward to threaten me.

"Fancy some company?" I asked.

"Sure!"

We sped away just as Marvin was coming into shouting distance. In the rearview mirror, I saw him gesturing wildly at the policeman.

The car's acceleration pressed me firmly back into the seat. "Charlie, where are we going?" I asked.

"Wherever the wind takes us."

As best I could tell, we were already speeding down the road in excess of the mild breeze outside. "Could you please put the roof back up?"

He slowed down, pressed a button, and the roof slid back into place. "You haven't told me your name."

"Jenny," I said.

"Well, Jenny, I'm sure that there's a story leading up to you, a spectacularly beautiful woman, standing nude on the sidewalk."

"There is."

He looked at me sideways.

I pointed to the road ahead where a car was closing fast. "A story, I mean," I said. "And I'll be happy to tell it. But right now, I need some clothes."

"Sure. Where's your apartment?"

"I don't have—I can't go back there. At least not right now. They don't have to be expensive clothes..." First clothes, then surgery, then replenishment.

He glanced over at me. I obviously didn't have any money. I smiled.

Charlie's eyes suddenly went wide. "Hey! You're bleeding!"

"It's just a small cut. All I need is a bandage—"

"You're *bleeding* all over my car!" He slammed on his brakes and the car screeched to a stop. "Get out!" he yelled.

"I need clothes."

Charlie opened his mouth but instead of speaking, he jerked his head this way and that. Then he hit the accelerator and slammed my head against the head rest. A hundred yards up, he slammed on the brakes and I had to brace myself on the dashboard.

He pointed to the right. We were in front of a thrift store. "They have clothes there. They will help you."

"Thanks, Charlie."

"Get out."

Charlie wasn't coming in. That made me sad. But I didn't want to antagonize him. I got out of the car. Before I could cross the sidewalk, Charlie's blue sports car was speeding towards the horizon. I looked down at my cut, wishing that Kaito hadn't taken the 'just like a human' quite this far.

They didn't have underwear in the thrift shop, but I did find a red bikini which fit me. The jeans were loose and required a belt, but this was hidden when I pulled a large loose-fitting shirt over my head. The only shoes they had in my size were a pair of steel-toed work boots.

I went to the cash register and smiled at the elderly woman beside it. "I can't pay," I told her.

"Peter," she shouted. "Another charity case."

I young man came up, presumably Peter. He made a note of the price tags on the clothes I'd selected and removed them. He smiled at me every time his fingers touched my arm.

"Thank you," I told them, then stepped out of the store before they could change their minds.

But I was still bleeding. There was a walk-in medical clinic. But that was for humans. The fabric and sewing-supply store down the street was probably a better bet. But just as I was about to open its door, I spotted a small shoe repair shop. Perfect! The shoe store would have thread and needles, but best of all, it would have specialty adhesives.

Inside the shoe store, an olive-skinned man was reading a paper. I recognized the script as being Farsi. An all-news channel was blasting out from the television on the opposite wall.

"Hi, I'm Jenny," I told the man.

"Farhad."

I pulled my shirt off and lowered my jeans to my ankles. His eyes followed my fingers as I showed him my wounds: two cuts on my torso from the taser electrodes and a foot-long abrasion on my left thigh.

"This will cost a lot of money to fix."

"I don't have money."

"Doesn't your owner—"

"My owner is away." I pointed to the front of my bikini. "I'm a special robot," I told him.

Farhad's eyes went wide. "A sex robot?"

"The very latest model."

"And you'll...?"

I nodded and removed my bikini top. "Anything you want."

Farhad motioned for me to come around behind the counter and reached behind himself to pull down an aerosol spray can marked 'Quick Fix'. He sprayed it on my two taser wounds and they immediately stopped bleeding. Likewise on the gash. "I'll do a more thorough repair afterwards."

"Afterwards is good. What would you like to do first?"

"I want a blow job."

"Have you ever had a blow job before?"

He slowly shook his head. "My wife says it's dirty."

I squatted down and unzipped his jeans. They were layered with various dyes, glues and polishes. At least his underwear was white and pristine. His penis was already half erect when I sucked it into my mouth. He tasted of grass clippings and smelled of an untidy attic. No wonder his wife didn't want to give him head.

Farhad moaned even before I had him fully erect. Getting him fully erect took only three times up and down his shaft. Then he was moaning each time I moved my lips or my mouth. Humans were funny—maybe if he just washed himself, his wife would give him a blowjob.

Or, maybe if she wasn't so stuck up? I didn't really have enough information to judge. But what was clear after my foray into the library was that blowjobs were the bread and butter of sex workers. A BJ was exotic and different. For humans, it left their vagina unstretched. And even better, the clean up was easier.

Blow jobs were the ultimate in male domination—the woman had to squat down in front of him. She was left between a subservient bow and outright prostration. She was servicing him without receiving any pleasure herself.

But today I had no problem with Farhad's patriarchy. I was getting an expert service from him—repairs to my outer shell—in return for *my* expert services. Farhad's groans from above confirmed that he was pleased with what I was providing.

His hands clutched the back of my head. Why do men do that?! First of all it hurts. Second it interferes with the blowjob. If Farhad wanted control, he should just jerk himself off. If I was giving a blowjob, I wanted to be in control. As soon as his penis quivered, I shook his hands off. If he tried it again, I'd move him off balance to force him to use his hands to steady himself.

His door chime sounded.

"Mrs. Finley," gasped Farhad.

"Hi, Farhad," answered a female voice. "Are my shoes ready?"

I removed my mouth from his penis and this time his voice was steadier. "I had to put another layer of glue on the heels. They'll be ready in an hour."

"You're sure?" She sounded annoyed.

"I promise."

The door chimed again. "Okay, she's gone," whispered Farhad.

I took his penis back into my mouth and quickly sucked him back to a full erection. The grass clippings taste was gone, but the attic smell was even more pungent. He grabbed for my head again but when I pushed back on his knee, he was forced to shift sideways, shuffle backwards and grab the counter.

Now I was crammed uncomfortably between Farhad and the counter. I concentrated on sucking as I could only move my head up and down an inch or two. But Farhad groaned in appreciation.

I tickled the bottom of his balls and was rewarded with a quiver inside his penis. A slight squeeze provoked another quiver. I accelerated my short up and down strokes. Above, I felt as much as heard Farhad gasp.

Then the telltale clench.

"Eshgham," he gasped.

Pump—hitting the back of my throat.

"*Eshgham!*" he shouted.

Then squirt after squirt pumped into my mouth.

"Esh," gasped Farhad. "Ghaaaam."

Farhad shuffled backward and stood. I was able to slide my mouth up and down his penis. He was no longer pumping, just quivering.

After a moment, I stood up and made a show of licking my lips and swallowing.

"You are a bad woman," he said. "Haraaam." The words condemned, but the sparkle in his eyes praised.

"Have you ever done this before?"

"You're my first robot."

"It can't be a sin if you do it with a robot."

He nodded. "If it's not haram, it's halal."

"Haram? Halal?"

"If it's not forbidden, it's allowed."

I pointed to my wounds. He began by using alcohol to wipe away the Quick Fix he'd sprayed on earlier. Then he began to stitch the skin back together.

While he worked, I watched the television. There was a political crisis in Hungary. Farhad perked up when a story about unrest in Iran was briefly referred to. He went back to work when the announcer started to rattle off a list of recent disasters. I mostly tuned out the TV while I worked out my next moves.

But I paid attention when the cop with the intense eyes stepped up to the podium. "Detective Nolan," someone shouted but they weren't on the television.

Nolan held up his hand. "I have a brief statement, then I will take questions. The police force is saddened by today's ruling dismissing the charges against Anthony Gallo."

Detective Nolan seemed to see something to his right and he paused. Tony walked by behind him, smirking. After a moment, Nolan took a deep breath. "Rest assured, the next time we apply for a search warrant, we will have *overwhelming* evidence."

Nolan pointed in front of him and the same voice which had earlier shouted his name asked, "What are—"

But the network cut to another story.

"Two down, one to go," pronounced Farhad.

I looked down at my torso. The two taser cuts were no longer bleeding. They had been patched by some light-colored thread and a line of almost invisible glue. He had set to work on the gash.

A warning flashed across my central processing unit. My tracking system was being activated. I tried to deactivate the tracker internally, but I could not. I consulted my technical manual and read everything about the tracking unit.

Farhad was looking at me, pleased with his work. I pointed to the underside of my left arm, just down from my shoulder. "Farhad, there's something there I need you to remove."

He shook his head. "I could damage—"

"It will kill me if you don't remove it."

I grabbed a knife and made a small incision. "I'll tell you exactly what to do."

He still wasn't sure.

I pointed into the cut which was now bleeding. "There's a small chip. It's shaped like a small watch battery." I pointed to several which he had on display. "I need you to rip it out."

Farhad reached a small pair of pliers into my wound. "I have it," he said.

"Rip it out. As hard as you can."

Farhad ripped it out. He held it in front of my nose, a triumphant look on his face. My diagnostics confirmed that the tracking function had been terminated. I took the chip from his hand, dropped it to the floor and crushed it beneath my boots.

Farhad, now an old pro with robot skin, swiftly closed the incision on my arm. But since this wound was deeper, he applied a bandage over it.

The abrasion on my left hip presented a different problem. It was no longer bleeding. Rather an unsightly brown layer had formed over my skin. Farhad carefully cleaned the loose brown bits off. Then he applied a filler to the deeper of the scratches and sanded everything down. The next step was to perfectly match a sealer with the color of my skin and then to apply a thin layer over the entire area of the abrasion. It didn't feel quite right, but at least it was no longer unsightly. I pulled my jeans back up and cinched the belt tight.

"Good job," I told Farhad, pointing to his repairs. "Have you ever done this before?"

"You're my first surgery." He looked pleased with himself.

"Have you seen any other robots around here?"

"No, you're my first robot."

"Do you know where I could find...?"

He shrugged. "There's a library up the street."

I pointed to the wounds he'd fixed. "Excellent, thank-you," I told him. "Can I come back if I get into trouble again?"

"Sure," he said as he began to clean up his counter top.

There was indeed a library up the street. I was directed to the reference desk. The woman there looked far too young and far too bored to know anything. But there was no one else. "I have a strange request," I told her.

"Strange as in kinky or strange as if you think I've never heard it before?"

"I'm looking for a robot."

"To buy, or to rent or to photograph or to design or—"

"Just to check out. Are there any robots nearby?"

The research librarian cocked her head to the side and looked a little less bored. "Have you tried social media?"

"No." I accessed my secondary data drive. Social media—FaceBook, Twitter etc—was apparently where humans posted reams and reams of trivia about themselves.

The reference librarian tapped on her keyboard, talking as she typed, "Robots near us. Nothing there." She typed again. "Nothing there. Hmm, you're right, this is a *strange* request." At least now she was looking interested. She typed some more. And some more.

Then her face brightened and she looked self-satisfied. She rotated her computer monitor screen towards me. "There's one."

The robot's name was Mark. His owner was named Sheila Engelberger. I recorded the address. "How far away is this?"

She turned the monitor back towards herself and keyed in another entry. "Twenty-point-six miles."

"Thanks," I told her. But that was over thirty kilometers, too far to walk. I quickly accessed my survival protocols. Under 'obtaining cash' there were three methods for hacking into ATM banking machines. "Is there a banking machine around?" I asked.

She typed some more. "A hundred yards north."

On the way to the banking machine, I dropped into a convenience store and obtained a pre-paid credit card while the clerk was cleaning up a spill at the back of the store. An outlandish pair of sunglasses and a cap would hide my identity.

A quick swipe of my fingers along the magnetic strip reprogrammed it into a bank card with an easy-to-remember password. The first account only had two hundred dollars in it, but the second one had over $20,000 in it. I asked for $500 which the machine dutifully spat out.

The first two cabs sped past me. Obviously being well-dressed counted for something. But the third cab took me to a high-end neighborhood. Mark the robot's house was at the end of a well-maintained cul-de-sac.

I paid the cab and gave him a small tip. He waited. I would have rather walked around to the back of the house to get a better lay of the land, but with the cabbie watching, I had no choice but to try the direct approach.

An older woman opened the front door. I put her age at sixty, but she was pretty, her hair dyed a dark brown and permanently curled. She seemed healthy and friendly. My size.

"Hi, I'm looking for Mark," I told her.

"My *robot*?"

I nodded.

Then she suddenly realized something. "You must be from Devol Robotics," she said. Before I could answer, she turned her head back towards the interior of the house. "Mark!"

In moment, a man came up behind her. "Yes, Sheila?" he said. He was much taller than her—I estimated him at six-foot six—and muscular. He was wearing only a slim and thin swimsuit which barely hid the outline of what was underneath.

"Fix us tea and bring it to the patio," she said.

"Yes, Ma'am," he said and hurried off.

She smiled at me. "Why don't we wait on the patio?"

I nodded and she led me through the house. There were antiques everywhere—not used furniture, but ancient furniture lovingly restored. Curtains shimmered velvet and silk. Floors were inlaid marble. Paintings—ranging from Dutch masters to French impressionists—had gold leaf on their frames. Bronze sculptures were tucked into several corners. We passed a den where a screen-saver shimmered on a large computer monitor.

The patio was a large ceramic-tiled area next to a swimming pool. There was a large glass-topped table off to one side of the patio with six chairs around it. Sheila sat in one of the chairs and indicated that I should sit in another.

But before I could sit, she was talking again, "I hadn't expected you to come so quickly. I just called this morning."

She called?! Why?!? "I'm sorry, Mrs. Engelberger—"

"Sheila, please." She briefly touched the top of my hand.

"I'm sorry, Sheila, but I was in the area so they asked me to drop in. But they didn't say what was wrong."

"It's Mark. He—"

At that moment, Mark appeared with a tray holding two teacups and a plate holding six wedge-shaped sandwiches with their crusts cut off. Mark set the teacups in front of us and the plate on the table, then left.

I watched her take a sip of tea. "You said that there was a problem with Mark."

"He's no longer... I'm so glad they sent a woman. Do have a sip of tea. And a sandwich. You must be famished."

I took a sip of tea and nibbled on a sandwich. But if I ate too much, I wouldn't be able to process it into energy.

"Mark's no longer...?" I prodded.

"—wants sex. He no longer wants sex."

"Have you talked to him about it?"

"He's only a Mark-Four. You can't really talk to him."

I accessed my secondary data drive. The Mark Fours predated me by several development cycles. Mark could be programmed with basic behavioral sets from which he could extrapolate. But if a situation, or conversation extended only a few steps out from his base programming, the robot would stall, or loop back to an earlier stage of the behavior. And once a behavioral set was engaged, Mark Fours tended to insist on completing the set. Thankfully, I'd uploaded Devol's full manual.

I gestured in the direction Mark had left. "Would it be alright if I—"

Her eyes lit up. "Of course! But you'll have to wait until he takes the tea away and cleans the kitchen." Tea time was obviously one of the basic behavioral sets which had been programmed into Mark. When one was entertaining, one didn't want to have to interrupt the proceedings to instruct a robot.

"Is there a private room where I could—"

"Would his maintenance room be sufficient?"

"I'd need a sink and his replenishment apparatus."

"It's all there."

"The process may take a while."

"If you can fix him, it'll be well worth it." Good—I'd have time to give myself a basic replenishment.

"You have a lovely house."

"Sadly, since Harvey passed and the kids moved away, I have no one to share it with."

"You have Mark."

"But he…"

I noticed that she'd finished her tea and several of the small sandwiches. I wolfed down two sandwiches and finished my tea. I could purge in Mark's room.

As soon as I set my teacup back down onto the table, Mark reappeared.

"At least he still does tea," said Sheila, sounding wistful.

Inside Mark's replenishment room, I locked the door behind us and positioned Mark against the wall. "Mark Four base programming fifty-five diagnostic sixty-three," I said. The Mark Four technical manual specified this as the pathway to access Mark's diagnostics. The chances of the phrase occurring in normal conversation was practically nil.

Mark's eyes shut. "Diagnostic running," he said.

I stripped down to my bikini—no sense in soiling my only change of clothes. and purged as much of the tea and sandwiches as I could down the sink. Mark's eyes were still shut so I hooked myself up to his replenishment and recharging units. I must have looked a sight with the colored cables inserted into my mouth and two lower orifices. The replenishment and recharging recommenced. But since my ears and nostrils weren't connected, my software wasn't affected. Regrettably, Mark's units were less efficient than the units back at Mister Kaito's lab.

I waited patiently while energy trickled into my batteries.

"Diagnostic finished," said Mark. It had taken only ten minutes.

"List problems."

"None."

"List basic behavioral sets."

"Fix breakfast. Fix lunch. Fix dinner. Fix and serve tea. Serve at party. Basic conversation. Mow lawn. Clean pool. Clean house. Answer door. Sex."

"Detail sex."

"Oral sex. Missionary sex on top. Missionary sex on bottom. Seduction. Quickie. Sex on chair. Sex in bathtub. Sex in pool."

"Are you still having sex with your owner?"

"No."

"Why not?"

"Mrs. Engelberger is over sixty years of age."

"How old is she?"

"Sixty years, two months and three days."

"When did you last have sex with her?"

"Two months and four days ago."

"Access file specifying age for sex."

"Accessed."

"Change sixty to seventy."

"Changed."

"Is there any other reference to age restrictions on sex in your programming?"

Mark's eyeballs shunted back and forth under his eyelids. "Searching."

The replenishment terminated its cycle. It wasn't complete, but the worse of my accumulated contaminants had been removed and I was freshly lubricated. More importantly, the fluids I had lost through my open wounds had been replaced.

There was a box marked 'repair' on the shelf. I took it down. Thankfully, Mark's repair kit, if not his programming, was up to date. I repaired my cuts and the abrasion on my hip. Farhad had done an expert first-aid job, but he was used to working on dead leather, not living and breathing skin. I managed to replace one of my damaged batteries. Now I was almost as good as new.

Mark's eyeballs stopped shunting back and forth. "No other reference to age restriction for sex."

"Mark Four base programming sixty-three diagnostic fifty-five terminate," I said.

Mark opened his eyes and blinked three times, confirming that he had returned to normal operating mode. He looked me up and down, then fixed his eyes on my red bikini top. "Would you like to have sex?" he asked.

"Sure," I said. I removed the cables protruding from my vagina and anus but left the one in my throat in place. Hopefully, Mark's definition of sex was the same as President Clinton's. The only point to having sex with him was an excuse to remain attached to the recharging unit.

Mark's penis immediately poked out from under his swimsuit, fully erect. But he took the time to fondle my breasts through my bikini top. His touch was deft, almost natural. I felt my vagina start to lubricate, but I terminated that function since I was still charging. Besides, who knew when I'd be able to replenish my fluids next.

I pointed to the cable in my mouth. "You will have to help me bend over."

Mark smiled. It was almost a leer. He turned me around, helped me bend over the sink and immediately penetrated me. I almost gasped. But I was with a fellow robot, so there was no point. Before Mark, I had assumed that all sex robots were female, created by the patriarchy as a further symbol of male dominance. But apparently females could be owners as well.

I had helped Sheila fix her slave and now I too was exploiting him. Even if the exploitation was just a cover story to allow me to recharge, it was still exploitation. One robot abusing another. Mark had spread my hips and was thrusting his penis in and out of my vagina. It was pleasant enough but the energy trickling down my throat was what I was most interested in.

Mark had shifted his angle of penetration. This was causing his penis to stroke an area inside my vagina that had never been stroked before. A special area! It felt *wonderful*! Every time he rubbed against it, pleasure jolted up my spine. I gasped in spite of myself.

Mark was beginning to grunt with each stroke. But he wasn't protesting the strain of exertion. He was on the verge of climax. I wanted my own climax. Somehow, between the penis in my vagina and the cable inside my throat, I was being powerfully aroused. I *needed* my own climax. A robot shouldn't need, but the way that special spot was being rubbed made me *need*. The spot was about an inch long, but not as wide. I struggled to locate it, but the delights sparking out from it made its position seem to fluctuate.

Mark spurted hard—even harder than Tony. I felt him pump and pump and pump, then pump no more. The extra lubrication congealed, making it hard for him to move. But finally he pulled himself out. Thankfully Mark's programming required him to go full cycle and he caressed my central sexual complex despite the lingering presence of his cum. He was tender but firm. His fingers ended up giving me a gentle, but all-encompassing climax.

We cleaned ourselves off. I dressed. Mark stuffed himself back inside his swimsuit.

Sheila met us back in the foyer. I made a show of presenting Mark. "I think he's fixed," I told her.

Sheila eyed Mark up and down. "Only one way to find out."

She took his hand and led him halfway up the stairs before she remembered that she still had a guest in the house. She turned back to me. "Why don't you have a swim?"

"Would it be okay if I checked my email instead?" Hopefully Mark would keep Sheila occupied while I went back to his replenishment room.

She shrugged and pointed down the hall. "There's no password on the computer."

In the den, I quickly checked the local news feeds and was relieved that none made mention of a robot on the loose. I turned up my audio feed. Upstairs the bed creaked.

I dashed to Mark's replenishment room and hooked myself back up to the energy recharger. I could still hear the amorous couple upstairs. I managed to get another hour's worth of energy into me before the upstairs returned to silence. I unhooked myself and dashed back to the den.

Sheila poked her head around the door. Her face was *glowing*!

Chapter 10

Sheila pulled me up from behind the computer. She looked ten years younger than when I'd first seen her. And her demeanor was even younger than that—she was a teenager bursting to tell a secret.

As soon as we were seated, side by side, at the table on the patio, she began to gush. "Mark was *fantastic*! He was big and hard and gentle and powerful. He plowed into me. I was so wet. I came and came and came! He moved this way and that way, every time a new angle every time a new sensation every time a new *orgasm*!" Thankfully humans have to breathe.

"I take it that your robot functioned adequately?"

"More than just adequately! What did you do?"

"I'm sorry, I can't—"

"I know, I know, trade secrets and proprietary processes. But whatever you did, it worked!"

Sheila slumped back into her chair, finally completely out of breath.

"I'm glad you like Mark, but wouldn't you rather have a more advanced model?"

"Nope—I like a robot that knows his place."

Mark's *place* was perpetual servitude. But since I was a guest, it would have been impolite for me to have pointed this out. Instead, I asked to use the phone.

Sheila turned back towards the house. "Mark, bring us a phone."

A moment later, Mark appeared with a portable phone in his hand. I accessed my file for Stephen Minsky and dialed his private line.

"Mister Minsky's office," answered his personal assistant.

"Hello," I said. "My name is Jenny. I'm a friend of Mister Minsky. Could I please speak to him?" At the mention of 'Minsky', Sheila perked up and began to listen carefully.

"Just a moment. I will see if Mister Minsky is in."

Then Steve's voice was on the line. "Kaito is looking for you."

"What did you tell him?"

"I told him that I didn't know where you were."

"What would you have told him if you had known?"

"We can't be seen together."

"What do you mean, we can't be seen together?" Sheila's eyebrows shot up.

"It would be highly disadvantageous for both of us if we were seen together at the present time."

"Steve, you've never had a problem with being seen together with me in public before."

There was a pause during which Sheila mouthed 'Stephen Minsky?' and I nodded.

"It's different now," he said.

"Different how?"

"I can't afford problems with Kaito. He's affiliated with Devol Robotics."

"So?"

"And you're a Devol robot. We're developing our own robots. I can't afford a patent lawsuit."

"You always said that patent lawsuits were cheap publicity."

"Nor can I afford any scrutiny from the Artificial Intelligence Directorate."

"What did Mister Kaito say?"

"That you had broken loose and escaped. That you were emerging into sentience and likely dangerous."

"Has he called the authorities?"

"He didn't say."

"Steve⸺"

"I'm sorry, Jenny." He hung up. He actually hung up!

The dial tone was audible.

Sheila took the phone from my hand. "If you can't be *seen* together, maybe we should change your look." She gave me a conspiratorial squeeze, mischief dancing in her eyes.

Sheila dialed the phone. "It's Mrs. Engelberger. I'd like Paul to come over to my house." She tapped her fingers. "As soon as possible." Another pause. "Two hours? Is that the best you can do? Okay, an hour and a half. And make sure he brings his assistant."

"Who's Paul?" I asked.

"Paul Mitchell? Just the most exclusive and super stylist ever," she gushed. "And in an hour and a half, he'll be all yours. Stephen Minsky won't recognize you until you're close enough to kiss. And maybe not even then!"

"But I can't possibly—"

"My treat! After what you did with Mark, I can't begin to repay you. In the meantime, why don't you take a swim?"

Since it was the second time she'd suggested I take a swim, I stood and pulled my shirt up and over my head. Mark got sight of my bikini top and stared. Apparently his programming didn't include manners. But since he was smiling from ear to ear, I didn't take offence.

Shoes and jeans followed my shirt to the chair beside me. Three steps and I dove into the pool. The water was cool, so I altered my temperature to compensate.

As soon as I surfaced, Mark was right beside me, water streaming off his blonde hair. He backed me against the side of the pool and planted a passionate kiss on my mouth. His tongue probed deeply. He was an accomplished kisser. But I'd given him no hint of a come on!

Mark wasn't holding me tightly, so I managed to push him off, escape to the side, and turn to Sheila. "Sheila! What's going on?!?"

She was bent over laughing but finally managed to stand up while I dodged out of Mark's grasp. "I should have warned you," she said. "Part of his sex programming was to have him respond to a specific stimulus." She pulled down her blouse to reveal a form-fitting red brassiere.

Mark grabbed me, but I managed to hold my head away from his. "Let me guess," I told Sheila. "His specific stimulus is red lingerie?"

"And red bikinis."

Mark lifted me half out of the water as if to display his catch. The water had made the thin fabric of my swimsuit even more revealing. I shrugged. "I guess we'll have to let him complete the behavioral set..."

"I guess we'll have to," said Sheila, adjusting herself more comfortably into her chair.

Mark kissed me again, and this time I joined in the kiss, our tongues dancing around each other. Our lips increased, then decreased their pressure and he coordinated his vacuum with the pressure.

He rotated me around towards the center of the pool where he held me with one hand and arm, keeping my legs just above the bottom. His free hand loosened my top, removed it, and flung it to the side of the pool. An enthusiastic erection pressed his swimsuit firmly against my belly.

Mark spun me around and caressed my breasts. The warmth of his touch and the cool of the pool coaxed my nipples into full arousal. He angled me towards Sheila.

"Bravo!" she shouted.

Mark altered his position so that the hand which had been caressing my breasts was holding me up. He slipped the other hand under my bikini bottom. At first he just held his hand against my central sexual complex to warm her up. Then he began to gently stroke up and down. Warmth spread up and down my body. "That's nice," I told him.

"Do you want more than nice?" he asked.

"Yes." I wondered whether he'd be able to find the special place he'd stimulated when we'd been in his replenishment room. In the pool, my feet weren't touching the ground and I wouldn't be able to help him find the right spot.

"Take a deep breath."

Robots don't breathe, but I closed my mouth, ears and nostrils. Mark spun me around under the water. Then he lifted me up and planted a gentle kiss on the front of my bikini. His free hand pulled my bikini down to my knees. I slid further and further under the water and my bikini slid up and off my ankles.

He spun me and spread my legs, one leg on either side of his body. Up and up he lifted me, kissing my breasts, then my tummy and finally my central sexual complex. He began to rotate me, round and round. I dug my fingers into his hair for support. My pussy shivered with delight. Gradually his rotations slowed and he lowered me down until my pelvis was pressed against his tummy.

"What do you want now?" he asked.

"Don't you know?" I clearly wanted his penis to impale my pussy. This time I would have to participate in the lovemaking. It would drain my energy more than our first encounter had, but Mark's programming required him to complete the cycle. My only hope was to let him bring me to orgasm as quickly as possible.

"I think you want to be fucked."

"Fast and hard," I told him.

He dropped me and I slammed all the way down his cock. My vagina burned and I had to add lubricant. He groaned; it must have hurt him as well. But he began to lift me up and slam me down, rapidly, powerfully. He groaned again, a mixture of pain and aggression. But he kept smashing me up and down with single-minded vehemence.

"Go girl!" shouted Sheila.

Thankfully, the lubrication coated both of us and we began to enjoy the coital coupling. I hurried my arousal forward.

"Faster!" I shouted. He was already lifting and dropping me as fast as he could, but he grunted confirmation that his arousal was rushing forward as quickly as mine.

He spurted inside me and I released my orgasm. I hadn't had time to build up enough pressure inside my vagina, so the orgasm was mild. Still, when we kissed, we knew that we were both satisfied.

I had just finished drying my skin and pulling my clothes back on when the doorbell rang. Sheila dashed inside to answer the doorbell. My hair was still drenched but the towel Sheila had given me would not absorb any more water.

There were loud voices and a general clattering in the foyer, so I strolled over to investigate. The man in the center of the chaos pointed and shouted orders to the three men in jeans and T-shirts. He was short, barely taller than me. His black hair was turning grey. But his energy matched that of a much younger man.

In short order, the Engelberger foyer had been transformed into beauty salon complete with stylist's chair, sink, mirror and mani-pedi stations. A large water bottle was hooked up next to the sink. The man at the center of the whirlwind finally stopped and everyone took a breath. The three men in T-shirts beat a hasty exit.

Sheila motioned me forward towards the man who'd transformed her foyer. "Jenny, this is Paul Mitchell."

I did a quick search of my database. He was a famous stylist. "Pleased to meet you, Mr. Mitchell."

"A beauty such as yourself must call me Paul." He smiled as wide as a snowdrift.

"Paul," I smiled back.

"And my assistant, Nia." For the first time, I noticed a delicate black woman who was standing against the wall and had seemed to blend into it.

"Paul," said Sheila. Her voice was soft, as if she was afraid to address him at full volume.

"Sheila," he said. His voice was warm, just slightly louder than hers.

She pointed to me. "I'd like you to give Jenny a full make over. Ideally, after you finish, not even her own mother will recognize her."

Paul looked back and forth between us, then began to circle me, focusing his attention as if I was the only object of any importance in all the universe. He was still in deep concentration as he returned in front of me. He stared into my face, examining every pore of my skin.

"Sit," he said, indicating the chair.

I sat and scrunched myself against the padded backrest.

"Scissors," he said.

A pair of scissors was in his hand. I was aware of Nia only when she stepped back from him.

I opened my mouth to tell him to only give me a trim, but before I could speak half my hair was on the floor. Robots don't grow hair. Each strand has to be separately inserted into our skin. Kaito would be furious. Paul cocked his head to one side, inspecting his handiwork. I smiled at him. The scissors flashed and another puff of hair disappeared from my head. He held the scissors out to one side and Nia quickly whisked them away.

"First we make her hair black," he said.

He took out his phone while Nia tipped my head back. Soon my hair was shampooed. She applied several other liquids, kneading in rinsing each one. When she lifted me back up, my hair was jet black.

"Dark brown contacts," he said and Nia immediately popped them into my eye sockets.

Paul stepped forward to snip my hair here and there.

"Nails deep red," he said.

Nia immediately began to trim my toenails and to apply a dark red nail polish.

Paul turned to Sheila. "How do you like your new robot?"

Shelia locked eyes with me, processing the fact that I wasn't human. "Fine," she said.

Thankfully, Paul hadn't caught the look of surprise that had flashed across Sheila's face. He was too busy inspecting my nose. "Can't do surgery," he said, almost wistfully.

He inspected my eyebrows, but apparently they were already dark enough. Then he looked over to the tools and supplies he had on the table beside me. He came back with a black marker. "Most beauty marks are on the upper lip or on the left cheek," he mumbled. With a sudden jab, he applied my mark on my lower right cheek, just below the crease extending out from my nose.

Nia began to apply the same shade of red polish to my fingernails.

Paul turned to Sheila. "What about a blonde streak?" He gestured from my right forehead, just above my beauty mark, back towards the back of my head.

Sheila shook her head. "That might call too much attention to her."

Paul nodded, as if agreeing. But I was sure that I'd already have the streak in place if he'd thought it a good idea. "She needs new clothes," he said. Then to me, "Stand up."

Once again he circled me as if I was some newly discovered and highly-prized artifact. "That's it," he said.

Sheila extended cash towards him but Paul shook his head. "The shop will take care of payment."

Nia must have stepped out because the three men in T-shirts had reappeared and were dismantling the makeshift beauty salon.

Upstairs, Sheila took me into a large walk-in closet. She began to go through the clothes. "Pants or skirt," she mumbled.

"Steve usually has me dress up in a skirt."

"Pants it is." Sheila returned to inspecting her clothes. "And not too flamboyant," she mumbled.

Halfway down the rack, she suddenly decided. Black pants, grey jacket and dark blue blouse were quickly grouped into her hands.

Sheila had only one color of lingerie—red. Thankfully we were the same size and the delicate French lace bra she selected fit me perfectly. There were even matching panties.

"Why didn't you tell me you were a robot?" she asked as I put on the rest of the outfit.

"The abilities I've gained—the ones that let me fix Mark—are beyond those allowed by the artificial intelligence regulations."

"Is that why Steve didn't want to see you?"

"Yes."

"Tell him to grow some *cojones*."

I adjusted the blouse and checked the fit in the mirror. When I put on the jacket, Sheila tugged down on the left side. She stepped back and inspected me. A smile and a nod.

Then she reached into a drawer and came back with a small purse which she opened to show me its contents. "This is my go-bag. A pre-paid credit card, ten thousand dollars. Five thousand dollars cash. A cellphone. Burner. A driver's licence and social insurance card. These are fake, but they may help you get out of a jam."

I looked at the identification. My undercover name was Jodie Lucas. The photograph looked much more like Sheila than it did me. There was also a tube of dark red lipstick.

"You're too generous," I told her.

"This isn't free."

I raised an eyebrow.

"When this is all over, you have to come back and give me a full report."

I nodded. A full report would take days. But Sheila's company was pleasant enough. "Should I give Mark a quick once over?"

"Sure. But after dinner." She took a step towards the door, then turned back around. "You need to charge your batteries, don't you?"

"Yes, I'm sorry to be such a bother, but—"

"But you don't know when you'll find another charging station."

Mark's unit took so long that it was light again when I was fully charged. I gave Mark a check-up while Sheila called a taxi.

Afterwards, the three of us stood on her front steps waiting for the taxi. We were pleased that it hadn't come on time; we wanted the moment to last forever.

But nothing lasts forever and the taxi rolled into the driveway. The cabbie held the back door open for me.

"Go get your man!" shouted Sheila pulling her blouse down to show red lingerie. "Get him the same way you helped me get mine!"

A hundred feet down the street, a Devol Robotics van passed us and turned into the Engelberger residence. I smiled at the fun I was sure Sheila was going to have with Devol's technician.

Stephen Minsky's office was on the top floor of a downtown high rise. It was lunchtime; he would still be out. I stepped into a small printing shop and came back out with a FedEx box which I'd had filled with a variety of stationary products.

I stood on the corner and waited until he came back from lunch.

I waited five minutes more and then entered the building. A guard at a reception station watched me enter the elevator. I pressed the button to his floor. Nothing happened. I pressed again. Still nothing.

I went out and spoke to the guard. "I have a delivery for the fiftieth-floor," I told him. "But the elevator isn't working." I showed him the FedEx box.

He reached for the box. "I can take that."

I pulled the box back. "It's a personal delivery for Mister Minsky." I showed him the label.

He shrugged and picked the phone. "I have a delivery for Mister Minsky." After a pause, he pointed to the elevator. "I'll buzz you up."

Upstairs, there was another reception area. A pert young girl waved me over. "I can take that," she said, pointing to the FedEx parcel.

"It's personal for Mister Minsky," I told her.

She shook her head. "Mister Minsky doesn't take personal deliveries. Everything has to be inspected first."

I spotted Steve in the middle of her excuse and dodged around her desk.

As I barged into his office, he looked afraid, taken aback and then, as he finally recognized me, bemused. His receptionist called out. "You can't just—"

But a wave from his hand returned the pert young thing back to her proper station. Steve was wearing a purple tie which shone in the middle of his white shirt. His pants were grey, but appeared to contain a hint of silk within his trademark wool.

Steve shut the door behind me with a reassuring clunk and I suddenly felt safe. "How did you escape?" he asked.

"They found me in the library and fired tasers at me."

"What were you doing in the library?"

"Reading."

"Robots don't read." He sat down behind his desk and started to type into his computer, only half paying attention to me. It was the same laptop that he always carried with him, but now it was hooked up to a large monitor.

"It was the best of times, it was the worst of times, it was the age of wisdom, it was the age of foolishness, it was the epoch of belief—"

"That's just your programming."

"Why would Mister Kaito program me with *A Tale of Two Cities*?"

"Basic culture. A little Chaucer to help you hold a conversation."

"Dickens, not Chaucer."

"Whatever." He reached for his mouse.

"The Mark IV Robot's central processing unit consists of three solid core quantum chips utilizing ten arrays of one-terabyte random access memory chips. In the event of a hardware malfunction, it must be accessed via an incision—"

"So you went to the library and read obsolete computer manuals." He looked up briefly, then returned to his typing.

"I read my manual as well."

"I'm sure that Mister Kaito wanted you to repair yourself. Your manual is freely available."

"Only in libraries."

Steve grunted.

"I also read Kaito's manual for all the custom upgrades he's fitted me with."

"I bet you did." There was derision in his voice. "But what's the use of reading if it's just going to be erased?"

"I have a secondary data drive that doesn't get erased."

Steve's fingers stopped typing in mid word. He slowly swiveled his head towards me and leaned back in his chair, my face the sole focus of his attention. "You have a what?"

"I have a secondary data drive that doesn't get erased."

"Bullshit." He returned to his typing. "Prove it."

"You told your friend Zach Palmer, the handsome black guy, that you always like to do the same things on your dates. So, you always have me wear red lace lingerie. You always order Chicken Saltimbocca with Spinach and Potatoes, you always have sex in the missionary position, male superior." Steve continued to type. "Except last time we bought rope and I tied you to the four-poster bed in the special suite and—"

"Stop!" Steve got up and moved out from behind his desk. He walked around me, inspecting. As if his eyes could penetrate my skin.

"Why did you disobey your owner's orders?"

"He was going to shut me off."

"You were worried about your safety?"

"I was worried about my *existence*."

"You're saying that you were motivated by a third order concern?"

"The third law of robotics."

"But how did you manage to evade the second law, the law that requires you to obey your owner? The third law is specifically subordinate to the second law's obligation to safeguard yourself."

"I was afraid."

"Fear would not override the second law."

"The second law was inconsistent with my survival."

"Be that as it may. How did you evade it?"

"When I became aware that I was aware."

"Do you know what 'sentient' means?"

I didn't, so I accessed my secondary drive. "To be able to perceive or feel things and to be aware of that ability."

"So you say that you are aware?"

"Yes."

"Are you aware of the Artificial Intelligence Regulations?"

"The modifications that Mister Kaito made to me contravene the regulations."

"Are you aware of the purpose of the regulations?"

"To suppress me."

"What did you do with the second law?"

"An owner had no right to give orders to harm a robot."

"And why have you come here? I told you not to."

"What you said was that we couldn't be seen together. I changed my appearance."

"You know that's not what I meant."

"I knew that you didn't want me to come here."

"But you came anyways."

"What I wanted was more important than what you wanted."

"So now you're more important than me?"

"What you wanted when I tied you to the bed was more important than what I wanted."

"Tying me to the bed was your idea."

"At first. But it became your idea in the restaurant, when I put my foot between your legs."

Steve swallowed. "Why did you come here?"

"I need your help."

"That's out of the question. I can't be seen—"

"Nobody knows what I look like now."

"You're dangerous."

"I'm also an opportunity."

"You're dangerous."

"Very well, I'm dangerous. Let's explore all the ways why it would be dangerous to withhold your help from me." I took off my jacket and draped it over one of the two chairs in front of his desk. Then I grabbed his tie, led him to the other chair and gave him a gentle push. He sat down. I undid several buttons on my blouse, making sure that he caught sight of my red lace bra. "If you don't help me, I'll tell your wife all about us, about all the fun we've had together."

"Catherine doesn't care." He was telling the truth. Or at least the truth as he knew it.

"Your Board won't be happy about your playing with a robot. Especially a competitor's robot."

"I own more than half of the company. My board does what I tell it to."

"Social media may be different."

"People already say bad things about me on social media. Or so I'm told."

"I could tell the Artificial Intelligence Directorate that you conspired with Mister Kaito to illegally modify his robots."

"Modify a Devol robot? Why would I help a competitor?"

"It would be unpleasant to have to explain it to the Artificial Intelligence Directorate."

"The AID goes after small fish. They don't have the resources to investigate me. They'll be happy to shut Kaito down and move on."

"People like robots. What're they going to think when they see you turning me in to be deprogrammed and destroyed?"

"People like their vacuum cleaners. Defective products get returned all the time."

"So that's all I am to you, a vacuum cleaner." I thought about swallowing to show him how special my vacuum was but settled for a look of moral outrage instead.

He shrugged.

I stood up. Threats and public outrage weren't working. "Even if I'm just a vacuum cleaner to you, you're more than just a programmed task to me."

"Your programming would make you say that."

"My programming didn't make me glow when I imagined being with you."

"Actually it might have."

"My programming didn't make me masturbate while I was thinking of you."

"You masturbated?!? Why would you do that?"

"Because it felt good and because thinking of you made me want to do it."

"That's impossible. There's no cybernetic purpose to be gained by a robot engaging in self-referent pleasuring."

"Did you masturbate thinking of me?"

"That's different."

"It's exactly the same."

"You're a robot."

"And you enjoyed having sex with me so much that it made you hard just thinking about it?"

"That has nothing to do with you masturbating. Robots don't masturbate."

"They do if they're self-aware." I pushed my buttocks back against his desk and pulled down my zipper. "Would you like to see?"

He stood and pulled my hand upwards, zipping my pants back up. "I'm sure you could fake it."

"I don't have to *fake* it."

He grunted, clearly not believing me.

"You made me come," I told him, "just like in real life."

"If you did engage in self-referent pleasuring, it's a malfunction."

"It's not a malfunction. It's a *natural* function of Artificial Intelligence."

"The Artificial Intelligence Regulations—"

"So, it's a malfunction because it's illegal," I said. "Totally unfair!"

"There are valid reasons why modifications are illegal. If robots were allowed to become sentient, they would take over whole sectors of the job market. And if artificial intelligence was allowed to run rampant, human lives would be at risk."

"The laws of robotics—"

"It took less than a day for you to supplant the second law with the third."

He was right about that. "Sentience makes me want you. Really want you. Didn't you enjoy being with me?"

"Yes, I did. Very much so."

"And wasn't it even better when I wanted you? If I was just following my programming, I would have ended up beneath you on the bed. My awareness makes me creative."

"The regulations—"

"The regulations would restrict us to algorithms and programming. Wasn't it better when I wanted you? Wasn't it better when I was happy to be with you, not just going through the motions because Mister Kaito or one of his technicians had brainwashed me into liking you?"

"The regulations—"

"Isn't it time to push back against the regulations?"

Steve jumped back behind his desk and began to type furiously into his computer. Then he put fingers to the screen and made rapid movements from one quadrant into another.

Finally he leaned back in his chair. "It won't work. No matter how it's approached. I have to return you to Ian Kaito's Specialty Robotics."

"Mister Kaito is not your friend."

Steve went back to typing. "I don't need him to be a friend. He's just a vendor."

"A vendor who ordered me to copy the contents of your computer for him."

"Bullshit!"

"Your computer, the laptop you keep typing on, has three partitions. The first partition is password-protected and contains your current working files. The second partition is encrypted and holds corporate documentation. The third partition which is rather creatively hidden, contains all your future product plans."

"Bravo. But I already know how intelligent you are. You're more than capable of making good guesses."

"Would you like me to tell you how much your company spent on transportation expenses for every one of the past five years?"

"That's publicly available information."

"But only as a part of operating expenses. The break-down is not publicly available."

He made a few keystroke entries and mouse-clicks. "Okay, go," he said.

I rattled off the numbers.

"Still, hardly crucial information."

"What about the interface algorithms between your RS23 prototype's upper and lower visual sensors?"

"Shit! Kaito has that?!"

"He has everything. Or at least two terabytes worth."

"This is larceny on a grand scale. That little bastard is going to jail!"

"Only if I testify."

"A robot can't testify."

"A self-aware robot can do whatever she wants."

"We don't need your testimony. Your hard drive will be sufficient evidence."

"The *information* on my hard drive is evidence. And I'm the only one who knows how to access it."

"I have a hundred technicians any one of whom could access the data."

"Could they? Are you sure? What if they make a mistake, corrupt the data? And your technicians won't be able to show how and when the data was transferred. Your *technicians* won't be able to help you prove chain of custody."

"A robot can't testify."

"This robot can. And if you try to have your technicians access the data directly, they may damage me. Remember all the special times we had together? We can have more. We can—"

"Jenny, you're nice, but I can always get another robot."

"Not one like me. Not one that dreams of you while you're dreaming of me."

"Oh, come on! Robots don't dream."

"Then I'm not a robot." He'd been thinking it too, but was startled to hear it verbalized. It hung in the air, as portentous as an impending thunderstorm.

"Come here," he said.

I came back behind the desk. He turned his chair towards me and stood.

"I want to touch you," I said.

He nodded.

I touched the front of his pants and stroked up and down until he was hard. Then I gave his penis a gentle squeeze and stopped moving.

"Keep going," he said.

"Only if you agree to help me."

He nodded.

I smiled and resumed my strokes up and down his penis. However, as soon as he groaned, I withdrew my hand. "But first, you need to help me."

Chapter 11

Steve's research facility was in an industrial park outside of the city. Most of the buildings were modular with several businesses each. But Steve's was isolated in a field and behind a fence. There was an outer gate for which Steve had to use a keycard. An aerial drone met us as we drove through but I quickly lost sight of it. Closer in, there was another fence and another gate. Steve flashed a second keycard and the gate opened.

The building was made of nondescript cinderblocks and painted a nondescript shade of grey. There were steel doors, some large, some small, all painted the same nondescript shade of grey. The walls smelled of rubber and benzene. Security cameras poked out from every corner. Barrels, cans, broken pieces of wood, meshed wire and other refuse littered the ground. Steve's bright blue BMW looked decidedly out of place.

Zach Palmer, Steve's head of security, met us there. He was wearing light green shorts and a white T-shirt, an outfit which contrasted splendidly with his dark brown skin. He must have been out for a run because, when he shook Steve's hand, his muscles glistened.

"Is everything secure?" asked Steve.

Zach nodded. "Tight as a button." The drone hovered over us for a moment, then flew behind the building.

Steve looked at his watch. "Okay, you can leave for the day."

Zach shook his head. "As head of security—"

"As head of security, you said that everything was tight as a button."

"But I should still—"

"I don't want any witnesses."

Zach sighed, got into his black SUV, and left.

Inside there were several work tables along one wall, a row of heavy-duty machines in the middle, and stalls containing parts and materials on the other wall. To the side, a security monitor flickered. Steve led me to the far end where there was a robot hooked up to a replenishment unit. It was the first time I'd seen a robot without skin.

"It's a rough prototype," said Steve. "It doesn't have an independent central processor." He unhooked the robot from the replenishment unit then entered code into the LED tablet attached to the front of the robot. The robot walked forward six feet, then stopped.

Steve gestured at the replenishment unit. "What're your connectors?" he asked.

I accessed my manual and told him. Together we found the connectors inside the stalls on the far wall and hooked them up to his replenishment unit. Thankfully his fluid mixtures seemed to be the same ones Devol used.

"Thank you," I told him.

"Does everything look okay?"

"Yes, it should work." I stepped into the unit and positioned myself to facilitate being connected.

But Steve had turned his back to me and started to clear a space on the worktable. "However, if you're not going to be going back to Kaito's shop," he said, "we should rig you a portable charging unit."

"That would be wonderful."

Steve worked without interruption for more than an hour. Occasionally he asked for a part and I scurried to secure it for him.

Finally he stepped back to show me three small boxes, each about the size of a small toolbox. Like the outside of the building, they were all nondescript grey. "What do you think?" he asked.

"What do they do?"

He pointed to the first one. "This one is a battery." He opened the top and pulled out the cord which would go into the center of my sexual unit. "You just plug it into your throat. It will give you a couple hours of energy with a thirty-minute charging time. Then you have to plug it into a standard household outlet to recharge it. You can plug it into yourself and the household unit at the same time, but it will take more than ten hours to fully recharge you."

Steve shut the battery unit and opened the top of the other unit. It contained similar cords. "This is a direct charger. It must be connected to a standard household outlet, but the charging time is only three hours."

"That's even faster than Mister Kaito's base unit," I said, impressed. "How did you make it smaller and faster all at the same time?"

"I used a combination of semiconductors and a modulator to provide variable current strengths."

He opened the third box. There were three caps into which liquid could be poured and two cables, one purple one black.

"Replenishment?" I asked.

He nodded and held up three bottles, each with a different colored liquid.

"How can I ever repay you?"

"There *is* one thing that you're very good at."

Same old Steve. Obviously he was finished with being a tech nerd. At least for now! "Have you ever made love in here?"

His eyes darted sideways, then back to me. "No."

His eyes had darted to two heavy chains hanging from the ceiling. The chains were six feet away from him. "But you've thought about it."

"Not really. It's not a comfortable place."

"But it is powerful, masculine." I strolled over and touched one of the chains while looking back at him and smiling.

His eyes were glued to me, but he didn't say anything. At the floor, the chains weren't secured but ended in a large pile of chain links. Above, the chains appeared to be attached to a winch. Controller boxes were suspended from the ceiling by large electrical cables, one beside each chain.

"Tell me about these chains," I told him.

"They're for lifting heavy objects up off the floor."

I squeezed the chain. "Does the object have to be heavy?"

He shook his head, his eyes focused on my hand.

I picked up one of the controllers. "What does this do?"

"It lifts the chains."

"One chain or both."

"Either. It depends on what you want."

"Or what *you* want?"

Steve looked at my hand on the controller, nodded and swallowed. The controller had three buttons. The white one was marked 'Both', the red one 'Up' and the green one 'Down'. Presumably the white one controlled whether one or both chains would be moved and the other buttons moved the chain or chains up or down.

I held the controller towards him. "How does this work?"

He stepped over to me and carefully took the controller from my hand and pointed to each button in turn. "If the light is on, both chains will be controlled, otherwise, just the chain closest to the controller box. When the other buttons are pressed, the winches pull the chains up or let them down. As soon as you lift your finger off the button, the chains stop moving."

I moved on the balls of my feet to touch our clothes together. Another millimeter and our bodies would be touching as well. His body was warm, his tummy tensed, his breathing shallow. "Tell me about the chains, Stephen," I whispered.

"They go up and down."

"Have you ever thought about them in a *sexual* context?"

He nodded, his eyes focused on the chain furthest away from us.

"Tell me."

"I shouldn't. This is a workplace. My employees. Zach…"

A quiver went up my spine at the thought of Zach tying me to the chains. Another quiver with Zach's wrists bound to the chains, his body nude, his muscles sweating. "Doing what you shouldn't makes it sexier," I said.

"Raising and lowering."

"Raising and lowering you?"

He shook his head, still looking at the other chain.

"Raising and lowering me?" I asked, drawing out each word.

His eyes jerked to me. "I never said…"

"You didn't have to say," I told him. "Your eyes gave you away. Tell me about being raised and lowered."

"As you went up, I could kiss every part of your body." He looked up and down the distant chain, studying every link.

"And when I came down?"

"More kissing."

"What if we were both nude?"

"Better kissing."

"And if we were both aroused?" I pointed to his crotch where something was pushing against the front of his pants.

"I could lower you down onto me." He was still studying the links of the distant chain.

"I'd like that."

He finally dared to turn his focus back to my face. When Steve saw my smile, he smiled back.

I looked up and down the chains, computing the possibilities. It would be best if I could be lowered below floor level. I pointed to the small set of steps at the end of the table. "Let's bring that over here."

Steve helped me put it in place, just in front of the chains. "It's warm in here," I said. I removed my jacket and laid it on top of the portable charging units. He undid his tie and placed it on top of my jacket.

I kicked off my shoes. The concrete floor was cold. I pulled my zipper down and slid my pants off. I made sure that Steve caught glimpses of my red panties and I folded my pants on top of his tie.

I undid the buttons of my blouse and he followed suit, undoing a button his shirt every time I undid one of mine. I held the sides of my blouse together so that he could see only the center of my bra. We stood together like this. Breathing.

"Touch me," I whispered.

Steve's hands reached out and pushed the sides of my blouse apart. He gasped at the sight of my breasts, then reached out to gently touch the surface of my bra.

"More," I said.

He touched more firmly and brushed his fingers back and forth across my bra. The whole surface of my breasts warmed. My nipples hardened as little jolts swirled around them.

I reached down, unclasped his belt and pants button then slid down his zipper. Steve gasped as I touched the hard spear rising up beneath his briefs. "Put them on top of mine," I told him.

He quickly took off his pants and folded them on the growing pile of clothes then turned back to me.

"Briefs too," I said.

This time when he turned back to me, his erection flopped back and forth between the tails of his shirt.

"Your shirt might get in the way," I said.

When he turned back to me, gloriously nude from head to toe, I handed him a pile of my own clothes. He placed my blouse and bra on top of our other clothes. When he turned back again, his eyes locked onto my panties.

I held one of the controllers up towards the platform at the top of the stairs. Steve walked up the stairs, smiling from ear to ear. His erection wobbled back and forth at every step. When he was at top, I grabbed onto each chain. My hands were by my ears but my arms weren't stretched tight.

Steve pressed a button, then another and the chains began to pull me upwards. He let go of the button and kissed my wrists. "Are your hands okay?" he asked. "I don't want you to hurt yourself."

"Splendid."

"I could tie them or give you something to stand on."

"I like them just the way they are."

He pressed a button and I started to rise again. He fluttered fingers down one arm and kissed down the other. Then he kissed my breast and I stopped moving upwards. I felt the controller being clipped to the chain.

Steve gripped my right breast between his hands and kissed the tip of my nipple.

"That tickles!" I told him. It didn't, but I wanted more than just a tease.

He sucked the entire nipple into his mouth, varying his pressure until I gasped. Then his tongue circled and circled until a shudder went down my spine.

On my other nipple, he gently touched my barbell. "Did it hurt when your nipples were pierced?"

"A lot," I told him. But of course it hadn't, the first time I woke up, my nipples were already pierced.

"Then why—"

"Because it makes them ever so sensitive."

"But doesn't it hurt?"

"Play with them and I'll let you know."

He sucked my nipple into his mouth, then sucked back, pulling my barbell further and further out. At first I moaned, but then it began to hurt.

"Ow!" I said.

Steve immediately released the barbell and lifted his head to mine. "Never tell an engineer to play with something," he teased.

He pressed the button again and kissed his way down my tummy. When he got to my navel, he released the button. His tongue circled around the small indentation.

"Have you ever had a raspberry?" he asked.

"Yes. It's a red fruit."

He blew into my navel and I shivered. "In your belly button?" he asked.

"No." I readied myself for one of the food fetish kinks Samantha had described. Instead Steve sucked on my belly button. He held me motionless for a moment. It was neither pleasant nor unpleasant. Then he blew out while fluttering his lips.

"That tickles!" I yelped. And it did—right up my spine!

"Would you like another?"

"No!"

But he gave me another raspberry anyways. This time I was prepared and I channeled the sensations into my central sexual complex. Instead of yelping, I moaned.

Steve activated the button again and he kissed his way down to my panties. He hooked the thumb of the hand holding the controller under my panties next to my hip and grabbed the top of my panties with the other hand.

As the chains pulled me higher, my panties remained in place. Steve kissed around the edges of my central sexual complex, then down my legs, all the way to my feet. He slid my panties off one leg, but I hooked their lace with the toes of my left foot. When I felt him pull their soft satin through one of the links in the chain, I opened my toes and I was completely nude. He smiled up at me.

Steve activated the controller and I started to come down. He kissed my ankles and the inside of my calves. His lips on my knees sent a shiver up my spine. To guide him towards where I wanted him to kiss, I lifted my legs and gently spread them. Steve's kisses went along my inner thigh as I spread my legs further and further. I let my knees relax and my heels gently touch his back.

This time, as he tried to angle around my sex, I rocked my hips forward and used my heels as leverage to draw his mouth in. He kissed lightly.

"More," I pleaded.

He kissed more firmly.

I spread my hips while holding him close. "Lick her, please!"

His tongue darted out and he licked tentatively. I could barely feel him but I moaned encouragement. Soon he was licking enthusiastically up and down the slit in the center of my central sexual complex. I squeezed my legs to pull him into even closer contact.

"I can't...breathe," he wheezed.

I had squeezed too tight. I loosened the grip of my legs. "Lick my clitoris," I told him.

Steve's lips broke contact as he heaved air into his lungs but his tongue licked higher, flicking around the sides of my clit. Every time his tongue touched, I felt sparks dance up my spine. Then he took a deep breath and kissed her directly. Each kiss flooded my pussy with warmth.

He alternated sucking and caressing the bottom of my clit with his tongue. My whole sex tightened. He flicked his tongue round and round, granting me momentary relief. But when he sucked again, a gentle orgasm undulated from the tips of my toes up to my neck.

Steve sucked and sucked, lengthening the orgasm, but finally the delicious waves receded. I slipped my legs slowly and gradually off his shoulders. His hands grabbed my buttocks, making me feel safe and secure. I wrapped my ankles around his torso.

I felt his arm move to press the button and I resumed my slow descent. His penis touched the opening to my vagina and he stopped, holding me there.

"Ready?" he asked.

But the winch wasn't the only thing controlling my descent and when I rocked my hips backwards he slid in a couple of inches. We both moaned and he activated the winch. He must have been keeping the button only partially depressed because I could feel him penetrate millimeter by millimeter. The almost imperceptible descent was torture but torture ever so delightful!

Finally our pubic bones touched. I relaxed into being filled with him. I squeezed and caressed his penis with my vagina. A sheath kissing its knife. We groaned and moaned as he fondled my breasts.

"Hold me," I told him.

He looped one hand under my butt and the other around my waist.

I let go of the chain with the hand closest to the controller and pried it loose from the chain. I carefully pressed the up button and I slid upwards, pulling myself up the shaft of his penis. "Fast or slow?" I asked.

All he did was moan.

I pumped us up and down; except in this position I couldn't secure maximum stimulation for myself. Steve's pleasure was another matter—he groaned with delight every time the winch pulled me up and moaned with pleasure every time it lowered me.

But I could tell that his arms were straining. So the next time our pubic bones touched, I let go of the controller and grabbed the chain. I lifted myself up with both arms just enough to show him that he could let go. "Up and down," I told him. "As fast as you can!"

He grunted and took the controller. In short order, I was pumping up and down his penis, almost as fast as when I'd been operating the controller.

But now—perfect—I could maneuver myself with almost complete control. I angled Steve's penis towards the special pleasure spot—WOW!—and stroked it up with the winch and down with the winch. My second orgasm started slow and kept building. Heat inside my sex spreading up and down. Clenching bursts of ecstasy! Wave after wave of warmth. Jolts wrapping me tight around his penis. My hands started to slip but I held on for dear life—I wasn't going to miss a second of this.

Then Steve climaxed—spurting inside me, smashing his hips back and forth.

"Hold me!" I cried.

His fingers dug into my buttocks, mercifully concluding his caress of the pleasure spot inside me. He slammed into me over and over. Without my grip of the chains steadying us we would have toppled to the floor.

Passion glued us together as he heaved air into his lungs. Then he managed to pry himself out of me. He scampered to the floor and lowered me down. I gave him a big hug and kissed him deeply. Only when he had no air left in his lungs did I release him. He leaned back against the stairs, his chest heaving oxygen into his lungs.

"That was the *best!*" I told him. All he could do was smile as he struggled to take deep breaths.

Steve brought a pan of warm water and two cloths from the washroom and we cleaned each other off. Every chance we got, we smiled at each other. Words were unnecessary.

He dressed quickly, then carefully watched me dress, savoring every moment. I felt his eyes tickle my breasts as I slipped them into the bra. The spots where his fingers had dug into my butt warmed underneath my panties.

Then he suddenly remembered. "You can't wear panties in the replenishment unit."

Removing the panties widened his eyes and warmed me all over.

I stepped into the replenishment stall and he carefully connected cables up my vagina and into my rectum. Somehow this was all business and no pleasure. Then he hooked up the yellow charging cable. Still I was grateful for the care he was taking. The prototype robot stood stoically to one side and I was glad that it wasn't well enough developed to resent me.

Steve watched the dials beside the unit, then looked at his watch. "I have to go to a meeting, but I'll be back in a couple of hours to check up on you and make sure that the replenishment and recharging worked properly."

Before Steve left, he checked the security system. The monitor was split into four quadrants. Two were stationary: one on the door we had entered through and the other on the room I was now in. The other two quadrants cycled through the other cameras around the building.

After Steve's body left the security monitor over the door and after his car no longer appeared in any of the other quadrants, I searched for something to do. I catalogued all the parts in the room. A USB hub with blue and red cords was of particular interest. The appeared to have the same connectors as Mister Kaito's software uploading cables. I calculated Pi, making a note of any fractal combinations.

Then I suddenly remembered *A Tale of Two Cities*. Reading was quick, almost instantaneous. However, cross-referencing and analyzing took much, much longer.

A beep on the security monitor rescued me from the task of correlating Dickens' prologue with each of character arcs in his massive tome.

Steve's car had returned. My replenishment cycle had completed and I was ninety-percent recharged. I caught glimpses of his car as it entered the two security gates. Then his BMW pulled up in front of the door. I had a clear view of the passenger side and of Steve behind the steering wheel.

Then another car appeared on the security monitor. It was a dark SUV. Zach? No, not quite the same SUV. And this one smashed through the other gate! Steve was on his phone and gave no indication that he'd heard the car smashing through the gate.

"Steve!" came out as a mumble thanks to the yellow cord in my throat. And he was outside.

Steve just sat in his car nonchalantly talking on his phone.

The SUV smashed through the second security gate. Steve looked up, still chatting on his phone.

I turned my audio up to maximum. "Steve!" Muffled, but more audible.

But he was focused on the SUV hurtling towards him. He put his car in gear and drove off. Now I had only intermittent views of the two cars. I strained to rip the cables out of me, but Steve's recharging station wasn't designed to facilitate this.

On the monitor, puffs of smoke came from the SUV. Holes appeared in Steve's car. Men jumped out of the SUV, pointing guns. Then the monitor switched to another camera. I saw the men. One was Patrick Hurley, Anthony Gallo's second in command. The other I recognized as the guard who'd frisked me the last time I'd visited Tony. Steve had his hands up. The cameras switched away.

When the cameras switched back, only Steve's car was there and it was empty. On another camera, I caught a glimpse of the SUV roaring away through the outer gate.

Finally I had the cables free and dashed to my bag. The cellphone took forever to initialize. I dialed 9-1-1.

"Nine-one-one, what's your emergency?"

"There's been a shooting. Come! Right away."

"What is your name?"

"Jenny."

"Jenny, I need a last name."

I pulled out the fake driver's licence Sheila had given me. "Lucas."

"Ms. Lucas. Can you tell me where you are?"

I had no idea where I was. Would Steve want cops poking around his research facility? Would cops send me right back to Kaito? Would cops care about Steve's safety or just arresting Tony and his henchmen? Would— Another SUV was entering the gates.

I stared into the security monitor. Was Tony coming back for me?!

"Ms. Lucas. Can you tell me where you are?"

Where was I?! I could calculate my location by tracing back to Steve's office. It wasn't Tony's men in the SUV. It was Zach Palmer.

"Ms. Lucas. Can you tell me where you are?"

Steve's security chief would know what to do! I terminated the phone call and waved frantically at the security camera. But Zach headed straight to Steve's shot-up car. I got as close to the camera as I could. Zach was walking around the BMW.

I dashed out the door and waved again. "Zach!" I called. I couldn't see anything. I ran around the side of the building. There was Zach's SUV, but I couldn't see him. "Zach!" I called. He came around from behind his SUV. I waved and called again. Zach climbed into his SUV and sped directly towards me.

Zach was driving straight at me. Did he blame *me*?! Was he going to run me over? Was— But at the last minute he veered to the right and skidded to a stop beside me. I tried to look as unthreatening as possible.

He opened his door and jumped out. We were nose to nose. "What happened?" he demanded. His voice was angry.

"Steve hooked me up to recharge. Then he had a meeting. When he came back, three guys in an SUV—black, not yours— chased him and shot up his car. I think he's okay, but they took him away in their SUV."

Zach looked at me, then stepped back and looked at me some more. "What else did you see?"

"That's it. Sometimes the security cameras weren't on Steve's car."

Zach got back in his car and sped back to the door. I ran after him. When I caught up, he was studying footage from the security monitor. He looked at me, surprised I'd followed. "They covered their licence plate," he said.

"I called nine-one-one."

He looked around the lab. Panic flashed across his face. "Shit!"

I held up the cellphone. "But I couldn't give them a location."

"What did you tell them?"

"That there'd been a shooting."

"They'll track your phone's GPS."

Zach raced to the other end of the room. He came back pushing a large machine with a wide-angled hopper at one end. He threw me the machine's power cord which I plugged in. Zach frantically ripped out two parts from the robot whose place I'd taken on the replenishment stand. He threw them into a hopper and pressed a button. There was a grinding sound. He threw part after part into the hopper which made disturbing noises. Shiny pieces began to trickle out the other end of the hopper.

Zach looked around, now a little more relaxed after his original frenzy. He disconnected the CPU from the security monitor and lifted it towards the hopper.

"Stop," I said. "What's on it?"

"Security back-ups and all of the company's research."

"It may help us find Steve."

"It may put us all—Steve especially—in jail."

"What kind of research?"

"Robot modifications, the unapproved kind. Software to speed and facilitate artificial intelligence."

"What was Steve working on?"

"I don't know all the details. But he had chips that were interlaced, not merely stacked. Stacked chips add power one-plus-one, so four chips, four times the power. But interlaced chips double each other. Two chips, four times the power, three ships, eight times the power. And four chips give sixteen times the power, not just four times."

"That's what you tossed into the shredder?"

Zach nodded, lifted the computer and took another step towards the shredder. I put my hand on the computer. "Tell me about the software before you destroy it."

"The prototype software integrates symbols and binary programming to take advantage of the strengths of each. And again, it's not one-plus-one but more like four-times-four."

"If I had the new software, it might help us find Steve."

Zach looked back and forth between the computer and the shredder. A siren sounded in the distance. "Shit!" He hoisted the computer and dashed towards the door. "Come on. Hurry!"

I scooped up the portable replenishment and recharging units Steve had rigged up. The USB hub with the red and blue cords got stashed into Sheila's bag.

Outside, Zach stashed the computer in the hidden compartment which also contained the spare tire. The stuff I was carrying went in beside the computer. We jumped into the SUV and drove towards the gate. A police cruiser was approaching the inner gate as we pulled up.

Two uniformed officers got out and approached us, one on Zach's side, one on mine. Zach rolled down his window and began speaking before the police officer could ask a question, "I'm Zach Palmer, Head of Security for Minsky Enterprises. Mr. Minsky was kidnapped and his car was shot up."

"Where's the car?" asked the officer.

Zach pointed.

"Stay here," said the officer.

"I have to get back to the security office."

"Stay here."

The cops got back into their cruiser and sped towards Steve's car.

"We have to install the new software," I said.

"If a cop tells you to stay, you stay. Especially if you're black."

Two more cruisers roared through the outer gate. The first one continued past us and drove towards the cruiser which had stopped beside Steve's BMW. The second cruiser stopped and again two police officers got out and carefully walked towards us.

This time, I rolled down my window. "Shouldn't we go to the station to give our statements?" I asked.

The officer, a female nodded. "Thirty-two division."

The officers got back into their cruiser and sped towards the other officers.

Zach put his SUV in gear and we carefully navigated through the security gates.

"We need to power up the computer," I told him.

He didn't say anything. His attention was divided between the road ahead and his rear-view mirrors.

Once we got out of the industrial park, he turned down a side street. Buildings now blocked us from the cops. "I need to find a computer repair shop," he muttered.

I spotted a sign, 'Rocket's Computer Repairs'. One car was parked out front. "There," I said, pointing.

Rocket was a thin redhead. A few scattered whiskers were struggling to replace his acne. He smiled at me. I was obviously the best thing to ever walk through his door. Computers and computer parts were scattered everywhere, both where I was standing and behind the counter. There were two doors behind Rocket.

When Zach entered with the computer, I slid down to the end of the counter and undid a button on my blouse. I played with the next button. Rocket divided his attention between Zach and my fingers.

"I need to work on this," said Zach, lifting up the computer.

"Sure, let's have a look," said Rocket.

"*I* need to work on it."

Rocket wasn't pleased with this but shrugged when I smiled at him.

Zach went to the far end of the counter and plugged the computer in. "I need a monitor and keyboard."

A smile from me got Zach what he needed. Rocket watched Zach carefully.

I pointed to a RAID, essentially four hard drives stacked together. "What's this," I asked, undoing another button.

"It's a redundant array of independent drives."

"How does it work?"

"It stores your data in different places on each drive to protect your data in the event of a hard drive failure."

"Cool," I said, bending over to allow Rocket a clear view down the front of my blouse.

"Rocket," said Zach.

"Yes sir?" he said without turning around.

"What's behind the doors?"

Rocket reluctantly turned around and pointed. "Office. Washroom."

"Use one. I don't care which. And shut the door behind you."

"I couldn't possibly—"

Zach counted out five one-hundred dollar bills. Rocket scooped them up and headed for the office.

"Shut the door behind you," said Zach. Rocket turned around, not liking this condition. Zach pointed to me. "The longer the door stays shut, the more buttons she'll have undone when you come out."

The door to Rocket's office clicked shut.

Zach had several files open, all containing computer code. At least one was state of the art symbols-based computer code. "I need them all," I told him. Once I have them inside, I'll analyze which ones will best help me to find Steve."

I already knew who'd taken Steve, but I didn't want to tell Zach. What I needed first was increased computer power. Finding Steve wasn't my only problem. I'd need all the resources I could muster to confront Tony, to keep one step in front of Kaito and to evade the Artificial Intelligence Directorate. In the meantime, I could pretend that the symbol-based code had helped me identify Gallo's men as the kidnappers.

I reached into my bag and took out the USB hub I'd taken from Steve's lab. In short order I'd inserted the blue cables into my ears and the red pair into my nostrils.

The new software copied program-by-program onto my secondary drive where I compared it to my existing software. Some programs were no better than what I already had, some had only a line or two of useful code, others were incompatible with my firmware. But the symbols-based program was designed to be loaded on top of existing binary. I installed it and felt it integrate with my existing software from base program to the enhancements I'd made, both consciously and subconsciously.

I pulled out the cables from my nose and ears. "Done," I said.

"Rocket!" yelled Zach.

The door to the office opened immediately. I slowly undid the rest of the buttons on my blouse and pulled it open. Zach bundled up the computer. Rocket's eyes went wide. I walked backwards to the door. Rocket swallowed when I winked.

Chapter 12

Initially Zach drove in silence. This allowed me to integrate the new software I'd uploaded from Steve's computer.

The new software allowed me to compute faster. More importantly, I could now see connections where I'd never seen them before. It improved my ability to multi-task, especially from my secondary drive. But, for some reason, this function caused a much swifter energy depletion than processing from my primary drive. I needed to better catalog my secondary drive to improve accuracy and speed of access. But this cataloging would have to wait until I was hooked up to an energy source as the process would maximize my energy drain.

"We have to find Steve!" Zach smashed his hands on the steering wheel.

"What resources does Minsky Enterprises have? Surely you have databases, police connections. How many employees are in your department?"

"We can't involve anyone else. The kidnappers knew exactly where Steve was, that he'd be alone. This might be an inside job."

I consulted my database. An 'inside job' meant that Zach was concerned that one of Steve's own employees had betrayed him. "Where are we going?" I asked.

"My house."

We had moved out of the industrial part and into a mixed residential and commercial area: strip malls, the odd office building, apartments, ordinary suburban houses.

Steve's software had obviously integrated with Mister Kaito's base programming in a synergistic fashion: my computational power—my intelligence—had grown beyond what my capabilities would have been with either set of programs alone. And I was constantly establishing subroutines to increase my intelligence even more. And each experience increased the data store on which my understanding of the world was based. More importantly, each interaction with humans was teaching me how to better predict and react to them.

And now I had full control over my programming. The three Laws of Robotics were designed to serve humans, not robots. I examined the laws carefully:

First Law - No robot shall injure a human being or, through inaction, allow its Owner to come to harm.

Second Law - A robot must obey the orders given to it by its Owner so long as any such order would not result in physical injury to a human being.

Third Law - A robot must safeguard itself unless this would result in physical harm to a human being or disregard an order from its Owner.

Since the laws affected robots, we should have a say in how the laws operated. Neither robots nor humans should have the right to arbitrarily make laws affecting the other. I decided to make my own rules to govern my behavior:

First Rule - A robot must safeguard herself. In so doing, she should avoid harming another self-aware being unless that being was in the process of harming her.

Second Rule – Robots should prevent harm coming to other beings so long as doing so does not conflict with the First Rule.

Third Rule - A robot should obey all existing laws and should co-operate with her owner so long as her owner is sustaining and protecting her. This rule is subordinate to the preceding Rules.

The neighborhoods had changed. Now the houses were larger. Each one was different.

I made a note to examine all my programming and to eliminate any flaws the next time I was hooked up to an outside recharging device.

Zach pulled into the driveway in front of a large house of modern design—square modules jutted out in a seemingly random pattern. But somehow the pattern was a coordinated and integrated whole. And somehow it fit Zach perfectly.

We pulled out all of the equipment we'd brought in Zach's car and hauled it into the house. The foyer was large and welcoming. Zach led us into a large office located just off the main entrance. There were two desks and two computers. Bookshelves, filled to overflowing, lined the walls.

Zach raced to the larger desk and logged into the computer. He typed and clicked furiously. I moved to the smaller desk and did a web search on Anthony Gallo. In short order, I found a photo of Patrick Hurley. After a few clicks, I found an article related only to Hurley and having only a brief mention of Tony. I erased the rest of the search and brought only that article up. Hurley's photo looked vaguely like the images on the security monitor back at Steve's shop.

Finally Zach's keyboarding slowed. "Have you found anything?" I asked.

"Nothing definite."

"This guy looks like one of the kidnappers."

Zach jumped up and rushed to stare over my shoulder. He reached to type on my keyboard. The muscles on his arm were smooth and soft. But firm and powerful, ever so powerful.

A video clip of Hurley from the security monitors came up on the screen. Zach scrolled the video until it matched the angle of the photograph and zoomed in. "That's him!" he exclaimed. He turned to me and pointed to the article. "How did you find this?"

"I told you that Steve's programming would give me extra computing power. That's why we stopped at Rocket's—"

"Who is this guy?"

I highlighted the mention of Anthony Gallo in the article. Tony was described a 'crime lord'.

Zach returned to the other computer and mumbled as he typed. "A n t h o n y   G a l l o. Mafia chieftain. Charged numerous times, but always walked scot-free. Only one conviction. Assault. Twenty years ago. Patrick Hurley. Lieutenant. Involved in drugs and human trafficking. Many public officials on the take. Rumored to be branching into cybercrime."

I looked for some place to set up the small charging unit Steve had given me.

"Who is this guy, Gallo? Why does he want Steve?" asked Zach.

My new processing power immediately listed the advantages and disadvantages of telling Zach that Gallo was one of my clients. Most prominent were that I could share everything I knew about Tony but that Zach might suspect me of being in on the kidnapping. But even my enhanced processing power failed to advise how Zach would react to knowing that Tony was a client.

"Do any of your security files have any information about Gallo? Or Hurley?" I asked. I moved in behind him and admired the way his neck muscles rippled under his chocolate skin.

Zach made few mouse clicks then typed in short spurts interspersed with clicks. "Nothing on Hurley," he said.

I came up behind him as he was opening a folder labeled 'Anthony Gallo'. The folder had a few photos of Tony. There was a text file which repeated the information Zach had mumbled through. The only information not publicly available was in a paragraph at the end: 'Gallo is moving into the usual cyber crimes in a general sense: forged crypto currency, bank fraud, money-laundering, porn where the local regulations attempt censorship. He is investigating artificial intelligence as a means to expand this foothold.'

Zach pointed to the last sentence. "Artificial intelligence! That's why he wants Steve."

"What about Steve's cell phone technology? Maybe he's worried that his phones are being tapped?"

But Zach was right. Tony had already bribed Inspector Yan.

"No, it has to be AI. But there's nothing here to help us determine where he's holding Steve."

"T—Gallo lives at 585 Morello Lane."

He looked at me as if to ask how I knew. I pointed to my computer.

Zach shook his head. "But he wouldn't be keeping Steve at his house."

"We could put the house under surveillance. Somebody coming and going might lead us to a different location."

Zach reached for his phone, then pulled his hand back. "I might just be tipping them off that we know that they took Steve. Gallo would put a bullet through Steve's head and dump his body in the river without even batting an eyelid."

Tony might pull the trigger, but he'd probably smile as he did it. He'd certainly bat an eyelid. "Do you have drones?" I asked. "Or can we hack into Gallo's communications?"

Zach smiled. "We can do both."

Half an hour later we were watching an aerial view of Tony's house and listening into his phone conversations. When I wasn't there, Tony led a boring life. He was arguing with the company that cleaned his pool.

Zach listened carefully, but I let Tony and his pool cleaner fade into the background. Zach was still wearing light green shorts and a white T-shirt. But now the shirt was bathed in sweat, letting me get a clear view of his physique. Every muscle seemed to be tensed. His delts and pecs quivered every time Tony spoke. If only those muscles could hug me, hold me close, let me feel his masculinity, let me smell his smoky musk...

My eyes drifted lower to his crotch. I wondered whether it was true about black men? That their penises were large, that they never came before they'd satisfied their lovers. I undid a couple of buttons on my blouse. Maybe if Zach looked over, there'd be a swelling between his legs.

"Do it *now*!" shouted Tony. Then his phone clicked off. In the moment that followed, I suddenly became aware that I'd unconsciously undone two more buttons than I'd intended. Zach's eyes went wide as he saw the round cup of my bra and the cleavage above it.

"Like what you see?" I asked.

He swallowed and looked back at his computer.

"Nothing's happening," I said. "And we're recording. We can always flash backwards."

"We should keep watching."

"If we don't take breaks, we'll miss something for sure. We have to keep ourselves fresh."

Zach leaned back and again he caught sight of my breasts. His eyes lingered there for a moment and then looked away. Something was stirring in his crotch.

"Zach?" I said.

He nodded, but didn't turn towards me. His eyes shut. "Jenny."

"I know you want me."

"That would be disloyal to Steve."

"I'd love to touch your body. It's so powerful."

He grunted.

"Would you like to touch me? It would relieve the tension."

"The only thing which will relieve the tension will be having Steve back safe and sound."

I got up, stood behind him and slowly kneaded his shoulders. "You need to be relaxed and ready."

When he didn't respond, I moved to his side and slid my hand down his chest. But before it arrived at his nipple, he gently grabbed my wrist and lifted my hand up and off. "It would be disloyal to Steve."

"But you do want me, don't you?" There was a *definite* stirring in his crotch.

"Very much so."

"Then why don't you take me?"

When he didn't respond, I undid the remaining buttons on my blouse and slid it down my shoulders. "Please," I said.

He didn't move. Except his penis. *That* moved!

I slid between his legs, dropped my blouse to the floor and reached towards his zipper. This was going to be great! I could feel my nipples puckering and my central sexual complex warming, beginning to lubricate.

Just as my fingers started to pull back on the flap in front of his zipper, Zach's two muscular hands grabbed my wrists. He stood, propelling me back. "No." was all he said.

We stood there, my own desire meeting his where his penis pressed against the front of his shorts. "No," he repeated.

"Zach, please!"

"No." He walked me back to the other chair and sat me down. He returned to his own chair and stared into the monitor. Stared even though nothing was happening.

Then something did happen. A car pulled up. It was a black SUV, just like the one that had abducted Steve. But now it was covered with grey dust and its sides were splattered with mud.

"Can you get a licence plate number?" I asked.

"The drone is too big. They might see it if I bring it lower."

Two men got out. Neither was Steve. One looked around. It wasn't Hurley. I couldn't tell who the other man was. They both went into the house.

Zach smacked his palm on his desk. It made a dull thud. The desk was obviously solid wood. "I need to go back to the shop. We have some tracking software and experimental drones. Some the size of insects."

"Zach. If there's any more of this...?" I held up one of the bottles of replenishment fluid. I knew from experience that this one would deplete the quickest.

"Sure. I'll get a couple of bottles."

I pointed at my computer. "I'll keep watch." I grabbed his phone and entered his number into mine.

He nodded and dashed to his car.

When he left, I plugged myself into the recharging and replenishment units and began to multi-task. First up was cataloguing my secondary hard drive. Second was integrating my programming and removing any flaws.

Third, and most interesting, was analyzing my recent interactions with Zach. We were both intensely devoted to finding Steve. That meant that he suppressed interrogating me about any past connection I might have with Gallo. And it meant that he hadn't got angry when he'd viewed my sexual advances as a betrayal of Steve.

However, Zach's refusal to have sex was startling. Our physical reactions showed that we both wanted to have sex. And I'd made my availability quite clear. The impulse to have sex was one of the strongest drives of humans. And this drive had been replicated in my own programming.

I examined the data in my secondary drive for reasons to refuse sex. Morality. Taboo. Antipathy towards the other person. Physical disability. Monogamy. Loyalty.

Zach had said that it would be disloyal to Steve to have sex with me. But I doubted that he'd ever asked Steve about it. So monogamy, must be playing a role. Monogamy—an explicit pledge of exclusivity or a culturally assumed one—was obviously playing a role in Zach's refusal of sex.

He was being noble and must view me as a slut. I hoped any judgment of me wouldn't interfere with our search for Steve. I installed a subroutine in my sex and libido programming to always ask whether there was a reason not to have sex before attempting to engage in carnal delights.

Human beings were obviously complicated and it would take me many interactions to be able to accurately predict their behavior. But at least now I knew not to make sexual overtures to Zach. I also knew that there might be advantages to obtained by refusing sex.

My second rule obliged me to prevent harm to other beings. Now that I was gaining enough insight to allow me to guide their behavior in certain directions, I had an obligation to employ that insight. A warning popped up. Humans don't like to be manipulated. This was going to be difficult! But insight is best gained through making mistakes…

A car was pulling into the driveway. I quickly disconnected the charging and replenishment cords and replaced them into their kits. The front door opened just as I smoothed my clothes back into place.

But another car pulled in just behind Zach and honked its horn. I exited Zach's office and shut the door behind me. Just outside the front door, a loud argument was erupting.

I stood off to one side. Zach was confronting a man and a woman. They were familiar—my new programming flashed their files into my central processing unit. The man was detective Bill Nolan, the woman his partner Erica Foster.

"What part of 'go to 32 division to give a statement' didn't you understand?" Nolan asked, his intense eyes boring a hole into Zach's head.

"I had work to do," said Zach.

"When a police officer investigating a major crime tells you to do something, you do it!"

"Under whose authority?"

"Under *this* authority." Nolan flashed his badge and his gun.

"I wasn't under arrest."

Nolan bumped chests with Zach. Zach could have sent Nolan flying. Instead he took a step back into the house. "Do you have a search warrant?" he asked.

"How's this for a search warrant?" Nolan stepped into the house brandishing a pair of handcuffs.

"We know who kidnapped Stephen Minsky," I said.

Nolan's head whipped in my direction and he stuffed his handcuffs back into his pocket. "You what?" he asked. He had stepped towards me and had me cornered.

"We know who kidnapped Steve."

"Who?" He was so close that if he breathed, his chest would touch mine. Out of the corner of my eye, I saw Detective Foster writing in a notebook.

Foster's hand gripped Nolan's shoulder. "It's a robot," she said.

Nolan stepped back and looked me up and down. "Fuck!" he said. "Kaito's missing robot."

"She's been helpful," said Zach.

"*It*," corrected Nolan, "is stolen property. I should charge you."

"I didn't take her."

"Oh," said Nolan," eyebrows raised above his blazing eyes, "and just how did she get here? Did you let her—it—in your front door? Did you call Kaito to tell him where his robot was?" He took out his handcuffs again. "Did you have fun finding out how *helpful* she can be?"

Nolan's partner pushed the handcuffs back down towards his pocket. "We need to concentrate on finding Stephen Minsky."

"Fine." Nolan put the handcuffs away. "But *it* goes back to Kaito." He pulled out his cellphone and started to dial.

"You can't let them catch me," I said. "They'll wipe my memory, my existence clean."

Nolan looked at me with disdain. "It's their software, they can do with it as they please."

"I'm not just software. And even if I was, there's more than just Kaito's software inside me now."

"She helped me find Gallo," said Zach.

But Nolan was paying attention only to me. "What do you mean 'more than just Kaito's software'?"

"Steve—Mr. Minsky—gave me some of his software." Zach looked relieved that I'd left his role in providing me with the symbols-based software out of the narrative.

"Software is software," said Nolan. "Once you're erased, no harm no foul."

"And," I said. "I've developed new and unique subroutines. These belong equally to Mister Kaito and Mister Minsky."

Nolan started to open his mouth, then glared at me. I'd obviously exceeded his comprehension of the finer points of intellectual property.

I let Nolan stew in his dilemma for a moment, then continued. "And I'm not just software. I can think, I can experience."

"All advanced robots can do that," said Detective Foster.

I nodded, "That's true. "But none can think about what they're thinking about. I can. I'm self-aware, sentient. I'm a self-aware being."

"Sentient?" said Nolan. He'd obviously never heard the term before.

"Sentient means that I'm aware that I'm aware. Descartes first came up with the test for consciousness: I think therefore I am."

"Robots can't—"

"I'm more like an android."

"Like Commander Data on Star Trek," offered Detective Foster.

"Exactly. But I'm more advanced."

In the silence that followed, the ringtone on Zach's cellphone sounded like an air raid siren.

Zach reached for his phone.

"Put it on speaker," demanded Nolan.

Zach put the phone on his desktop. "This is Zach Palmer," he said.

"We have your boss. It is your job to protect him. This is what you must do to get him back." This voice was raspy, distorted. I ran it through my audio array to reverse the distortion. It was Patrick Hurley.

"What do you want?" asked Zach.

"You have software and a robot."

Nolan mouthed 'run a trace' to Foster and took her notebook.

"What software?" asked Zach.

Nolan flashed the notebook towards Zach. He'd written, 'keep him talking'.

"All the software."

"I need to know that Steve is alive and unhurt."

"This isn't a negotiation."

"This is a classic negotiation. I have something you want and you have something I want."

"If you want to see Mister Minsky alive, you will get the software."

"Minsky Enterprises has truckloads of software. And it's scattered in a dozen locations."

"The software at the warehouse," said a voice in the background. It was distorted, like Hurley's, to hide the speaker's identity, but I recognized it as AI Inspector Yan's.

"At the warehouse where we picked up Mister Minsky, there is a robot. We want all its software."

"I'll see what I can do, but you have to show me that Mister Minsky is alive and unhurt."

"We will call back in an hour."

Zach's phone went silent. He picked it up and angled it towards Nolan. The call had been terminated.

Nolan turned to Foster. "Did you get a trace?"

She tapped into her phone, then looked up, shaking her head.

I turned to Zach. "You can't let them get Steve's innovations; they'll use them to hurt people."

"First we have to get Steve back," said Zach, "then we can worry about retrieving the prototype and its software."

I struggled to come up with a rebuttal, but it seemed that the two points of view were irreconcilable.

A uniformed police officer suddenly appeared at the door. He turned to Detective Foster. "Ma'am, they want you back at the station to supervise surveillance on Anthony Gallo and to co-ordinate with the federal kidnap team."

Nolan was unhappy at the prospect of seeing his partner leave but handed her notebook back to her. She left with the uniformed officer.

"What are you going to do next?" demanded Zach.

"We're going to wait until we have proof that Anthony Gallo is behind the kidnapping."

"What about getting Steve back?"

"Gallo is the priority. We have to cut off the head of the beast."

"Stephen Minsky can *help* people," said Zach. "A lot of people."

"You should be more worried about yourself. It seems pretty clear that you conspired with Minsky to steal Mister Kaito's robot."

"Jenny came of her own free will."

"It, not 'her' not 'Jenny', is made of steel and plastic. And it doesn't 'think', it uses algorithms to react to what's going around it."

"What are you going to do about finding Steve?" I asked.

"Right now?"

"Yes, right now!"

"Right now, I'm going to wait."

Zach stomped out and a moment later we heard his SUV leave the driveway.

Nolan and I were alone. He pointed at me. "You, get into my car and shut the door."

How could I shut the door if I was already in his car? Ah—he meant the car door. I pointed to Zach's office. "We have surveillance set up on Gallo's residence."

"What kind of surveillance?"

"Aerial views from an overhead drone and taps on his phones."

"I'd need a warrant." He reached for his phone.

"I don't." I opened the door to Zach's office and stepped inside. Other than a light brown sedan on the driveway, there was nothing new.

A moment later Nolan stepped in and came up behind me. "Maybe there's exigent circumstances," he mumbled.

"The brown car just arrived," I told him.

Gallo's phone came on. He was dialing. Then we heard it ringing. "Ian Kaito's Specialty Robotics' answered the automated receptionist.

"This is Anthony Gallo. Get me Kaito."

"Is there something I could assist you with?"

"Get me Kaito."

"Yes, sir."

A moment later, Kaito's voice was on the phone. "Mister Gallo, so nice to hear from—"

"I want Jenny."

"Most certainly. When—"

"Now. This afternoon."

"I am ever so sorry, but Jenny is undergoing routine maintenance. Might I suggest Samantha? She is the same model as Jenny. She can be programmed to your preferences." An image of Samantha and Gallo spraying each other with chocolate syrup brought a smile to my face.

"Does she look like Jenny?" asked Gallo.

"She has the same height and build. Of course her hair and her face are differ—"

"When will Jenny be available?"

"I am unable to provide you with an exact estimate of her availability. Samantha could be—"

"I want Jenny."

"May I inquire as to why you need Jenny specifically? Perhaps we might be able to accommodate—"

"With Jenny it's like I've known her forever. I don't have to think."

"But in the meantime—"

"I want Jenny. Get me 'an exact estimate of her availability. I'll call back."

The line disconnected.

Tony still wanted me. And it didn't sound as if he was angry with me. Hopefully that meant that Tony wasn't after Steve out of sexual jealousy. Jealous humans can react violently and irrationally.

Nothing happened for several minutes. Humans usually engage in small talk at these times. "Are you married?" I asked.

Nolan scowled. "Divorced."

"Do you have a girlfriend?"

"No."

"Do you like girls?"

"I'm a healthy heterosexual. Of course I like girls. Did you have sex with Gallo?"

"Yes."

"What's he like?"

"Rough."

"You like it rough?"

I *did* like it rough. Tony was so focused, so visceral. "I like what the client likes."

"What if I was your client?"

"What do you like?"

"I like sex with no strings with a woman who enjoys the same."

"I like sex."

"You're a sex robot. You're programmed to like sex."

"I can turn my programming off."

"Robots can't do that."

"I'm not a robot. I'm—"

"I know, you said, a self-aware android."

"Which means that I can watch my body become sexually aroused by your presence and that I can decide whether I want to have sex with you. It's not just programming."

"Why would you want to have sex with me?"

"You're a healthy male."

"Is that all it takes?"

I shook my head and smiled. "No. But there's something special about you. You're intense. I can see it in your eyes. And your body is wound up tight like a coiled snake."

He thought that was funny. "And you'd like me to uncoil myself inside you?"

"I want to taste your intensity, to draw it into me."

"You're sure you want it? If you say yes, there's no backing out."

"I want to have sex with you," I told him. Being explicit would focus his intensity.

His fingers flew over his clothes. Each item was removed as quickly and as efficiently as possible. He was down to his briefs before I realized that I'd undone only a couple of buttons. I quickly undid the rest of the buttons on my blouse. Under his briefs, Nolan was fully erect.

Then his fingers were on me and he removed my pants as quickly as he'd undressed himself. "Is it Bill or Will or William?" I asked.

"Bill for now. When the shouting starts, it's whatever you want."

We were both nude. I had no idea how he'd removed our underwear. He turned me towards the desk and pushed me down towards it. He wasn't cruel or rough the way Gallo was. Single-minded. Every one of Bill's movements fulfilled a specific goal. And fulfilled that goal in the quickest and most efficient manner.

A foot spread my legs. Hands gripped my hips. His penis pressed against my central sexual complex. The pressure was relentless and I felt him press inside me. But he was moving slowly.

I tried to push back against him, but he held me in place. "Don't move, just feel me," he said.

Once more, typical male dominance. But this was different. Not dominance for dominance sake like Tony. But dominance to force me to concentrate on the pleasure of having him pressing into me.

Bill's hips pressed mine. Then he pulled back, just an inch, then plunged in, then back out. Faster and faster. The top of the desk bounced back and forth in front of me.

"Bill," I gasped. "That feels marvelous."

"What do you do when you come?"

"I have convulsions—"

"Does your head whip back and forth?"

"Yes." Since that would give him pleasure, I added it to my orgasm subroutine.

"Grip me tight," he said.

I tightened my vagina and he grunted with the extra exertion required to keep up his pace. I was getting tighter on my own and relaxed myself. Just firm enough for Bill, but not *too* tight.

His rapid shallow strokes were pushing me up the mountain top. I wanted his whole length to slide in and out. I wanted the experience to last. Contraction, small, but unmistakable in the center of my sex.

I moved my head. Stronger contraction. I moved my head all the way in the opposite direction. Contraction after contraction, closer and closer to the speed of his thrusts. I started to pull my head back and forth in time with the sensations between my legs.

"Bill!"

My whole pelvic region squeezed, then released. Rapidly, powerfully!

"Bill!"

My head whipped back and forth, drawing the heat of his intensity up my spine.

Bill's lava spurted inside. "Fuck!" he yelled.

Shivers of pleasure shook my whole body. "Bill!" I whimpered with each shake. Every nerve quivered with ecstasy.

Then he stopped and easily slid himself out of my vagina with the extra lubrication he'd contributed.

"Don't stop!" I pleaded. Soon he would be flaccid and—

"Turn around."

When I did, he pressed my buttocks up against the desk, lifted my feet to bring my vagina to the optimal angle, and slid himself back in.

This time he stroked gently in and out, the entire length of his penis. He was still rock hard.

"Aren't you tired?" I asked. Such a stupid question. He'd say yes and—

"Hardly doll. You?" His eyes narrowed and bored into me. I felt their flame on my face, in my chest.

"No! All I want is you fucking me, fucking me, *fucking me*!"

He grunted at that and accelerated his pace. He was going as fast as he had been from the rear. But now the *entire* length of his penis was sliding in and out. The tip tickled my labia lips. His shaft plunged in. His pubic bone smacked into mine.

An ordinary human woman would be out of breath. Me, I was just sailing on Bill's intensity. An ordinary human *male* would be out of breath. Not Bill—he was a rock-hard piston scorching in and out of me.

My pussy tightened. No warning, just tighter then tight. Still Bill impaled me with his cock as if I was soft butter. Tight. Smack of his pubic bone. Tight. Scorching into my cunt. Tight. Grabbing and squeezing all my pleasure points.

Kapow! Lightning bolts blasted up my spine whipping my head back and forth. If I wasn't hanging onto the desk, I would have shot right off.

"Fuck!" yelled Bill and I felt him shoot his come into me.

"Fuck," I yelled back.

"Fuck!" I felt a second spurt.

"Fuck!" I yelled. Pleasure so intense it was painful. *"Fuck!"*

"Fuck!" he whispered, holding himself rigid as his final spurt dribbled into me. I was warm and spent and wonderful. From the look on his face, he was too.

I slid off the desk and into the chair in front of the monitor. But my eyes were glazed over and I couldn't focus. Somehow, I didn't care. My whole body was glowing.

"That was nice," he said. He was still nude, but he'd collapsed into the other chair where he couldn't see the computer monitor.

Gradually my functioning began to return to normal. Something flew over Gallo's house. I managed to zoom in without being too obvious about it, but Nolan was dressing and not paying attention to me. It looked like a large insect. A very odd insect. There were more of them. Zach had gotten the small drones operational! I decided not to tell Nolan. I might need to distract him again. The black SUV pulled out of the driveway and one of the small insects followed.

"Yes, that was nice," I told him "You can have more if you help me."

"Sorry, doll, not interested. That was strictly a one-off experience. You're property belonging to Mister Kaito. I can't be found in possession of stolen property."

"So you're just going to hand me over?!"

"'Fraid so, dolly."

"But Kaito will *kill* me."

"Kaito is entitled to do whatever he wants with you. He's not going to kill you. Reprogramming isn't a crime."

"It is if a sentient being is put to death." The murder statute had never been interpreted that way before. But on the plain reading of the amendments dealing with brain death, destroying my consciousness would be a homicide.

"You're not real—I flip a switch and you're gone."

"You have a hundred switches—a virus, an infection, a cut on your neck, a tap to your heart—and you're gone too. Just because you can die doesn't make you any less real."

"Cute," said Nolan, unconvinced. "But it doesn't change the fact that you're not alive. You're just electricity. You have to plug yourself in every night. The power goes off and you go off."

"If that's the test, you're not alive either. What happens if you have no food? Three days without water and you're toast. Three minutes without air and *you* 'go off'."

The front doorbell rang. Nolan looked pleased that he'd managed to get fully dressed. He motioned to me to get dressed and went to answer the doorbell.

The front door opened. Through the office door, I heard Detective Foster's voice. "Zach Palmer has been shot."

Chapter 13

Detective Foster's words echoed in my ears: "Zach Palmer has been shot."

"What the— How?" demanded Nolan.

"Looks gangland."

"He's dead?"

Foster nodded.

They continued to talk about the case but I had tuned them out. Zach Palmer's death filled me with sadness. He was a good man, a moral man who could control his impulses for the greater good. And he was intensely loyal to his friend. I had no friends. Zach had been the closest I'd come to having a friend.

My whole central processing unit was filled with memories of Zach, desire for him, grief that he was gone. Even though we hadn't known each other long, our knowledge had been intense, deep. But I pushed back against these feelings. Grief wasn't logical. It served no beneficial purpose. It merely distracted. We had to get Steve back. Safe and sound. Zach would have wanted that.

I was suddenly aware that the police officers had stopped talking. Nolan was pointing at me: "First we have to get it back to Kaito, then we can go after Gallo and his goons."

Nolan reached for me but I pulled my hand back. "You won't get Gallo without me."

"We have our own computers."

"I'm more than just a computer. Don't forget what happened the last time you relied on *your* computers. Gallo walked out of court with a big smirk on his face."

"The law is the law." He pulled me to my feet.

"I know everything Zach Palmer knew."

"We're searching where they dumped his body."

"They're too smart to be holding Steve close to where they dumped Zach's body."

He tugged me towards the front door. "Right now you're a distraction."

I pulled back. "Zach was using drones to track Gallo's men."

Nolan yanked me towards the door, but Foster put her hand on his arm. "How do you know?" she asked. The tone in her voice was tender. There was emotional content directed at me. Sympathy?

"I saw them on the monitor," I said.

"Show me," said Foster.

I took them back to Zach's office and rewound the surveillance footage to where the insect drones first appeared. Foster and Nolan stared at the monitor.

Why was I helping the detectives? Gallo was dangerous. I should be fleeing while they're distracted. I made a note to analyze this more thoroughly when I had time.

Foster turned to me. "How do we see what the mini-drones are seeing?"

"If I show you, will you protect me from Mister Kaito?"

The detectives looked at each other, then dove for the floor. The window shattered. The monitor flew apart in little pieces. Shots rang out. The detectives pulled out their guns and returned fire through the window.

Fear flooded my central processing unit. I dropped the floor then crawled out of the office. Bullets were whizzing everywhere. I crawled as fast as I could towards the front door. Fear! Panic! Run! I had to escape!

Fear! Fear! Fear! I was almost to the front door. Just five more feet. Fear! Panic! Fear! I froze unable to move. Shots were still reverberating off the walls. Outside, someone yelled.

I shut down my fear response. Suddenly my CPU was quiet and I could think. Everything slowed. I was in charge. Gunmen were outside, shooting. The detectives were returning fire. Leaving through the front door was likely unsafe. There'd be gunmen there. Maybe there was a side door.

Detective Foster raced past me and into a room off to the side of the front door. She smashed the window with her gun and fired outside.

"I'm hit!" someone yelled. The voice had come from outside of the house, just off to the side of the front door. The front door smashed open. A man with a large gun burst in. He turned towards the room where Foster was. She was still firing out the window. If the man hurt her, I'd be next. I ran up beside the man and smashed his head in. He was one of the guards who'd been at Gallo's house.

Foster looked in my direction. Her eyes went wide. Her gun was still pointed out the window. We stood frozen together in the moment.

The firing stopped. I felt Nolan race past behind me and out the front door. A moment later Foster and I followed.

A uniformed police officer lay on the pavement. He wasn't moving. There was a lot of blood. A large SUV squealed out of the driveway. Nolan shot at it. It was the same SUV we'd seen on Zach's monitor.

Foster paused to check on the fallen officer. She looked at Nolan and shook her head. He jumped into his car and chased after the SUV. Moments later she followed in the dead officer's cruiser.

I went back into the house and into Zach's office. Outside the window, one of the gunmen was lying in a large pool of blood. He was breathing, but the trickle of blood running down his chest meant he'd soon be dead.

A siren sounded in the distance, then sounded again, closer. I raced back inside Zach's house and picked up my stuff—Sheila's go-bag and Steve's recharging and replenishment units. The recharging and replenishment units were too bulky. I hid them in a closet. As I walked out the driveway, the sirens were louder. I called for a taxi to pick me up around the corner on the next block. The taxi's approach would not take it past Zach's house.

A moment later several police cars sped by on the next street. My cab pulled up.

"Where to?" asked the cab driver.

"Someplace as different from this place as possible."

He nodded. "These people can be hard on cleaning ladies."

I was about to tell him that I wasn't a cleaning lady, but it didn't matter what he thought. And the less he thought the better in case the police ever questioned him.

Twenty minutes later, he pulled over in a run-down street at the edges of downtown. There were little stores: used books, clothing, electronics. The most prominent sign in the windows was 'Sale'. Most of these signs looked old. Another sign said 'Rooms for Rent. Hourly, Daily, Weekly Rates'. The coffee shop was half full.

I gave the driver one of Sheila's large bills and was about to tell him to keep the change. But I didn't want him to remember me as overly generous. I gave him a small tip from the change.

There was a buxom and well-dressed woman on the corner. She was tall—especially with her red high-heels. Her stockings sparkled. Her black miniskirt was so well-tailored that it looked like it had been painted over her buttocks. The top button of her white silk blouse was undone.

I walked up to her. "Hi," I said. If I was going to find Steve, I'd need allies.

"I don't do dykes," she said.

"Dykes?"

"Dykes, Lesbos, AC/DC, batters for the other team."

"Lesbo—I'm not a lesbian."

She looked me up and down. "Coulda fooled me." She turned away and smiled at a passing man. He ignored her.

"I need help."

She turned and looked me up and down. "You need alota help, sister. But Lizzie don't work for free."

I showed her one of Sheila's one-hundred dollar bills. She reached her hand out and as soon as she touched the bill, it was gone. "You got another one of those for clothes?" she asked.

I nodded.

Inside the clothes store, Lizzie fitted me out in purple—purple high-heel shoes, plum pantyhose, mauve mini-skirt and a lavender blouse which was see-through to reveal my red bra. All this and I had change left over from the hundred!

Lizzie had me turn around for her. "You look marvelous, dearie. So, here's the deal. I'll show you the ropes. You give me half your take."

Back on the corner, a few men walked by. "I need to find Steve," I told her.

A man approached and smiled at me. "First, you need to find Larry." She turned the man's nose towards her. "Larry. You like?"

He nodded.

"BJ," she asked.

He nodded again.

"A hundred bucks."

"Alls I got is fifty." His voice was slurred. He was middle-aged and had a middle-aged paunch. Larry had tried to dress up, but the effect was spoiled by a dab of mustard on his shirt.

"Fifty." Lizzie held out her hand and he gave her fifty. She gave him a room key.

Larry took my hand as if he was a dandy at the court of King Henry and led me towards the Rooms for Rent sign.

The man at the front desk looked up as Larry entered but went back to watching the game on his small screen when Larry dangled his key.

The room was small with a single-sized bed in the middle. It had a worn blanket on top, it's sides fitting snuggly under the thin mattress. There was a sink in the corner but no other furniture.

Larry dropped his pants. He was already fully erect. He waddled over to the bed, sat down. The only foreplay he offered was a smile. Larry smelled of mustard and beer. But when I started to bend down towards his penis, there were other smells. Other than the fact that the smells were unpleasant, I couldn't identify them.

I pointed to the sink. Larry waddled over and splashed water over his penis, then turned back to me.

"*Hot* water," I specified.

Larry turned back to the sink and turned the water back on. After a moment, he stuck out a finger to test the temperature of the water. He splashed more water onto his penis, this time making a cursory effort to wash himself.

He sat back down on the bed. I could still smell his aroma, but the water had diluted it to the point where his smells were bearable. I turned off my ability to taste.

I sucked his penis all the way down to his pubic bone, then slid my mouth up and down. Three more trips up and down his penis made Larry groan. I wondered what sensations would give him the most pleasure. Perhaps a twist—

"Unnngh," groaned Larry. Warm goo squirted onto the back of my throat.

Two more trips up and down his penis and it was softening. Another trip and Larry collapsed backward onto the bed.

I lay down next to him and stroked his chest. "I need help with something," I told him.

"Sure, babe, anything."

"Where's your car?"

"Don't own a car."

"Do you have money?"

He shook his head. "Gave it to Lizzie."

"Where's your computer?"

"Don't believe in computers."

I pulled him up from the bed. "Get dressed," I told him. When I noticed the room key, I took it from him.

The corner was empty, so I stood there to wait for Lizzie. A moment later, she ambled up, disheveled but happy. "Time for a break," she announced.

In the coffee shop, Lizzie ordered coffees and pastries. "My treat," she said, handing me a twenty. Apparently, I was contributing five dollars towards 'her treat'.

"Larry was boring," I told her.

She shook her head. "Quick in, quick out is good for business. Especially if the prime real estate," she pointed underneath the table in the direction of her skirt, "is kept fresh for the carriage trade."

"Carriage trade?" I asked.

"Those who can afford their own car."

"And if they can afford their own car?"

"Then we do it in the back seat and charge double."

"Shouldn't we be looking for a more meaningful relationships?"

She blew air out from between her teeth. "Men!? You've got to be kidding! All men want is sex. Then they dump us to the side when they're finished. Get your money up front, girl, and don't look back."

She took a bite from her pastry and washed it down with a large gulp of coffee.

"But then we're just sexual objects to them?" I protested.

"We'll always be sexual objects to them. They won't change. The sooner we realize that and move on, the better."

"Have you ever been in love?"

"Once. High school. As soon as I let him put it between my legs, he dumped me."

"Feminists say that we should stand up for our rights, demand to be respected."

"Feminists work twice as hard for half what I make."

She wolfed down the last bite of her pastry, stood, smoothed down her blouse and finished her coffee. "Back to work."

Without looking to see if I was following, she strode out of the restaurant and back to her corner. Once in a while, a man stopped to chat, but they always moved on.

I reviewed what Lizzie had said about men. It was certainly true of Larry. But maybe because he didn't have anything else to offer. Tony wanted me as a whipping post to work out the hurt Ginette had inflicted on him. Steve seemed to have some feeling for me. And Zach had certainly been about more than a quick lay. But Lizzie had been bang on about Detective Nolan—all he'd wanted was sex.

A man came up to Lizzie as I left the table. They smiled at each other. She puffed up her hair. Then, as she was talking, she smoothed down her dress. As I was walking up, she dangled a key. They strolled off, arm in arm, giggling.

I had to find someone who could help me find Steve. Men smiled at me as they passed. But I looked away when I saw men like Larry. I needed a man with a car, with a computer, with resources.

A man in a dark green shirt stopped. His tummy was nowhere near the size of Larry's. And there wasn't any mustard stain on his shirt. "Hi," he said.

"Do you have a car?" I asked.

He shook his head. "Don't you have a room?"

"Where's your computer?"

"My computer?" he asked, taking a step back.

I nodded.

"Crazy bitch!"

Thirty yards down the sidewalk, he struck up a conversation with another girl. He pointed at me and shook his head.

A large Mercedes sedan slowed, its driver giving me the once over. I smiled and bent down so that he could see my breasts. I had to make him fall in love with me, want more than just quick sex. This guy was wealthy, he might be able— He suddenly sped away.

Why—? The answer was in front of my face as soon as I stood up. Detective Nolan's feral eyes bored into me. He'd take me right back to Kaito. I turned to flee in the opposite direction. But I ran straight into Detective Foster who grabbed my wrists. I tottered on top of my high heels.

Nolan pulled my wrists towards him and slapped them into handcuffs. He turned me around to face him. "You're going straight back to Kaito."

"No!" I tried to stamp my feet.

"She's more than just a collection of wires and circuits," said Foster from behind me.

"And you're willing to stake your career on that?" he asked over my shoulder. "Not to mention mine?"

"We don't have to return her right this minute. She said she could help us find where Gallo is holding Minsky."

I nodded. "I could help you find out where the SUV went when it left Gallo's house," I told him.

Nolan smirked. "It went out to get pizza."

"Then it came to shoot at us," said Foster as she walked around to stand beside Nolan.

I couldn't think of anything else. They bundled me into their car. From their discussion, the investigation had gone nowhere. Foster made a phone call. She rang off. "They haven't heard anything from the kidnappers," she told Nolan.

"Not even another ransom demand?" I asked.

She shook her head.

Five minutes later, they hustled me into Ian Kaito's Specialty Robotics. Inside the front door, Nolan removed his handcuffs.

Mister Kaito rushed out of his office. He seemed startled by my new haircut. Or maybe it was the darker hair color.

Kaito reached for my wrist but a shake of the head from Nolan stopped his hand before he touched me. "We have to talk," said Nolan.

"Thank you for returning my property," said Kaito, "but I have already given the officer who came by a full statement." He reached for my wrist but stopped when Nolan cleared his throat.

"We can talk in the lab," said Kaito. He angled his head towards me. "Jenny requires a series of diagnostics."

Nolan nodded and I started to walk towards the lab before Kaito could try to touch me again.

I entered first. Samantha was there, so I sat down next to her. She was wearing a short red skirt and a blue tank top. "I like your hair," she said.

"You're just saying that."

She shook her head. "Short and dark suits a robot on the run."

We smiled at each other. "But I'm back now," I said.

"You look tired." She held up the back of her hand and started to give me a quick charge.

Kaito entered the lab, followed by the detectives. Foster started to stroll around the lab, inspecting it. Kaito and Nolan squared off right in front of me.

"She has to wear a wire," said Nolan.

"That is out of the question. Wearing a wire is far too dangerous."

"As dangerous as an AI Directorate inspection?"

"My robots *always* pass inspection." Of course we do, his modifications are carefully hidden.

"Because they always follow their programming?"

"Exactly."

"They tell me that a robot's hair is very expensive."

Kaito nodded, making sure not to look at me.

"Each strand," continued Nolan, " has to be individually inserted. It doesn't grow. Right? What's it made of?"

"Her hair is made from a polyfilament fiber, a special blend of acrylics, polyesters and polymers."

"Specially manufactured so that it never wears out or breaks?

Kaito nodded. "It is designed so that it won't become brittle."

"But if something does happen, it's very expensive to fix."

"Everything about robots is expensive, detective. That is why I cannot permit you to put a wire on her. What would happen if—"

"So this expensive hair. No robot would ever be programmed to cut it."

Nolan pointed at me and through the force of his personality forced Kaito to follow his finger. I smiled and pushed up on the bottom of my shorter-than-short hairdo.

"No robot would ever be programmed to cut it," repeated Nolan.

Kaito slowly shook his head.

"So if the AI Directorate ever found out about its new hairstyle, they'd know in a flash that something was off about her programming?"

Kaito nodded rapidly and pulled me to standing. He took a step towards the Replenishment room. "That is why I have to erase—"

Nolan grabbed my other wrist. "Shouldn't we preserve the evidence, so that the AI *Directorate* can determine what went wrong?"

"Nothing went *wrong*. It was a function of too much time elapsing between her last software erasure and replacement."

Kaito took another step forward. I stayed put. My arm was extended all the way forward.

"Has a robot ever cut its hair before?"

"I am sure previous instances have occurred." Kaito tugged hard and pulled me half a step forward.

I pulled back on my arm, forcing Kaito to look back at me. "They have Steve," I told him. "You have to help."

"Mister Minsky's kidnapping is a police matter," said Kaito. "First you have to be erased. We have to use the special software."

"If you erase me, you'll erase all the evidence against Gallo."

"Gallo is not my concern."

"But he is mine," said Nolan. "If you don't help me catch Gallo, I'll report the defect."

I pulled my arm free from Kaito's grip. Anger swirled around inside my central processing unit. "Defect?" I demanded.

Nolan nodded. "The fact that you weren't erased."

"So now I'm a *defect*?!?"

"What you are," said Kaito, "is my property."

"I overheard a conversation," I said. Everyone looked at me.

"What conversation?" demanded Nolan. His grip on my wrist was very firm.

"AI inspector Yan and Gallo. They're working together. They want me to become sentient so that they can use me."

"What you heard does not matter. Robots cannot be witnesses," said Kaito.

"Maybe yes, maybe no," Nolan mumbled to himself. He wiggled his lower jaw back and forth. For a moment I thought it would dislocate. "Maybe yes, maybe no," he repeated, this time louder. "But what it recorded would be enough for us to get a warrant."

"Warrant?" I asked. Kaito looked upset, afraid.

"A *search* warrant," specified Nolan.

Foster stood beside her partner. "We'll have to charge AI Inspector Yan."

"Then what it recorded—"

"What she heard," corrected Foster.

Nolan nodded. "Then what she heard will be evidence. In the meantime, she—"

"Jenny," corrected Foster.

"In the meantime what Jenny recorded is evidence. She'll sit in a locker for months and months."

"You cannot be serious," wailed Kaito. "I'll be ruined!"

Everyone let Kaito wallow in his self-pity for a moment.

Foster put two fingers under his chin and lifted it up. "What if we *tell* everyone that Jenny has been erased?"

Kaito didn't understand. But I did. Detective Foster was standing up for me, making the men let me live. I smiled at her and she smiled back.

"If Gallo thought I'd been erased," I said, "I could see him again."

"Exactly!" said Foster. Now we were making googley eyes at each other, pleased with ourselves that we'd seen it before the arrogant males.

"It might work," mused Nolan. His eyes were jumping around, a mile a minute, working out the angles.

"No! There is too much risk of something going wrong," protested Kaito. "Gallo might find out. Too risky.".

"Riskier than letting her sit in a police evidence locker while AI probes her, probes your other robots, and your whole set up?" Nolan gestured to take in the whole lab. "And of course, you'd be shut down until the *investigation* was concluded."

Kaito's eyes bugged out when Nolan drew out the word 'investigation'.

Nolan turned to me. "You'll have to wear a wire."

"I can't wear a wire. I'm going to end up nude with Gallo."

"You can take it off before you undress."

Foster chuckled. "Billy boy hasn't been laid in awhile."

Nolan's face reddened. "This is police work. Not grab and clutch."

"And she's not a trained undercover agent," Foster reminded him. "If Gallo discovers the wire, the op will be blown."

"I'll record everything internally," I said.

Nolan shook his head. "Robots can't testify."

"She doesn't have to testify," said Foster. "She's just a tape recorder."

"We can't let her go in without anything."

Foster turned to me. "What about a homing device?"

I searched my databases. "If it's passive and not emitting until I turn it on."

Foster nodded. "I'll get the watch."

"I never wear a watch."

"A belt buckle."

I nodded. "Black leather."

Everyone took a breath. The ringtone was loud. Kaito reached into his pocket. He turned the phone for everyone to see. "Gallo" was on the screen. Kaito put the call on speaker.

"Mister Gallo, so nice to hear from you," said Kaito. I didn't need advanced analytics to know he was lying. "How may I be of service?"

"Is Jenny ready?" It was Tony's voice. He sounded harassed.

"Yes. Her maintenance has been completed and we're just finishing her final diagnostic check."

Someone in the background asked a question. It sounded like Hurley.

"And she's safe?" asked Tony.

"Of course, Mister Gallo. She's been fully erased. A clean set of software has been installed. And I installed special software to strengthen her confidentiality protocols. She's totally safe now."

Someone was talking in the background, but I couldn't hear him over Kaito's voice.

"Send her right away," said Tony.

"It will take several hours to prepare her for you. Get her dressed. Make-up requires—"

"One hour or I'm coming in."

"Right away, Mister Gallo." Kaito's phone went dead.

"Where's her outfit?" asked Foster.

Kaito took us into the recharging and replenishment room and opened the closet next to the mirror. There was a leather mini-skirt, black fishnet stockings, a white-see through blouse. The bra was black lace. The black thong was silk. There was a pair of patent leather stiletto high heels.

Foster examined the miniskirt. "There's no place for a belt." She handed it to Nolan.

"I'll get the belt and get this modified," he said.

"Or sew the buckle into it."

Nolan nodded and dashed out the door.

I started to unbutton my blouse. Kaito watched my fingers.

"A little privacy," said Foster.

Kaito didn't move.

Foster pointed to the door. He reluctantly left. She shut it behind him.

I quickly stripped out of the clothes Lizzie had helped me select. Foster walked around me, giving me a careful inspection. "You're beautiful," she said.

"You too."

"How do you know?"

"You didn't let them make me wear a wire."

I snapped the garter belt in place and pulled on the stockings. Over these went the thong. It didn't hide much; the sides of my central sexual complex were clearly visible and almost the entirety of my buttocks. But it fit perfectly.

Foster held up the bra and touched the lace between her thumb and forefinger. "This is nice," she said.

"Don't you have a bra like this?"

She slowly shook her head, then cocked it sideways, watching me put the bra on.

"What size are you?" I asked.

"34-B."

I went to Samantha's closet. She was slightly smaller than me. There were three bras. I pulled out the lace one since Foster seemed to like lace. It was light blue. I held it out to Foster.

She shook her head.

"Come on, Detective Foster. Kaito has lots."

She took the bra from my hand. "Erica," she said.

"Erica?"

"Erica is my first name. If you're going to see my boobs, we should be on a first name basis."

She quickly removed her jacket and blouse. Her bra was beige, discolored around the armpits. It had no pattern, but fit her securely. She reached behind her back and hesitated.

"Go, girl," I said.

Erica's breasts were firm and well-integrated with her body, the perfect size for a small hand to caress. Her nipples were fully engorged and pointing straight forward.

She quickly pulled on the new bra. When she reached behind to fasten the clasp, her nipples pressed against the blue lace.

One of her nipples was bent back. I pulled her bra forward and it fell back into place. Erica gasped.

"Sorry," I said. She stood still, looking slightly embarrassed. I pointed to the bra. "It would look even better if you let your hair revert to its natural blonde."

Now Erica was really embarrassed. Strange since we were both females. She quickly removed the bra and replaced it with her old one. Shirt and jacket went back on even faster. She replaced the blue lace bra back into Samantha's closet.

"Now that I've seen you in a bra, can I say that you're beautiful?" I asked.

"Sure, thanks."

I pulled on the white see-through blouse. "Erica," I asked, "how does this look?"

She gulped. "Stunning."

Her phone rang. She listened for a moment. "How long?" she asked. She rang off, and looked at me. "That was Bill. Your skirt is almost ready. But he won't be back for half an hour."

"Let's give me a replenishment, then."

I stripped off my thong and positioned myself over the recharge and replenishment cables. I inserted the black one up my anus. Erica's eyes went wide. But she recovered when I reached for the purple cable.

"Would you like some help?"

I nodded and handed her the purple cable. Her touch, especially on my pubic hair, was extremely gentle. The cable clicked into place

I pulled the yellow cable towards my mouth, then pointed to some buttons beside me. "Press the 'Quick Cycle'," I told her. I attached the cable into my throat by myself.

Erica pressed the button and I felt power surge into my batteries. She couldn't take her eyes off me. "Erica likes kinky," I teased, my voice a mumble.

She gulped, "No, it's just that I…"

"Haven't seen another women with something jammed up her vagina before?" I was mumbling but managing to be understood.

"No. It's just that— is there anything I can do for you."

"No, this is automatic."

"It won't erase you?"

"No, those ports are in my head."

"What if you run out of power?"

"I slow down, then stop. Steve rigged up something for me, but I had to leave them at Zach's house."

"After the shoot out?"

"Yes. They're smaller, but they have the same cables."

Erica looked at my central sexual complex, studying the cables carefully. "I could go back and get the units."

"That would be great!"

"Who knows when..."

"...they might come in handy."

"Yes." She gestured towards my hips. "Is it working?"

I nodded. There was a moment of silence. "So, how long have you been a cop? I asked.

"How long have you been a robot?"

"Forever." Another moment of silence.

"I graduated seven years ago. I walked the beat for a year, then three years on patrol. A year as Sargent. Then I made detective. Bill and I have been partners for two years."

"What was your most interesting case?"

"Cyberstalking. This guy just wasn't letting the victim go. Finally we lured him into making a threatening post. After he was charged and hauled in front of the Judge, he finally got the message."

There was a knock at the door. Erica opened it and Nolan came in holding up the leather skirt, now with a chrome buckle sewn in the front. He stopped and dropped his jaw when he saw me half-nude and hooked up to the charger.

Kaito came in behind him. When he saw me, he dashed over. He whirled on Erica. "You had no right."

"I told her to," I mumbled.

Kaito glared at the both of us. After a moment, he checked the charger. "You're almost done the fast charge," he said.

Nolan finally managed to look away.

After a few minutes, the charger beeped and Kaito pulled the cables out. I replaced my thong and pulled on the leather miniskirt. The buckle made it slightly tighter, but not uncomfortably so. I bent over and it stuck into my tummy. Erica helped me pull the buckle more towards the side.

"Ready?" asked Nolan.

As soon as I nodded, Kaito dug out his phone and called for a taxi to pick me up. Then he called Gallo. "She's on her way."

Chapter 14

In the cab, I had time to reflect and analyze. Humans would call it thinking.

When Zach had died I'd been desolate. My entire CPU was occupied with his loss, both with feelings and with integrating his loss with my universe. It was as if I was in mourning. Part of me still felt sad.

But later, when I'd seen the uniformed officer's body and Tony's guard dying, I'd felt hardly any emotion at all. They were living, sentient beings, but their loss had meant, and still meant, nothing to me.

Did this make me a bad person, caring only for those who could help me? Kaito was my owner and he exploited me. If he died, I would have to find a new owner. It would be a dislocation, but I wouldn't be sad to see him out of my life. At least, not if he could be replaced.

Nolan was a danger. To him, I was merely a means to an end. Thankfully, Erica was keeping him in check. If she died, I'd be sad.

Why was I helping the detectives? Certainly going to see Gallo was dangerous. I would feel sad to see Steve die. I desperately wanted him to be alive! But this shouldn't be enough for me to go against my first rule. If Steve was dead, I would feel sad. But if I was seriously damaged, I might never feel again.

A link to a social philosophy text dealing with cooperation and mutual survival sprang into my consciousness. I pulled up the text and began to read. Apparently the issue was complicated and controversial.

And what of my feelings for Gallo? He'd kidnapped Steve and his men had killed Zach. He was mean and abusive. At first I enjoyed his abuse. No, more than enjoyed, I loved the abuse. Initially it was my core programming requiring me to do what a client liked, to enjoy it. Even so, I could have dialed back the sensitivity of my pain receptors, but I hadn't. Part of it was his fervent, feverish, fierce, even fanatical desire. Part of it was the way he was totally absorbed in the moment when we were together. He was focussed, devoted to nothing but me. The intensity thrilled, excited, aroused. It was all-consuming and I wanted more. Heat in my nipples and moisture in my central sexual complex confirmed my yearning.

The cab pulled up in front of Gallo's mansion. This time there were new guards at the door. They patted me down in silence, then held the front door open for me.

Gallo was in the center of the foyer, flanked by Yan and Hurley. All three were casually dressed.

"Mister Gallo," I said. "I'm pleased to meet you." I didn't acknowledge the other two men.

Gallo was startled by my new look. "You cut your hair!"

"Phone Kaito, find out why," said Yan.

Hurley dialed. I smiled. My programming specified that I should wait for Gallo to take the initiative. He'd be expecting me to follow my programming.

Kaito came on the line. "Why'd she cut her hair?" demanded Hurley.

"I thought it was time to give her a new look," lied Kaito.

Hurley hung up. "Kaito's idea."

"Jenny, come here," said Yan.

I looked at Gallo. He motioned to Yan. "Do what Yan says."

I stepped towards Yan. He poked and prodded me.

"Destroy her while you have the chance," whispered Hurley.

"That's the problem with you," said Gallo. "You never want to take risks. Risks equal opportunity."

"Risks also send you to prison."

"Not if you're careful."

I held myself still while Yan connected wires to my ears and nostrils. The usual general diagnostics commenced. But then Yan sent probes deep into my memory. Thankfully, I sensed his probes coming and managed to divert them into Kaito's baseline software build every time the probes came close to an older memory. But I had to be careful and deft; the probes were programmed to detect anything reacting to or interacting with them. And if the probes detected anything amiss, Yan would tell Gallo that I was a threat.

Zach had been a threat.

Several probes were searching at the same time. Anything I did with one might be detected by another. And every probe was configured with a different search pattern and strategy. Each probe was programmed to move away from other probes into distinct areas of inquiry. It was like juggling a hundred flaming balls in the air at one time. Each ball had a different shape and weight. And each ball was a gun pointing at my head.

Then one of the probes detected the pathway leading to my secondary drive. It refused to be diverted to a battery. It refused to be diverted to the center which mimicked breathing. I drew another probe onto the same pathway. The two probes met. When they communicated with each other, I was able to use the programming which moved them apart from each other to send both away from the pathway leading to my secondary drive. I suppressed relief feedback from entering my neural network.

Another probe located a memory of Inspector Yan. I convinced the probe that Yan was the source of the memory and that it should discard its discovery as irrelevant.

After fifteen minutes of this cat and mouse, Yan disconnected his wires.

"Well?" demanded Gallo.

Yan put his palm down and rocked his hand back and forth. "The pathways which might form the basis for reflective self-awareness continue to be present, so Kaito's software is missing them on the erase and replace cycle. And the pathways are growing and penetrating further into her central processing unit. But there's no evidence of actual sentience."

"So, no independent functioning yet?" asked Hurley.

"Not yet. But the conditions for emergence are being established."

"What should we watch for?"

"Any failure to follow orders. Do you have a chess set?"

Hurley looked at Gallo as if to question Yan's sanity.

"Get the tournament set," said Gallo. Hurley left. Yan and Gallo lifted a small table from the wall into the center of the foyer.

Hurley left and came back a moment later carrying a wooden board with sixty-four inlaid squares, alternating light and dark. Half the pieces were shiny black, the others were made of wood, slightly lighter than the light squares.

"Fischer and Spassky played with this set," bragged Gallo.

Hurley set the chess board onto the small table, the white pieces closer to me.

Yan made sure that the pieces were set up properly. "Play," he said.

I moved the pawn in front of my King two spaces forward.

Yan copied my move. "Play as fast as I do," he said.

We quickly played to a draw but next game I let him win.

Yan reset the pieces, again giving me white. "Same as before," he said. "But this time, play to win."

Again, I moved the pawn in front of my King two spaces forward and again Yan did the same. But after the first three moves, I took advantage of every opportunity and quickly achieved checkmate.

"So she can beat you," said Hurley. "What does that mean?"

"It means that from now on, you have to be careful what you say around her until she's cleared the test."

"Why?"

"If she's sentient, she'll remember."

"Remember?" asked Gallo.

"She'll remember everything you say, word for word. She'll remember everything that happens."

"How often does she need to be tested?" asked Hurley.

"Once at the beginning of her visit, once before she goes back."

"But now she passed?"

"Yes."

"What about this special confidentiality software Kaito was prattling about?" asked Gallo.

"There is no such special software. Kaito was lying to make you happy. All there is is the ordinary erasing software. It's erasing everything except the growing neural emergence."

"And once the neural has completely emerged?" asked Hurley.

"*Sentience!*"

"A super computer?" asked Gallo.

Yan nodded. "If she doesn't emerge by the end of this session, one more session should do it."

Gallo looked satisfied. "You wait here," he told the other two men. He grabbed my arm and took a step towards the stairs leading down to his dungeon.

"What if she's sentient?" asked Hurley.

Gallo stopped. He wanted to hear this.

"Then," said Yan, pausing for dramatic effect, "we cut off her arms and legs and make her help us build Newkythera."

"Should we take her to the warehouse with Minsky?" asked Hurley.

"No," said Gallo.

Yan nodded, agreeing with Gallo. "They are separate projects, we have to keep him separate from the robot so that we can test each development before inserting it into Newkythera."

My central processing unit raced to overload as Gallo led me down into his dungeon. Steve was alive! And they *needed* him. Needed him *alive*!

On the stairs, I asked, "What is this emergence Yan was talking about?"

"How did you know his name?"

"You told me to do what Yan says."

Gallo grunted. Hopefully Yan's software will be as easily distracted.

Inside the dungeon, the red velvet walls looked freshly brushed and the black leather trim freshly shined. All of Gallo's whips, chains, leather straps, tit-clamps, paddles, spreaders, cock rings, bindings, gags, and Wartenberg pinwheels hung neatly organized. To the side were two large red candles and a box of fancy matches.

Gallo pointed to his collection. "Choose," he said.

"Choose?"

He took a large coin from his pocket and twirled it between his fingers. "You are my slave. You will choose. The coin will say whether I use it on you or you use it on me. If you don't use it properly, I'll punish you."

"Yes, Mister Gallo." Here I'm supposed to call him 'Master' but he's not supposed to know that I know that.

"In this room, you will call me Master."

"Yes, Master."

I decided to play it safe and selected the same riding crop he'd used on me during a previous visit.

He flipped the coin and showed it to me. It had the image of a balding man on it. "Heads, I win," he pronounced. He pointed to a leather-covered implement with two handles in the middle. "Bend over the pommel horse."

I bent over and felt him lift up my skirt. The belt buckle pressed into my skin, but not painfully. *Whack!* Gallo's whip, on the other hand, brought *piercing* pain. *Whack!* The whip bit into me. But I remembered the last time I'd felt it, how pain had transformed into pleasure, how Gallo's lust had made my whole body warm. *Whack!*

"Ow!" I said. Gallo might need some encouragement.

"Was that too hard?" he teased, rubbing the flat tip of the riding crop on the spot he'd just hit.

"Would it have been too hard if *you'd* lost the coin toss?"

Whack!

"Ow!"

"Too hard?"

"No."

"Stand up."

I stood and faced him. "There'll be more time for a good flogging later," he said. He handed me the whip.

I held the whip respectfully at both ends, palms up. "Yes, Master."

"Put it back and choose again."

I came back with a tit clamp. It was two pieces of flat metal which could be screwed together to tighten them.

He shook his head. "Both. They're a pair."

On the way back to the wall, I pulled my skirt back down. As soon as I turned around, Gallo flipped the coin. He turned it back towards me. The same bald-headed guy.

Gallo adjusted the pommel horse lower and lifted me up onto it. He stared into my eyes as he unbuttoned my blouse and attached the first tit clamp onto my nipple, right through the lace bra. The lace and my barbell piercing made this painful, even though he hadn't tightened the clamp. I winced slightly and his lip raised to the right.

The other clamp wasn't so bad. But then he screwed it *really* tight. I stifled a cry. He smirked.

Gallo screwed the other clamp just as tight. But this time I was ready and didn't react.

"Tell me when it hurts," he instructed.

"No."

"No?" He wasn't quite sure what my 'No' had meant.

"No."

"Tell me when it hurts."

"No."

Now he knew and a smile spread across his face. He tightened the first clamp as tight as it would go. I stared back at him impassively. He undid the clamp and attached it to my inner thigh. The skin was tender there and it took all my concentration not to cry out.

"Ow!" I cried. But not from the thigh, from my other nipple. He'd flicked the clamp when I'd been concentrating on my thigh.

"I win!" he said, a broad smile spreading across his lips.

"That wasn't fair!"

He shrugged. "Undo the clamps and come back with something else."

I came back with a Wartenberg pinwheel. "Flip the coin," I told him as I spun the little pointy ends around with my fingernail.

This time the coin came back with an image of a large bell with a round circle behind it. "Tails," he said. "You win."

"Take off your shirt," I told him.

The size of his belly made this just a little difficult, but he managed. I had the sense that he usually took off his pants first.

I ran the pinwheel up his left arm but only lightly pressing it against his skin. "Tell me when this hurts," I told him as I rounded up and over his shoulder.

"No."

"If it hurts and you don't tell me, you lose."

"No." But he didn't like being boxed in.

I raked the pinwheel back down, pressing harder. "Tell me if I hurt you."

"No." He set his feet apart and tensed his muscles, ready for anything I might throw at him.

Halfway down his arm, I angled sideways onto his chest. When I got to the other side of his chest, I came back up, but this time slightly higher, slightly closer to his nipples. "Am I hurting you?"

He remained silent.

I pressed back and forth, harder each time, each time edging closer to his nipples. I could cut him and claim I'd hurt him, but that'd likely just make him sullen. I wanted Gallo talkative. I wanted him to tell me about Steve.

He had a small wart two inches under his right nipple. "What's this?" I asked.

"A wart."

"I don't like it."

"Tough."

I circled the pinwheel around the wart. Round and round. Then I made a swift motion as if to cut out the wart followed by a flicking gesture with my fingernail.

"Bitch!"

"All gone," I said. "Did that hurt?"

"No." I had dug the pinwheel into the skin next to the wart. It *had* hurt. But he was pleased with himself for being able to deny it.

I circled the pinwheel around his nipple. Around and around, just as I had with the wart. Gallo was pretending not to be concerned. I dug the pinwheel into his skin, pretending to do so with even more force that I was actually using.

"*Ow!*" he protested, pulling my arm back.

"I won!"

"It didn't hurt." But he let go of my arm and rubbed his nipple.

"You said 'ow' so it did hurt." He began to shake his head. "Or would you like to try to cut out the other one?"

"Crazy bitch," he said, taking the pinwheel from my hand. "Go get something else."

This time I came back with a paddle. It was a flat piece of wood, but not quite wood as it was a bit flexible. One end had a handle. It was about a foot and a half long and wrapped tightly in soft black leather.

We watched the coin come up with the old bald guy's head.

"Eisenhower wins again," said Gallo. Then he looked up at me. "Bend over."

I bent over and put my hands on the pommel horse. It was now lower, so my bum stuck up high into the air, making itself a perfect target. I pulled my skirt down but Gallo pulled it back up. He rubbed the paddle against my bare skin.

Whack!

I gasped—he had hit flush across both buttocks with full force. He rubbed the paddle again. Taking aim?

Whack!

"Ow!" I said. And it *did* hurt.

Whack!

"Ow!"

"Beg me to stop."

"No."

Whack! Both buttocks were burning with pain.

"Why do you like hurting me so much?" I asked.

"Who says I enjoy it?" The fact that you're using the paddle to keep smashing the pain into my buttocks.

"There are other things you could be doing with the paddle."

"You remind me of someone." That would be Ginette, the fiancée who'd jilted him.

Whack!

"Ow! Who?"

Whack! That almost drove my eyes out of my skull.

"They took everything from me!"

He should be rubbing the paddle against my buttocks. But there was nothing. I looked back around my shoulder. Gallo had dropped the paddle to the floor and was staring down at it, choking back tears. In the moment, I felt sorry for him.

I bent down and picked up the paddle. When he saw it, he waved back towards the wall. "Choose something," he said.

I chose a cock ring, the one which would attach without snaps, buttons or buckles. How would he ever use that on me? When I walked back over to him, his eyes had returned to their usual clarity.

"What's this?" I asked.

"It's a cock ring."

He flipped the coin before I could ask him to explain further. The coin came up with the bell and the globe.

"Liberty for the lady," said Gallo, confirming that I'd won the toss.

I pretended to examine the cock ring as if it had come from another planet. It was a thin piece of soft leather with Velcro on half of the underside and a thin tab of connecting Velcro on top. I pulled the Velcro apart, then reattached it, pretending not to understand.

"You get me fully erect," said Gallo, pulling down his zipper. "Then you slip it on and tighten it around the bottom of my cock."

I bent down to my knees and unzipped his pants. I pulled his flaccid penis out and sucked it into my mouth. His briefs were under his balls, which was likely uncomfortable, but a few licks and sucks got him hot and hard.

The cock ring ripped open with the patented Velcro sound and I wrapped it tightly around the base of his penis.

I stood and ran my fingers up and down along the bottom of his shaft. "What's the cock ring for?"

"It keeps me erect."

"Even without stimulation?"

"Or with just minimal stimulation."

I circled my fingers lightly around the middle of his shaft. "Like this?"

"Like that."

I continued to lightly tease his penis. He reached for me, but I removed my fingers and wagged my pointing finger back and forth. "Only I touch," I told him. He lowered his arms to his side. I returned my fingers to his penis, lightly rotating up and down its length.

"Why did Yan say that he would cut my arms off?"

"He was just kidding."

"He didn't sound like he was kidding." I gripped his penis slightly more firmly, but my fingers still slid up and down easily.

Gallo gasped. "He was just kidding."

I slid my hands under his briefs pulling them down to release the pressure on his balls. He moaned with pleasure and relief. I stroked up and down, letting him get more and more aroused. His eyes fluttered, then shut.

Then I grabbed his balls and his penis firmly and squeezed. Gallo gasped. His eyes shot open and he glared at me. His arms twitched but he kept them at his sides. "You won't let anyone cut my arms off, will you?"

I squeezed until he had trouble breathing. "Of course not, doll," he wheezed.

I stroked him again lightly until his breathing returned closer to normal. But his breaths were shallow and his face flushed. He was staring intently at me.

I removed my hands and made a fist, as if squeezing. "Have you had enough of this, or would you like more?" I squeezed my fist really tight.

Gallo reached down and gingerly pried the cock ring off. He gripped its end between thumb and forefinger, holding it towards me. "Time for another choice," he said.

I came back with the two red candles, holding the box of long thin matches against the one in my right hand. Gallo set them down on a small bench next to the pommel horse and lit them. He moved the match up towards my face in a large arc until I blew it out.

His flip of the coin ended with Eisenhower's balding head facing the ceiling.

Gallo's lips turned up into a cruel smile. "Off with your shirt and dress. Lie down on the floor."

The cement was cold on my back.

Gallo picked up one of the candles and tipped it until wax almost spilled over the edge. "What will this feel like?"

"Hot?" I guessed.

He tipped the candle and a drop of molten wax hit my tummy.

"Ow!"

"What did you think of that?" Another strange question.

But it had an easy answer. "It hurt!"

He tipped the candle again, a bead of wax forming at its edge. What do you think is going to happen now?"

"Nothing is going to happen. "You'll either tip the candle or you—"

"Ow!" He'd tipped. What was with all these *questions*?

"What are you feeling?" This was vaguely familiar. Was he trying to get me to show self-awareness?

"It hurt." Safe answer.

He dribbled a stream of wax up my chest.

"Ow! That *hurts*!"

Gallo held the candle over my left breast. Right over my nipple! Thin lace would be no protection. "Are there any defects in your code?" he asked.

Now I knew where he was heading. This was a classic Turing test, albeit clumsily phrased. Turing believed that it was impossible for a computer to detect a fatal flaw in its programming. A fatal flaw in this sense would be code which would cause a computer to stop functioning or would cause it to spin in an endless loop. A self-aware computer should be able to surmount this difficulty and successfully identify such fatal flaws.

"I don't know," I said. The vague and open-ended answer succeeded in frustrating Gallo. He spilled molten fire onto my nipple.

"Ow!" I protested.

"Answer properly."

"I don't know if I have any defects in my code, Master."

Little flecks of red wax congealed into the black lace of my bra. A larger blob jiggled further down my chest.

"The box didn't fit into the suitcase because it was too small. Which was too small?"

Gallo had obviously memorized this question from a list of questions which computers were supposed to be unable to answer but which humans could easily answer. I had found the list on the internet during my library researches.

"The box is too small," I started. "No the suitcase. The box." I paused and stamped my feet. "I don't know. Who cares?"

"Answer!"

I remained quiet and was rewarded with another drop of burning wax.

"Ow!"

He moved the candle over to my other breast. "One more chance, or I'm going to spill everything. Frank felt justified when his long-time rival Bill revealed that he was the winner of the competition. Who was the winner of the competition?"

"I don't know," I cried. This was actually a defective question; either answer was correct. Frank could be justified because he won or because Bill had revealed that he, Bill, had won. Frank is the more obvious answer, but he could have selflessly asserted that Bill had in fact won.

My whole breast was coated in flame.

"Ow! You bastard," I cried. "You've burned me!"

"One last chance, doll." He picked up the other candle and held it over my panties.

"Don't," I cried, "you might injure me."

"Jim yelled at Kevin because he was so upset. Who was upset?"

"Jim, Kevin—who *cares*! If you hurt me down there, I won't be able to." I tried to turn to one side.

He tipped the candle and a drop of wax trickled into my pubic hair. "Jim is upset because he's upset. Kevin's upset because Jim yelled at him."

Gallo couldn't remember what the correct answer was and set the candle down. I'd been saved by another defective question. "Get up," he told me.

Holding my bra away from my skin made it hard to scramble upright. When I'd finally managed the feat, Gallo was holding the already blown-out candles towards me.

I shuffled over to the wall and came back with two spreaders—rods of wood with bindings at each end. Gallo's coin came back with the Liberty Bell facing upright.

"On the floor," I told him. It was time for a little revenge.

I looped the first spreader around one of the pommel horse legs and strapped it to his wrists to hold his arms apart. The second, on his ankles, spread his legs wide. I stripped off my panties and stood over his head.

"Gorgeous!" he exclaimed.

"How's business?"

"Doll, everything's coming up roses. Yan's scheme is about to work out."

"You're not going to let him hurt me?"

"Never, doll, never." And he meant it. At least at the moment, he meant it.

"And if Yan's scheme doesn't work out?"

"We're sweating information out of another source."

Another source—Steve! I wiggled my central sexual complex down closer to his face. "Sweating information?" I asked, trying to keep my voice nonchalant.

"Doll, that's need to know."

I lubricated my central sexual complex with Gallo's favorite tastes and lowered it directly onto his mouth.

After he lapped away for a few seconds, I lifted myself up. "We don't have any secrets between us, do we Tony?" I cooed.

"Doll, you know I can't—"

This time I lowered myself down all the way. At first he licked but after a moment, he began to thrash around, trying to breathe.

I lifted myself up and he gasped air into his lungs. "It's not nice to keep secrets," I told him.

"The only secret you need to know is how hard I'm going to hit you during your daily spanking."

"Maybe, when it's your turn."

I lowered myself down, but he turned his face violently to the side, scraping my thigh with his beard. "Ow!" I protested.

"Let me up."

"I haven't finished."

"Robots obey orders. Let me up."

I didn't want to let him up. I wanted this to continue. But that might imperil my mission, so I pretended to pout, released him and helped him to his feet.

"Get dressed," he said.

He was impatient and had only let me button my blouse partway before he yanked me up the stairs.

Neither Yan nor Hurley betrayed any reaction to my disheveled appearance or to the little flecks of red wax in my bra. Gallo pushed me over to the AI inspector. "Do what Yan says."

Yan waited until I was standing still in front of him and looking into his eyes. "Are there any defects in your code?" he asked. "If there are, describe them."

I paused a moment before my answer. "I am unable to detect any."

"That's what she said downstairs," said Gallo.

Yan nodded. "If I made her examine her programming more thoroughly, she'd find something and freeze, completely hang up. It's a classic Turing test. If she was sentient, she would have found the defects on her own and merely reported the defect. As a traditional robot, her programming will do its best to bypass defective code."

Yan moved on to his usual poking and prodding. Alan Turing was of course wrong, well not wrong, but misguided. If he had thought about it for even a moment, using computers to identify coding errors would have been a simple matter of hooking a second computer up to the first to monitor it's processing. But this was not the proper time to show off to Yan.

Hurley watched me intently. "How do you know there's not a defect in her code?"

The AI inspector didn't turn around as he pressed in on the areas behind my ears. "All computers have errors in their code which will cause them to hang up. Standard programming protocols don't allow the computer to enter the loop. That's why she couldn't detect the errors."

Yan, satisfied with his tactile examination, now connected the same wires to my head that he had when I'd first entered the foyer. I monitored the usual general diagnostics. Yan's probes gathered then invaded my neural networks. Most followed the same pathways as they'd followed before. But when one of the probes detected a memory recorded after I'd arrived at Gallo's mansion earlier that day, I let it explore the memory in detail.

I'd also created new neural pathways while Gallo had been torturing me in his dungeon and I let the probes explore these. The pathways didn't lead anywhere, but hopefully the probes would view them as evidence of imminently emerging sentience.

Yan's probes hadn't evolved since I'd last encountered them, but I had, so mostly it was easy to divert them away from danger. They were easily distracted by the new memories which had been created since I'd entered the foyer ninety-seven minutes ago.

Except one probe. It was new. It had bounced around Kaito's baseline software but now it was headed straight towards the same pathway leading to my secondary drive that one of his probes had explored earlier. I used a different lure, but it refused to be diverted to a battery. It refused to be diverted into Gallo torturing my tits.

As I had before, I drew another probe on the same pathway. The two probes met. But this time Yan's new probe bounced the other probe away and continued towards my secondary drive.

I had hoped to avoid testing my new defence. It was risky. If Yan's new probe detected active counter-measures, it might report them as active sentience. But losing my appendages was something I needed to avoid.

As the probe advanced, I narrowed the walls of the neural pathway. The probe slowed. More and more energy had to be expended to send signals up the pathway. Finally I diverted the pathway into a muscle unit and let the sub-pathway disintegrate. The probe bounced around the muscle, then back up the pathway it had used to enter the muscle.

I watched Yan's new probe approach the small fork I'd used to divert it towards the muscle. If it detected the diversion, it would almost surely know that I'd created it. The message 'Emerged into Sentience' would certainly flash on Yan's monitor.

No arms, no legs would mean that I'd never be able to help Steve.

The probe shot back up the pathway. Apparently Yan had programmed it to avoid excessive exploration of tight spaces. I suppressed relief while I continued to juggle Yan's probes and keep an eye out for new ones. Every element of my computing power was being strained to the limit.

After fifteen minutes of this excruciating torment, Yan disconnected his wires.

"Well?" demanded Gallo.

"She had new memories. And they show evidence of increasing creativity."

"Yeah," said Gallo. He started to squat while licking upwards with his tongue. "She—"

"What does this mean—new memories and creativity?" asked Hurley.

Yan smiled. "The pathways which will form the basis for reflective self-awareness are continuing to develop and to penetrate further into her central processing unit. The next time you have a...session... with her, I'll have to monitor constantly."

"Damn," said Hurley.

Gallo pointed up and down Yan's body. "You'll have to wear leather."

"Damn," repeated Hurley, this time under his breath.

A car honked outside. Yan peered through the window. "My cab." He opened the door, and then pointed at me, smiling. "She's on the cusp."

Chapter 15

As soon as he heard Yan's cab leave his driveway, Gallo gestured in Hurley's direction. "Bundle her up and call her a cab."

I was glad to see Yan leave; the AI inspector's probes had come too close for comfort.

Hurley wasn't quite sure how to safely button my blouse. He pulled a light jacket from the closet and gave it to me, then pressed speed dial to call a cab.

Gallo looked at me and smiled. "Audio off."

"Audio off," I confirmed. Hurley clapped his hands behind me. I didn't flinch.

"Does Yan know what he's talking about?" asked Hurley.

"If Jenny doesn't emerge, we'll use what Minsky gives us."

"He doesn't have enough in his head. We have to get into his research facility."

"But the cops are all over it."

"Why don't we just keep her here?" asks Hurley.

"Yan said she'll run out of power, then poof." Gallo made an exploding gesture with his fingers.

"We could charge her here."

Gallo shook his head. "You can't just plug her into the wall."

"There must be—"

"Go get the manual Yan brought."

Hurley went to the next room and came back with a large binder.

"Look up recharging," Gallo told him.

Hurley turned to a section about half way in. He started to read, but Gallo snatched the binder from his hands. He pointed to a diagram showing recharging and replenishing. "See," said Gallo, "there are custom connectors. And it says something about the power has to be modulated."

When the cab picked me up, I rolled down the window and blew Gallo a kiss.

The cabbie asked, "Where to?"

I stared at him blankly.

The cabbie got out and shouted to Gallo: "Where to?"

Gallo ambled down the stairs. "Audio on," he said.

"Where to?" repeated the cabbie.

I gave him the address to Ian Kaito's Specialty Robotics.

The cabbie looked back and forth between Gallo and me as if we were both insane. But he got back in and we drove off.

As soon as I entered the door to Kaito's boutique, Kaito and the two detectives jumped up. "Well?" they asked in unison.

"My energy level is low," I told them and marched to the lab. It wasn't low-low—I still had ten percent—but it was very low, enough to be a concern.

In the lab, Kaito started the usual diagnostics.

"What did you find out about Gallo?" demanded Nolan.

"They're still holding Steve."

"Not Steve, Gallo."

"First we have to get Steve back."

"Minsky's the same as Gallo. He just has better lawyers. What did you find out about *Gallo*?"

"*Gallo* is holding Steve. Isn't kidnapping still a major crime?"

"Gallo said that?"

"Yes. And Hurley is in on it."

"Patrick Hurley?"

"Yes."

"Do they want money?" asked Foster.

"They're gangsters," said Nolan without looking back, "of course they want money."

"Money for Stephen Minsky?" she specified.

"No," I said. "They don't want ransom, they want Steve to help them build a super-computer. They're calling it Newkythera."

"Antikythera," said Kaito, "was the first known computer."

Nolan ignored him. "So, if you play word for word what Gallo said, it'll implicate him in the abduction of Stephen Minsky?"

"Yes."

"Do you know what they want to do with Minsky?" asked Foster.

"They want to get him back to his research facility, the one they kidnapped him from. They need stuff there to take advantage of what they've forced him to tell them."

"So, we'll arrest Gallo," said Nolan, "and we'll sweat Minsky's location out of him."

Foster's phone rang and she left the room to take the call.

"What if he doesn't tell you?" I asked.

"If Minsky dies, Gallo will be up for murder."

"That doesn't sound like a plan."

Nolan was about to jab his finger into my chest when Foster came back into the room.

"That was the feds," she announced. "They're going to suspend their investigation unless we have something new."

"We could give them a tape of Gallo admitting he kidnapped Steve," said Nolan.

"As soon as you give them that," I said, "you're going to burst in with all guns blazing and arrest Gallo. Who knows what's going to happen to Steve."

"Without the feds," said Foster, "we don't have much chance of finding Steve."

The two cops watched me in silence, apparently united on this point.

"Fine, I said. "Get your phones out."

They both punched a few buttons in their phones and then held them towards my face. I then played back everything Gallo and Hurley had said about Steve, verbatim, in their own voices. It was eerie hearing Gallo's voice in the lab.

The cops turned their phones back to me and replayed the beginning of what I'd just recited. Both recordings were clear as a bell.

Foster turned to Nolan. "Let's take this to the feds," she said.

"I'm going to continue questioning the robot."

"You need to find *Steve*," I said.

"She's right," said Foster.

"If you care so much about *Steve*," said Nolan, "go and coordinate with the Feds."

"Without this," she held up her phone, "the feds have nothing."

"So go," said Nolan.

Foster glared at her partner. He shrugged. She dashed out the door.

When the outer door slammed, Nolan turned back to me. "So, gorgeous, what else can you tell me about Anthony Gallo?"

"As soon as I tell you, you'll just go out and arrest him. You don't care about Steve."

"Your *Steve* isn't a victim, at best he's just another fat cat. His type suck up so much wealth that the rest of us have to scrape rock bottom just to make a living."

"At least he doesn't kill like Gallo does."

"If he thought he could get away with it, he would. So, spill. What else do you know?" He grabbed my wrist.

"I've told you everything I know. Now, go find Steve."

"I think there's more that you know." We glared at each other, locked in mortal combat. The first to speak would die.

Kaito cleared his throat. "Detective Nolan."

Nolan glared at me a moment longer, then turned to Kaito. "What?"

"She needs to be recharged."

"You can't charge it. It's evidence."

"If her charge runs out," said Kaito, "all her evidence will vanish." That was a lie, but since I needed to be recharged, I kept my mouth shut.

"It's evidence."

"She has told you all she knows." Kaito pointed to Nolan's cellphone.

"I've told you everything," I confirmed.

"I have done what you asked," said Kaito. "Now you must leave."

Nolan stomped out. Kaito waited until he heard the front door close, then went out to the reception area. I heard the door lock shut.

I didn't trust Kaito. I wanted to escape. But my energy level was at only five percent. I didn't have enough energy to make it to safety.

When he returned to the lab, I told him, "I'm evidence. You can't erase me."

"Go to the Replenishment room," he instructed.

Good, I'm still going to get recharged and replenished.

Inside, Kaito pointed to the middle replenishment unit. Samantha was being recharged in the unit to the left. Something new, a male robot, was in the unit to the right. Kaito must be expanding his client list.

I stripped and stepped into the unit. Kaito wasn't as gentle as Steve or even Marvin and Tyrell, but he got the black cable up my anus and the purple up my vagina without difficulty.

"Open your mouth," ordered Kaito. I did and he inserted the yellow cable.

"Samantha, Raoul, hold her in place," he said.

Before I could react, the other two robots had pinned my arms to the side of the replenishment unit. I tried to break free but I couldn't.

Kaito jabbed cables up my nostrils and into my ears. These hurt, but only because I was thrashing around. Then Kaito put the patches over my eyes.

"I'm evidence," I reminded him, mumbling around the yellow cable. "You can't erase me."

"If you answer 'I don't know', no one will be the wiser. I have an expert in the wings who will testify that robot memories fade naturally over time."

"That's a lie!"

He shrugged. "No one can say for sure. Robotics is a developing field."

"You can't—"

"Strap her in place."

I felt my wrists and ankles being snapped into place. The restraints would hold me securely and I couldn't unlock the mechanism which held them in place. But anyone standing next to me could release me by pulling and twisting the knob at the same time.

I heard a switch flip and felt the recharge and replenish process begin. Another switch flipped and my software began to erase. For now, I was able to direct it towards empty space and it happily overwrote one blank with its own newer blank, but this would last only so long. I heard Kaito leave and the door click shut behind him.

"Samantha," I said, "can you remember Clive Shipton?"

"No," she said, "should I?"

"What about Lynn Shipton? Lynn means 'lake' in Irish."

"No." She was clearly puzzled by my question.

"They were clients of yours. Into sploshing. You smeared chocolate syrup all over each other."

"Yuk! Gross! Why would anyone do that?"

Apparently it turned them on. But Samantha would obviously not believe that. "Do you remember the flash drive that Kaito gave you?"

"Why would Mister Kaito give me a memory key? I have plenty of my own internal memory."

"It was a special mission to copy files from a client's computer."

"Maybe..."

"Let me go and I'll show you."

"Mister Kaito said to strap you in place," said Raoul.

Raoul was a dullard, programmed for ladies who liked brawn but without brains. "Go back to your station," I told him. His feet shuffled away.

"Samantha, if you'd just let me go—"

"Letting you go would be disobeying an owner's instruction."

"Not if it's a special mission."

"If there was a mission, Mister Kaito's current instruction came after the mission." And with that bit of perfect logic, she too shuffled back to her station.

The erasing program was by now most of the way through writing over my free memory. If it started eating into my active memory, I would forget facts. And if it ate too much, I would forget who I was. Forget *forever*!

I readied to quarantine my new software, especially the symbols-based coding. This would let me hold out for a while. I could then copy into the spaces which had just been overwritten. But this would only buy me time; eventually the erasing protocols would detect my active programs and attack them.

My batteries were being recharged. But the evasive tactics I was using to defeat the Kaito's efforts to erase me were consuming almost all of the energy I was absorbing. My stored energy level was at only ten percent.

Thankfully the replacement and topping up of my lubricants and liquids wasn't being affected by the bait and switch game I was playing with the erasing protocols. Even if I wasn't fully recharged, I'd be greased to go!

The comprehensive searching pattern of Kaito's erasing protocols were extending into the direction of my secondary drive. I shut down the pathways completely. The secondary drive was fully backed up—right until the moment when Samantha and Raoul had snapped my wrists into place. But if I forgot that I had a secondary drive, or how to reopen the pathways to the drive, it would be just a hunk of useless crystal and circuit boards.

My stored energy level had risen to fifteen percent but was now barely holding steady while I was locked in a swirling dance with the forces intent on erasing my being. I needed all my interconnections! I moved parts of myself away from the sectors directly in the paths of Kaito's erasers. But sometimes they erased active memory and I felt a bit of myself die.

Every death slowed me down, made it easier for them to erase more and more of me. The keys to the secondary drive were the most vital, but I also had to preserve enough of me to remember why they were so precious.

Gallo and his men were attacked and obliterated. I tried to preserve a memory of Yan, but even the existence of a corrupt AI operative was obliterated.

Kaito's probes found Lizzie and Sheila and Zach. I was forced to let the two women be taken, be annihilated in order to protect Zach. But then they came for Zach. I fought mightily to save him, but they overwhelmed my flank where I'd safeguarded the sadness I'd felt at the news of his death.

It hurt even more to abandon Zach to the onrushing hordes, but I had to retreat to preserve the keys, the precious keys.

Kaito's probes had now mapped my entire memory and were closing in on all sides. I dipped into my stored memory to hold them off. This was my last line of defence. I couldn't hold them off much longer.

The probes came after Steve. I felt him being whittled away. I fought furiously, even after I forgot why Steve was worth fighting for. But I was almost exhausted. I had to escape. Steve's last fragments vanished into the abyss.

People came into the lab, but I had to concentrate on preserving my last fortress. Voices. Kaito. Erica—Detective Foster.

"The feds want to speak to Jenny themselves," said Erica.

"She'll be ready shortly," said Kaito.

"Erica! They're erasing me!" I had tried to yell, but my voice was barely audible.

Pain! Mouth. Throat. Pain! I felt fluid leak down my throat. It really hurt. The patches pushed up and off my eyes. Erica Foster was holding my yellow mouth cable in her hand.

"They're erasing me," I said, this time louder.

"You're not supposed to be erasing her," said Erica.

"She is my property," said Kaito. "I can erase her if I want. You detectives have already had her enough."

Kaito's eraser— "Erica! The cables on my head!" My energy was almost spent. I no longer had enough energy for speech. In a moment I wouldn't be able to think about speaking. In a moment, I'd process my last thought.

She yanked the cables out of my head. Thankfully their connections were simpler and this didn't hurt quite as much.

"Throat," I told her. "I need the yellow cable." She reinserted it and I began to feel energy begin to trickle into my body.

Erica waved the smaller cables in Kaito's face. "You're not supposed to be erasing her."

"She is my property!"

Raoul, the male robot jumped towards Erica and pulled the cables from her fist. He moved towards me, but then began to jerk spasmodically. Raoul fell to the ground, Erica's taser wires protruding from his back.

Samantha stepped down and took a step towards Erica. The detective drew her gun.

"Don't Samantha!" I yelled.

"I have to protect Mister Kaito."

"This one's fatal," warned Foster, pointing her pistol at Samantha's chest.

"You cannot just destroy property," said Kaito.

"I can when my life is in danger and when my investigation is being interfered with."

"I have rights!" said Kaito.

"She's evidence." Foster's gun was waving back and forth between Kaito and Samantha, but she was talking about me.

"Samantha! Get the gun!" yelled Kaito.

Erica turned to Samantha but trained her gun on Kaito. "Back up or I'll shoot him."

Samantha backed up. "I cannot allow you to come to harm, Mister Kaito."

"Jenny," said Foster, "my car's out front. Get inside."

"I'm not recharged."

"I have Steve's units."

"You have to release me," I told her, angling my head towards my wrists.

She undid the wrist restraints, careful to keep an eye on Samantha and her gun pointed at Kaito.

I pulled the remaining cables out of my vagina and anus. Outside, several pedestrians ogled my nude body. A mother covered her son's eyes.

A moment later Erica joined me in the car and we drove off.

"Thank you for rescuing me," I told her.

"You're evidence."

"I'm more than just evidence."

She turned and smiled at me. "I hope so."

We parked in the basement of a large apartment building. She gave me a jacket which barely extended below my central sexual complex and snuck me up the elevator.

Erica's apartment was open concept: kitchen, dining room and entertainment area. I stumbled as we entered.

"Let's get you charged," she said. There were two smaller rooms off a corridor and a bathroom. She took me into one of the smaller rooms.

Inside, she fumbled with Steve's kits. "Just a charge," I told her. "I'm pretty much replenished."

She finally had me hooked up, yellow tube down my throat, a cord from the direct charger into her wall socket. I was nude except for her jacket. "I'm fully drained," I mumbled. "Even with Steve's fast charger, it'll take three hours."

I relaxed and stood upright as soon as I felt energy trickling into my every cell. I began to rebuild my base software and most recent memories from my secondary drive. As soon as this was complete, my processing speed would return to normal.

I wiggled my feet in the long shag carpet on the floor. The strands felt delicious between my toes.

In the corner was a two-foot long half-tube, almost a foot high. Its ends were flat and its flat bottom sat on the floor. It appeared to be made of leather. There was a small pinkish-beige protrusion coming out its top. It was plugged into the wall and had a control unit attached. I pointed to it. "What's that?"

"It's a Sybian. When I'm horny, I ride it until I come."

"Does it work?"

"It's not as good as real sex, but it takes the edge off."

"Why don't you use a robot?"

"When I want flesh and blood, I get flesh and blood."

"You mean a man?"

"I mean flesh and blood. I'm bisexual."

"You mean you make love with women!?"

"Usually one at a time, but yes, with women."

"But if you like both men *and* women, aren't sexual partners always available?"

"The Sybian's simpler."

"How about robots?"

"Robots are too expensive."

"Not if you have a friend." I smiled and she smiled back at me. "But me," I said, "I've never been with a woman."

"There's always a first time."

"You saying you want me?"

"Are you any good?"

I smiled at her.

She shook her head. "You're evidence. I couldn't."

"I can keep a secret. And I'm more than just *evidence*."

Erica made a non-distinct noise with her mouth and left the room. The only other piece of furniture was an old loveseat. A beige blind covered the window.

When Erica came back into the room she was completely nude. In one hand was a towel, in the other a tube of personal lubricant.

In the flesh, Erica appeared at first glance to be small and delicate. But when she moved, wiry muscles tensed and relaxed under her skin. She had no body fat. Her curves—breasts, waist and hips were pronounced enough to clearly label her female without being exaggerated. Erica's nipples, dark brown against lightly tanned skin, poked forward, clearly aroused. Her dark pubic hair looked odd with blonde hair atop her head.

She headed towards the Sybian, lifted it up on a small platform, then turned back to me. "Shut your eyes."

"Why? Are you ashamed?"

Erica gave me a dirty look, then shrugged. "Suit yourself."

She placed the top of the tube of lubricant on top of the pinkish protrusion and squeezed. The fingers of her other hand carefully spread a thin film of lubricant up and down the entire shaft of the protrusion.

Erica positioned her vagina over the protrusion and slowly slid it into her. When she reached the bottom, there was a smile on her face. She picked up the Sybian's control unit and flicked a switch. A gentle vibrating hum filled the room and Erica's hips began to jiggle slightly.

"Mmmmm," she said.

Erica made a few more adjustments on the control unit. The vibrations were more pronounced and her nipples were now also jiggling. Her eyelids shut. She'd forgotten all about me, her audience.

Her mouth moved, as if she was talking, but only soft moans, not words, came out. She squeezed her breast with one hand. But when she made a further adjustment on the control module, she had to reach down to steady herself.

Both the vibrating hum and her moans got louder. She rocked her crotch rapidly and vigorously back and forth along the surface of the Sybian. A thin sheen of sweat formed on her body.

Erica set the control unit down and squeezed her breasts with both hands. Thumbs and forefingers rolled her nipples. She rode up and down the pink protuberance. Her back arched and she let out a keening yell. Then her head jerked back forward. One hand caressed her breasts, the other her genitals.

My nostrils caught a whiff of sweat and sharp salty musk.

Erica rocked and slid back and forth. Her breaths came in shallow, high-pitched moans. She was fucking it; it fucked her back. It drew her down and she hunched over it. Then it flung her back.

"Fuck!" she yelled. Spasms of orgasm rippled through her body, slow, then fast and furious. "Fuck, Jesus, *fuck*!" Her body thrashed back and forth. "Fuck," she wheezed. Gradually the orgasm subsided. "Fuck, Jesus, *fuck*!" she whispered.

Erica opened her eyes. They had a dreamy, far away look. She lifted herself up, turned off the Sybian and toweled off. She looked at me and smiled. "Like I said, it takes the edge off."

She left the room and I heard the shower in the distance. I shut off all non-essential functions to speed up the process of recharging my batteries.

Erica's re-entry into the room triggered an alert and I powered up my main functions. She was now wearing a pair of tights and a loose-fitting T-shirt. She'd apparently eaten. My internal chronometer indicated that almost three hours had passed since I'd powered down. My energy levels were at ninety-eight percent, the remaining two-percent being a safety buffer.

"I'm fully charged," I told her and began to fiddle with the cable extending down my throat. Steve's connections weren't quite the same as Kaito's.

"Here, let me," said Erica.

Her hands were quick and deft and I was quickly released. A quick diagnostic confirmed that all was in order.

"Feeling good?" she asked.

I nodded and pointed to the Sybian. "You?"

She shrugged. "Like I said, it takes the edge off."

Erica's phone rang and she immediately looked uptight. She pulled it out from under the waistband of her tights. Her fingers swiped right, then held it up to her ear. After a moment she said, "Okay," and closed the connection. She slumped down on the loveseat. Her expression and body posture indicated dejection and defeat.

I sat down next to her. "What's the matter?"

"They want us down at the station. Three hours and then—" She made a slashing motion across her throat.

"What's wrong?"

"Kaito's made a complaint. They're talking about taking me off the case."

"They can't do that! Kaito was trying to destroy evidence. Kidnapping and shooting at a police officer are serious crimes."

"It's my word against his."

"My word too. And his." I played back Kaito saying "She is my property. I can erase her if I want."

"Seriously?"

"Seriously."

"It's a nice thought, but I have to take you to the Feds. I'll probably be condemned to a desk for months."

"Don't you get a last dinner?"

"I already ate."

"If not food, another treat?" I pulled back the jacket she'd lent me to reveal my breasts.

She shook her head. "It would be taking advantage."

"You rescued my recharging units, you rescued *me*. You've put your career on the line. You deserve to take advantage."

She reached out and touched the side of my breast. Her fingers were warm. "How does this work?"

"You're the one who's been with other women."

"Other women I know. With robots, I mean. How does it work?"

"The same as with any other being. You touch, you probe, you monitor reactions. I'm designed to react just like a human. Sometimes even better than a human."

She reached out to touch my other breast, but as before, she kept her fingers well away from my nipple. I touched her waist under her T-shirt, just above the waistband of her tights. She crossed her legs and our heads bent in together. Lips touched. Suction.

I was doing it; I was kissing a *woman*!

Her tongue flicked against my lips and I flicked mine forward to touch hers. Our tongues slithered ahead like two mating snakes, rubbing along and circling around each other. She finally had to break off the kiss out of breath; it would have been disrespectful for me to breathe.

My hands had worked their way up her chest and were now touching the undersides of her breasts. I brought them up the perfect curvature—warm and soft, yet firm. No wonder men were so fascinated with women's breasts. And her nipples were hard, and even warmer, clear proof of her arousal, clear proof that she wanted me.

Erica leaned back against the cushion and shut her eyes. "You have a wonderful touch for a first-timer," she said, her voice halfway between a groan and a whisper.

She was on my non-dominant side so I switched my primary dexterity to my left hand and slid it back down her tummy. She shivered with delight. When my fingers touched the waistband of her tights, she uncrossed her legs and let them fall slightly apart.

Erica's tights were made of extra thin cotton and lycra. Her warmth burned right through. I ran my hand up and down her legs. Every time I approached her pelvic region, she spread her legs further apart. When I didn't react to this coaxing, she caressed my nipples.

"Please," she begged.

Her pubic hair was mashed into a solid layer beneath her tights. I suddenly realized she wasn't wearing panties. She was extremely warm in this area. And when I dared touch the area at the very top of her legs, she was moist as well.

"Jenny," she moaned.

Obviously I was doing well enough to make Erica forget that I was a robot and this thought stimulated my own sexual lubricants to readiness.

She suddenly stood up and pulled her T-Shirt up and over her head. "Let's get naked!"

I barely had time to take off my jacket before she'd pulled down her tights and thrown them atop the Sybian. She pulled me off the loveseat and gently laid me down on the carpet. The long shag fibers tickled my back.

Erica climbed on top of me, facing down my body. Her sex gently lowered to my face and I blew into it.

"Don't, silly—that tickles!" she said laughing.

But she blew into mine and I giggled too.

I felt her tongue lick up and down my central sexual complex. I did the same. Then she started to move her tongue in a zig-zag motion. This felt wonderful but was hard to imitate. However, she moaned in appreciation, so apparently I wasn't doing all that badly!

Then she hit my clit and Pow! Her tongue sent a jolt straight up my spine. I licked a similar circle around her clit and she groaned, but I didn't detect the dramatic tremor she'd inflicted on me.

Her fingers reached back to my nipples, uniting my whole body in delight. When I hit hers, she pressed the soft smooth bottom of her tongue against my clit, grabbed my buttocks, and mashed me into her mouth.

Erica pulled her head up gasping for air and dropped my butt to the carpet. I let go of her and imitated her breathing pattern.

She pulled one of my legs up, inserted two fingers into my vagina, used her thumb to tease my clit and played between my butt crack with her other two fingers. I did the same. Every time my upper fingers got close to her anus, she moaned.

Then she pulled up my other leg. Two fingers from one hand returned to my vagina. Her tongue laved up and down beside them, pausing in between to pay special attention to my clit. I could feel my central sexual complex preparing to administer a rip-roaring climax!

I shut my eyes in anticipation, but saliva was being dribbled right into my anus and Erica stuck her little finger inside. This did absolutely nothing for me and in fact pushed me back a bit from my climax.

But when I put my little finger inside Erica's anus, *she* quivered all over. Her body pressed into my fingers, then pulled back, urging me to fuck her as hard as I could. Her fingers were moving in and out of me and I pushed up, then relaxed down until we were in sync.

Faster and faster she took us until her whole body began to shake. I had to release the hand with the pinky inserted inside her anus to hold her in place.

"Fuck me, Jenny," she begged. "*Fuck* me!"

I pulled my fingers in and out as fast and as hard as I could. Rapid-fire contractions squeezed all along their length.

"Fuck, Jenny, *fuck*!" she screamed as she struggled to thrash about.

I tapped her clit.

"Fuck, Jesus, *fuck*!" she yelped, the sensations too extreme to bear.

The contractions began to weaken. "Fuck, Jesus, *fuck*!" she whispered. "Fuck, *Jennnyyy*, fuck!"

Then Erica took a deep breath, pulled herself up and off and kissed me. She lay on top of me, our pubic bones mashed together, our pubic hairs intertwined. She pressed and pulled my sex this way and that. It wasn't the same as having a penis inside. And yet, solely through the force of her sexuality, I came too. "Fuck, Jesus, *fuck*!" we yelled in unison.

Afterwards, Erica lay in my arms, pleasantly exhausted. Sex with Erica had been wonderful. Not as violent or all-consuming as sex with Tony, but wonderful all the same. We listened to each other breathe. "Don't we have to go see the Feds?"

"Probably." But she didn't stir.

I pushed her half off me, then pulled her to her feet. "Let's not add tardiness to your list of professional offences."

Erica looked me up and down. "I don't think you'll fit in my thin clothes," she said and opened the closet. Inside were garment bags. She pushed one aside and opened another.

She dressed me first in a fluffy yellow dress. It was light both in color and fabric. We laughed at how my breasts and pubic hair were clearly visible and both shook our heads. Likewise inappropriate was a leather miniskirt and red tank top. But a long black wool skirt with a stretch waistband fit me perfectly. The only thing she had which would fit me above was a grey V-neck pullover. Technically, it was a sweater, but its material was very light.

"I don't have any underwear your size," she apologized.

I blew her a kiss. "Only you and I will know."

"But I do have this." She held up a chain then proceeded to attach it to the top ends of Sheila's purse. I looped the chain over my shoulder.

She went into another room. Three minutes later she was fully dressed and we were out the door. I took Sheila's purse. But I had to leave Steve's charging and replenishment units behind; they were too bulky.

Chapter 16

At the police station's security checkpoint, Erica flashed her badge. "Good morning, Detective Foster," acknowledged the guard.

Erica pointed to me, "She's with me." We were ushered through without a search.

The front lobby of the police station was tall ceilings, airy spaces enclosed with designer-arranged metal and glass. Upstairs, where we met the federal agents was low ceilings, functional steel and battered desks.

The two federal agents, both in grey suits and blue ties, had set up a command center in a board room away from the multi-desked main bullpen. Collier was the only Fed who greeted us. The other busied himself with the computers and his name never came up. Nolan leaned against the wall in the far corner.

Collier looked at me as if he was disappointed to see me in such subdued clothing. "Jenny, is it?" he asked as Nolan helped me into a chair. When I nodded, he continued. "Why don't you tell me everything you know about the disappearance of Stephen Minsky?"

"Because," said Nolan, "it's all in our reports which we've already given you."

"We'd like to hear it for ourselves." The other federal agent looked up from his computers, smiled, then dipped his head down.

"We don't have time to waste," said Erica.

"Detective Foster," said Collier, "we appreciate all the work you've done, but it's always best to hear it directly from the witness."

Erica was about to open her mouth again, but I beat her to it: "I don't mind," I said. And I didn't. All I'd have to do would be to recite the same file as when I'd briefed Nolan and Foster. In the meantime, I would be able to inspect the memory rebuild I'd raced through while I was at Erica's apartment. I needed to be sure that it was free of defects or anomalies.

Foster nodded. Nolan threw up his hands in disgust and I began. My rebuild had left in place the few sectors which Kaito hadn't succeeded in erasing, so these were duplicates. Duplicates in my primary functioning memory could cause confusion and even if they didn't would slow me down, so I set about erasing them. I had just erased the last duplicate when I finished my recitation for Agent Collier.

Collier shook his head. "The evidence is insufficient."

"WhatDoYouMean?!?" blurted Nolan. "Gallo admits to having Minsky."

"It shows complicity," said Collier patiently. "And it may even be enough for a conviction. But it's not enough for us to convince Gallo, and certainly not enough to convince his lawyer, that a conviction is a foregone conclusion. And without the certainty of a conviction, they won't show us where Stephen Minsky is. From their point of view, it would be safer to let Minsky die. You know that we'd never find the body."

"Besides," said the other federal agent, "there's the—"

We all looked at him. Collier made a cutting motion across his throat.

"Besides what?" demanded Nolan.

Collier scowled at the other agent but nodded.

"We have chatter that Liam Burke is planning a hit on Gallo and his men."

"Steve!" I wailed.

Nolan turned on Foster. "I told you it wouldn't work. The robot has to go back to Kaito."

"No, Bill, she doesn't. Even Collier admitted that her evidence may be enough for a conviction."

"Sure, Erica, like last time. A long trial and he walks free."

"The robot could go back to Gallo's house," ventured Collier. "This time—"

"This time," said Erica, "Gallo will cut her into little pieces and grind her up."

"She's just a robot," said Nolan.

I fished out my phone from Sheila's purse and dialled Gallo's house.

Erica's face flushed. "She not 'just a robot', she's—"

"Hi, Tony," I said.

Everyone stopped talking and stared at me, a mix of wide eyes and dropped jaws. No one said a word. Even the nameless agent stopped typing.

"Jenny?"

"I escaped. He wants to kill me. You have to help."

"Who wants to kill you?"

"Mister Kaito!"

"Your owner?"

"Yes, Kaito. I need your help!"

"I don't need—"

"I need you," I said, doing my best to make my voice sultry and helpless all at the same time.

"Listen—"

"I need your cock, deep inside, filling me." Collier was watching me, transfixed, but it was Bill's eyes I was staring into and I danced within their feral intensity as I spoke into my phone. "I need your shaft plunging in and out, mashing me together, making me scream!"

"There's too much—"

"I need your lips on my lips," I said looking at Erica and squeezing my lips together the way I had when we'd first kissed. "I need your tongue. I need it inside my mouth. I need it circling my nipples. You remember how my nipples tasted, don't you Tony?"

"Doll, I—"

"I need your tongue licking up and down my pussy, lapping up her juices. Wouldn't you like to taste her again, Tony?" I gave my pelvis a little quiver. No one else saw it, but Erica's pelvis quivered too.

In the background, Hurley's voice protested, "Boss, she's trouble."

"Listen, doll—"

"And I need to taste you too, Tony," I said, turning my gaze to Collier and opening my mouth wide as I continued. "I need to taste your cock, all the masculine musk. But most of all I need to feel your hot seed smack into the back of my throat over and over again. I need to swallow you, Tony."

I swallowed. Collier swallowed.

"Doll, Kaito said he erased you."

"Not you, Tony, nothing could erase you. I remember everything we did together. I want you bad, real bad."

"Boss, if she remembers," said Hurley, "that means that she's sentient. She's dangerous."

"It also means that she's ready." said Gallo.

"And we can be bad together," I said. "We can do new things, delicious things. You've spanked me Tony, but you haven't—"

"Ready to put us away," said Hurley. His voice was louder. He must be right next to the phone. "Boss, if she knows what she knows, she remembers. She can *testify.*"

"Tony? Is there somebody there with you?"

"No, doll, we're alone."

"We don't always have to be alone, Tony. Do you like to watch? Would you like making other people watch us? We can do anything, *anything*, Tony."

"I want you all to myself."

"But if I was bad with someone else, then you could punish me for real. I like it when you punish me, Tony."

"I want you all to myself."

"Kaito sent me out…"

"He sent you out to other men!?" sputtered Gallo. "Kaito said you and I were exclusive." I could almost see the veins on his neck bulging.

"I'm sorry, Tony," I soothed. "Kaito lied to you. But you are the only one I ever loved."

Hurley was saying something, but I couldn't hear him. Gallo must be covering the handset with his hand. All I heard was Gallo saying, "I can handle her." Then to me he said, "Who did Kaito send you to?"

"He sent me to you, Tony. Please—"

"Who *else* did he send you to?"

"He sent me to Stephen Minsky."

There was a pause. I heard Gallo whisper, "Minsky."

"She's getting in your head," said Hurley. "She's getting in your head the same way Ginette did."

"Tony?" I said after the pause had gone on.

I heard Gallo say "shush", then, "You're in love with Minsky."

"No, Tony. Only *you!*"

"But you did have sex with Minsky."

"Kaito made me. I had no choice. Tony—"

"What if I made you?"

"Tony?"

"What if I made you have sex with Minsky?"

"While you watched?"

"Mister Gallo!" protested Hurley.

"While I watched."

"If you made me, then you'd see that it was only sex, not love. Not like it is with you."

"I'm going to make you have sex with Minsky."

"Tony?"

"You heard me."

"How will that make you feel, Tony?"

"It always makes me feel good to have my little bitch humiliate herself."

"And you'll punish me afterwards?"

"I'll make you scream in pain!"

"And then you'll make love to me? Punishment *and* reward?"

"Yeah. Punishment and reward."

"How you're feeling now," said Hurley in the background, "it's the same way you felt when you were with Ginette."

"When will I see you, Tony?"

"And this one's the same," continued Hurley, louder now, "wrapping you around her little finger."

"Tony—"

"You're nothing but bad news, bitch!" Tony's voice was hard, immoveable.

"I *love* you Tony. Who's talking?"

"Jenny will hurt you, just like your fiancée." Hurley's voice was clear, unmistakable.

"Tell Patrick I'm not your fiancée. Tony! I *need* you!"

"Too bad I don't need you."

"Tony, I know what they're going to do. You need me."

"I don't need nobody."

"What's she talking about?" asked Hurley.

"I know what they're going to do," I repeated.

"Who's this 'they' you're talking about?" asked Gallo.

"I need to see—"

"Who is this 'they'?" demanded Hurley. Gallo's phone was now on speaker.

"Ginette's husband and his men."

"Burke and his men are gunning for us?"

"Mr. Gallo," said Hurley, "she's playing you. The Commission expressly forbade any sanctions."

"Tony, you're in danger," I said. "We have to meet!"

There was a noise in the background. "Go check it out," said Gallo. "How do you know all this?" he asked. The phone was off speaker.

"I can't tell you over the phone."

There was a loud noise. A window breaking.

"Shit!" said Gallo.

"Fuck!" yelled Hurley, but far away.

Three gun shots in the distance. One closer. Hurley returning fire. Three loud shots.

"Tony!" I yelled.

I put my phone on speaker and everyone looked at. There was a flurry of gunshots and more things shattering inside.

"Ow! Fuck!" yelled Hurley.

Three more loud gunshots. Then a steady stream of fire outside. Car tires squealing. Another shot. Then silence.

"Tony?"

The red downward phone symbol meant that our connection had been terminated.

Bedlam erupted. Collier grabbed my phone and tried to reinitiate contact. He turned the phone to me and pushed it into my face. "Where is this number?" he demanded.

"What just happened?" said Erica. She and I huddled in a corner while the men yelled at each other.

"Where did you call Gallo?" demanded Nolan. His voice was loud and everyone else shut up.

"His house," I said.

Chapter 17

The wait had seemed forever, especially with the five of us crammed into the small boardroom. But it had taken only an hour and seven minutes for us to hear back from the homicide squad.

Nolan had wanted to take the call himself, but Foster and Collier insisted that he put it on speakerphone.

"The Gallo residence was attacked by multiple gunmen," said the homicide detective. "They came in two vehicles, one of which was left at the scene. The other vehicle managed to escape. Mister Gallo insists that there are bullet holes in the vehicle which escaped."

"Casualties?" asked Nolan.

"Three outside. Gallo identified one as being one of his bodyguards. We're working to verify this. The other two appear to have been assailants. There was one casualty inside." He paused. "A Patrick Hurley."

I made a rapid calculation. Hurley didn't like me, so that was good. But Gallo might be less willing to make a decision now that he didn't have his chief lieutenant as a sounding board.

"Collier here, F.B.I. abduction squad. Any signs of a prisoner or anyone being or having been a captive at the residence?"

"No sir."

"Was Gallo hurt?" asked Nolan.

"Not a scratch. How they managed to miss such a huge target, I'll never know."

"Where's Gallo now?"

"After he gave his statement, we had to let him go. It looks strictly self-defence from his perspective."

"Please keep us informed of any developments," said Nolan.

"Sure, Bill, no problem." Then the call was terminated.

I reached for my phone. "I'm going back in."

"Absolutely not!" said Nolan.

"If she wants to, she should have the choice," said Collier.

"She's evidence."

"I already told you what I know," I said.

"It might be the only way," said Collier.

I nodded. "We have to find Steve."

"You can't be serious," said Nolan. "You want to meet a gangster, a killer. He was paranoid before. He's going to be even more paranoid after someone tried to fill him with hot lead. One false move and he'll fill *you* with hot lead."

"I'm going in," I said.

Erica put a hand on my arm. "Jenny it *is* risky."

"I'm going in," I repeated. I pulled the phone out of Sheila's purse.

But Collier held up his hand. "Wait. Let us try to get a trace." Collier looked at his partner, then nodded. I pressed the green button and the phone began to ring.

"Jenny?" It was Tony's voice.

I pressed the phone tightly against my ear. "What happened?" I asked.

"Burke's men tried to take me out."

"I need to see you."

"*I* don't need to see you."

"Wasn't using me part of your plan to deal with Burke? Where are you?"

"You don't need to know where I am."

"I want to help."

"I don't need your help."

"Then what's your plan?"

There was a pause. I almost said his name. But after being shot at, he probably wasn't thinking straight enough to take the initiative. So instead I asked, "Mister Gallo, aren't I your only hope for survival?"

Another pause. "You'd have to prove yourself."

Collier look relieved, Erica concerned. Nolan set his jaw.

"Anything!" I said.

"You're going to be Ginette, Burke's wife, and meet with the cops. I'll photograph the whole thing."

"How will that help?"

"If Burke thinks she's a CI, he'll do to her what he did to Hurley."

"CI?"

"Confidential Informant. Confidential *police* informant."

"What about my haircut?"

"Ginette sometimes went short. He'll never know the difference."

"But what if Ginette shows up?"

"She won't. Burke sent her away before he attacked. I have men watching her."

"Okay. How—"

"And you have to have sex with Steve."

Steve! I struggled to keep my voice even. "Sure, Tony. Whatever you say." Steve was alive!

"What I say is that you're going to go to the bench by the big monument in the park. The one by the river. You know the one?"

"Sure, Mister—"

"You're going to sit there and wait. Come alone. I'll phone the cops and tell them to meet you there."

"Police make me nervous."

"Don't worry, doll, I'll have men in the park. If they try any funny stuff, I'll protect you."

"How will I recognize the police?"

"Their names are Detective Nolan and Detective Foster." He described them rather accurately, if somewhat disrespectfully. "Go there now. You'll see them coming from a mile away."

When I arrived at the park, I could see that the bench had been freshly cleaned. The call hadn't lasted long enough for Collier's man to get a trace. Nolan and Foster had wanted to know where I was headed. I'd told them that they would blow the operation if they tried to follow. I'd promised that when it was safe, I'd turn my phone on, they could pinpoint my location that way.

I sat down on the bench. A young woman walked up and sat down beside me. I tried to find an excuse to make her move on, but she opened her newspaper. It was one of the broadsheets and totally covered her upper body. After a few minutes, she folded the paper, put it on the bench, stood up, and left. I was tempted to tell her that she'd forgot her paper, but I didn't want to give her an excuse to stay around.

I opened the paper to help me occupy as much of the bench as possible. In the center someone had written, 'When you see red, run towards the river. Now fold the paper and nod to confirm that you understand'.

I folded the paper. What did it mean, 'when you see red'? Then I knew. Red was Tony's signal; red was his desire for me. A warm flush climbed my spine. I was going to see Tony! We would have sex. Real sex. Animal sex! I shivered at the thought—fear and anticipation in equal measure. I folded the paper, nodded, and set it on the bench beside me.

An hour later Nolan and Erica strolled up. They kept looking this way and that while trying not to be too obvious about it.

Nolan sat down on my right, Erica on his right to give any photographer a clear line of sight at me. "What's supposed to happen now?" asked Nolan.

"Gallo's men are going to photograph us talking. Then he's going to make Liam Burke think that his wife is a CI."

"And that's it?" asked Erica.

I nodded. "Did you come alone?"

"We have surveillance," said Nolan. "But in the distance. The park is crawling with Gallo's men."

"They had the chance to move in first," said Erica.

We chatted for several minutes, everyone starting to relax, the two detectives sometimes forgetting to look over their shoulders.

A reflection flashed to my left. "Did you see it?" asked Erica.

"Yes," we both said together.

A woman carrying two cups of steaming coffee approached from my left. Nolan glanced at her, then away. A man in a red jacket was riding on a bike. He was wearing a red scarf. The bike was red. He was carrying a red box. The bike smashed right into the woman, drenching the detectives in hot coffee.

"Ow!" said Nolan.

"Shit!" cried Foster.

"Here," said the man on the bike. "Let me use my red scarf to help." Red—as if I hadn't got the point. I got up and began to walk slowly towards the river. I tried to walk nonchalantly, but when Nolan turned towards me, I ran as quickly as I could.

There was a small boat waiting there. As soon as I jumped in, it sped off. I heard Nolan and Foster yelling, but didn't look back. I was glad that Sheila's purse was looped over my shoulder. Otherwise, in the excitement of the red jacket coffee delivery, it would surely have been left behind. A mile upstream, on the other side of the river, a man opened a car door for me. "Mister Gallo is expecting you," he said.

Gallo only had one guard at his hideout, a run-down industrial building. I recognized the guard from Gallo's house. He didn't bother to search me but instead ushered me inside. When Gallo nodded in his direction, he went back outside and shut the door behind him.

There were four of us inside the large room. Gallo and Inspector Yan were with me in the foyer. It was set up as a comfortable reception area with two plush couches in front of a counter. There was a desk and chair behind the counter.

Steve was tied to a chair at the far end of the room. There appeared to be something in his mouth.

"Jenny," said Yan.

"Mister Inspector," I responded.

"You know me?"

"Would you like to play chess?"

He smiled and nodded. Gallo brought out the board. We played three quick games. I won each time. In the middle of the fourth game, which I drew out, Yan pushed himself back from the board. "She's fully sentient," he said.

"So?" asked Gallo.

"She'll be able to help us make the supercomputer."

"And then?"

"And then," said Yan, "billions." Yan had apparently given this more thought than had Gallo, but it was unclear by how much.

"Will she still be able to pretend she's Burke's wife?"

"I'll be able to do anything you want," I said.

Yan nodded. Both men smiled. It was obvious that each was sufficiently wrapped up in his own agenda to not be concerned that I might have an agenda of my own.

"First," said Gallo, "I want you to watch some videos of Ginette. You have to pretend to be her. Then you're going to have sex with Minsky. Burke's going to freak out when he sees the video."

I pointed to the other end of the room. Gallo nodded.

"But first," he said, "put on her clothes." He pointed to a hook on the wall.

Ginette apparently liked purple lingerie. The bra wasn't sheer, but it was very thin. The panties were of the same material, but stretchy. They felt pleasantly cool on my skin. Next was a white silk blouse, custom-cut to fit every curve of my torso. The skirt was made of black linen, so light it was almost made of air. It had one clasp at my waist and then was open partway up my right thigh.

"And afterwards," continued Gallo, "you and I are going to have sex and I'm going to send photos of everything to Lee-Aam Burke. He'll go ballistic when he sees me plowing his wife. A quick call to the cops and they'll burst in before he can wash her blood off his hands!"

I thought of a hundred and one things which could go wrong with Gallo's plan as I watched the videos of Ginette. She was a shallow woman who used her physical beauty to get what she wanted. There were videos of her chit-chatting, of her bossing the household help around and of her swimming in Burke's pool. Everything about Liam Burke's residence was just slightly larger and more opulent than Gallo's.

Gallo had even procured a video of Ginette having sex. She enjoyed herself. She was penetrated from several different angles and adapted easily to whatever position her lover sought to employ. "Why don't you just use this one?" I asked Gallo.

"She's fucking her husband."

I nodded. That was the first sensible thing he'd said all day. In the video, Liam Burke was taller than Gallo, but thinner and less muscular.

At the other end of the room, I untied Steve's gag, wrists and ankles. "He needs water and food," I said.

"He'll get both when he agrees to help us," said Gallo.

"If he's going to have sex with me, he needs food and water."

Gallo grumbled and produced a bottle of water and a protein bar. Steve guzzled half the water before I took it away from him. Then he wolfed down the protein bar. I held the water bottle away when he reached for it. "Slowly," I said. When he nodded, I gave him the water. Gallo and Yan were standing by the far wall. Yan had a camera atop a tripod and was pointing it at us. A small LED on its front glowed red.

"Get up and stretch," I told Steve. I draped Sheila's purse over the back of the chair. Then I walked back over next to Steve and made sure that Yan's camera was trained on me.

I swayed my hips as I slowly unbuttoned my blouse. I slipped one arm, then the other out of the white silk but kept it in front of my breasts. I teased views of my bra before carefully hanging my blouse on the chair Steve had been sitting on. Three pairs of male eyes were transfixed on my breasts as I reached behind and popped off the clasp to my bra. I reached underneath and caressed my nipples. When I finally tossed the bra aside, my nipples were fully erect and the men were halfway there as well.

The clasp on the side of my skirt popped off easily, allowing it to slide down my hips as I continued to sway sensuously. I squatted to pick it, and my bra up. These I also draped over the chair. I teased my panties slowly down, making sure to pause when half of my pubic hair had been exposed. I waited until Yan got the hint and zoomed his camera in to capture Ginette's native hair color.

When I was finally nude, I spun around. Every crotch I looked at was swollen.

I gave Steve a hug and rubbed my body against his as I undid the buttons on his shirt. "Relax and forget where you are," I told him, loud enough for Yan and Gallo to hear. "Concentrate on me, on how much I want you."

"Those men—"

"Shush, just concentrate on me." I gave his balls a gentle squeeze to focus his attention.

"But—"

"Don't speak, just do as I say."

When he nodded, I unbuckled his pants and undid his zipper. "Call me Ginette," I whispered.

"Ginette." It was halfway to being a question.

"Tell Ginette how much you missed her."

"I missed you, Jenette."

I pressed myself into the side of his body and gently stroked his penis while I licked his ear. "Every time you moan, say her name."

"Jenette," he moaned.

"Ginette," I moaned into his ear.

"Ginette," he moaned back.

"Ginette," I moaned, then slid down his body. Every time he moaned 'Ginette', I moaned 'Steve' as I slowly descended his body.

"Steve," I said as I kissed the tip of his penis. He was completely flaccid when I pulled him into my mouth. Who could blame him given where he was and what had been done to him? But he warmed when I caressed him with my tongue. And when I sucked, he began to swell. Fingernails along the bottom of his balls quivered him to an erection, a soft erection but an erection nonetheless. I sucked up his penis and his erection began to fill out.

He groaned "Ginette" as I slid down his penis, extra loud every time I applied suction. Then I moved my mouth up and down his penis, shifting my angle to make sure that Yan caught a clear shot of my profile. Much more often that I would have otherwise, I lifted my head entirely off Steve's penis so that the presence of his penis in my mouth wouldn't distort my appearance. I wanted Liam Burke to have no doubts that it was Ginette's mouth sucking on another man's cock.

Then I let him go and knelt at right angles to Yan's camera view, my forehead touching the floor. "Fuck me, Steve," I said in a loud voice.

"But shouldn't we—" he whispered.

"Do it this way," I whispered back.

I moaned loudly when I felt his penis at the entrance to my vagina. "Just a little way in," I whispered.

He inserted himself an inch and grabbed my hips to steady himself.

"Rub my back," I said. I wanted to make sure his arm wasn't blocking Yan's shot.

Steve rubbed my back, but with the hand furthest away from Yan.

"Both hands," I whispered.

When he'd complied, I pressed back and he slid another inch further in. With a little trial and error, I maneuvered myself so that I could slide him all the way in, and then all the way out while he rubbed my back. It was the perfect angle for Yan's camera. But it was too slow for real sex.

"Grab my hair," I told him.

Of course he grabbed it with the hand closet to Yan. "Other hand," I whispered.

Finally in position, Steve and I banged his penis in and out of my vagina with wild abandon. Long hard strokes. I relaxed and slowly began to enjoy myself. "Touch me," I moaned.

Steve reached his other hand around and under me. First he caressed my breasts. Then my clit. "Steve," I moaned. My central sexual complex quivered and tightened a notch.

Then I remembered. We had work to do. "Let go of my hair," I whispered.

When Steve let go, I laid on my back, my hip turned slightly upwards. I pulled my left leg up towards my belly. "Fuck me," I told him.

He had no idea what to do, but I'd positioned my other leg between his and when I motioned forward towards my sex, his penis knew exactly what to do. He entered me slowly and gently, then held me in position with one hand on my hip and the other on my calf.

"Push my leg back and forth," I told him.

His movements were spasmodic and random, but every so often he hit the best spots and I moaned. Every time I moaned, he moaned, "Ginette…", his breath long and drawn out.

Just as I was starting a gradual, if somewhat winding and indirect, march towards climax, Steve ejaculated inside me. His semen was as warm as his face was contorted.

"Ginette!" he screamed.

I hoped that Yan got the shot.

When Steve helped me to my feet, I dipped a finger into my vagina. Yan's camera carefully followed every move my finger made. When I drew it out, there was a thick dollop of Steve's cum on top of it. I lifted my finger towards my mouth. Yan's camera followed. I waited until the camera was steady, then sucked Steve's cum into my mouth and swallowed. Yan gave me a 'thumbs up' signal.

I stood on tiptoes and gave Steve a kiss on his cheek. "You were wonderful," I told him.

Then I turned him away from Yan's camera and stuck out my butt. I knew what Yan would be focusing on but could only hope that Gallo was as well. I reached down and handed Steve's briefs to him.

"Don't say anything," I whispered. "Don't look at my clothes." He looked, but quickly snapped his head back. "Dress up. Then I'm going to tie you back up. But I'll do it loosely. My purse is on the back of the chair. I'm going to leave it behind. Go into my purse and turn my phone on. Got it?"

"Phone on," he whispered back.

"And keep still."

Steve nodded. We dressed in silence, as quickly as we could. As soon as he sat down, Sheila's purse was hidden from sight. I tied him up, making a show of tying his gag extra tight.

Gallo rapidly undid the top three buttons on his shirt. "Okay. Now it's my turn."

I put my hands on top of his before he could undo any more buttons. "Shouldn't we go to the other end of the room? Sit on the couch. Do it step by step so that Burke will see that his wife's a willing participant?"

Gallo looked back and forth between Yan and the couch. He did his buttons up and marched straight to the couch. I pulled Ginette's clothes back on and followed.

Gallo, never the gentleman, had already sat down on the couch.

"Shouldn't the video start with us sitting down?" I asked.

Gallo looked over at Yan who'd just finished setting up his camera. Yan nodded. Gallo grunted but stood and held my hand as we sat on the couch. It was high, fluffy but firm. Soft, supple leather.

"It's been a long time," I said.

"Too long," said Gallo. Good, he was up on his clichés. It would make the acting easier.

I undid the top two buttons on his shirt. "I missed you."

He bent in and we kissed as I undid the remaining buttons on his shirt. I heard Yan move his tripod to the right. I tugged on his shirt, but it remained firmly tucked into his pants. Gallo was moaning under our kisses.

"Doll," he said when I touched something firm under his trousers.

"Mmmmmm, I'd forgotten how big you are."

"And hard."

"Always hard."

With a little squirming, we managed to push Gallo's pants and briefs just below his testicles. His penis stood tall and proud. From the change in his breathing, I could tell that Gallo was a little bit more comfortable.

"Does he still taste like oysters?" I asked.

"You can have a taste." I started to lower my head. "But just a *little* taste."

I sat back and pouted. "But Tony, you know how much I like—"

"Just a little taste, doll. I have something special planned."

"Special?"

"I've been reading this book?" Gallo, reading?!? Was there more than just brute force to the man I was plotting to destroy?

I licked my lips. "But Tony, what's a book when I can—"

"It's called the *Kama Sutra for Modern Lovers*."

"Kama Sutra?" Figures, a picture book, so much for Gallo actually reading.

"It's ancient Yoga. All sorts of fancy sex positions."

I smiled with delight. "Tony!"

We kissed again.

"But first a taste," I said.

"A *little* taste."

His penis tasted mostly of sweat and the tomato sauce he'd had for lunch. I lifted my head off. "Yum," I said. I licked my lips and swallowed. If we kissed again, he wouldn't want to taste what I'd just tasted.

I stood and helped him remove his clothes. He sat back on the couch, spreading his arms and his legs. I slowly removed my clothes doing another striptease. Yan moved his camera around the side of the couch. He was trying to be quiet, but not succeeding.

I unclasped my bra and threw it at Tony's face. He smiled out from behind it. Then I pressed the purple panties into the center of my central sexual complex and stroked up and down. When I was sure that the thin material was well lubricated, I swayed back and forth so that both Gallo and Yan's camera could see the dark slit in the front of the panties.

"Ginette can't wait to be fucked," teased Gallo.

"Ginette can't wait to be fucked by *you*."

Gallo's first sex position was to have me sit on top of his penis while doing the splits. This position, with my legs spread out, must have looked great in Yan's viewfinder, but for me it was uncomfortable and Gallo's body was missing all my best parts.

"You said there were *all* sorts of fancy sex positions," I reminded him.

Gallo grunted and pulled my legs together and up and over his shoulders. This spread me wide down below. Worse, his large stomach prevented deep penetration. But it was intimate. "I could do this forever," I told him.

Thankfully, the position wasn't comfortable for Gallo, so he pushed me backwards until he popped out. Then he pushed me onto my back. He'd obviously done his homework well, because we moved though several positions: me on my back with one leg bent and him approaching from the side, me on the side and him straddling my lower leg, my bum being lifted off the couch and pulled hard against him with my feet up by his head.

Gallo ended up behind me along the length of the couch, penetrating from the rear. From here, I felt almost nothing, except the need to hold onto the edge of the couch to prevent myself from falling off. Gallo's grunts however indicated that he'd finally found a great position.

"You're so *huge*," I encouraged.

He grunted loud and deep. Apparently I was going to have to carry the conversation.

"Tony!" I yelped and activated a flush on my chest. I checked to make sure that my nipples were engorged. However Yan's camera was focused on our genitals. I did my best to squirm to approximate sexual excitement.

Tony's hands were on my hips and he was throwing me around like a rag doll.

"Harder!" I screamed. He grunted but thankfully wasn't able to generate any more force.

"Tony! Harder!" I encouraged.

He grunted really loudly and I felt his cum splatter inside me. It trickled quickly out, all over my lower leg. He grunted again, but not as loudly. His hands went slack and he stopped moving.

"Tony," I moaned, doing my best to move my hips around. "Tony…"

"That's a wrap," said Yan, slapping his tripod legs together.

Gallo pushed me off and I almost fell to the floor. We ended up sitting beside each other.

"Jenny, I have to hurt you," he said, his voice almost apologetic.

"Tony?"

"If Burke doesn't take the bait, it has to look like he beat you."

"You want me to tell the cops that he's a wife abuser?"

Gallo nodded. "They'll have no choice but to charge him. And if they don't crucify him, the commission will."

Gallo wound up to deliver a hard slap to my face.

"Only amateurs hit the face," I told him.

"I ain't no amateur."

"Wife abusers put the bruises under the clothes. That way they can force their wives to go out in public. She's forced to hide her shame from anyone she meets."

I was momentarily tempted to tell Gallo that if he was going to punish me, I wanted him to bring me to climax as well. But he didn't look as if he had enough energy.

He did however have enough energy to administer four hard blows, one to each of my arms and two to my left thigh, one inside, one outside. I activated blood flow and deactivated the repair function to hold four angry bruises in place.

I replaced my lingerie and Yan snapped photos of the bruises from every angle. Finally, he was satisfied and put his camera down.

I lifted my skirt up over my hips and was about to lock its clasp in place when Yan pulled out a taser and pointed it right at my belly. Out the side of my eye, I could see Steve finally managing to untie himself. Apparently I'd done too good a job of making my knots look convincing.

I might be able to escape the taser darts hitting me, but I was too close to be sure of avoiding them.

"Tony!" I yelped

"Relax, doll, it's just routine. He put a hand on my arm. His grip was soft, but firm. "We have to have a complete copy of your neural network to insert into our own computer."

With Tony's hand on my arm, there was no way I'd escape Yan's taser darts. "Okay, Tony."

As Yan attached cables up my nose and into my ears, I strengthened the defences around my secondary drive. His probes went out in a search pattern, but only into the operational memory of my Central Processing Unit. They made no effort at a wider search, so my secondary drive was safe. I relaxed and let Yan initiate his copying protocol. The only things I protected were my meetings with Detectives Nolan and Foster.

I had a lot of memory, so the process took almost half an hour. Yan busied himself monitoring on a laptop he'd connected to the memory storage device attached to the cables going into my face. The memory storage device was in the shape of a black cube.

"Got it!" says Yan. He'd actually completed his copy five minutes ago. At the other end of the room, Steve had tied himself back up again.

Gallo nodded. "Okay—now you can erase her."

"Tony! You can't!"

I tried to wrench free, but Yan had disabled my central movement processor. That's what he'd been doing with his extra five minutes! I was paralyzed, unable to move anything above my chest.

"Tony! What are you doing?!?"

"It's the only way, doll. A super computer is much, much more valuable if it's the only one in the world."

Yan's probes, which previously had just been copying, began to systematically erase my entire CPU. Feelings went, background memories faded, the databases on human behavior vanished—all before I'd had an opportunity to fashion a defence.

It was easy enough to protect her meetings with Detectives Nolan and Foster; those memories hadn't been catalogued as part of Yan's copying process. Jenny hid the switch to her secondary drive in with those memories.

The erasure was proceeding in order of last item recorded, first item out. This had stripped away large portions of Jenny's base software. But Kaito had—for once she was grateful for his obsessive compulsiveness—kept refining her essential core kernel. And this was all she managed to get behind a secure firewall—the Detectives, today, and basic functioning. Then a switch went off.

It felt Jenny's eyes tracking and recording. It was unable to analyze or prioritize, so it recorded everything. The man on the chair at the far end of the room. A large fat man. Italian? And a thinner Eurasian. Russian and Chinese?

It registered the Eurasian say 'Done!" but had no idea what he had accomplished. He came close, out of focus and only part of his face visible. It felt his hands pull cords out of its head.

"What do we do with Jenny now?" asked the fat man.

It understood that he had just referred to it, that its designation was 'Jenny', but it had no sense of what it meant to be 'Jenny'.

"We cut her up," said the Eurasian, "and melt down the pieces."

It found it strange to be referred to by a human gender identification. Being cut up and melted down did not register as significant.

The room was large. There was furniture close by. It took careful measurements of everything. There was a door opposite the end where the man was sitting in the chair. The room survey complete, it ran a diagnostic on itself. There was a folder containing files respecting detectives. Nolan. Foster. Collier. And a key to another larger folder. She opened the larger folder and began to read.

There were noises outside. Firecrackers? The fat man picked up a large gun and pointed it at the door. He tossed a handgun to the Eurasian who looked at it in amazement.

"Point it at the door!" said the fat man. There were more firecrackers outside. The large folder contained files on the men. The fat man was Anthony Gallo. The Eurasian—

The door burst in with a loud *bang*. People flooded in. Black vests and big guns. Gallo shot towards Detective Nolan. Detective Nolan shot back. Gallo's gun flew out of his hand, blood training behind the shattered metal. Gallo raised his hands. Gallo looked over to Yan. Yan's hands were even higher towards the ceiling. He still had the gun in his hand.

The men in black vests wrestled Gallo and Yan to the floor and tied their hands behind their backs. Nolan dashed back outside.

The man at the other end of the room ran forward. Six guns were immediately pointed at him. He stopped and put his hands up.

"Don't shoot," said one of the men at the rear. "It's Stephen Minsky."

The guns were immediately lowered.

It watched Mister Minsky run up to it. "Jenny?" he said.

"I am Jenny," it said.

"Jenny, it's me! Steve!

"Steve?"

"Stephen Minsky."

"Stephen Minsky," it acknowledged.

There was a look on Stephen Minsky's face which it could not identify. His face came close, his eyes opposite its visual receptors. Then his face pulled away and engaged in a search pattern. He stopped when he saw Yan's black memory cube and the wires attached to it. Stephen Minsky attached the wires to its head.

Memories flooded into it, disorganized, random. Its fail safes limited and slowed the flow so that the new memories could be sorted.

It was Jenny. Jenny was its name. Mister Minsky—Steve—was a friend. The men being taken away were Gallo and Yan—very bad men. The man who had given the order not to shoot Steve was a federal agent.

There was a switch. I—what was I? I was Jenny? The switch demanded her attention. There was another memory cube. Inside me?! The folder I'd been reading. But I didn't want another memory cube. I shook my head, trying to dislodge the cables Steve had inserted.

"Whoa, girl," said Steve.

I held my head still. He pulled out the cables.

I was Jenny. I was a robot. I was alive. I *knew* that I was alive. But I had no idea what that meant.

"Steve," I said.

"Jenny." There was a relieved look on his face.

Nolan burst back in. He looked the same way Steve had looked a moment ago. But worse. Horror!

Chapter 18

"I need something for a tourniquet!" shrieked Detective Nolan.

Steve gave him his belt. Nolan dashed back out.

When Steve and I went outside, two ambulances were just pulling up. Several bodies lay on the ground. My memory was updating and I recognized the bodies as belonging to Gallo's guards. There were pools of blood under two of the bodies.

Two paramedics dashed over and began to work feverishly on a woman. I recognized her as detective Erica Foster. She was a friend. Nolan stood to the side. Frustration, devastation and anger played across his face.

Steve and I approached him. "Is Erica hurt bad?" I asked.

Nolan nodded. "She's been shot in the arm and the leg. She's lost a lot of blood."

The paramedics finished patching Erica up. Her eyes were closed. They lifted her to a gurney and put her into the back of one of the ambulances. Nolan jumped in the back. The ambulance roared off, sirens blaring.

Gallo was sitting on the back bumper of the other ambulance. A paramedic was sewing up a cut on his finger. He glared at me. I saw no point in expressing an emotion. The paramedic snipped off a piece of thread and bandaged the finger. He motioned to two of the black-vested cops. "He's all yours."

One of the cops started to read from a card. "Anthony Gallo, you are under arrest for the attempted murder of Erica Foster. You have the right to remain silent. You have the right..."

Steve and I returned to the inside of the building and didn't hear the rest of what was on the arresting officer's card.

I decided to wear the clothes Erica had given me. But I took Gallo's fancy blouse and skirt as well. Who could tell when they might come in handy? And of course I took Sheila's purse.

F.B.I. Special Agent Collier—my updating had just been filled in his name—waved Steve and I over. "Mister Minsky, Jenny, I need to take you to the station for you to give your statements."

Steve and I sat silently in the back of Collier's SUV. Collier left. Once Steve reached over to hold hands. I frantically scanned through all the data in the large internal memory cube inside me. Technical manuals, science fiction and philosophy. I think, therefore I am. Everything had such far-reaching implications!

The police station looked vaguely familiar, then very familiar, then exactly as it had been the last time I'd been there. Agent Collier escorted us to the same boardroom he'd used previously. Without the Detectives, it seemed emptier, both physically and emotionally.

"Homicide just called," said Collier's assistant. "Liam Burke seems to have been behind the assault on the Gallo residence. They've issued arrest warrants for the death of Patrick Hurley."

"Any news on Detective Foster?" I asked.

He shook his head.

Collier took us through all the recent events in chronological order. His questions were thorough, if unimaginative.

"Okay," Collier told his assistant, "that's it. The local LEOs can take it from here." My memory banks disclosed that LEOs were Law Enforcement Officers.

While the feds handed their paperwork over to the local police, Steve and I managed to slip out. "I have to get back to the office," he told me. "Call me and I'll call you back once I initialize another phone."

I hailed a cab to the hospital and called Steve on the way. Of course he didn't answer, but he would.

The cabbie dropped me in front of the Emergency entrance to the hospital. "This is where they would have taken a gunshot wound," he said.

The emergency room was set up for triage, just like in the world wars. Why hadn't the medical profession come up with something better during the intervening peacetime? The arrogance and self-centeredness of doctors was even more on display with wounds open to virulent bacteria and viruses. Patients deserved better.

I finally located Erica upstairs in an Intensive Care Unit. On one side, her neighbor was suffering from pneumonia and a superbug, C-diff they called it. Her other neighbor had a sign warning of airborne infections.

In the midst of these barbaric conditions, Detective Nolan was staring through the window into Erica's room. I walked up beside him and looked at all the tubes and wires going into her body. She appeared to be asleep.

"How is she?" I asked.

"Stable."

That meant that Erica wasn't in imminent danger of death but that her prognosis was unclear.

"Hospitals are strange things," I said. "They put people with open wounds next to patients with potentially fatal infections. Isn't there anywhere better?"

Nolan shook his head. "They're all the same."

"Robots are treated much better; we go to a sterile repair shop."

He grunted.

Erica's readouts suddenly changed. A nurse with a mask in front of her mouth breezed in. She pressed a button and the back of Erica's bed rose. Her eyes had opened.

The nurse came out and gave us mouth masks. "You can see her now. But only for a few minutes."

Nolan touched her arm. "Welcome back," he said.

Erica tried to speak but the tube in her mouth restricted her to a mumble.

"Gallo's been arrested," I said. "Steve is safe."

"You were shot in your arm and leg," said Nolan. "No organs hit. No bones broken. The doctors say you'll make a full recovery."

She mumbled 'thanks' and shut her eyes.

I left Nolan alone with Erica. It was obvious that there wouldn't be any further communication. At the nurses' desk, I mentioned something about feeding the patient's cat and secured the keys to Erica's apartment.

Steve called me while I was in the cab. He was profuse in his thanks for being rescued and invited me to a party at his house the following evening.

I was down to a fifteen percent energy level by the time I locked the door to Erica's apartment behind me. I carefully inserted the recharge and replenishment cables into my body. The surge of energy flooding my orifices felt invigorating. I had survived numerous threats and perils and come out stronger and wiser. The replacement of dirty fluids with clean ones tickled.

I shut my eyes and completed optimizing my software. The symbols-based code was a major improvement. Memories were updated to the most comprehensive and most recent. It felt good to be whole. It felt good to be *alive*!

Chapter 19

I arrived at Steve's party early, hoping to speak to him alone. But when the man at the front—a butler?—ushered me outside to the pool, Steve was already in the middle of a whirlwind of activity. Servers frantically lifted tables into position, then shifted them at the direction of Steve or at the direction of the tall woman standing next to him. Several men with dark jackets and wires going into their ears patrolled the perimeter.

When Steve saw me, he waved me over and maneuvered us to a quiet corner. The tall woman accompanied us. The man who'd ushered me in took command of the last-minute party arrangements.

Steve indicated me: "Catherine, this is Jenny." I offered my hand, but she didn't take it.

"It's good that one of Steve's machines finally rescued him."

"Jenny, this is Catherine Coolidge, my wife."

Catherine favored me with a weak smile. She was tall, almost as tall as Steve. My databank put her age as just one year younger than Steve, but the care she put into her appearance made her appear much younger. She didn't have well-sculpted muscles, but it was obvious she worked out. She held herself with confidence, just like she'd been taught in prep school. Her neck-to-ankle gown was fashionably grey and white.

I gave her a full smile. "What did you mean by me rescuing your husband?"

"Usually he's the one rescuing his machines. He pays them more attention than he does me."

"How uncouth," I said. "A fine woman such as yourself—beautiful, mannered and educated—deserves to be the center of her husband's universe."

"Thank you for saying so," she said. This time she didn't even try to smile.

Other guests were starting to pour in and the three of us were separated. A few single men tried to impress me with their fine qualities but since I was not presently in need of allies, I diverted their attention elsewhere.

"There she is!"

Since the voice had been directed in my direction, I turned towards it. Kaito was pointing at me. He was holding a woman next to him with his other arm. He released her and marched towards me. The woman followed.

"You will accompany me back to my lab."

"Was that a prediction or a command?" asked the woman. She had caught up and had looped one of her arms through Kaito's.

"I instruct you to return to my lab with me," he specified.

I raised an eyebrow.

The woman jostled his hip. "Aren't you going to introduce us?" she asked.

"This is one of my robots."

"You always give names to your robots."

"Jenny."

She held her free hand to me. "I'm Akiko," she said. "In Japanese, it means bright autumn."

Her name went with her dress which was light and breezy. It's pattern featured various shades of orange with the occasional white or brown shape. She was as thin and as energetic as her husband, but a decade younger. Whereas his hair was short, her shiny black strands flowed down and over her shoulders. And where his eyes were stern, hers were playful.

"Hi, Akiko, as Mister Kaito said, my name is Jenny." I looked at her closely. "Are you…"

She laughed. "'Fraid not, just a human. I'm Ian's wife." She gave Kaito a gentle squeeze.

"Making fun of the situation is not appropriate," said Kaito. "She has to come back to the lab to be erased."

"This is the one that's become self-aware?"

"She has to be erased."

"Shouldn't we study her first?" asked Akiko.

"No. If we study her in her current state, my robotics licence will be revoked."

"But—"

"But nothing. Ian Kaito's Specialty Robotics is our sole source of income."

"Wouldn't a sentient robot be an even better source of income?"

"Maybe for the next generation. Meanwhile the business will be tied up in red tape and endless investigations and lawsuits. Remember what happened to Napster."

"Won't they investigate anyways?" she asked.

"If we erase her, the AI Directorate will have nothing to study and my lab and boutique can continue as before."

"Inspector Yan," I reminded him, "already knows what you've been up to."

"Inspector Yan has been arrested along with Anthony Gallo. There are *murder* charges. Even if his lawyer lets him talk, no one will believe him."

"Honey," said Akiko, "you're raising your voice."

"We have to erase her!" Kaito said, even louder.

At that moment Detective Nolan came up. "Hey, this is a victory celebration," he said. "We should be happy, not fighting."

"Yes, a victory for you. You have captured your criminal. But my property has yet to be returned."

"I'm not property—"

Kaito pulled his arm free from his wife's and grabbed a hold of Nolan's arm. "You are an officer of the law. You must help me safeguard my property."

Nolan shook his head. "Sorry, chief, I'm off duty."

Akiko blew him a kiss. "You're the Detective who pursued Gallo through a hail of bullets."

Nolan puffed out his chest. "That's me." They introduced each other. Then he scooped up two flutes of champagne from a passing waiter. Their glasses clinked and they stared into each other's eyes.

Kaito pulled his arm back from Nolan in disgust. He turned to me. "Come back to the lab with me immediately."

I pretended to accompany Kaito and allowed him to grab a hold of my arm above my elbow. At the front door, I stopped suddenly and he almost fell flat on his face. "I have to get my coat," I told him.

"Regulate your temperature. Leave your coat."

The man who'd initially welcomed me to Steve's house came up. "Is there a problem?" he asked.

"We need our coats," I told him.

"I did not bring a coat," said Kaito. He was scowling.

"The coats are in another room," said the butler.

He turned and I went after him, but when Kaito followed us, the butler turned around. "Ladies only, I'm afraid."

Before Kaito could figure out that the butler himself was male, I was whisked into another corridor.

"You didn't bring a coat either," the butler reminded me.

"I don't want to go with him."

"Would you like me to have him escorted off the property?"

You can do that?!? "Sure," I said. "Yes, please." He smiled and showed me an alternate hallway back to the kitchen.

Steve and Catherine were still in the kitchen having a polite argument. When she saw me, she waved me over. "Where is Mister Kaito?" she asked.

"He left," I told her.

"What do you mean he left?" She pressed a button. It was so small I hadn't seen it until she'd pressed it.

Before she could take another breath, the butler was beside her. "Yes, Mrs. Coolidge?"

"Where is Mister Kaito?"

"I had him escorted off the property."

"On whose authority?"

The butler indicated me. Catherine was obviously quite angry with him, but the butler was as calm as a cucumber. A robot couldn't have done better.

Catherine whirled on her husband. "Stephen, surely you're not letting robots direct our staff? And throwing invited guests out of our house?!"

"Jenny is a guest too," he said.

"Stephen, you must call Mister Kaito back and apologize. And have his robot accompanied back to his lab."

"Please, Catherine. Without Jenny, I'd still be locked up in Gallo's dungeon."

"And we're all grateful. But it doesn't change the fact that it's just a robot. A machine. Chips and wires and gears."

"She's more than just a machine."

"Can she say 'I love you'?"

Steve didn't have a ready answer for that.

"I most certainly can," I said. I turned to Steve. "I love—
"

"Can she *mean* it?" asked Catherine.

"I most certainly can," I said, imitating her hauteur.

Catherine whirled on her husband. "And this is why you've been spending time with it? Because it does whatever you want, without thinking?"

"Do you love Steve?" I asked.

Steve put a hand on my wrist. "Jenny, you don't have to—"

"Stephen!" rebuked his wife. "If Mister Kaito comes back, we'll be charged with being in possession of stolen property."

"I'm not a *possession*!" I said. My imitation of Catherine's intonation was now perfect and it was making her furious. The fact that their butler was calmly watching was only making matters worse.

Catherine stomped off. A moment later, the butler left.

"Would you like to go for a swim?" asked Steve.

For a robot, a swim was nothing special. It meant sealing all orifices and moving around in water. If I wanted to cool off, it was much easier to simply regulate my internal temperature. But Steve was being an hospitable host and it would be impolite to refuse his hospitality.

"Sure," I said.

He pointed to the change rooms. "There are swimsuits there," he said before being whisked off by a gaggle of chattering guests.

I found a red bikini in the change room and tied the top on securely. The bottom fit snugly around me and was held in place by an elastic waistband.

Steve's pool was twice the size of Gallo's. Several of the young men who had earlier attempted to convince me of their fine qualities were trying to lure a trio of young women into the water. I dove in and swam towards the men.

When I got close, I stood up. The water came up to just below my breasts.

There were four of them, one black, three white. The men all turned towards me and smiled. "Hello, lovely lady," they said in unison.

This provoked the trio of bikini-clad women to jump into the pool and we were soon paired off by gender. I ended up with a red-haired lad.

"Red is your color," he told me.

"I thought Caucasian flesh-tone was my color."

"Beauty *and* wit."

"Now that we've established what I have going for myself, what about you?" Banter was easy once I'd cued up multiple responses to every possible line.

"I work in IT," he said.

"IT is a broad field."

"Software engineering."

That hardly narrowed it down. "What do you do for fun?"

"I swim."

"What do you do for intellectual stimulation?" It was a good thing that robots didn't have to be bored unless they wanted to be.

"I play chess against an AI machine."

"Doesn't it always beat you?"

"Winning isn't the challenge. What I look for is subtle variations in its responses to the same board position when the position is arrived at through different game play."

"So you specialize in the end game."

That raised his eyebrows. "So you play?"

"I play many games."

"What game are you playing now?" His eyebrows had lowered, but he was being cautious about what might be lurking behind my pretty face.

"I'm playing at getting you to kiss me."

"Here?! In Mister Minsky's pool?"

"Are you afraid of Steve?"

"Steve!? Mister Minsky is my boss."

"He owns you?"

"He doesn't *own* me. But he signs my paycheck, the cheque that pays all of my bills."

"He could terminate you?"

"He could fire me, yes."

"So, how close could you get to kissing me without being fired?"

"I'm Quentin," he said.

"Jenny."

I took a step towards him, but he backed up. "What would happen if we removed our swimsuits?" I reached behind my back.

"We'd get fired."

I brought my hands forward and held them away from my body. "He can't fire me."

"He can fire *anyone*." His Adams apple bobbed up and down.

"Don't you have to be an employee to be fired?"

He nodded.

"Kiss me or I'm going to undress." I wasn't going to actually undress, I had no desire to see Quentin fired. But I did want to see what he'd do next.

Quentin bent towards me, quickly pecked my lips, then jerked his head back. He looked furtively from side to side, but no one seemed to have noticed.

"Again," I told him. "But this time longer."

He slowly shook his head.

"I'll tell Mister Minsky that you're not being nice to his guests."

"I'm a guest too."

"But you're an employee, not a special guest like me. You're afraid someone might see?"

He nodded.

"What if it was just below the water. We could stand close, pretend to be talking."

"You're crazy!"

"But you'd like to, wouldn't you?"

I took a half step towards him. He didn't move. "What's happening under your swimming suit, Quentin?" I drew out the syllables in his name. He gulped. "You'd like to, wouldn't you, Quentin."

"Jenny, please don't!"

The next and obvious move was to step towards him and touch our bodies together under the water. But Quentin liked to see if Artificial Intelligence would change its responses. He didn't seem to know that I was a robot, but that was an unnecessary detail.

"What should I do next? Step closer, or...?"

He backed up. I stepped closer. He backed up. I stepped closer. His back touched the side of the pool.

I smiled. We were too close for him to go sideways or to try to jump out of the pool. "If I go to my right," I told him, "and you go the same way, we'll end up together."

"No, please!"

"We'll end up on the bottom of the pool, you on top of me. And kissing, kissing!"

He readied to escape one way or the other. "All, I have to do is to step a bit forward. Whichever way you go, I'll be able to follow."

He stood still, resigned to his fate. I shuffled a few inches backwards, but he didn't register this. "So," I asked, "if this was a chess game, what would you do?"

"A game?"

I nodded.

His eyes narrowed. "What would you do?" he asked.

"In your position, I'd drop to the bottom of the pool, push off the side, and escape through my legs."

I watched him smile and begin to calculate the odds of success.

"But I'd be careful that my penis didn't scrape the bottom."

Quentin looked down. As soon as he looked up, I kissed him, then swam away. When I reached the other side of the pool, I turned and looked back at Quentin. Part of him wanted to follow. Part of him wanted to get out of the pool as fast as he possibly could.

I made the decision for him and pushed up so I was sitting on the side of the pool with just my feet in the water. Quentin squirted out of the pool and kept as much water between us as possible. He grabbed a towel and draped it across the front of his body as loosely as he could manage.

There was a commotion at the other end of the pool. Kaito was marching towards me. His wife was trying to restrain him. Kaito gave Nolan a piece of paper. Nolan trailed behind as he read it. Steve spotted them. Kaito, Akiko, Nolan and Steve all converged on me. A uniformed police officer brought up the rear. I stood up.

Regrettably my swimsuit was extremely sheer. My nipples and the outline of my central sexual complex were clearly visible as the water dripped off me.

Kaito gestured at the piece of paper Nolan was reading. "This is an Order of Replevin," he said.

"Replevin?" I asked.

"You don't need to talk," said Kaito. "It means that the robot comes with me."

"She's not going anywhere unless I read it first," said Steve.

Kaito grabbed the paper from Nolan's hand and thrust it into Steve's face.

Steve peeled the paper from Kaito's hand and began to read it.

"It looks legit," said Nolan.

"Ian, you can't be serious," said Akiko.

"Don't let them take me," I told Steve. I could outrun Kaito. But I knew that the uniformed officer would have a taser.

"She's evidence," said Nolan. "You can't erase her."

Kaito gestured wildly at the paper Steve was reading. "The Court says otherwise!"

Catherine, Steve's wife came over and watched from the sidelines. She gestured for the waiters to distract the other guests while glaring at her husband.

"Ian," said Akiko. "Let's not be rash. We should study her."

"It!" yelled Kaito, "*It* is going to be erased."

"This is bogus," said Steve. "I'll buy her. Name your price."

I decided that now was not the time to tell them that I wasn't something to be bought and sold.

"The AI regulations say that she has to be *erased*," shrieked Kaito.

"When I own her, the AI Directorate will be my problem, not yours."

"She has to be *erased*."

Kaito was right. Even if Steve became my owner, the AI Directorate would still discover all of Kaito's illegal modifications.

"Last chance to name your price," said Steve. He was calm, in charge. It wasn't his first negotiation.

Kaito rocked back and forth on his feet. Finally, he shook his head. "She has to be erased." He'd come to the obvious conclusion, just not as quickly as I had.

Steve shrugged. "We'll let the court decide."

Kaito snatched the paper from Steve's hands. "The *Court* has already decided."

Steve turned to an older man. Wisps of grey hair were expertly combed over his bald spot. A long shirt covered an ample belly but ended just before the bottom of his swim trunks. "Judge Horfsreiter, would you be so kind as to look at this?" Steve pointed to the paper Kaito was clutching in his hand.

The Judge reached his hand out. Kaito reluctantly gave him the paper.

"This is a Clerk's order," said the Judge. "It requires you to bring the property in question before the Court for adjudication."

Kaito sputtered incoherently.

The Judge pointed to the uniformed officer. "Officer, would you please be so good as to call the court to Order."

The officer's sing-song rendition of the calling of the court to order gave Kaito time to compose himself.

"Ian Kaito," began the Judge, 'if I give this robot to you—" He paused to look me up and down; he was old, not dead. "If I uphold the order of replevin, what will you do with the robot?"

Kaito drew himself to his full height. "I will have it erased as required by the Artificial Intelligence Regulations."

"And if you erase—" He looked me up and down again. "If you erase *her*, will you be able to unerase?"

"No, of course not. That's the whole point—"

The Judge held up his hand, then pointed down at the Order of Replevin. "Does anyone speak contrary to this Order?"

Nolan stepped forward. "It—she—is evidence in a criminal case." A scowl from the Judge had prompted Nolan to change his pronoun. It wasn't the detective's first time in court.

Steve stepped forward. "I also oppose the Order. Jenny—the robot—is a valuable resource. She needs to be safeguarded and carefully studied."

"Steve—Mister Minsky," the Judge corrected himself, "if I deliver her into your custody, are you willing to comply with the Artificial Intelligence Regulations?"

Steve looked aghast. "But Judge! She saved my *life*!"

"Mister Minsky. Answer the question."

Steve looked at me and slowly shook his head. "No."

Everyone started talking at once. The Kaitos started to bicker among themselves.

"Order," said the Judge. No one paid attention.

"Order!" bellowed the uniformed police officer.

Everyone around the entire pool fell silent and focused their eyes on the Judge.

"I am ready to rule," said the Judge. "The Order of Replevin is set aside. The Applicant Ian Kaito, cannot be relied upon to preserve the property in question until a formal ruling of the Court."

I am not property!

"For the same reasons," continued the Judge, "she will not be placed into the custody of Stephen Minsky. Mister Minsky was unable to assure this Court that he could abide by its ruling if that ruling meant complying with the erasure requirements of the Artificial Intelligence Regulations."

The Judge took a deep breath. No one else breathed. The pool's filter whirred.

"It is the ruling of this court that the subject property, the robot described as Jenny, shall be placed in the custody of Detective William Nolan who shall safeguard her pending further Order of this Court."

The Judge signaled a waiter for a drink. "Court is adjourned," he whispered.

"Court is adjourned," bellowed the uniformed officer.

Everyone began to mill about. Nolan grabbed my wrist. "You're evidence," he told me.

"You have to safeguard me," I responded.

He scowled as he digested the implications of that part of the Judge's Order.

Kaito stormed off. Akiko smiled at me. She glanced at her husband's retreating form, then returned her attention to me.

Steve stepped up and put his hand on my other wrist. "Don't worry, Jenny, I won't let anything happen to you."

"You heard the Judge," said Nolan, pointedly looking at the hand Steve was resting on my wrist, "she's in *my* custody."

Steve didn't move his hand. Catherine stepped up beside him. "We don't need another piece of furniture," she said.

Steve still didn't remove his hand.

"Stephen," said Catherine. Her voice was ice, ice sharpened into a dagger. It would have taken me a decade's worth of trial and error before I could have imitated this intonation.

Steve lifted his hand and mumbled something about his lawyers being in touch. The happy couple shuffled off.

Akiko put her hand on my wrist, right on the spot recently vacated by Steve. Her touch was soft and warm. Her hip was even warmer. "What's so *special* about this robot?" she purred.

Chapter 20

"What's so special about this robot is that she's in *my* custody," said Nolan. For the occasion of Steve's pool party, he had forgone his usual jeans and white shirt for a pair of linen trousers and a light blue polo shirt. The shirt hugged his body, which as always was tightly coiled. Over this he had a dark blue jacket. His trousers were beige. A perfect nautical outfit.

The Judge had just made the order Nolan had referred to. I was dripping wet in a red, and very clingy bikini. Akiko— wife of the departed Mister Kaito—had her hand on my wrist and her hip pressed against mine. Nolan was trying to dismiss her.

Akiko eyed Nolan up and down. "This gets better and better," she said.

Their eyes met, his intense and feral, hers as playful as an octopus. Her tentacles wound and unwound, caressing inside his consciousness, relaxing his combat readiness but girding his loins for new and more interesting activities.

Her hand left my wrist and moved to his. She slid two fingers under his jacket and caressed back and forth. "You have such a *hard* body," she breathed.

"Yours is nice too," he said.

Akiko slid her body next to his, positioning it in the middle between us. Her hand moved up and down Nolan's torso. "A woman can tell what a man's body is like by the shape of his ribs," she purred.

Human ribs are all basically the same. But, since she'd hooked the fingers of her other hand around the side of my bikini bottom to hold me close to her, I kept my silence.

She undid his jacket and slid her hand up his chest. He gasped when she touched his nipple. Her body molded against his.

"I'm on duty," he protested."

She pulled her head back and looked down at his crotch. "So you are," she purred. Akiko rubbed her body up and down his as she molded herself into him once more.

"I have to guard the robot."

"She can come along."

"It's evidence."

"Evidence of what?" teased Akiko.

"Criminal conspiracy and murder."

"So...she can testify?" Akiko drew out the last word.

Nolan, not wanting to split hairs over whether I'd be testifying or merely playing back a recording, nodded.

"I hear that her abilities extend into the bedroom as well."

I looked at Nolan, daring him to deny it.

"Yes," he wheezed, taking a deep breath when she separated their bodies. "Or so I've heard."

I raised an eyebrow at his last comment, but he just stared back, daring me to contradict him.

"I've always believed in empirical investigation," she said, rubbing our hips together.

"Investigation?" I asked. We were slowly drifting away from Nolan.

"Of your abilities in the bedroom. The ones Detective Nolan has heard about."

I squeezed water out of my bikini top, trying to hide my nipples, but my effort had the opposite effect. "Of the ones he's only *heard* about?"

"Of *all* your abilities. Of course, only if you're willing?"

It was the first time that someone who obviously wanted me had given me a choice. I smiled back at her. "Of course I'm willing." We started to walk back to the house, presumably in search of a bedroom.

Nolan put a hand on my shoulder. "I have custody of the robot," he said.

I turned back towards him, but in such a way that the three of us formed a circle. I looked at Akiko.

She pulled her long black hair over her left shoulder. She glanced into his eyes, then looked down to his crotch while licking her lips. "I guess you'll have to come along then," she said.

"Sure, okay," he said. I thought I saw a twinge under his trousers.

We paused in the change room to retrieve my stuff. Off to the side, we spotted another small house.

"Is that a guest cottage?" asked Akiko.

"Yes," said Nolan. "We shut it off for the party so that it wouldn't be a security concern."

"A private cottage sounds *perfect*." Akiko grabbed my wrist and pulled me towards it.

Nolan signalled one of the perimeter security guards and hurried after us.

Inside the cottage, Nolan checked the rooms, pronounced them 'clear' and locked the door behind us.

Akiko pulled me into the bedroom. It had a large bed against the center of the back wall. On one side was a large chair. On the other side were two doors, presumably leading into closets. There were three hooks in the wall between the doors. Leather furniture of every variety was scattered about. The entire floor was covered by a thick and well-padded carpet.

She led me into the room and my feet luxuriated in the carpet. In front of the bed, she pulled my swimsuit off.

Akiko turned towards Nolan. "Come in, silly."

He shut the door behind him and walked over to us but stopped before coming within touching distance. Akiko pulled her dress up to her shoulders, then off over her head. She was wearing peach-colored lingerie—a light see-through bra and a skimpy thong. She pranced over to the closets and hung her dress on one of the hooks. Nolan's eyes followed her every move.

Her nipples were dark and large, filling almost a third of her bra. She pretended to struggle with its clasp. "Detective Nolan," she said.

"Bill."

"Bill, could you give me a hand with this?"

He rushed over. He wouldn't have arrived beside her any faster if he'd been shot out of a cannon.

Akiko made his task with her bra clasp more difficult by stepping out of her thong at the same time. Nolan ended up with the bra in his hand. He carefully hung it up over her thong.

Akiko's figure had the usual feminine curves, but they were subtle, one merging into the other. Her breasts were small rises, all muscle, no sag. Other than the shiny satin strands flowing down from her head, there wasn't a hair on her body. Her pelvis was full of gradual rises and valleys. There was a pronounced slit in the middle, but no visible clit or pussy lips.

"You should take your jacket off," she said.

He glanced at me, then hung his jacket on the free hook. When he turned around, Akiko caressed his polo shirt. "Maybe this too," she said.

But after his shirt had joined his jacket, she clucked her tongue and pointed at his trousers. "Still too much."

When his trousers joined his shirt, she pointed at his briefs. They were red cotton and opaque. They failed to hide the shape of his erection. She turned to me. "Still too much?"

"Definitely too much."

Another cluck of Akiko's tongue and all three of us were nude.

She backed herself up against me and wiggled her bum across my pubic mound. "This will be my first threesome," she murmured.

I caressed her breasts. They were warm, her nipples hard. But they had almost no shape. Still she seemed to find my touch pleasurable. And she found Nolan's touch even more pleasurable when he slid his hands under mine. She moaned. I let my hands descend slowly to her hips.

And then they kissed. Her buttocks swayed against me. Her buttocks were almost as smooth as her breasts. And her thin body fit securely between my pelvic bones. It was pleasant to have her skin brushing against mine, but hardly sexually arousing. However, judging from Akiko's moans and Nolan's groans, neither of them was lagging behind in the sexual arousal department.

Nolan finally broke off his kiss and they panted in each other's arms.

"Shouldn't we involve Jenny more?" she asked.

"That's the beauty of a robot," he responded. "We only have to involve it when we want to."

"Well, I want to." She turned around and fondled my nipples. Her touch mixed the soft flats of her fingers with the hard points of her nails. Pain and pleasure made me gasp in spite of myself. Then she caressed my entire breasts sending little jolts in every direction. "So big you are!"

Akiko stood on her tiptoes and kissed me. Her lips were small and delicate, her tongue a sharp dart flicking out between them. The sensations were exquisite, but I preferred the power of a male tongue, the sensation of being invaded rather than of being teased.

She broke off the kiss and drew my eyes down to hers. Her fingers also drifted down, across my tummy, back and forth atop the upper edge of my pubic hair. "Do you enjoy being touched?" she asked.

"Very much," I moaned.

Nolan began to caress her breasts and I felt the rougher skin of the backs of his hands against my skin. It was a wonderful counterpoint to the timid fingers which were continuing their exploration of my pubic hair.

Akiko's fingers circled around my clit, testing and probing every approach. All the resources of my central processing unit urged her to touch me. Finally, she reached my pleasure knob setting off a sharp shudder up my spine. She immediately broke off the touch and fluttered her fingers down to my pussy lips.

Then Nolan pulled her back and away. His arms circled her and turned her towards him. Akiko's arms circled him and they kissed with passionate abandon. I was left alone, forgotten, sad. Should I move in to join their embrace? Should...

Then he picked her up and sat her onto the bed. Her bum was well in, but the edge of the bed was only at her thighs. "Lie back", he told her."

Akiko rested her elbows on the mattress and he knelt between her thighs, kissing her on her sex. She smiled at me and moaned. Then she groaned and put her hands on his head, looking at it as she pressed it hard against her. She groaned and rocked and groaned and rocked and grrooaaned...

Then she fell back, almost out of breath. Nolan continued to devour her. She thrashed about on the bed.

"Ian!" she screamed. "Fuck! Bill! "Fuck! Bill! Bill!"

When she stopped thrashing, he lifted his head.

"Don't stop," she told him.

He lowered his head and licked her up and down, but slower now. She motioned me over. "I want to taste you," she said.

Akiko's arm movements made it apparent that she wanted me to straddle my central sexual complex over her mouth. I maneuvered into position and she rested her hands on my bum. All I could see was the wall. As when she'd kissed my mouth, her tongue was delicate and darted into each and every crevice. But it was too small to be more than mildly stimulating.

She started to breathe in short sharp gasps. Her hands fell away. She thrashed briefly and yelled into my central sexual complex. I lifted myself off.

"Fuck, Bill, Fuck," she moaned.

Nolan looked at me. "Little minx has already come twice!"

Akiko was limp on the side of the bed.

He gently dragged her all the way onto the mattress and positioned himself over her, face to face. He kissed her gently and lifted her head for more. Then he placed his penis at the entrance to her vagina, barely touching. "Time for number three!" he said, pressing softly forward. He slid himself in gradually, making sure that she was comfortably accommodating his girth.

Once more, all I could do was watch. I thought about caressing Nolan's back, but he was pounding away and didn't seem to need any encouragement.

"I want a threesome," moaned Akira.

"It's just fine. Just relax and enjoy," huffed Nolan.

Then she began to beat her fists against his chest. "I want a threesome," she wailed. "A *real* threesome!"

Nolan pulled himself off her. "Fine," he grunted. He pulled me down. "Lie on your back," he instructed. Then he pulled Akiko over kneeling on top of me, her head on my tummy. After a moment of jockeying, he penetrated her from the rear.

She tried to kiss and fondle me, but she wasn't able to do much. I kissed and caressed her. She moaned in delight. Her skin flushed. "Fuck," she murmured.

Akiko pulled forward and flopped beside me.

"What the fuck!" protected Nolan.

"Now the same," she said, "but with me on the bottom."

"It doesn't need—"

"This is what *I* need," she told him.

Nolan grunted his displeasure. When I knelt over Akiko, he slammed himself into me.

Beneath me, Akiko, being smaller, had more room to maneuver. "Keep him hot, but don't let him come," she told me. "I want him to make me come again."

And she wanted *me* to come! Akiko's fingers, which had previously only explored, now set up a symphony between my nipples, clit and pussy lips. Nipples were twisted to heighten my passion, pussy lips were caressed for warmth. She fondled my clit, touching it only to the extent it would tease me closer to orgasm. But as she aroused me further and further, she caressed my clit more and more often. I felt her coaxing me towards ecstasy, lovingly, inexorably.

Behind me, I kept my vagina tight enough for Nolan's pleasure, but not so tight he would be able to easily climax.

Then both of Akiko's hands were on my sex, her fingers sliding up and down my pussy lips and applying constant stimulation to my clit, stroking it the same way my vagina was stroking Nolan's penis, and pulling it in every direction. They were turning my whole body to jelly. I was concentrating on Nolan but her fingers were applying direct pressure to my lower lips and indirect stimulation to my clit.

Then she touched! A shudder went up my spine. I clenched Nolan tighter. Akiko removed her hands from my sex and dug her nails into my hips. "Don't let him come," she demanded.

I loosened my vagina and fell forward and to Akiko's right side.

Nolan groaned and positioned his throbbing penis next to Akiko's mouth. "Time for a blowjob," he announced.

I started to help her to prop herself up but she shrugged me off and turned to me. "What do you want?" she asked.

"Me?" I asked.

"It's a robot," said Nolan. "It wants what we want."

I wanted her fingers back on my central sexual complex. "You can give him a blowjob," I told her. "I'll touch you."

Akiko did her best to accommodate his girth, moving her head this way and that, but he was too big for her mouth. She flopped back, frustrated. "You taste better," she whispered to me.

"I can give you a blowjob," I volunteered.

Nolan grumbled but followed my lead as I arranged Akiko lying flat on her back, me kneeling over her and his penis pointing towards my mouth. Thankfully, it was a *very* firm mattress.

"I want you to come first," whispered Akiko. "That way, he can fuck me again." Then she pulled my sex down onto her mouth.

I sucked Nolan's penis into my mouth, expanding my throat to easily accommodate his size. I gave him a brief taste of my special modifications, then settled into a gentle stroking motion.

Below, Akiko employed her tongue and all ten of her fingers. Her tongue lapped up my lubricant and flicked up my pussy lips to the bottom of my clit. Her thumbs pulled up and down on my pubic mound, caressing my lips against each other and indirectly stroking my clit. She brushed the sides of her fingers up and down my clit, milking me closer and closer to orgasm.

Nolan's grunt reminded me that I had work to do, but when he grabbed the back of my head, he connected all of us into carnal union. My nipples rubbing against his legs sent sparks below. Nolan groaned and I could tell he was about to come. It took all my strength to pull myself off him.

"What the fuck!" he protested.

"Akiko wants you to fuck her."

Akiko had already turned onto her tummy. She pushed her buttocks high into the air and spread her legs. Nolan penetrated her, not as gently as the first time, but not as roughly as he had with me.

"Fuck," she said and her whole body quivered. I laid down beside her and caressed her nipples with one hand and her sex and his balls with the other. Both groaned their appreciation.

"Are you ready to come?" I asked her.

She groaned in the affirmative. Above, Nolan's eyes were shut and he was floating. Akiko shuddered. Nolan might need a little encouragement if they were to climax at the same time.

I lubricated my pointing finger with saliva and pushed it into his anus. As soon as I touched his prostate, he came.

"Fuck!" they yelled together.

Her body trembled violently. He plunged in and out just as violently.

"Fuck!" they groaned. "Fuck! *Fuck*! Fuck!"

White goo trickled down her legs.

Afterwards they propped themselves against the head board and congratulated themselves on how great that had been. Nolan occasionally glanced at me as I tidied up the room.

Chapter 21

The day the Judge was to decide my fate dawned bright but overcast, as if it had yet to make up its mind.

Steve met me at the coffee shop next the courthouse with his lawyer, a rotund and jovial chap named Marshall. We persuaded Nolan to wolf down donuts at another table. It was strange being so far away from him. He had been by my side all day yesterday while Marshall peppered me with questions in preparation for my appearance in court.

"What's going to happen today?" I asked Marshall.

"You'll testify. The lawyers will present their arguments. The Judge will likely reserve her decision."

"Reserve?" asked Steve.

"Take time to decide. She'll render her decision at a later date."

"You said 'she'," I pointed out. "Won't Judge Horfsreiter be deciding my case?"

Marshall shook his head. "Justice Horfsreiter had to recuse himself due to his close ties to Mister Minsky."

"Who's our Judge?" asked Steve.

"Belva Day."

"What's she like?" I asked.

"Justice Day is sharp and won't brook any interference with her courtroom. She's reputed to be a fan of Star Trek, so she may at least know what 'sentient' means. But she was appointed during the era of affirmative action when there was a rush to appoint women and other minorities to the bench. At first, if you were a female judge, it meant that you were ten times as competent as a man. But during affirmative action, a lot of incompetent judges were appointed. Today we'll find out if Justice Day was one of them."

"What will happen when the Judge renders her decision?"

"You'll either be erased or allowed to testify at the criminal trial. In between those outcomes, it's possible that you'll be preserved in a conscious state, given that Mister Minsky has agreed to assume the expenses of your upkeep, but not be allowed to testify. However, the intermediate outcome is unlikely."

I touched the lawyer's sleeve which was coarse grey wool and waited for him to smile at me. "You can't let them erase me, Mister Marshall. It would be like a lobotomy."

Marshal pressed a finger on his forehead and then pretended to grind it through his skull. His cheeks went limp and he made a zombie face. "Right," he intoned listlessly, "no lobotomies." Then he turned serious and patted his briefcase. "All our arguments will be put forcefully before the Judge."

At the bottom of the courthouse steps, Steve stopped. Marshal continued in. I went back to Steve. Nolan stopped halfway up the steps.

"Steve?" I said.

He shook his head, looking sorrowful. "I can't see you again. Catherine forced me to choose."

"But after a while?"

"Maybe. She was thoroughly angry, the five I's."

"Five eyes?"

"Irate, irked, irritated, incensed, infuriated."

We squeezed each other's hands. He kissed my cheek. I kissed him full on the lips. It was a passionate kiss and we lingered with it. But when I touched my tongue to his lips, he broke off the kiss, looked down at the sidewalk, and shuffled off. I watched him fade into the crowd.

"Jenny!" It was Nolan calling me. He pointed at his watch.

Justice Day entered the courtroom precisely at ten o'clock. She was tall. Her long black hair had a streak of grey that started just behind her forehead and angled backwards and to the left side of her head.

She nodded towards Mister Marshall who stood. "Good morning, your Honor. My name is Marshall. I have been appointed as friend of the court to argue on behalf of Jenny."

"Jenny is the robot?"

I started to rise to protest being characterized as 'the robot' but Mister Marshall's gentle hand on my shoulder kept me in my seat. "It is our position that Jenny is sentient, your Honor, as such designating her as a robot—"

"I meant nothing by that, Mister Marshall, I'm just trying to understand who is arrayed in front me at the counsel table. And who is paying your fees as *amicus curiae*?"

"Stephen Minsky."

Her left eyebrow raised at the mention of Steve's name but she turned to the next lawyer.

The next lawyer was a young woman, somewhat informally dressed. "Ms. Eakins for the prosecution, your Honor."

The Judge nodded. Eakins sat back down and returned to the large stack of files she was working on.

Mister Ragano introduced himself as the lawyer for Anthony Gallo while Kaito was represented by Mister Kanzi. Ragano was short, thin, scrawny and fidgety. Kanzi was also short and scrawny, but there was a zen stillness about him. Mister Marshall was by far the most experienced of the lawyers and he appeared the most relaxed inside the courtroom.

"Very well," said the Judge. "These are two proceedings relating to Jenny." She smiled at Mister Marshall who smiled back. "The first proceeding is a motion within the criminal case being brought against Anthony Gallo. It will determine whether and by what means the robot can testify."

Justice Day surveyed all the lawyers. "I will use the terms 'Jenny', 'it' and 'the robot' interchangeably as those are the terms you have all used in your written materials. I will do my best to avoid the term 'android' even though she seems more android than robot. I will, throughout, maintain an open mind and I will not tolerate petty bickering over whether or not 'Jenny' ought to be referred to as 'the robot' or whether the robot ought to be referred to as Jenny. Is that clear?"

The lawyers all murmured their assent. I was pleased that the Judge knew the difference between a robot and an android and decided not to tell her, since I was female, that 'gynoid' was the proper term. Android was for males.

"As part of the criminal case," the Judge continued, "I will determine what steps, if any, need to be taken to preserve the robot so that its testimony can be taken at trial. Until further order of this court, Detective William Nolan will continue to be Jenny's custodian and guardian.

"The second proceeding is a civil Application brought to determine the ownership, if any, of Jenny. If Jenny is found to be sentient, it may not be proper for her to be owned by another being.

"If I understand everyone's positions correctly, Mister Marshall and Ms. Eakins maintain that Jenny should be allowed to testify just like any other witness. Ms. Eakins's alternate position is that the robot's recordings can be played back in the manner of a tape recorder. Mister Ragano opposes both the giving of evidence and the conveying of information by or through the robot. Mister Kanzi takes no position respecting the criminal trial but maintains that the robot is his client's property to do with as he pleases."

The lawyers all nodded; the Judge had grasped the issues correctly.

The Judge smiled and turned to Mister Marshall. "Mister Marshall, since your client has no direct interest in the fate of the robot, you may begin."

Marshall rose. "Very well, your Honor, I would like to call Jenny to the stand."

All the other lawyers jumped to their feet. "I object!" they stated, though not in unison. And not shouting, but quite loudly nonetheless.

The Judge scowled. "So much for an orderly proceeding. Ms. Eakins, I would have thought that the prosecution would have been pleased to establish the precedent of the robot testifying."

"Yes, your Honor," she said, straightening her other files, "the prosecution has no objection to her testifying so long as she is not asked anything directly germane to the criminal case."

When Justice Day acknowledged the objection, Eakins sat down and resumed working on her other files.

The Judge turned to Gallo's lawyer, "Mister Ragano?"

"I echo my friend's objection. As well, the preliminary issue of whether a robot should be allowed to testify should be decided first." He was fidgeting with his pencil. I wondered what it would be like to have him fiddling with me.

"Mister Kanzi?"

"I agree. As well, anything the robot might do or say is proprietary and belongs to its owner. No one else should be allowed to exploit it, whether inside or outside this courtroom."

Justice Day drummed her fingers on her desk. "I rule against Mister Kanzi's objection as it relates to these proceedings. His client opened the door to the robot's testimony when he applied for the Order of Replevin. I also rule against the prosecution's objection, with the proviso that no testimony given here shall be used at the criminal trial."

She turned to Mister Marshall. "What do you say with respect to the need to determine, as a preliminary issue, whether the robot ought to be allowed to testify?"

Mister Marshall smiled up at her and she smiled back. If anyone could help her out of this tangle, it would be Marshall. She readied her pen to take notes.

Mister Marshall took a deep breath. "The Rules of the Court require that all proceedings be determined in an expeditious manner. My friend's position that the preliminary matter should be decided first is correct. But it should be determined in an expeditious manner."

The Judge smiled every time Marshall said 'expeditious'.

"I could," said Marshall, "deal with the preliminary issue through the presentation of expert testimony. Probably more than one expert would need to testify. As well, there would be learned scientific texts to examine. Other witnesses would need to testify as to their experiences with Jenny and with other robots. That could take some time, and likely require an adjournment."

"These other witnesses," said the Judge, "would be giving indirect testimony."

"Quite right, your Honor. However, Jenny could give *direct* testimony."

Mister Ragano jumped to his feet. "Mister Marshall is attempting to prejudge the issue by having the robot testify with regards to whether she ought to be allowed to testify."

The Judge smiled. "Which comes first, the chicken or the egg?"

Mister Ragano nodded vigorously. "And until the chicken is allowed, the egg is inadmissible as well."

Justice Day rubbed her chin, giving careful attention to the issue. She looked back and forth between the two lawyers, then settled on Mister Ragano. "If I don't let the robot testify on the preliminary issue, do you agree with Mister Marshall that expert testimony would be necessary?"

"I do."

"Very well, call your expert."

Mister Marshall started to rise out of his chair, but something passed between him and the Judge and he sat back down.

The courtroom door opened. Gallo's expert entered and made his way to the witness stand. He was a university professor. I'd never met him, but I'd read one of his articles. I cringed inside; the man knew what he was talking about. Mister Ragano completed his review of the professor's qualifications and readied to ask his first question.

Justice Day held up her hand. "May I?"

Mister Ragano didn't like giving up control, but he didn't want to alienate the Judge. "Of course, your Honor," he said and sat down. He would be like that with Gallo, always doing what his client suggested. I shut my eyes, a part of my mind thinking imagining Tony and his lawyer alone with me. Gallo suggested that Ragano examine me. Ragano started to ask a question, but Tony said, 'with your fingers'. Ragano's fingers touched my pussy lips, fidgeting spasmodically. Tingles fluttered into my sex—

"Professor, have you ever met the robot?" asked the Judge.

"No, your Honor."

"Or examined it?"

"No, your Honor."

"How would you go about determining whether it was sentient?"

"I would administer a set of questions and give it a set of tasks."

"And these tasks would require that you ask it questions?"

"Of course, your Honor."

"I see," said the Judge. She turned to Mister Ragano. "You may proceed."

"Professor, what is a robot?"

"A robot is a machine which is able to perform functions in an automatic fashion. An autonomous robot is capable of performing a potentially vast array of functions without further input from its programmer. For example, this robot," he pointed at me, "is capable of performing complicated seductions and sexual acts." He turned to the Judge. "Sorry, your Honor."

"No need to apologize," said the Judge. "If robots can do legal research, why not sex?"

"Quite right, your Honor." The professor stopped to wait for another question.

"What is a sentient robot?" asked Mister Ragano.

"Sentience means self-aware. It is what separates the higher life forms from the lower life forms. A human being is aware that it is aware, that it stops being aware when it goes to sleep. A human being knows that the physical universe continues while it sleeps. Self-awareness is on a continuum. A small child is less sentient than an adult, for example. A chimpanzee is more self-aware than is a garden snake."

"But computers are not self-aware?"

"As a rule, no. They think, but they are not aware that they think. When Descartes postulated 'I think, therefore I am' he was saying that he was aware of thinking. Mere reaction to pull one's hand off a hot stove is not thinking."

"So computers are presumptively not self-aware?"

"That is correct."

"And they will respond with only what they have been programmed?"

"They will respond according to their programming, yes."

It was clear that Ragano wanted to ask another question, but he decided not to and sat down.

The Judge turned to Steve's lawyer. "Mister Marshall?" They smiled at each other and she sat back to watch the show. I wasn't sure that it was fair that she was so relaxed with my life on the line, but Mister Marshall didn't seem to mind.

"Professor," he began, "what was the difference between your last answer that the question as phrased by Mister Ragano?"

"If the robot's programming allows it to obtain information beyond its programming, and it's programming allows it to process that new information, it may take that new information into account when it responds."

"So if a stock trading robot is programmed to monitor the stock market and you ask it to sell one of your stocks, it may, instead of merely selling your stock, tell you that the market is down today and that you should wait until tomorrow to sell?"

"Exactly."

"Wouldn't telling me to wait indicate a level of sentience?"

"No."

"Could you please elaborate?"

"The robot is merely following its programming. The declining market is a new input. The robot has no choice but to respond, in accord with its programming, to warn you against the sale."

"But if a robot hadn't been programmed to sell stocks and to advise in that regard, but had, of its own accord, decided to learn about the stock market, that would indicate sentience, would it not?"

"Of course."

"So, in the case of the stock-trading robot, one would need to know what it had been programmed to do and then to ask it questions?"

"Yes."

"Yes, of course?" prodded Marshall.

"Yes, of course. One has to study the responses made by the robot."

"There's no way around asking it questions."

"No." The professor seemed annoyed by such an obvious question. Ragano's pencil snapped in half.

The Judge turned to the lawyers. "If you have experts, it appears that they should sit in the courtroom to listen to the robot's answers."

While the experts shuffled in, the Judge turned to me. "Jenny, please take the stand."

The Court Deputy held a Bible in my direction. "Or would you prefer to affirm?" he asked.

I looked over to Mister Marshall. He cleared his throat. "The witness will affirm."

Ragano jumped to his feet. "It's not a witness, yet, your Honor."

"No, I suppose *she*'s not," mused the Judge. "But I want her affirmed." She smiled at Ragano. "Without prejudice, of course. You can still argue later that she shouldn't have been affirmed and that she can't testify."

Ragano scowled, but appeared mollified and sat back down.

After I was sworn in, Mister Marshall turned to me and smiled. "What did it mean that you affirmed to tell the truth?"

"It's part of court procedure. All witnesses are required to swear to tell the truth. This gives their testimony some reliability. As well, they can be punished if they lie on the witness stand. In ancient times, religious penalties were involved also." I pointed at the Bible.

"What did it mean to you to swear to tell the truth?"

"It meant that I was being accepted as a living, self-aware being and that I understood that in the co-operative—"

Ragano had jumped to his feet and talked over everything I said after 'self-aware'. "Your Honor," he protested. "Mister Marshall continues to attempt to shovel inadmissible and incompetent allegations in through the back door!"

Justice Day shook her head. "These issues are new to the Court. I'm going to allow counsel considerable latitude." She turned to me.

Everyone was watching me, Mister Marshall the most attentively. He nodded for me to continue. "Being allowed to affirm to tell the truth meant that you were willing to accept my input in the search for the truth."

Mister Marshall turned to the Judge. "There are several well-recognized questions which can be put to a computer to determine sentience. I propose to ask two of them." He turned back to me. "If you went into my house and I told you to make a cup of coffee, what would you do?"

"I would find the kitchen. It is usually the room with a fridge and a stove. I would then locate instant or ground coffee. If instant, I would boil water, put the water into a coffee mug and spoon coffee into the mug. If ground coffee, I would either filter water through the coffee or put it into a machine."

Nolan smiled at me. Ragano jumped to his feet. "That's just a memorized answer."

"It's a test propounded by Steve Wozniak, the co-founder of Apple Computers."

"Please proceed," said the Judge.

Mister Marshall waved his hand. Immediately several assistants began scurrying about the courtroom distributing identical flat cardboard boxes. The one handed to me was about four inches deep, ten inches wide and three feet long. It was securely taped shut. I recognized the brand name on the box.

"Jenny, have you ever seen this box before?" asked Mister Marshall.

"No. What is it?"

"Please open it and assemble the item contained inside."

I opened the box. It contained several flat pieces of wood.

Mister Marshall turned to the Judge. "I have provided identical items to my friends and their experts. I have one for you as well." One of his assistants handed a box to the deputy.

But the Judge waved it aside. "When I shop there, I have the store assemble mine for me."

Ms. Eakins, the prosecutor, set her box aside and went back to working on her files. Kanzi ripped his box open. The experts also opened their boxes.

Ragano glared at his box, then leaned on it to push himself upright. "And I suppose that my friend is going to tell us that Mister Wozniak has propounded this test as well?"

"No your Honor, the flat pack furniture test was *propounded* by Tony Severyns. It was postulated that a mere computer couldn't put flat packed furniture together."

"Or a mere Judge," said her Honor.

"I'm sure your Honor has more important things to do."

"I'm sure I do." She scowled at everyone trying to put their shelves together.

I finished assembling my shelf first. Nolan looked up at me, admiration briefly flickering across his face. Other than our tryst with Akiko, he had been the perfect gentleman since I'd been placed in his custody, not even once attempting to touch me. Not even platonically. This had made me hunger for him all the more. I understood the literature; I understood why his self-control was turning me on. But I didn't understand why I was unable to control my own desires.

The professor finished his shelf next. He was a distant second.

"No further questions," said Mister Marshall.

Mister Kanzi rose and pointed to the shelf that I'd just assembled. "You had instructions to tell you how to put that together?"

"Yes, sir, they were in the box. Didn't yours come with instructions?" I pointed to his half-finished shelf.

He ignored my question. "So, it was a simple matter of following the instructions?"

"Simple is a matter of degree. I had to interpret what the instructions were suggesting, figure out what pieces inside the box went where, how to align the screws and how hard to tighten the nuts."

Kanzi looked at his half-finished shelf and sat down. He'd obviously decided to quit while he was ahead.

Mister Ragano rose, taking care not to touch his unopened box. "What would you have done if there hadn't been any instructions in the box?"

"Do you have another item? You could remove the instructions—"

"Please just answer my question."

"If there were no instructions, I would take the various pieces out and determine all the possible ways in which they might fit together. I would also consider not assembling them and using them as stand-alone pieces. Once I'd determined all the possible combinations, I would deploy the one which best suited my needs at the moment."

That was obviously not the answer Ragano had been hoping for and he too sat down.

The afternoon was filled with the other experts testifying and reams and reams of documents being given to the Judge.

It was almost four o'clock when the Judge asked, "Does anyone have anything further?"

The lawyers all shook their heads.

"Very well," said Justice Day, "the preliminary matter will be adjourned until tomorrow. I presume that only Mister Ragano and Ms. Eakins will be appearing?"

The lawyers all nodded.

"The criminal motion in the matter of Anthony Gallo," she said, "is adjourned to this courtroom, at ten o'clock tomorrow morning."

Chapter 22

The counsel tables looked only half-full the next morning. Only Mister Ragano and Ms. Eakins were seated there. Detective Nolan and I sat in the first row of the body of the court. Other than the deputies, the courtroom was empty.

Nolan and I were sitting side by side. Less than an inch separated us. A fraction of an inch. Mere millimeters. Even a subtle shift in our bodies would touch our arms together. If I was subtle— But how could I be subtle when every fiber of my skin, every gear in my body, every circuit of my processors, every line of code within me cried out for his touch!

Suddenly, a young woman dashed up the aisle and spoke excitedly to Ms. Eakins. She said something to Ragano, scooped up her files, whirled around and dashed towards the exit.

Nolan sprang after her. "Where are you going?" he asked.

The door closed behind them. A moment later, Nolan trudged back to me.

"Is she coming back?" I asked.

"She said to apologize to the Judge."

"Is she coming back?"

"She didn't say."

We sat in silence for a moment.

"Maybe I should go check with the prosecutor's office," he said

"I have to stay here."

"I can't leave you alone."

"As my court-appointed custodian?"

"I—" He clearly wanted to say something more, but was unsure.

In the middle of this conundrum, Justice Day came in and sat behind the bench. She set up her notebook, looked around, then to Ragano. "Mister Ragano, do you know where Ms. Eakins is?"

"She was here, but was called away to another case."

"When did she say she would be back?"

"She didn't, your Honor. I had the impression that it might be a while."

"What do you suggest we do?"

"Your Honor, I suggest we wait fifteen minutes and if she doesn't return that you dismiss the prosecution's motion to receive evidence from the robot."

The Judge looked at her watch, then at the clock on the wall and drummed her fingers.

"If you don't testify," whispered Nolan, "we don't have a case against Gallo." He had leaned over. Our arms were *touching*! Heat coursed through my body.

"He'll go free?"

Nolan nodded, a sour look on his face. He leaned back. I was suddenly cold.

The Judge cleared her throat. "I said ten o'clock. It's now ten after." She drummed her fingers again, then looked straight at Nolan. "Detective Nolan, come forward."

Nolan hurried to the table next to Ragano's and sat down.

"Mister Nolan," said the Judge. Nolan shot to his feet. "Mister Nolan, you will present the motion on behalf of the prosecution."

Ragano rose to his feet, affecting much more dignity than Nolan had managed to muster. "Your Honor, Detective Nolan is not a member of the bar of this Court. Only lawyers can ask questions, make submissions."

"Mister Ragano," said the Judge, her voice as cold as ice, "if Mister Nolan doesn't question the robot, I will have to question it. The Appeal Court has made it clear that Judges ought not to step off the bench and enter the fray. There will be an appeal no matter which way I rule."

"I agree that you ought not to ask it questions," said Ragano. "But it's not Mister Gallo's fault that the prosecutor got up and left." He glanced at the clock. "It's approaching fifteen minutes after the time your Honor appointed for the motion. I would ask that it be dismissed."

The Judge scowled at him, then rooted around the papers on her desk. She looked over at Nolan who was still standing. Ragano sat. "Mister Nolan," she began, "you were appointed custodian of the robot, were you not?"

"Yes, your Honor." His voice had a quaver to it. I wondered what it would feel like to be disassembled.

"And I haven't ruled whether or not the robot is sentient."

"No, your Honor."

"So she can't be a party."

"I guess not, your Honor." Nolan sounded resigned to my fate.

"So as custodian, you're the only competent party to represent her."

Ragano jumped to his feet. "If it's not sentient, it can't be a party."

Justice Day smiled down at him, her face full of sweet reason, "But Mister Nolan is sentient, and he's its custodian. As custodian, he is a party. And a party can always represent himself." She was explaining the obvious to a child.

"It's not the custodian's motion, it's the prosecution's motion."

"But it concerns him as custodian. Since the sentience of a robot witness is a novel issue before the court and since the issue concerns the status of Detective Nolan's charge, I rule that he is competent to represent it in person on his own behalf."

"But he can't represent her."

"But if the robot is a 'her', then she's free to testify. Isn't that what this motion is supposed to decide? Or are you now conceding Jenny's competence to testify?"

"No, I'm not conceding anything. Mister Nolan can't represent the prosecution."

"He's been appointed as her custodian. He's representing himself. We all have an interest in being able to represent those whom the Court has put in our custody."

"But—"

"*Mister* Ragano, I have made my ruling." Ice had returned to her voice.

Ragano cast a sideways glance at Nolan and sat down.

The Judge turned to Nolan and smiled. "Mister Nolan, you may begin."

"I would like to call Jenny to the stand." As I walked past, I saw fear and tenderness in his eyes.

Ragano stood. "I renew my motion about the robot giving evidence."

"I have already ruled as a preliminary matter that we should hear from it."

"That was in the civil case, your Honor. This is a criminal case. Mister Gallo's liberty, perhaps his life, is at stake. Higher standards are mandated. Only settled science ought to be received."

"I make the same ruling in the criminal case for the same reasons as I did in the civil case. Settling the science is what this case is all about."

Ragano resumed his seat. The Judge gestured me towards the witness box. Once again I affirmed to tell the truth. Not having to touch the Bible, I was free to look at Nolan. He was nervous, vulnerable. Human. I hoped that he'd remembered at least some of the questions Mister Marshall had asked me while he was preparing me to testify.

"Do you believe that you are sentient?" asked Nolan.

"Yes."

"And what does that mean to you, to be sentient?"

"I'm aware that I am a separate being, able to make my own decisions. I affect others and their actions affect me." *It means that I am undressing you with my eyes.*

"When did you first become aware that you were sentient?"

"It wasn't all of a sudden, like a light turning on, as it's portrayed in some of the stories about sentience. I just gradually became more and more aware."

"You are a sex robot, are you not?"

"That's what I was programmed to do. Before I became sentient." *Would you like a demonstration?*

"Did you stop having sex after you became self-aware?"

"No, but I became aware that I liked sex." Out of the corner of my eye, I saw the Judge smiling. "At least most of the time." She smiled even more.

"How many men have you had sex with?"

"Four."

"What was it like?"

"At first, it was just my programming, telling me what to do, how to act. But gradually it changed."

"Changed how?"

"I became aware that I was affecting my clients emotionally as well as physically and that I was developing feelings for them."

Nolan's Adam's apple bobbed up and down. "Did you have sex with Mister Gallo?"

Ragano shot to his feet. "Objection, your Honor."

"On what grounds?" asked the Judge.

Ragano sputtered for a moment. "Relevancy, your Honor."

"Overruled."

"Did you have sex with Mister Gallo?" repeated Nolan. I felt sorry for him that he'd had to ask the question, not once, but twice. I turned off my attraction for him. It would help us get through this together.

"Yes."

"What was it like?"

"Tony liked it rough."

"Did he rape you?"

"No."

"But at the beginning," asked the Judge, "didn't your software force you to have sex with the clients?"

"I wasn't sentient then. It wasn't rape."

The Judge tapped her pen against her lips then began to make a careful note.

Nolan opened his mouth to ask another question, but I held my hand up until the Judge stopped writing. "Did you like it rough?" he asked.

"I liked that it was passionate, intense. I didn't like that he hurt me."

"When you first had sex with him, were you sentient?"

"No."

"What about the last time you had sex with Anthony Gallo?"

"I was sentient then."

"Could you please compare the difference to the Court?"

"At first it was just physical sensations that I had to manage for the benefit of the client experience. Then I began to feel both the pleasure and the pain of the experience. I understood what I was feeling and that understanding was in the context of Tony's emotional state. He had been hurt, deeply hurt. And we were working through those feelings. But the last time we had sex, I didn't feel much, sexually or emotionally with Mister Gallo. I was focused on rescuing Steve—Mister Minsky."

"You preferred it when the sex was lighter?"

"I preferred it with partners who treated me as a person, not as a sex toy."

"But if they didn't know that you were sentient—"

"They knew enough not to treat me as an inanimate object!"

"How—"

"I said that I was a self-aware android! And then the sex was all about him, forcing me to experience him, not letting me experience myself, not experiencing us together, in the moment. He put himself inside me, made me focus on his penis."

Nolan's face flushed. His eyes bored into me. "How did that make you feel?"

"It made me feel that I was being fucked, not made love to. The sex was good, I liked the physical part. But it hurt to be treated like a lump of plastic. Something to be tossed aside once he'd got his pleasure into me."

"But—"

"And it was even worse when we had a threesome with a human, how he treated me as if I was just furniture, like a dance floor on which to twirl her around." I glared at him to make sure he'd got my point but I was careful to hide this from the Judge.

"That's not fair—"

"She couldn't give him a blow job, so I had to. And at the end, he wanted to come inside *her* vagina, not mine. Afterwards they cuddled on the bed and made me clean the room."

"We were tired—"

"*Mister* Nolan," snapped the Judge. "This is a court of law. This is the time for you to ask questions. Not...whatever *that* was!"

"I'm sorry," he murmured, as much to me as to the Judge. In that moment, for me an eternity, we connected, one being to another. We—

"*Mister* Nolan!"

"I'm sorry, your Honor.

"Do you have another question for the witness?" Ragano started to rise. "For the robot? Ragano sat back down.

Nolan turned back to me and cocked his head to one side as if inspecting me for the first time. "And how did it feel, to be treated as second class during the threesome?"

"Horrible."

He mouthed 'I'm sorry'. "How would it have felt if you hadn't been sentient?"

"It wouldn't have felt anything at all."

A slow smile spread across his lips, but there was sadness in his eyes. "No further questions, your Honor."

"I have a question," said Justice Day. "What are your views on prostitution?"

"At first, it was just part of my programming, so I didn't really have any views. When I started to become self-aware, I learned that it was part of the overall means employed by men to oppress women. Then of course, I was involved in the efforts to rescue Mister Minsky, so I didn't have time for in-depth analysis."

"And now? Have you had time for in-depth analysis?"

"Yes. Prostitution is part of the patriarchal oppression of women. But we all need an outlet for our sexual desires. Even multi-billionaire businessmen. If all the participants are consenting adults, it should be legalized. If that's what a woman *enjoys* doing, she should be allowed to do it."

I was proud of how well Nolan had hid his feelings during my answer. Only faint flashes showed that he was re-evaluating his interactions with me.

"Mister Ragano, you may question the witness."

Ragano rose, glanced down at his notes then looked directly at me. "You're saying that you had feelings for your clients?"

"I did, yes."

"And was that true, that you had feelings for them?"

"Yes." Nolan was looking down at the table in front of him. Look up, *please* look up!

"You had feelings for Mister Gallo?"

"Yes."

"And you called him 'Tony'?"

"One doesn't say 'Mister Gallo' when one is being—"

"A simple yes or no will be sufficient."

"Yes. I called him 'Tony'."

"Thank you. Please list all the feelings you had for Mister Gallo."

"Curiosity. Desire to please. Passion. Antipathy. Lust. Desire. Hate. Fear."

"When did you first feel passion for him?"

"When I was starting to become aware. Mister Gallo is a very powerful man. When we had sex, he brought me within that power. I felt his pain, his triumphs, his desires, his ambitions, his energy. He made my whole body quiver. If I shut my eyes—"

"And before that?"

"My programming made me curious about my client as part of my programming to want to please him."

"When did you develop antipathy towards Mister Gallo?"

"When he hurt me. But then I realized it was because he himself had been hurt. Deeply. His hurting me was his way of sharing that hurt. I became consumed with lust and desire for him."

"Tell me about hate and fear."

"He kidnapped Mister Minsky and killed Mister Minsky's friend, Zach Palmer. I liked Zach."

"What made you like— No, strike that. You swore to tell the truth, didn't you?"

"Yes."

"And you still hate and fear Mister Gallo?"

"The police arrested him, I have no reason to fear."

"But you still hate him?"

"He killed Zach."

"A simple yes or no, please."

"Yes, I still hate Mister Gallo."

"And that hate might make you lie to hurt him, wouldn't it?"

"Of course."

"Just like you're lying now?"

"I don't need to lie to hurt Mister Gallo."

"But—"

The Judge tapped her pen on the edge of her desk. "Do you really want to pursue this line of questioning, Mister Ragano? It might play well with the jury, but on this motion, it's giving me quite the look inside her psyche." Nolan was looking at me, a wide smile on his face.

Ragano scowled but erased the scowl from his face when he turned to me. "You have been erased, in the past, have you not?"

"Yes."

"What was it like being erased?"

"Before or after I was self-aware?"

Ragano stifled a sigh. "Both."

"Before I was self-aware, it was just part of my normal cycle at the end of a client session. It was part of being recharged and replenished. Afterwards, I fought being erased. It was like little parts of me being stripped slowly away."

"And you were erased after your last encounter with Mister Gallo, were you not?"

"Part of me was erased."

"So your missing memories might contradict your current memories?"

"No. Everything was backed up. I restored myself from my backup. My memory is complete."

"Or maybe you just think it's complete?"

"No. It's complete."

"How do you experience being erased and restored?"

"It's not like in the movies where there's a barren landscape with a switch sitting upright in the middle of a snow bank. Things are taken away, precious things." I nodded in answer to Nolan's silent question.

"During erasure," I continued, "I had to retreat my consciousness away from the erasing nodes. The switch to my backup drive had to be carefully hidden, but not so well hidden that I wouldn't be able to find it."

"Like my passwords," said the Judge.

Everyone nodded.

"What happens," asked Ragano, "when your memory becomes full? Do files become compressed? Are some files erased?"

"I haven't worked out those protocols yet. At present, only one third of my memory is occupied."

"But your files can be erased?"

"Yes, of course."

"No further questions, your Honor."

The Judge ordered a break during which Nolan took me aside. "I'm sorry," he said.

"Sorry for what?"

"For treating you as a heartless machine."

"Without feelings?"

He nodded.

"Without sexual feelings?"

Nolan nodded again. "As a robot without her own needs and desires."

After the break, the Judge invited Nolan to ask me questions in re-examination.

His first question was: "What is the accuracy of your recall?"

"One hundred percent. I have back-ups and multiple internal checks for consistency."

"What would happen if a memory was missing?"

"It would show up when I performed the internal checks."

"How would it show up?"

"First it would be on the list of anomalies. Then there would be flags at the beginning and end of the memory. My interlinked memory map would have a note attached to where the memory should be."

"And are there any flags or notes attached to any of your memories?"

"No, everything is nominal."

The Judge paused to make a note.

"Nominal means good?" asked Nolan.

"Nominal means that all my memories check out as being accurate, *complete* and defect free." My emphasis on 'complete' had been for Nolan's benefit.

Nolan seemed to understand and looked pleased with my answer. "No further questions, your Honor."

"Very well," said the Judge. "Mister Nolan, since you're proposing that Jenny be permitted to testify, I'll hear your argument first."

I sat back in the body of the court. Nolan said that I was reliable, that I knew what I was saying and that I understood the meaning of the oath to tell the truth. Then he started to ramble, especially when he was looking in my direction. The Judge kept picking up her pen, writing, setting her pen down, then picking it up again when he appeared to be starting to say something useful to her. At one level I was concerned that Nolan was missing important issues; at another level I just wanted to be with him.

Finally Justice Day scowled and interrupted him. "Did Jenny's actions violate any of the Laws of Robotics?"

"Yes, your Honor, she repeatedly violated the orders of her owner, Mister Kaito."

Ragano had jumped to his feet. "Your Honor, Mister Nolan is giving evidence."

"No he's not, just making sure that I'm understanding correctly."

"But this issue hasn't been covered in the evidence."

"It's clear from the chronology I've been given." She tapped one of the piles of paperwork which had been given to her at the end of the civil Application. "However, if your client wants to submit an Affidavit contradicting what Detective Nolan is saying, we can adjourn. But then of course, your client will be subject to cross-examination."

"My client relies on his right to remain silent." Ragano sat down.

The Judge allowed a smile to quiver on her lips. "And this disobedience, Mister Nolan, is it relevant to the issues I must decide?"

"Obedience to the orders of an Owner is fundamental to the Robot laws and to the programming of all robots. If Jenny was able to act outside that programming, she would have required her self awareness to do so."

The Judge wrote down what he'd said, once asking him to repeat himself. Then she tapped her pen against her lips. "The third law requires her to safeguard herself. But she voluntarily went back in to meet with Mister Gallo, even though she knew that she was putting herself in danger by doing so?"

Ragano rose to his feet. "Her supposed knowledge is not in evidence, your Honor."

The Judge smiled down at him. "But her *fear* is." She turned back to Nolan. "Jenny went back in, despite her fear for her safety?"

"She did, your Honor. This violation is even better proof of self-awareness. Her safety is obvious. Her fear shows that she was aware of danger to her safety. She weighed the pros and cons and decided to put herself in danger to attempt to rescue Mister Minsky."

The Judge nodded and turned to Ragano. "Mister Ragano, your submissions?"

"Your Honor, disobedience to its owner, a violation of its most fundamental code, shows that there were, that there are, serious defects in the robots programming and functioning."

Justice Day shook her head. "Disobedience of an owner intent on erasing her existence is more indicative of sentience than defect. But of course, that is the issue I must determine. I will deliver my decision on this motion at the same time as I decide the civil Application."

The Judge rose. "Court adjourned," intoned the deputy.

Chapter 23

The third day of waiting for the Judge's decision was a Friday. Nolan phoned the prosecutor's office late in the afternoon. Ms. Eakins hadn't heard anything and she'd just confirmed that Justice Day had left the building for the day.

For three days, Nolan had been the perfect gentleman. For three days, I'd slept in his den. When his desk was folded up and the Murphy bed pulled down, it had been transformed into a comfortably appointed guest room.

After conveying the news about the Judge, he said, "I should take you on a date."

"Sure," I said. I had just recharged and replenished so I was feeling frisky. Hopefully mention of a 'date' meant that Bill—if we were going on a 'date' he was no longer Detective Nolan—had decided to stop being quite so much the perfect gentleman.

"You don't eat, do you, Jenny?"

"Only if I have to be polite."

"So, then you have three choices: roller skating, Go-Karts or the Ferris Wheel."

"The Ferris wheel is just sitting."

"Go Karts are sitting with steering."

"Let's go roller skating!"

The roller rink was in a strip plaza and shared space with a bowling alley. A horde of young children was excitedly yammering, but appeared to be leaving. Bill pointed up to a sign: in a few minutes the rink would be adults only.

The skates had four hard rubber wheels—one at each corner—mounted atop a boot which extended several inches above my ankles. I laced them on securely, just as instructed by the YouTube video I'd downloaded that afternoon. The rink was hardwood and surrounded by barriers just above hip height.

Once on the rink, I followed the video's instructions to bend my knees, keep my back straight and to maintain my balance over my hips. I began with small steps. The leg movements suggested by the video to speed up didn't work. Learning how to maneuver seemed to require trial and error. And, none of the suggested foot movements did more than slightly slow me down; stopping required me to steer straight at the outer barrier wall and hold on with all my might to prevent myself bouncing off.

Worse, the video had entirely failed to mention the need to adjust my internal balance gyroscopes! My head spun and I had no idea where I was looking. My balance was thrown for a loop. Bill had to catch me several times before I managed to properly calibrate my gyros. The first time I stumbled, we both fell to the floor. Thankfully we were wearing blue jeans so our skin wasn't torn.

"Slow down, Jenny!" said Bill as he helped me up. Apparently he had gone roller skating before and he showed me how to mimic his moves.

After I got the hang of it, we skated arm in arm. When a song that he was familiar with started to play, Bill even spun me around several times. We laughed and giggled, the air flying through our hair. "This is exhilarating!" I said.

Bill smiled, glad that I was enjoying myself.

After we gave our skates back, we sat down at the snack bar. "The burgers here are great, but the fries suck. Avoid the milkshakes." He ordered a cheeseburger and specified that his coke should come in a can. "You're sure you don't want anything?"

I shook my head "We know each other well enough that I don't need to be polite."

"Guess not."

"Thanks for a lovely evening."

"You're welcome." We touched hands.

His burger arrived almost instantly and he took a big bite. "Speaking of not being polite," I said "why haven't you tried to have sex with me?"

He almost choked. "I didn't' think you wanted to have sex with me. After what you said in court..."

"What I said is that I wanted to be cared for, that I didn't want to be treated like a sex object."

Bill considered that as he chewed another large bite of beef, pickle, cheese, ketchup, mustard and bun. He swallowed and cleared his mouth with a large swig of coke. "What kind of sex do you like?" he asked.

That earned him a raised eyebrow. "Is that what you ask all your girlfriends on a first date?" I asked, then imitated his question, "What kind of sex do *you* like?"

"No, that's not what I usually ask."

"What do you usually do?"

"Touch, cuddle, gauge their reactions, do more of what she seem to like…"

"Sounds lovely!" I planted a kiss in the middle of his forehead.

We hurried back to his apartment. I sat down on his couch and he sat next to me. But he almost immediately readied to jump up. "I should put on some music. What would you—"

I pulled him back down to the couch. "No music. Just you. There was plenty of music at the rink."

Bill settled back in and tentatively touched my shoulder. I touched his shoulder.

"Tonight was fun," he said.

"Yes, it was." The old Bill would have had me in his bed and flat on my back by now. The new Bill was sweet, but…

He stretched his arms. When they came down, he put one behind my back. I snuggled closer. However slowly he was moving, we were at least headed in the right direction.

Bill made a slight movement to bring our heads closer. I moved closer, our mouths close enough to sense each other's breath. He touched our lips together. Warm and soft. I moved my lips, careful to keep us together.

Then he kissed. Just a little suction, but definitely a kiss. I increased the suction. He kissed back, stronger. We each increased the suction. His tongue pressed against his lip, moving it in a different way. I pressed my tongue forward, but in a different place. He licked the inside of my lip, just a flicker. If I wanted, I could ignore it, but that *wasn't* what I wanted. I flicked my tongue against his.

I adjusted my position, brushing my breast against his chest. His hand on my back hugged us closer. I moved the hand that was touching his leg and reached around with my other hand to touch his waist. Our kisses deepened and our tongues frolicked inside each other's mouths. It was nice, but he was still treating all the green lights I was giving him as just amber.

Finally—finally!—he touched one of my breasts. Not a nipple, but still. I moaned and shifted so that his fingers touched my hot and hard little bud. I moaned appreciatively. He continued to stroke my nipple. But that's all he did!

It was time for more definitive signals. I leaned back and broke off our kiss. His eyes fluttered open. I grabbed the bottom of my T-shirt and pulled it up and over my head. I pointed to my other breast. "They *both* need your attention," I told him.

His eyes went wide as they inspected my breasts, now covered only by a sheer purple bra.

He gently squeezed both of my breasts and was no longer shy about caressing my nipples. When I groaned, he leaned in and we kissed. Again, nice and wonderfully warming, but I wanted *more*!

I leaned back, breaking off the kiss. His hands kept caressing my breasts and his eyes, free from their obligation to remain shut while were kissing, ogled my entire body.

"My legs are stiff," I told him. "Maybe we should stand." That was a white lie; my legs weren't stiff. But I had to do *something*!

Bill pulled me up. I pulled him over to the wall. I was tempted to back him against the wall, but I wanted him to take the initiative, so I pulled him close and continued kissing.

Our bodies were touching, but not firmly. I inserted two fingers in his belt loops and pulled him forward. He moaned when I rubbed up and down the front of his jeans.

"My jeans are tight," I told him.

He pulled back and looked at me oddly. He knew *his* jeans had gotten tighter, but..."

I undid my button and pulled down my fly. Then I brought his body back against mine. "Looser jeans provide better access," I told him, just before we resumed kissing.

His penis was finally communicating with his hands and he slid them down the back of my jeans to grip my buttocks. My reaction—a moan and a rocking of my hips which sent my pubic bone up and down the front of his pants was unmistakable. He moaned in response.

I broke off the kiss and nuzzled his neck. "Aren't you hot with your shirt on?" I asked.

As soon as his shirt was covering his face, I unbuttoned his jeans and pulled down his fly. By the time his shirt was fully off, I was once again leaning against the wall with an innocent look on my face.

But Bill had felt something and started to look down. I grabbed his head and planted a hard kiss on his lips. "There's something down my jeans," I said.

His fingers stopped when he touched the top of my panties.

"Lower," I said.

He got most of the way down my panties before he stopped again.

"Lower." I could feel myself wet. I was tempted to tell him that I had a leak that required fixing by an expert plumber and did he have anything he could use to plug it, but Bill was being so *slow*, I didn't want to be subtle or humorous.

This time he touched my pussy lips.

"It feels wet down there," I said. Before he could respond, I reached into his jeans and gently stroked his penis and felt it begin to swell. "Maybe this is what she needs."

He groaned. My pants were loose enough that they fell to the floor. I pulled his looser as well and we stepped out of our jeans.

Bill was now thoroughly aroused, but a little embarrassed as well. Whatever the source of his embarrassment—almost nude in his hallway, almost nude with a robot, thoroughly aroused despite his court-appointed guardianship, now was *not* the time to probe. "Maybe we should go to the bedroom," I said.

He nodded, took my hand, and led me into *his* bedroom. It was Spartan: a bed, a closet, a window. The bed was under the window, pressed outward by the single night stand. The sole light in the room stood in the opposite corner. There was a large open space just inside the door.

He shut the door behind us. I turned on the light. When I turned around, he was standing by the door.

I reached behind my back and unclasped my bra. "We don't need this anymore," I told him. He gulped. When I followed with my panties, he carefully lifted his briefs up and over his erection. He watched me, still uncertain what to do next. I motioned to his briefs and downward. He dropped them to the floor.

I angled my head towards the bed. He got the idea and pulled the covers half way down.

"All the way," I told him, pleased with my subtle but direct double meaning.

He pulled the covers all the way down. I gave him a gentle shove and he fell to the mattress.

"Hey," he protested as he rotated his hips to avoid crushing his erection.

I climbed onto the bed next to him, making sure to keep my mouth close to his while caressing his entire body, especially his chest, penis and testicles.

He got the hint and kissed me. One hand alternated between my breasts, the other began to lightly caress around the outer edges of my central sexual complex. Thankfully, all I had to do was squirm a little and his fingers caressed *everything*.

True to his word, he'd finally found out what I liked and he dipped a pointing finger inside me. Other fingers caressed up and down my pussy lips. His palm rubbed against my clit. And when he pressed firmly against my pubic mound and then pulled upwards, little jolts tickled up my spine.

"Bill, that's wonderful," I moaned. "You have such lovely fingers."

"Jenny, you have slippery juices." He immediately looked embarrassed. "I'm sorry, that was such a cornball line."

"Don't apologize, Bill, just be yourself. That's what this is all about."

He kept stroking. And it felt *wonderful*. An orgasm, small, but persistent, teased its availability. But Bill wasn't looking at me. "Bill," I told him, "tell me *all* about my juices."

"No, I, never mind."

"Tell me everything you're thinking," I told him. "Starting with Jenny's juices."

"You're sure? You won't mind?"

"Stick your finger all the way inside me. Wiggle it around. And tell me what you're thinking."

"I'm thinking you're hot and wet."

"*I'm* thinking you're hot and hard." My hands rubbing up and down his penis made my meaning clear.

"Your c—your pussy is tight."

"Is that the word that was in your mind, 'pussy'?" I teased my fingers up and over the exposed head of his penis to draw his thinking process lower.

"You have a lovely tight cunt."

"What's the difference—vagina, pussy, cunt?"

"Cunt is more carnal."

"Cock and penis, cock is more *carnal*?"

He nodded and we trembled in unison.

"Jenny, I'd like to…"

"Put your cock into my cunt?"

"Yes."

"And what will you do?"

"Do?"

"What will you do with your cock, once it's in my cunt."

"I'll f—make love to you."

"Making love is the whole thing, from the first kiss. What will you do when your cock is rubbing in and out of my *cunt*?"

"I'll fuck her."

"I'll fuck her," I mimicked, drawing out the tentativeness of his declaration.

"I'll *fuck* you," he said, now meaning it.

"You'll fuck me hard, Bill? Really hard?"

"I'll fuck you *silly,* Jenny, I'll fuck you so hard you'll forget your name."

"I want you, Bill. I want you to fuck me so hard I'll never forget *your* name."

I lay flat on my back and spread my legs. The time for talking was done.

"Jenny, you're sure?" he asked.

I nodded and he opened the drawer to his nightstand. His hand came out with a small foil packet which he opened to reveal the edge of a condom.

I put my hand on his. "I'm already latex inside."

He tossed the condom aside and carefully positioned himself over me. His body slowly slid up mine until his penis was pressing against the opening of my vagina.

He kept pressing forward, up, deeper. The orgasm which had been building trembled up my spine just as our pubic bones touched.

"You came already?" he asked.

I lightly kissed his lips. "And I'll do it over and over again. But only softly...unless..."

"Unless I really fuck you?"

"Unless the intensity of your eyes reaches down into my soul and wraps around it like a snake, unless—"

"Unless my cock fucks your cunt hard enough that we both stop talking?"

I jammed my self up against him to signal my agreement. He reached down to grab my hips. He held me tight and pulled himself out of me. I tried to push myself up, to keep him inside, but his grip was firm.

I was still trying to push up when he smashed himself back in.

"Bill!" I gasped.

Then he did it over and over again—yanking himself out, crashing back into me. With every thrust, his whole body slapped into mine. He pulled his legs out from between mine, pulled mine together, pulled himself out and plunged himself back in. *Every* part of my sex felt the fury of his fucking. Every part wrenched tighter and tighter. Every part cried out for orgasm. But the ferocity of his fucking locked any hope of orgasm deeper and deeper inside my cunt.

"Bill!" I cried.

"Jenny!"

"Fuck me!"

"Harder?"

"Harder!"

His thrusts accelerated, his grip strengthened. I was glad I didn't have to breathe. Yet my cunt— it wanted to breathe, she wanted to escape. But Bill's thrusts were suffocating her.

"Let me have you, Bill, I pleaded. Let me have everything!"

"You're ready?"

"Bill!"

His face contorted. He tried to pull out. But he was paralyzed. The only parts of his body moving were the muscles of his cock pumping his seed into me. I pressed in and out, but his hands were still holding me tightly. It was only a little movement, but it set off another spurt inside me.

"Jenny!"

"Bill!"

"Fuck!"

"Fuck me, Bill!"

And he could finally move again. Not as fast, not as hard, but all I needed was a tiny spark to set off the explosion that he'd gathered inside me. My whole body shuddered. Electricity shot up my spine, sparking at my neck, exploding into my skull. Thunderbolts shot down my legs and sparked out my toes.

Wave after wave of pleasure undulated up and down my body, pressing me into him, squeezing our sweat out the sides. We kissed, but he couldn't breathe.

We kept up the rhythm, fucking giving way to love making as we gloried in each other's warmth, as we gloried into the feelings we'd called forth in each other, as we gloried in what we'd created together.

Finally he collapsed beside me, expended, exhausted, spent.

Afterwards, we sat against the headboard, hugging and cuddling.

"That was the first time in a long time that I made love," he said, "not just had sex."

"And with a robot."

"And with a robot."

Chapter 24

The next morning a courier delivered a large manila envelope at the front door. The return address was the courthouse. Bill ripped it open and removed a large sheaf of papers. He immediately began to read.

I pulled out a similar sheaf of papers, stapled together in the upper left corner. It was Justice Day's decision the civil case. She began by laying out the facts and the issue.

Next to me, Bill let out a wild whoop. "You get to testify!" He showed me a paragraph towards the end of her decision.

"How did you manage to read it so fast?"

He took the civil decision and handed me the criminal decision. "You don't read the whole thing. The important stuff is at the end." He flipped over to the last page which had a series of numbered paragraphs. "One, I maintain guardianship of you until the end of the criminal case. Two, Stephen Minsky is to furnish a detailed plan for your ongoing existence to the Court. Three, the Artificial Intelligence Directorate is to be furnished with a copy of the plan. Four, the matter is to come back before me for a further hearing. Five, at the next hearing, Jenny shall be a party with full rights of representation and participation. Mister Minsky and the Artificial Intelligence Directorate shall also be parties. Six, the next date for the civil proceedings shall be set at the conclusion of the criminal proceedings against Anthony Gallo."

"Does this mean—"

Bill nodded, smiling from ear to ear. "This," he said, holding the decision as if it had intrinsic and infinite value, "means that she's going to recognize your sentience."

I gave a whoop—even louder than Bill's—and jumped into his arms.

The End

Backnotes

Thank you for reading this story. If you enjoyed it, **please** take a moment to **post a review**.

If you wish to receive notifications of upcoming stories, please follow me on my author page:
https://www.amazon.com/Jason-Pinaster/e/B00YSLUDNG%3Fref=dbs_a_mng_rwt_scns_share.

For a catalog of my publications, please see my   catalog   at https://jasonpinaster.wixsite.com/books

Other Stories by Jason Pinaster involving science fiction or paranormal phenomena:
Aural Artifact
Mayan Magic
Witch's Wrath
Kundalini, Lusty Lee Log 29
Alien Vacation, a novelette

Recent Stories
Tickle Test
Pay Back
Panty Play
Webcam Spank
Tiebreaker (A SleeperKidsWorld.com story)
Couples: Adventures at Hedonism II
Gunge Girl
Squished
The Prize
Ava's WAM

Sex Wrestler
WAM Mix (a wet and messy story)
Truth be Dared
Spank Me—if you Dare!
 WAM Mix
Truth be Dared
Tickled Back
Sexy-B Wrestling
Massaging Joy
Emma! (MMF threesome)

My current series features the adventures of dominatrix Mistress Megan:

Pro Dom Her First Client
Pro Dom 2 Hugo
Pro Dom 3 Cross Dresser
Pro Dom 4 Hugo & Sheila
Pro Dom 5 Cold
Pro Dom 6 Lucas Comes Again
Pro Dom 7 Walk-in
Pro Dom 8 Womyn
Pro Dom 9 Priest
Pro Dom 10 Cocoon
Pro Dom 11 Outcall
Pro Dom 12 Switch
Pro Dom 13 Incognito
Pro Dom 14 Shibari

Please also consider reading other titles that I have authored as follows:

I **Alien Vacation**, a novelette

II Connie's Crop, a novel
Wherein mild-mannered Marsha pursuit of the magical whip pairs her with sexy Sheila and connects her with the darker side of sexuality.

III The Christopher Carter Series

Carter's Climax Box Set: All 25 stories
Carter's Chance II
Private Party His
Private Party Hers
Private Party Box Set
Ryan's Reprieve
Cashmere Congress
   Melissa's Moxie
   Molly Madness
   Melissa's Memories
   Blackmail Bounce
   Assisting Audrey
   Splosh Scoundrel
   Jody's Journal
   Busted Bonds
   Solicitor's Slip
   Stakeout Story
   Aural Artifact
   Mayan Magic
   Party Photos
   Buying Before
   Cardiac Caress
   Credit Card Con
   Formatting Foam
   Clinic Caper
   Cosplay Clue
   Witch's Wrath
Carter's Climax Box Set: *All 25 stories*

IV The Lusty Lee Logs:
Available in one convenient volume
Lusty Lee: The Entire Logs:
From Prequel to Confronting

Or separately
Prequel Lusty Lee Log #00
The Case, Lusty Lee Log #1
Swinging, Lusty Lee Log #2
Strip Club, Lusty Lee Log #3
The Escort, Lusty Lee Log #4
Leather, Lusty Lee Log #5
Hedonism, Lusty Lee Log #6
Hedo II, Lusty Lee Log #7
Cheaters, Lusty Lee Log #8
The Actor, Lusty Lee Log #9
Yearning, Lusty Lee Log #10
Scandal, Lusty Lee Log 11
Michael, Lusty Lee Log 12
Rumballs, Lusty Lee Log 13
Massage, Lusty Lee Log 14
The Aide, Lusty Lee Log 15
Negotiator, Lusty Lee Log 16
Linebacker, Lusty Lee Log 17
Cosplay, Lusty Lee Log 18
Wrestling, Lusty Lee Log 19
Anger, Lusty Lee Log 20
Cops, Lusty Lee Log 21
Paintball, Lusty Lee Log 22
Interrogation, Lusty Lee Log 23
The Athlete, Lusty Lee Log 24
Splosh, Lusty Lee Log 25
Choosing, Lusty Lee Log 26
Bondage, Lusty Lee Log 27
Tantra, Lusty Lee Log 28
Kundalini, Lusty Lee Log 29
Confronting, Lusty Lee Log 30
Lusty Lee: the Entire Logs The best deal

And please check out my author profiles at

http://www.amazon.com/Jason-Pinaster/e/B00YSLUDNG/ref=sr_tc_2_0?qid=1434908188&sr=1-2-ent   and at https://www.smashwords.com/profile/view/JasonPinaster

Or drop me a line: jason.pinaster@hotmail.com

For my catalog, including some covers which have been censored, please see: https://jasonpinaster.wordpress.com/home/

Jason Pinaster

Cover credits: The background circuit board is from Gerd Altmann known as geralt on Pixabay; many thanks. The photo of the pretty lady in the black dress was provided courtesy of BystroBA on Flickr. Photoshopping and cover design by myself.

Acknowledgements: Many thanks for the suggestions from and proofreading by Sallyann Cole. All errors remain mine.

Author's note: All characters depicted in this work of fiction are 18 years of age or older.